PURSUIT

—OF—

WINGS
OF GOLD

RONALD C. FISH

ISBN: 978-1-63950-268-4 (hc)
ISBN: 978-1-63950-249-3 (sc)
ISBN: 978-1-63950-250-9 (e)

Writer's Apex

Gateway Towards Success

8063 MADISON AVE #1252
Indianapolis, IN 46227
+13176596889
www.writersapex.com

THE HEAVENS WERE THE GRANDSTANDS, AND ONLY THE GODS WERE SPECTATORS. THE STAKE WAS THE WORLD. THE FORFEIT WAS THE FIGHTER PILOT'S PLACE AT THE TABLE, AND THE GAME HAD NO RECESS. IT WAS THE MOST DANGEROUS OF ALL SPORTS....

—ELLIOT WHITE SPRING
AMERICAN ACE

CONTENTS

INTRODUCTION

This is the first book in a two-book series "The Tupi Field Series". The series is kind of like Archer meets TOPGUN. In the first book, three characters, all of whom bring their own special baggage to the story, strive to become Marine Officers, jet pilots, pilots who do the hardest thing a pilot can do land a jet on the pitching deck of a carrier at night and in bad weather, and, finally, TOPGUN Aces. Ricky hates all politicians who have run up a national debt of 34 trillion dollars and delivered a future we all are likely to live through. Carmen hates all Chinese Communists, but especially the ones that machine-gunned her Dad right in front of her as a child. And J.J. hates anybody who can pass his jump serve. The three become fast friends as they endure the rigors of training to become Marine Officers and jet pilots. Along the way, there are many hijinks, some steamy sex, many new friends are made, and love accidentally blooms between two of the main characters. The female readers will love this love story, and they are forgiven for skimming over the technical details of wing loading and thrust-to-weight ratios.

For the exciting conclusion of this story in Book 2 featuring a carrier battle between the U.S. and China over the Tupi Offshore Oil Field, including: the dogfight at Top Gun; the gang of aviators partying in San Francisco; a big dogfight at Red Flag; skiing in Vail with the lovely Amber Wong, consigliere to the mob; President Parry, an honest man with guts who was willing to do what was right for country regardless of the political cost to him personally, stopping payment of interest on the T-bills and U.S. bonds owned by China and the Chinese going apoplectic as a result; the Chinese ambassador to the U.S. being called before the president and lying about China's intentions; mysterious Chinese activity at the underground shipyard at Hainan discovered by KH-11 satellites; the Chinese armada setting sail around the Drake Passage, Cape Horn at the southern tip of South America; the U.S. sending liquid methane powered ramjet Aurora spy planes searching for the Chinese fleet; the nuclear raid on and destruction of the missile launch complex at Xichange Satellite Launch Center in Sichuan Province, China; the targeting and knockdown of Chinese satellites following the Chinese knocking down all our spy and communication satellites; the CIA finding the GinWui rootkit installed the Chinese hacker Wicked Rose one all government computers; the nuking of French and British carriers heading for the battle by a Chinese boomer; U.S. Virginia-class stealth submarines that take out the practically invisible Chinese Kilo-class submarines and the Chinese boomers; FEL laser weapons development to shoot down aircraft and missiles and use of it to melt the arming and ignition system of the 5 kiloton nuclear warhead of the DF-21 ASBM fired at the U.S.S. Nimitz; action by the MARSOC raiders using an insect swarm of drones to find the Chinese ASBM hidden in warehouses in Porto Alegre; a SEAL team taking out the Chinese crew of an offshore oil rig; Ricky getting into hack for telling the brass he would not lead the second raid on the carrier killer missiles; the brass relenting after they figures out that what he was talking about was true; Ricky and J.J. and Carmen figuring out the unique strategy to overcome the unique anti-stealth radar system defense of the missiles and leading the raid that took out the Chinese DF-21 carrier killer missiles; and the rest the action of the gripping battle between China and the U.S. Incidentally, Ricky, after being shot down and going into a coma, recovers and finds the love of his life. All this action and more is found in book 2.

Here is what two readers who read both books said about these books:

"When I read The Tupi Field and really didn't know what to expect. To my surprise and delight, it was a kick ass novel for a first time writer. It starts with a Chinese missile fired at long range from a stealth jet at one of the Marine pilots flying an a F/A-18 Hornet. He beats the missile after running out of propellant trying to follow his juking. But it gives a close-up look at modern aerial combat and the inventive way of using the F-35 for its 360-degree infra-red search and track system to complement the Hornet. The novel traces the trials and tribulations of three Marine jet pilots, one of which is a woman, in their quest to become jet pilots. The Tupi Field has lots of action in the air and the hotel rooms!!! Ron's characters are well-developed, interesting, exciting, and fun. This futuristic view of the world as we run out of energy and start fighting over what's left is sobering and scary. The jet and weapons technology classes that the pilots attend in the middle of the book are pretty deep for the average person, so you may find yourself skimming over those pages so you can get back to the actual battles, and the steamy relationships !!! Along the way, there is lots of kidding, some steamy sex, a whole lot of hijinks, and a Navy pilot who becomes their best friend. The book revolves around the challenge the pilots face in dealing with the technical superiority of the Su-30KII flankers and the fearsome capability of the Chinese DF-21 "carrier killer" anti-ship ballistic missile. The Chinese put up a clever anti-stealth defense to our raid to take out the missiles resulting in a loss of all our planes on the first raid, but our Marine pilots figured out what the Chinese were doing a devise, a daring raid to take the missiles out. I had a great time reading this book, and you will too."

PROLOGUE

May 1, 2034, 10 nautical miles off the Brazilian Coast at Porto Alegre, 740 miles southwest of the massive Tupi (now Lula) oil and gas field

Carrier Battle

"Cheetah-2 is spiked." Captain J.J. "Scud" Saleen, yelled into his radio. Scud did not sound like his usual laid back California surfer self. All five of the pilots in Cheetah flight sensed it. Something was wrong in a big way. Scud never sounded like that. Captain Saleen was locked up by the airborne search radar of an inbound Chinese J-20 stealth jet, but he could not see the stealth jet on his radar. "No returns on my screen. No idea where this guy is. Does anyone see him?"

"Negative. Nothing here." Woody called. The rest of the Cheetahs checked in one by one all reporting they saw nothing on their radars. Three excruciating minutes went by with everybody peering into their radar displays. Nothing.

Finally SWAT radioed from her F-35 Lightening, "Cheetah-5 has him Scud. He just flew into range of my DAS." She was referring to her Distributed Aperture System, a 360 degree Infrared Search and Track system in all Lightnings. Carmen was flying the only fighter which was DAS equipped in Cheetah flight. "It's a J-20 stealth, 320 degrees from Bullseye for 70, angels 42. I am linking him." Carmen radioed indicating she was linking the target information on the inbound Chinese stealth jet from her DAS system to the Super Hornets.

"Roger that SWAT. Looking. No joy." Scud replied.

"He just fired a missile! Heat signature is Adder. Outer edge of that missile's envelope." SWAT sounded agitated. Here voice had gone up half an octave.

The information that the missile was an Adder was very valuable to Scud. The Adder -- the Nato code name for the Russian-designed Vympel R-77, also referred to as the "AMRAAM-ski", was a medium range, radar-guided missile similar to the AIM-120 AMRAAM with a range of between 40 and 80 nautical miles.

The information that the inbound missile was an Adder told Scud several critical things. First, he now knew that the missile was being fired from approximately its maximum range and that it would be low on energy to maneuver as it got closer to him. He also knew that it was a radar-guided missile so it would be flying to an initial point the Chinese pilot had loaded into it from his stealth jet's airborne radar. Scud knew the Adder would fire up its on-board terminal guidance Doppler search radar when it reached the initial point to find Scud's jet and lock onto it.

J.J. knew that if he got further away, and started a series of high G turns, the missile would expend most of its kinetic energy (airspeed) in making high G turns to track him. Because it was fired from maximum range, it was possible the rocket motor would burn out or be low on fuel by the time it reached him, and the missile would not be able to maintain its Mach 4 overtake pursuit velocity for the intercept.

"Scud going defensive." Captain J.J. Saleen radioed as he banked the Hornet into a 2 G left turn to put the missile on his six, unloaded the jet, and pushed the throttle past its detent into full afterburner. The gentle turn was designed to not bleed off his airspeed and kinetic energy. He wanted to build his airspeed and energy rapidly so as to gain an advantage over the missile when it arrived. To accelerate rapidly, he pushed his stick over to achieve zero G. This unloaded the jet. By unloading to zero G, Scud minimized drag and maximized acceleration. When a wing is generating zero lift, it generates zero parasitic drag. J.J. wanted to build the kinetic energy and airspeed of his jet to put more distance between him and the missile in hopes its rocket motor would burn out before it reached him. J.J. wanted maximum energy for his jet and for the missile to be low or out of propellant when it arrived. He did not want it to have sufficient fuel to rebuild the kinetic energy it would lose in the tight turns it would have to make to intercept him.

"Roger that Scud, looking for trailers." SWAT replied.

When the range to the missile was 20 miles from intercept, J.J. reefed the jet over hard into a 7 G left turn to a heading that put the missile directly on his right beam. Scud hit the defensive countermeasures button and dispensed chaff and flares as he reefed the jet over hoping to confuse the missile's guidance system into homing in on the chaff or flares.

The missile was not fooled and turned hard to reestablish a lead pursuit angle. Scud reefed the jet hard right this time right toward the missile screwing up the missile's tracking solution and forcing it to make another hard turn. Just as it finished turning, Scud reefed the Hornet into a 7 G right turn to put the missile on his left beam to fuck up its tracking solution again and try to disappear into its Doppler notch. More chaff and flares. The missile turned hard again and was not fooled. It was coming fast.

"Goddamit, this thing is still tracking me. The Commie bastards must have changed the seeker head to infrared," J.J. thought to himself. There had been unconfirmed intelligence reports that the Chinese had modified some of the Adders to have infrared seeker heads instead of Doppler radar terminal guidance systems. Fear had started to set in. J.J. was starting to question his decision to become a pilot.

He did a quick calculation in his head and estimated that at Mach 4 or 3044 miles per hour, he had 23 seconds to live. He started a silent count and said the Lord's prayer and he rolled the jet into a hard 7 G turn toward the missile and dispensed more chaff and flares.

The missile turned again and continued to close on him. It was a generation four missile that was difficult or impossible to defeat with maneuvers or chaff or flares. Its guidance system was programmed to reject targets like flares and chaff that were not moving as fast as a real target would be moving.

Snapping back to reality, J.J. thought to himself, "Time for a Hail Mary." He deployed the An/ALE-55 block II fiber optic towed decoy. The ALE-55 towed decoy was an electronic warfare countermeasure decoy designed to protect jets from radar guided missiles like the Adder, the PL-12 Sino AAMRAM and heat seekers like the AA-11 Archer and the AA-10 Alamo heat seeking variants.

When he saw the decoy fully deployed, Scud chopped the throttles to idle and continued his turn into the missile. By chopping the throttles to idle while the decoy was out, an infrared missile could be caused to miss the jet and hit the decoy instead.

The missile was still tracking. J.J. mashed the button on the throttle to deploy more chaff and flares.

"Notch right Scud, it is still tracking you," Carmen radioed.

"Negative, it's a heater."

"What?"

"Chicoms changed the seekers to infrared."

"Holy shit." SWAT exclaimed

"That's what I said too."

Scud yanked the Super Hornet hard into another 7 G turn to force the missile to make another very sharp turn and dissipate more of its energy. It still had plenty to spare.

J.J. strained against the heavy G load of the turn, but when he finally saw the missile, his heart practically lept out of his chest. Scud saw that its rocket motor had burned out. It was still coming fast, but not as fast as it had been while its rocket had still been burning. Scud had added about 20 nautical miles to the distance the missile had to fly to the intercept point. Those 20 miles saved J.J.'s life, because he had succeeded in getting outside the missile's maximum range.

However, the missile was still gliding at Mach 3 now, and his Super Hornet was only traveling at 1369 mph —its flat out top speed. J.J. pulled into a hard right turn He saw the missile start to slow down and bleed off its energy as it pulled hard left trying to match his 7G turn. Just a few seconds before impact, Scud rolled left and pulled the stick just far enough to put his wing's lift vector on the missile. Then he pulled the stick back hard into his lap to turn hard toward the missile giving the missile an impossibly acute turn to the correct intercept point. Instantaneous water vapor clouds formed above Scud's wings as the pressure drop from the huge lift the wings were generating in the hard turn instantly condensed the water in the air to cloud. He spent most of his kinetic energy in that move, but when on the defensive, it is frequently smart to spend it all and live to fight another day.

Scud's desperation last second move almost broke his jet, but it had succeeded in exceeding the missile's capability to turn. The missile overshot and flew by him. Now at an impossible pursuit angle, low on kinetic energy, and out of fuel, the missile was unable to maneuver further for another intercept.

"Cheetah-1 is clear." J.J. thanked his guardian angel as he watched the missile fall harmlessly into the ocean below. But this dogfight was far from over....

The Brazilian sky was that impossible blue found only at 35,000 feet— and filled with missile smoke trails -- everywhere. The biggest jet dogfight in history raged as the carriers, cruisers, destroyers and hunter-killer attack submarines of three Chinese super carrier battle groups locked horns below with the supercarriers *U.S.S. Carl Vinson*, the *U.S.S. Ronald Regan* and the *U.S.S.* Nimitz and their supporting ships of the Southern Expeditionary Force. The Americans were trying to achieve air superiority over the Chinese in the Porto Alegre area in order to destroy a missile battalion of anti-ship ballistic missiles the Chinese had hidden on portable truck launchers in Porto Alegre. These anti-ship ballistic missiles were sinister weapons to which the American fleet had little or no defense. These Chinese anti-ship missiles were forcing the three American supercarrier battle groups of the Southern Expeditionary Force to stay 1500 nautical miles away from the three Chinese supercarrier battle groups currently dominating the coast of Brazil off Porto Alegre. Three more Chinese supercarrier battle groups were floating in the massive Tupi deepwater oil and gas field to the north of Porto Alegre. Three American supercarriers *U.S.S. Enterprise*, the *U.S.S. George W. Bush* and the *U.S.S. Harry S. Truman* and their battle groups were hovering just out of range of the Chinese anti-ship ballistic missiles far off the coast of Rio De Janeiro. They were waiting for the Southern Expeditionary Force to take out the ASBMs so they could attack the Chinese supercarriers dominating the Tupi Field.

The Chinese had invaded Brazil in May and had seized control of the Tupi field and diverted its oil and gas output to their own purposes causing a major worldwide energy panic. The American Expeditionary Forces could not stage an amphibious assault to free Brazil from Chinese control without air superiority. And the Americans could not achieve air superiority without attacking and sinking the six Chinese super carriers. Attempting to conduct an amphibious assault on the beaches of Brazil without air superiority would result in a bloodbath of epic proportions.

The Brazilians had fought hard and well, but had only lasted two weeks against the massive Chinese invasion force with aerodynamically superior Russian-designed fighters.

J.J. knew the Americans were fighting valiantly, but were losing. For the first time in history, the Americans were fighting with carrier-based F/A-18 fighters that were inferior in all respects to the Russian-designed Su-30MK2 Flankers and the navalized stealth fighters the Chinese were flying. Years of overspending in Washington and the ballooning national debt had forced the defense budgets to be cut drastically. New weapons systems and the development of a navalized American F-22 stealth fighter had fallen to the budget axe. The F-35 was supposed to be America's navalized stealth fighter, but it was a multibillion dollar clusterfuck.

The Flankers, with high thrust-to-weight ratio, low wing loading, canards and vectored thrust were fearsome weapons in the hands of a skilled pilot. J.J. and the rest of his Navy and Marine Corp pilot buddies knew the Flankers were far faster and more maneuverable than the American Super Hornets and F-35s they were flying. With their AESA radars and larger numbers of air-to-air missiles, the Chinese Flankers were shooting down the American F/A-18 Super Hornets in droves. To make matters even worse, the Chinese had developed a navalized version of their J-20 stealth fighter which was invisible to the Hornet's X-band search radar and the radars of the American AWACs radar planes. The Americans had only the F-35 as a carrier-based stealth plane, and it was a dog compared to the jets the Chinese were flying. J.J. knew this pissed off Carmen, his fellow Marine aviator. Captain Carmen "SWAT" Nicoise was at that moment flying an F-35 in a loose deuce about 2 miles off J.J.'s wing. J.J. had gone through Top Gun with Carmen, along with his best friend Captain Ricky "Woody" Magnusson, USMC, who was at that moment lying in a medically induced coma on a hospital ship.

The threat of nuclear war between the U.S. and Chinese in this battlespace at this moment was not only *real but imminent*. POTUS had already nuked the Chinese mainland missile launch facilities after they shot down our spy and communications satellites in preparation for their invasion of Brazil. In retaliation, the Chinese had used nuclear-tipped anti-ship ballistic missiles to sink the all the ships of French and British coalition super carrier battle groups that were steaming toward the Tupi field to aid of the U.S.

J.J. and the rest of the expeditionary force knew this was the pivotal moment in history. If the Chinese prevailed, the supplies of oil and gas from the Tupi field would remain diverted to China, and the economies of most of the rest of the countries in the civilized world would crash and burn. This was a fight to the death. J.J. was ready to die for the cause if necessary.

Chinese MIGs, AWACs and stealth fighters emblazoned the Brazilian sky with a primordial insistence that it is *they* that would win the world's first energy war.

Cheetah flight was a flight of four Marine Corp F/A-18 Super Hornets and one Marine Corp F-35 Lightning flying CAP 1 (Combat Air Patrol) on a high perch over the an XB-47 spoof AWACs and the real AWACs which was to provide the big picture to the SEAD, bombing and CAP elements assigned to the mission of destroying anti-ship ballistic missiles the Chinese had been hiding at Porto Alegre.

"Scud, Cheetah-5, I have him. He just flew into range of my DAS." announced Captain Carmen "Swat" Nicoise, USMC. She was flying an F-35 -- the only 360 degree Infrared Search and Track system equipped fighter in Cheetah flight. Carmen, an exotic Eurasian beauty queen with two black belts, was not a person to fuck with. Her call sign "Swat" as in S.W.A.T., came from a memorable night back in Pensacola when she was out drinking with the boys.

Carmen hated the Chinese communists with a white hot passion even though she was half Chinese. Her father had been the police chief in her city. He had been investigating underworld connections between Triad and corrupt Communist Party leaders in an effort to crack down on corruption in his province. The Communist Party politicos had contracted with the Triad, the Chinese Mafia, to kill her father. One night while Carmen was riding home with her Dad from an official function, Triad thugs had boxed their car in and dragged her father out into the street. They brutally machine gunned him to death right in front of her. Carmen wanted every Chinese communist motherfucker to die an excruciating death.

Carmen loved to fly the F-35's Distributed Aperture System (DAS), an Infrared Search and Track System (IRST) with no equal. With its network of six infrared cameras staring constantly outward in all directions her plane, it was like having super powers. The DAS gave Carmen a 360-degree infrared view of the battle space. These cameras could detect the heat signature of a stealth fighter out to about 50 miles, and could detect missile launches even further out. To J.J.'s benefit, Carmen's DAS had detected the inbound Chinese stealth jet. The data of the six merged infrared camera images was visible to Carmen on her VSI helmet-mounted display. Carmen linked the data to the Super Hornets over her Link 16 digital data link. They could not see her 360 degree world on their Multifunction displays, but they could see where she was looking. Carmen could look through the floor of her jet or directly behind it through the engines and structure behind her cockpit through the miracle of digital image processing which displayed on the inside of her helmet visor the portion of the 360 degree image from the infrared cameras where she was looking.

The DAS tracks every aircraft within range with sufficient accuracy to provide a safe off-boresight, lock-on-after-launch missile shot with any data-link equipped missile such as the U.S. AIM-120 AMRAAM "slammer". "Off-boresight" means the F-35 does not have to be flying toward the target. If the pilot can see the target and lock onto it with the DAS, that information could be uploaded to the missile for launch.

"It's a J-20 stealth, 320 degrees from Bullseye for 70, angels 42. I am linking him." Carmen radioed indicating she was linking the target information on the inbound Chinese stealth jet from her DAS system to the Super Hornets.

Bullseye was a code name for a reference point on a map, the position of which only American Navy and Marine Corp pilots knew. From Bullseye, the position of enemy targets could be stated in relative terms. That way, only U.S. pilots could understand the radio position call. Chinese pilots listening in who did not know where Bullseye was would not know if the U.S. pilots had located them yet or not. In this case, Bullseye was the commercial airport on the northeast side of Porto Alegre about 4 miles from the target area, so J.J knew the inbound Chinese stealth jet was about 70 nautical miles away at 320 degrees from the commercial airport at 42,000 feet. It would not be visible yet. But he knew where to look for it.

"Roger that Swat. Looking. No joy." J.J. replied.

"He just fired a missile. Heat signature is Adder. He is pushing that missile's envelope." Carmen sounded cool, calm and collected. All the Cheetah pilots smiled inside their oxygen masks. They were all thinking to themselves if Carmen could handle this life and death situation with such aplomb, they had better man up. And man up they did. They were the best of the best.

The information that the missile was an Adder was very valuable to J.J. Adder -- the Nato code name for the Russian-designed Vympel R-77 (also referred to as the "AMRAAM-ski"). It was a medium range, radar-guided missile similar to the AIM-120 AMRAAM, the world's premier air-to-air missile, with a range of between 40 and 80 nautical miles.

The information that the inbound missile was an Adder told J.J. several critical things. First, he now knew that the missile was being fired from approximately its maximum range and that it would be low on energy to maneuver as it got closer to him. He also knew that it was a radar-guided missile which was flying to an initial point the Chinese pilot had loaded into it from his stealth jet's infrared search and track system. Scud knew the Adder would fire up its on-board terminal guidance Doppler search radar when it reached the initial point to find Scud's jet and lock onto it.

J.J. knew that if he got further away, and started a series of high G turns, the missile might expend most of its kinetic energy (airspeed) in making high speed turns to track him. Because it was fired from maximum range, it was possible the rocket motor would burn out or be low on fuel by the time it reached him, and the missile would not be able to maintain its Mach 4 overtake pursuit velocity for the intercept.

"Scud going defensive, turn and burn, notch" J.J. radioed.

"Roger that Scud, looking for trailers. I am moving in tight." Carmen replied.

"Be my bait baby and there is a bottle of scotch waiting for you on the boat."

"Better be if I am going to be up here like a sitting duck while you play hero."

Doppler Notch Explained

J.J. knew that because the Adder's on-board terminal guidance radar was a Doppler search radar, it would have a Doppler notch into which he could disappear. Doppler search radars depended upon relative velocity of the target to the radar platform, which was the missile in this case. Anything with zero relative velocity could not be a target to the missile guidance system's idiot-savant logic. That is the wisdom behind flyng into the Doppler notch. A jet which either dives straight down, flies straight up or turns to keep the missile on the 3 o'clock or 9 o'clock beam position is perpendicular to the flight path of the missile and has no relative velocity to the missile. Such a jet disappears in the radar's filters.

J.J. started a series of violent 6 G turns to make the missile turn hard and dissipate its kinetic energy. J.J. watched the range between him and the heat signature of the missile decrease on his linked display as he strained against the crushing G forces caused by his violent turns.

JJ defeats Adder

When the range to the missile was 20 miles from intercept, J.J. pulled into a 2 G turn to a heading directly away from the missile. The gentle turn was designed to not bleed off his airspeed and kinetic energy. To accelerate rapidly, he pushed his stick over to achieve zero G, and pushed the throttle into full afterburner. By unloading to zero G, he thought, he could minimize drag and maximize acceleration. When a wing is generating zero lift, it generates zero parasitic drag. J.J. wanted to build the kinetic energy and airspeed of his jet to put more distance between him and the missile in hopes its rocket motor would burn out before it reached him since it was fired from maximum range. Accelerating rapidly would also give him a critical energy advantage when the missile arrived. J.J. wanted the missile low or out of propellant. He did not want it to have sufficient fuel to rebuild the kinetic energy it would lose in the tight turns it would have to make to intercept him.

J.J. gave Carmen the kiss off sign and rolled inverted and dove straight down, cutting his throttles to idle to cut his heat signature. "Break right notch Swat," J.J. radioed.

Carmen reefed her jet over into a hard right turn to put the missile on her beam and hopefully disappear into the other Doppler notch.

The missile was not fooled.

"Fuck, this thing is still tracking me. The commie bastards must have changed the seeker head to infrared," J.J. thought to himself. There had been unconfirmed intelligence reports that the Chinese had modified some of the Adders to have infrared seeker heads instead of Doppler radar terminal guidance systems. "At least Carmen is off the hook," J.J. thought with relief. Fear had started to set in though, and J.J. was starting to question his decision to become a pilot.

He did a quick calculation in his head and estimated that at mach 4 or 3044 miles per hour, he had 23 seconds to live. He started a silent count and said the Lord's prayer. He watched his airspeed rapidly build while the missile continued to close on him. It all seemed like a bad dream.

Snapping back to reality, he deployed the An/ALE-55 block II fiber optic towed decoy. This was a last ditch Hail Mary. J.J. was desperately trying to extend his lifespan.

The ALE-55 towed decoy was an electronic warfare countermeasure decoy designed to protect jets from radar guided missiles like the Adder. The block II improvement to the ALE-55 also protected its host jet from heat seeking missiles like the new Adders by presenting a heat signature like the host. By chopping the throttles to idle while the decoy was out, an infrared missile could be caused to miss the host and hit the decoy.

The decoy's on board electronics provides radar jamming of search radars in acquisition mode, and detects the change in radar signals when a radar lock has been achieved. The decoy analyzes the best jamming technique to use when a lock by the missile launch platform search radar has occurred and emits the best type jamming signals to break that lock. If that does not work and the decoy detects the change in radar signals indicating a missile launch has occurred, the decoy begins transmitting appropriate jamming signals to jam the missile's on-board radar. If that doesn't work, the decoy starts transmitting signals that present a bigger radar cross-section than the host.

The decoy tries to jam incoming radar pulses of the missile's on-board Pulse Doppler radar, by re-creating them in the decoy's signal processing circuits as "spoof" signals. The "spoof" signals transmitted back to the inbound missile have slightly different frequencies and slightly different reflection timing than the actual Pulse Doppler signals reflected from the host. The changed timing and frequency tells the missile's guidance system the target is moving at a different speed and is at a different range than the actual speed and range of the host jet. This screws up the guidance system calculations and causes the missile to miss altogether or hit the decoy. Since the "spoof" signals are stronger than the actual reflected signals, the missile's guidance system locks onto them rather than the actual reflected signals.

The missile was still tracking J.J. in his vertical plunge despite the electronic countermeasures of the decoy—because it was a heater. J.J.

pulled out of his dive and mashed the button on the throttle to deploy chaff and flares.

"Notch right Scud, it is still tracking you," Carmen radioed.

"Negative, it's a heater."

"What?"

"Chicoms changed the seakers to infrared."

"Holy shit." Carmen exclaimed

"That's what I said."

J.J. yanked the Super Hornet hard into a 7 G turn toward the missile to force it to make a very sharp turn and dissipate a lot of its energy. It still had plenty to spare.

J.J. strained against the heavy G load of the turn, but he finally saw the missile. His heart practically lept out of his chest when he saw that its rocket motor had burned out. J.J. had added about 20 nautical miles to the distance the missile had to fly to the intercept point. Those 20 miles saved J.J.'s life, because he had succeeded in getting outside the missile's maximum range.

However, the missile was still gliding at Mach 4, and his Super Hornet was only travelling at 1369 mph —its flat out top speed. J.J. saw the missile start to slow down and bleed off its energy as it pulled hard left trying to match his 7G turn. Just a few seconds before impact, J.J. rolled left and pulled the stick just far enough to put his wing's lift vector on the missile. Then he pulled the stick back hard into his lap to turn hard almost toward the missile giving the missile an impossibly acute turn it had to make to intercept him. Immense instantaneous water vapor clouds formed above his wings as the pressure drop from the huge lift the wings were generating instantly condensed the water in the air to cloud.

J.J. desperation last second move almost broke his jet as well as his neck. But J.J. had succeeded in exceeding the missile's capability to turn. The missile overshot and flew by him. Now at an impossible pursuit angle, low on kinetic energy, and out of fuel, the missile could not maneuver further for another intercept.

"Cheetah-1 is clear." J.J. thanked his guardian angel as he watched the missile fall harmlessly into the raging ocean battle below.

The water below was over 5000 feet deep – and full of submarines stalking each other and the flattops, cruisers and destroyers above. The Chinese had brought six small, virtually silent Chinese Kilo-class electric-diesel submarines along with a couple of ballistic missile submarines. These Chinese boomers had been loaded with antiship ballistic missiles with which the Chinese planned to destroy the U.S. carrier battle groups. The fearsome Chinese DF-21D Anti-Ship Ballistic Missile was nuclear-tipped and capable of sinking a super carrier, or any other ship for that matter, from 1500 nautical miles away. The U.S. had no weapon specifically designed to defend against it although a laser-based weapon had just been installed on some of the carriers. The laser weapon had never been tested against the DF-21D ASBM.

The boomers had been waiting to sink the U.S. carriers and their escorts before they got to the Tupi field. But they were gone now. The American *Virginia*-class hunter-killer attack boats had sunk them. Using a slick new stealth technology that bent sonar waves around the American subs, there were no reflections. The U.S. attack boats had snuck up on the boomers, and sunk them from very close range with Mark 48 torpedoes. The Chinese boomers never had a chance.

The *Virginia*-class boats now had to find and sink the Kilos before they sunk the American carriers or the American submarines themselves.

The Kilos, loaded with supersonic Sizzler anti-ship missiles and nuclear-tipped torpedoes, were silently lying in wait to ambush the American ships. The tiny Chinese kilos were lurking in the sonar shadows of undersea mountains and lurking near drilling platforms that corrupted sonar signals. The Kilos, with their anechoic tile lined hulls and fins, absorbed active sonar sound pulses rather than reflec them. They were virtually invisible to the American anti-submarine forces searching for them.

How We Got to this Point

The world had come to this point through a concatenation of factors. First among these was the failure of western as well as eastern governments to impose any energy conservation standards on their populations or tough mileage standards on their auto manufacturers. Citizens of the U.S., China, India, Japan, the European countries and the Central and South American countries continued to drive their SUVs and trucks, generally alone, oblivious to the fact that the world was running out of oil. They did not want to hear the words "conserve", "shared pain" or "sacrifice" from their leaders, and so their leaders, fearing a failure to get re-elected, never spoke them. No legislation forcing conservation was passed.

It was not really the public's fault. It is hard to know the true facts as a general member of the public. But the governments knew and the big oil companies knew. The governments did not want to start a panic, so they remained silent. The big oil companies did not want to crash their stocks, so they too remained silent. And so the good citizens went merrily along, oblivious to the fact that their end was approaching much faster than they thought. If you asked the average person on the street in 2021 how much oil he or she thought was left, the answer would be generally 100 or 200 years. Wrong. It was 18 years. Most people thought they would be long dead before the world ran out of oil. The reality was that because the world was running out of oil, that was going to make them dead. With no gas to run the tractors and combines and no oil to make the fertilizer, crop yields were plummeting. With no diesel to run the big rigs to get what was produced to the population centers, starvation and food riots were inevitable.

As oil fields dried up, some new fields were found and some new techniques like horizontal drilling and hydraulic fracturing, but it was not enough to stem the inexorable rise in demand. Wishful thinking, head-in-the-sand leaders both political and otherwise either ignored or did not understand the math of geometric progression in the world's population and the rising demand created by China's efforts to raise one billion people out of poverty.

A few forward thinking people chose to drive gas sipping hybrids, small electric cars or small, fuel efficient turbo diesels, but it was too few and now it was too late. The massive energy guzzling infrastructure to grow our foods and deliver them to our population centers, power our cities, fuel our transportation had not been converted to other energy forms.

Despite the fact that the United States had 300 years worth of coal in 2034 and was the Saudia Arabia of natural gas, nothing on a commercial scale had been developed by then to convert trucks, tractors, planes and cars to run on natural gas or synthetic fuels made from gasified coal. The Nazis had developed a process to make synthetic motor fuels from coal during World War II when the allied strategic bombing campaign had decimated their refineries at Ploesti and elsewhere. A South African company, Sasol, had picked up the technology and commercialized it during the apartheid embargoes of that country, but, aside from that, nothing had been done in the West to adopt the technology on a widespread scale.

Now it was too late. The massive North Sea and Prudhoe Bay oil fields had been sucked dry. Prudhoe Bay had been discovered in 1968 and had a capacity of 25 billion barrels of oil and had 25×10^{12} cubic feet of recoverable natural gas, but that was all gone now. Production at Prudhoe Bay had started in 1977 when the Alaska Pipeline was build and peaked in 1979, and died out in 2029 with a whimper. Mighty British Petroleum, which ran the field, declared bankruptcy in 2034 and threw thousands of people out of work.

The massive Brent and Forties oilfields had been discovered in 1970 in the North Sea along with a number of other smaller fields, some in British waters, and some in the waters of the Netherlands, Germany, Denmark and Norway. It was estimated that the mighty Norwegian fields of the North Sea held more than 54% of the sea's oil reserves. But by 2007, more than 60% of the oil in the Norwegian fields and more than 70% of the oil in the British fields in the North Sea had been extracted and production was falling. Because of accelerating demand in the U.S., China and India, the North Sea oil fields suffered the same fate as Prudhoe Bay and ran dry in 2034. Shell and Phillips Oil however avoided bankruptcy by developing massive wind turbine farms in the English Channel in time to forestall the precipitous drop in their cash flows from sale of North Sea oil when the fields ran dry. Decades of over consumption had done the same thing to the Saudi and Libyan oil fields.

Gasoline had reached $25 per gallon by 2030 and the price was climbing daily. Unrestrained consumption and a lack of any common sense or forethought whatsoever had brought the industrialized economies of China, India and the West to their knees. The high cost of energy was leading to massive disruption in the markets. Inflation was running at record levels, and shortages of food had led to food riots in Ghana, Senegal, Shanghai, Sudan, Ethiopia, Beijing, Paris, Rome, Athens, London, New York, Los Angeles and Miami. Stock markets around the world were tanking. It was clear that the precipitous decline in oil production was going to be a near extinction event for the human race.

And now it had come to war with China over the oil and gas in the massive Lula oil and gas field 125 miles off the coast of Brazil. China had been preparing for this day for years, acquiring from the Russian Federation a fearsome array of fourth generation fighters and developing their own fifth generation stealth fighters and drones. They had also developed a fearsome new weapon called an Anti-Ship Ballistic Missile that could knock out a super carrier 1500 miles away in one nuclear punch.

National Debt Effects

In the meantime, the U.S. had fallen behind in its weapons development and advanced fighter programs. Production of the deadly F-22 Raptor, feared by Air Forces all over the world, had to be stopped at 183 because of budget shortfalls. Of those, only 127 were operational in 2026. The U.S. Air Force tried to order 150 more in the face of the rising threat from the Chinese J-2 Stealth fighter and the Russian PAK-FA fifth generation fighter and continual improvement of the avionics and engines of Su-27 and Su-30 thrust-vectoring Flankers China had acquired from Russia. However, the massive spending by Democrats on social programs and Obamacare precluded the acquisition, and our carrier-based and land-based fighter arsenal fell farther and farther behind the relentless Chinese development programs.

The politicians in Washington had opened the door to let Wall Street run wild with derivatives in the Commodities Futures Modernization Act of 2000. In that legislation, all Bucket Shop statutes were preempted thereby rendering them unenforceable by the states. These Bucket Shop statutes were the last hope to regulate derivatives which are a form of bet allowing the holder of the derivative to make a bet on the change in value of something he or she did not own. Bucket Shops were places one could go in the 1930s and place speculative bets on how the value of a stock that the better did not own would change in the future. Bucket Shops led to massive speculation on the stock market. After the crash of 1939, they were outlawed. The Bucket Shop statutes where the last line of defense against the derivatives, otherwise knows and Instruments of Financial Mass Destruction. The Bucket Shop laws gone, and since Wall Street spread 300 millions dollars a year around Capital Hill in campaign contributions and lobbying expenses, they always got their way. The Bucket Shop statutes were wiped out with a single stroke of President Clinton's pen in 2000.

Having opened the door to run wild with derivatives, Wall Street did exactly that. There was big, big money in derivatives. Wall Street loved them. If you graduated from MIT or Stanford or some other prestigious school with a PhD or other strong background in math, you could get a job with Morgan Stanley or other big wall street firm writing these amazingly complex, mathematical nightmares called derivatives and make huge money. Far more than you could make taking any regular job. These people were called Quants, and they dreamed up and wrote derivatives for every conceivable speculative bet an investor might choose to make. Credit Default Swaps became a massive, invisible iceberg that hit the ship of state and sunk it. Wall Street banks had leveraged themselves out way beyond what was prudent and reasonable. The Wall Street firms were buying any and all mortgages regardless of whether the borrower could pay them back. The mortgages were bundled into Collateralized Debt Obligations and sold to unsuspecting investors who had no idea the underlying mortgages were junk. The result was a huge credit bubble that eventually burst when people started defaulting, and led to one of the worst real estate and stock market crashes in history. The economy was in the tank and tax revenues were way down as people lost their jobs and corporations earnings fell. All this happened just as social program spending was starting to rise with the aging of the baby boomers.

The U.S. government was helpless to shore up the economy. Politicians, fearing a depression, precipitously passed bailout legislation and gave billions of dollars to the banks and auto companies to shore them up and prevent their collapse. These massive bailouts of the financial system and auto industry in 2008 pushed the national debt to record levels.

The U.S. government was already in debt trouble in 2008 with massive unfunded liabilities imposed by the social security, medicare and military pension systems. To keep afloat, the feds were selling massive amounts of T-bills and other government bonds and debt obligations to governments around the world, including huge numbers of U.S. government bonds and T-Bills to China.

Meanwhile politicians, acting in the own self interest and, fearing loss in the next election, did little to curb government spending. This ultimately pushed the U.S. government to the verge of bankruptcy and the unthinkable – default on their debt obligations and huge cuts in social security and medicare obligations.

The feds really had no choice. There was simply not enough money to go around. Developments of new fifth generation fighters and defensive weapons systems fell by the wayside, as U.S. government struggled to pay at least part of their obligations to the baby boomers under the social safety net programs passed in a different era.

As a result, the U.S. forces squaring off against China were, for the first time in recent history, equipped with weapons systems that were inferior to those of their enemy.

The U.S. economy's debt crisis could have been lessened or averted by legislation in the 90's and first decade of the millennium to implement government funding on developing alternative energy sources. The government could have passed more legislation to encourage massive private investment in all forms of alternative energy development. Such investments would have led to whole new industries springing to life and creation of millions of jobs. These millions of jobs would have generated huge amounts of tax revenues for the federal and state governments. But it had not happened.

The government could have passed legislation forcing high mileage standards on the automakers and limiting the maximum speed limit to 55 MPH and encouraging conservation with financial incentives. But that did not happen either. Now the world was running out of oil, and the first energy war had begun.

Its not like anybody could have seen it coming. As of 2008, it was estimated that peak oil had been passed and that there was only about 38 years of oil left in the world based upon known reserves and then current rates of consumption. The problem with that estimate was that it assumed no growth in the Indian and Chinese economies, a flawed assumption to say the least.

China's economy was growing at a rate of 10% per year, and they were on an absolute tear building entire cities and millions of miles of new road. Simultaneously, massive development and manufacture of new weapons systems was going on. All this burned oil. The Chinese were burning massive amounts of fuel in their headlong rush into the future, and they desperately needed more. China, having been opened to the West by Nixon in 1972, steadily grew as its low labor rates attracted many of the manufacturing jobs formerly performed by U.S. workers. Essentially, almost everything was made in China by 2020. This led to a large increase in the size and wealth of the middle class in China, which in turn led to increased demand for cars, gas and other goods and services, all of which took energy to produce and ship.

Ross Perot's made a famous admonition to the American people in opposition to the NAFTA treaty to listen for the "giant sucking sound" of U.S. jobs going to Mexico. That turned out to be partially true, except the jobs went mostly to China, and the giant sucking sound was the sound of the oil fields around the world be sucked dry by white hot demand for energy.

The development of horizontal drilling and hydraulic fracturing to extract oil and gas from shale formations slowed down the inevitable, but the geometric progression of the world's population, and growth of the middle classes in China and India with their voracious appetite for energy meant the piper would eventually have to be paid. And now it was time.

It was the defaults on U.S. government bonds and T-bills owned by China and the Chinese economy's insatiable thirst for more oil that pushed the communists over the edge of peace into the abyss of war. The Chinese were desperate for oil imports to keep their industrial complex running, and their food production from falling off. Food riots were starting to break out all over China, as the dwindling supply of oil forced Chinese food production down.

Description of Tupi Field

The only bright spots in the world's oil picture were the massive, deep water Tupi oil and gas field off the coast of Brazil. For no particular reason, the Brazilians had renamed it the Lula Field in the 2000's. The Lula field was gigantic and located in the Santos Basis 160 miles off the coast of Rio de Janeiro in Brazil. Because of the extremely deep water, oil and gas were very difficult and expensive and dangerous to extract from the oil fields in this basin. Deep water drilling rigs capable of drilling on the ocean floor at a depth of 6600 feet and then through 16,000 feet of salt, sand and rock were very expensive to build and leased for more 3 million dollars a day in 2020. This caused the oil companies to delay in exploiting the Lula field until they were out of other options. As one of the world's largest oil field discoveries in the last 60 years, and as yet not fully exploited, it was the crown jewel of the world's oceans and a coveted prize. The communists of mainland China did not think it should be left to Petrobras and Brazil to own and control. The massive natural gas companion field Jupiter only 32 miles away, sweetened the prize. Nobody knew their plan but them.

But now at 35,000 feet and 500 knots, J.J., Carmen and the rest of Cheetah flight were fighting against all odds to preserve our way of life and their very lives. It had been a long and difficult process to get to this point. They were Top Gun fighter pilots—the best of the best, but they had struggled mightily to transform themselves from nuggets to supersonic assassins.

CHAPTER 1

THE BASIC SCHOOL-MARINE OFFICERS ARE MADE NOT BORN

November 10, About Five Years Before
The War With China Starts – The Basic School,
United States Marine Corps Base, Quantico, Virginia

To marines everywhere, November 10 is an excuse to party. November 10th is the birthday of the Marine Corps, and Marines, when they are not tending to business, don't really need much of a reason to party. This year was no exception.

Every year on the birthday of the Marine Corps, the instructors of the Marine Corps Training and Education Command as part of the "training" of the young Marine Officers hosted a banquet of epic proportions. After a lengthy and well-lubricated happy hour, dinner started with before dinner aperitifs and a toast to the platoon commanders. Dinner was served with wine and more toasts followed. There were toasts to the company commanders, the battalion commanders, the commanders of the First, Second, Third and Fourth Marine Divisions, the Commandant of the Marine Corps, the Joint Chiefs of Staff, the Secretary of the Navy and the President. Dinner concluded with Cognac and the traditional cake cutting ceremony. The first piece of cake was given to the oldest Marine present who then gave it to the youngest Marine present. The evening concluded with the reading of Marine Corps General Order 47, General LeJeune's birthday message to Marines everywhere and another Cognac toast to the Marine Corps itself.

RICKY INTRODUCED

Second Lieutenant Ricky Magnusson had started training at The Basic School at Marine Corps Base Quantico, Virginia five months earlier after having received his commission as an officer in the Marine Corps from the ROTC unit at Northwestern University where he earned a Bachelor of Science in Electrical Engineering graduating *summa cum laude*.

Ricky was sitting at dinner next to Second Lieutenant Carmen Nicoise, and Second Lieutenant J.J. Saleen. They had become fast friends over the first five months of trial by fire at The Basic School. TBS was not for slackers. The Marines did not want slackers or quitters in their officer corps.

Ricky was raised partly in Grand Rapids with his Mom and Dad and partly in the country on a dairy farm where he had been helping his uncle run a dairy farm since he was 13 after his grandfather had a stroke. Ricky was no stranger to hard work. When he was on the farm during the summers, he got up at 5:30 every morning to milk the cows. Then he would work all day till sundown driving tractors plowing, disking, bailing hay, driving the combine, taking grain to the mill in the truck. On the farm, nobody paid much attention to the niceties of when it was actually legal to drive.

Ricky was a show-me kind of guy with a prodigious work ethic, a quick wit, a quicker smile. He had no respect for slackers, posturing or bullshit in general. If you were a hard worker and smart he respected you and he would bend over backwards to help you. If you tried to blow smoke up his ass, you were toast.

Ricky was a ruggedly handsome gayblade who always kept a spare girlfriend around in case his number one girlfriend wigged out. How he juggled them and kept them both happy nobody quite understood.

When Ricky was growing up, times were tough in Grand Rapids. Ricky's Dad died a broken man. He never could find decent work again after he was laid off at 55 from the machine shop where he worked as a machinist. Ricky's Dad has lost his job as a result of the greedy Wall Street Investment bankers over-leveraging their firms, kiting worthless derivatives called Collateral Debt Obligations based upon liar loan mortgages that should have never been made. This reckless and fraudulent conduct caused the whole financial system to melt down in a crisis of confidence. As the morass unfolded and the stock market crashed, people lost the equity in their homes as home values plummeted. People started walking away from homes they once loved, because, in the new Wall-Street-Created reality, their mortgages were far more than the homes were worth. CEOs were panicking and laying people off in droves, and people started defaulting on their loans and losing their homes to foreclosure and declaring bankruptcy. Consumer confidence crashed. Factories closed, towns declared bankruptcy.

The bad news everywhere scared people to death. As a result, people simply stopped buying cars and pretty much everything else. The near bankruptcies of the Detroit automakers affected everybody in Michigan. The machine shop where Ricky's Dad worked got 95% of its work from General Motors, and when they almost went bankrupt and had to be saved by the government, almost all the machinists were laid off. Ricky's Dad was among them because he was older and made more than the younger machinists. When his Dad looked for work, he found that nobody wanted a 55 year old man. Even though that was highly illegal, it was the reality of the workplace, and nobody could prove it was happening. He tried a few odd jobs here and there, and even tried to open his own handyman business, but times were tough, and he had to close his doors.

It broke Ricky's heart to watch his Dad fail. He loved his father and his mother. They had been kind and loving parents and had always been there for him when he was down and needed help. He loved them so much, it made him cry to see them suffer. His Mom had to humiliate herself stripping at a seedy club in Grand Rapids just to make ends meet. Ricky's Mom was a MILF in her mid 40's. She used to cry at night, but she put on a brave face to talk to Ricky when he was young and give him little pep talks. She encouraged him to study hard and work hard to make people like him. She always told him if he worked hard and smiled and was genuinely interested in other people, they would like him. And she was right. They did. He had many great friends who were friends for life. He helped his friends whenever they needed it, and they returned the favor.

Ricky had a white hot hatred of the Wall Street investment bankers for what they had done to the country, and a total disgust for the gutless, corrupt politicians who could not find any fraud in what they did and who did not prosecute any of them. He was pretty sure that last part was because the Wall Street bankers spread 300 million dollars of lobbying money around Washington, D.C every year. The Wall Street bankers owned hundreds of Congressmen and Senators on both sides of the aisle, spreading money, tickets, junkets and women around liberally through their highly paid lobbyists. If they wanted a law passed, they had their lobbyists write it. If they wanted a law watered down, they had their lobbyists contort the language in committee so that it could not really hurt them.

Ricky watched the whole thing unfold on CNN. He chuckled at how all the big wigs rolled up in their blackout limos and then either said or did nothing effective to fix the problem. Always the blackout limos. Anybody with power in Washington always arrived in a blackout limo.

Ricky could not fathom how anybody in their right mind could build a debt instrument based upon undocumented mortgages, and then sell it to customers and not tell them what the debt instrument was actually based upon. Ricky thought to himself, "Are you kidding me? Let me get this straight--the borrower only had to verbally state how much money they made per year and not prove it. Then a big pool of these mortgages would become the underlying 'value' of the bond? What bullshit! So then these Wall Street assholes went out and kited these 'Collateralized Debt Obligation' to investors all over the world without telling them the truth about what its underlying 'value' was. Ricky thought to himself, "That was worse than fraud, that was criminal. Those Wall Street scum-bags intended to steal people's money, because they had to have been virtually certain those loans were never going to be repaid. But they did not really care, since they made their money up front when the deal closed. How the investor made out was irrelevant to them. They were even betting against these 'liar loan' borrowers being able to repay their mortgages so that they would make even more money if they were right and the borrowers did not repay the loans. Scumbags! If that is not evidence of criminal intent, *i.e. mens rea*, then, what is? How could that NOT be fraud? And yet not a single U.S. attorney thought it was. Something was very wrong with that picture.

So Ricky lost faith in the system and became a scoff law. Ricky had no use for any Wall Streeter or any politician, and disliked authority figures in general. He only respected people with integrity and those who did an honest day's work or who actually sweated from physical exertion in their jobs. He liked people who built things and who had courage, values, conviction and loyalty and patriotism. He vowed to some day become a leader in his country with unquestionable integrity that would do what was right for the people regardless of its effect on his own personal fortune or career.

Ricky's observations about Wall Street and about how the politicians bailed them out and coddled them after they ruined the whole country, well the whole world really, just kept reverberating in Ricky's head every time he thought about the struggles his Mom and Dad had to endure. It just infuriated Ricky. His animosity toward authority grew as he grew older, and he had to struggle to control and hide it. His goal was to excel in the system and someday become a great leader, but first he had to game the very system he despised to get to the top.

School was not as hard because he respected teachers. Where he was to have more problems later in life was with authority figures who tried to impose their will upon him for no good reason, reasons he did not agree with or reasons he did not understand. He was just about to run into this problem in a big way in the Marine Corps. Ricky did not know it now, but in order for him to become a Marine Officer, get into Pensacola, make it into jets and become a fighter pilot, all things that he was about to figure out he wanted to do, he had to game the system big time. He was going to have to figure out a way to get control of his attitude, because the United State Marine Corps is an unforgiving place, and it will kick you in the teeth in the blink of an eye.

Ricky developed a habit as an energy miser among his other oddities because of his interest in engineering and energy and peak oil. He was very concerned about the world not being ready for the end of oil, and that the end of oil would be an extinction event. He became obsessed with that issue after having attended the Telluride Film Festival one year and having listened to a talk given by the author of an excellent book called The Long Emergency. That was in 2010, and Ricky concluded the end of oil would be about 28 years away given the continued growth of China and India. He was extremely worried, because he did not see the leadership in Washington or anywhere else in the world doing the things they needed to do to get ready for the end of oil. Many things needed to be done in the areas of conservation and development of alternative energies. Many industries needed to be launched in areas including hydrogen, nuclear, tidal power, wind, solar, and conversion of the fleet to run on natural gas biofuels and synthetic fuels manufactured from coal. Those industries would create millions of jobs, but the politicians just did not see it, or somehow could not figure out how to do it. It was very frustrating for Ricky.

So he became an energy miser, and did what little he could. He would always turn lights off in rooms nobody was in, and drove his extremely fast cars at 55 MPH much to the annoyance of other drivers except when he was feeling frisky. Then he would blow by them like they were standing still, putting his foot into his supercharger like he was trying to reach orbital velocity.

Ricky drove slowly because he knew two things that adversely affect gasoline consumption that very few other drivers knew —first: that drag is proportional to the square of the speed, and aerodynamic drag is one of the biggest factors in gasoline consumption; and, two: that rapid acceleration of a heavy car is very wasteful. In fact, about 78% of the total energy consumption of a car is overcoming its own inertia, i.e., getting it off the line. So Ricky accelerated slowly, and that also greatly irritated drivers behind him. They would roar around him giving him dirty looks or shaking their fists at him. He just flipped them off casually, and smiled.

But because cars consumed so much energy starting and stopping, Ricky also had the bad habit of only slowing down and not fully stopping at many stop signs if he could see clearly that there was no danger of a collision. Because he was a big time scoff law, he viewed a stop sign as more a suggestion than a mandate if he did not see a cop around. That cost him his license a couple of times.

Ricky wanted more than anything to make his parents proud of him, and to make something of himself. He wanted to be somebody the whole country could look up to and respect as a leader with integrity. He worked like a dog to make that happen. It was to take him many years and a war, and a grievous injury and much schooling. But when his Mom finally died, she looked up from her death bed into his handsome face, took his hand, took the hand of his fiance', smiled her angelic smile and, still beautiful after all the years, said with one of her last breaths, "My son, she's lovely, I am glad you finally found somebody after all those women and all these years. I knew that the country would one day need courageous and honest men like you, men with integrity that would not be afraid to step into the breach and fight for all of us when the time came. I knew that you would be one of those men who would always stand by and fight for your values. Your Dad and I love you very much and I could not be prouder of you Son. God bless you."

"Thank you Mom. I Love you. I am glad she got a chance to finally meet you. She is actually more beautiful on the inside than she is on the outside. That is why I picked her. I just know that if you had time to get to truly know her, you would come to love her like I do."

Ricky's Mom passed away shortly after that, and Ricky never forgot those words. He tried to live up to them the rest of his life.

CARMEN INTRODUCED

Second Lieutanant Carmen Nicoise was an exotic, petite woman of Chinese-Spanish descent. But at her very core, Carmen had a boiling cauldron of hatred for the Chinese government. Her Dad was the police chief of Shanghai when she was a little girl and living on the mainland with her Chinese-Spanish Mom and her Chinese Dad. Her Mom was a teacher at a private Catholic elementary girls school that Carmen attended.

Carmen's Dad had been investigating a corrupt Communist Party official who had been taking bribes to grant licenses to foreign corporations to do business in Shanghai. The party official had put a contract out for a hit on her Dad using one of the Triad gangs that ran the underworld in Shanghai. One night as he was returning home from dinner with some of his police friends, three cars full of 14K Shanghai Triad gang members pulled up behind his car and one passed him and stopped blocking his car from the front and rear on a busy street. The third car pulled up alongside his car. There was no escape. Three gang members in ski masks got out of the third car and machine gunned Carmen's Father's police car from front to rear, shattering all the glass. They then pulled Carmen's Father out and brazenly machine gunned him to death in cold blood in front of a thong of startled onlookers.

The Communist Party official then manipulated the system so that Carmen's Mom was denied her death benefit and denied the pension she was entitled to as the result of her husband's many years of devoted service to the Communist Government. The corrupt Communist Party official still was not done. He got Carmen's Mom fired from her teaching job, and orchestrated a campaign to have her ostracized from society.

Almost penniless and with nowhere to turn, they used almost all of their savings to hire a Snakehead gang member to smuggle Carmen and her Mom out of the country. They went to Canada. Carmen's Mom met an Asian engineer from Microsoft who was vacationing in Vancouver and fell in love and married him. Carmen and her Mom and her new step father moved to the Seattle area near Microsoft's headquarters, and Carmen's Mom became a U.S. citizen after a couple of years.

When Carmen turned sixteen, Carmen's Mom arranged a marriage for her to a young Asian Microsoft engineer. The marriage was a disaster and Carmen was miserable. The young engineer was addicted to online gambling and Vicodin™ painkillers, and squandered most of their money. After struggling with his addictions for a year, Carmen realized it was a lost cause, and divorced him. She did get a green card out of the marriage though, and ultimately became a U.S. citizen.

Carmen's stepfather got transferred to Microsoft's Silicon Valley offices, so the family moved to Santa Clara when Carmen was starting her junior year in high school. Carmen's Mom was a good teacher, and her English was excellent. The Administrators at Mitty High School in Santa Clara, California, an exclusive, private Catholic high school, were both fascinated and horrified at her story and they decided to hire Carmen's Mom as a teacher and let Carmen enroll as a junior. Unfortunately, the Carmen's Mom's marriage disintegrated, so they were alone again. They struggled to make ends meet on a teacher's salary in pricey Silicon Valley. They took jobs picking fruit on the weekends, and babysitting whenever jobs became available to make extra money.

Carmen's Mom was a Tiger Mom before that was even a thing. She drove Carmen to excel in school and work hard in all things. She taught her manners, but she also taught her how to fight dirty. She insisted Carmen take martial arts training in addition to playing sports. Carmen's Mom taught Carmen to take herself seriously and not to take any guff from anybody who did not also take her seriously. She taught Carmen that she could do anything anybody else could do and being a girl was no excuse. She would tell Carmen, "No weakness, no whining, no manipulating of men with your beauty, no excuses. Just do it like you know you can. Always carry your own weight and never accept anything you did not earn. It will be offered to you because you are a beautiful girl. But you are NEVER to take it. You EARN it. GOT IT?"

"Yes Maam."

Carmen's Mom was also adamant about having pure Asian grandchildren. She was not a racist. She just did not want to have any half-breed grand kids, and she put a great deal of pressure on Carmen not to date men if they were not Asian. She absolutely insisted on this, and Carmen felt the pressure in a big way. This was a huge problem, because Carmen was a doll, and men of all stripes were constantly hitting on her.

As a result the strict upbringing by her educated, articulate tiger Mom and her disciplined, stern-but-loving-and-gentle police chief Dad, Carmen was a truly outstanding young woman. She was articulate, smart, well mannered and had solid values and a prodigious work ethic. Her academic record was impeccable with a high GPA and leadership demonstrated in many extracurricular activities including student government and team sports. She was lucky enough to win an appointment to the United States Naval Academy after interviewing with California Senator Paul Bond. She earned a Bachelor of Science in Aeronautic Engineering, graduating *magna cum laude.*

But all that discipline and hard work left Carmen with an OCD side and somewhat lonely and a healthy dose of repression which was just bursting to get out. She turned most men down because they were not Asian, and of the Asian men she went out with here, she found that most were either too short, too arrogant or too boring to hold her interest. So she did not date much and never had had a serious relationship. Up until this very night, the birthday of the Marine Corp, November 10, 2021, she was still almost a virgin.

Carmen had joined the Marines because she wanted to have an adventure for one thing, and she also wanted to kill as many Chinese Communist motherfuckers as she could for another. She also wanted to prove that women could be damn good fighter pilots. She had heard of incidents of sexual harassment in the Air Force, and she just had a feeling that the Marines were different. Carmen felt that, in the Marines, if you made it to the "yellow bars" and you proved you could "haul the mail", it did not make any difference if you were yellow, green, pink or blue, they would let you do your job no questions asked and no bullshit. She was right about that.

But more than anything, she had joined the Marines because she knew that it was in the cockpit of a Marine jet fighter where it was more likely than not that she could put the wood to the Chinese Communist douche bags she hated so much. She had been watching the political situation and the supply and demand situation in the world deteriorate over the past 5 years. She noted how the Chinese were quietly making deals all over the world for commodities like aluminum, copper, coal, wood, water, tar sands, liquefied natural gas, oil, etc. She watched as the world population grew as a result of growth in Brazil, Russia, India and

China and noted how the numbers of the middle class grew inexorably larger placing ever greater needs on the limited resources of the world. Carmen knew that there was eventually going to be a war between the U.S. and China over resources, and she wanted to be in a position to kill a bunch of the little commie bastards. Yes she was a hate monger when it came to the Chinese Communists. She hated them with a white hot passion.

Other than that somewhat incongruous trait, Carmen was unselfish, generous, compassionate and respected hard working people of all sorts. Carmen especially loved intelligent, hard working, good-looking, witty men in particular. She had no love for slackers. Because looked like she had been a Raiderette in a former life, guys had been treating Carmen like she was something special ever since she could remember. Literally thousands of them had flung themselves up against her garden wall and burst into flames to no avail. She just laughed at their goofiness. It took a lot to impress Carmen, because Carmen was no slouch. What really turned Carmen's head was a guy with the confidence and intelligence to realize that guys had been doing this to her for her entire life, and who treated her like she was no big deal and expected her to do her part, carry her fair share of the load and not expect any special treatment or favors.

Carmen prided herself in not taking advantage of men despite the fact that it was ridiculously easy. She believed that all relationships were partnerships, and she insisted on carrying her own weight.

Carmen was a bit of a hot-head. Her brain was going Mach 3 all the time and it had a tendency to overheat. This should not have surprised anybody who really knew her.

Carmen had a quick, razor sharp wit, and was not afraid to break out the sailor talk when the situation called for it. She could also be kind of intimidating when she gave you the dagger look even though she was so small. Despite the fact it looked like you could just take a deep breath and blow her away, you couldn't. She had two black belts and years of martial arts training behind that look. When you got that look, your best move was to do a 180 and sound the retreat unless you wanted to spend the night in the ER.

J.J. INTRODUCED

Second Lieutenant J.J. Saleen was a classically handsome, brown-haired, blue-eyed, six-packed, totally-ripped 6' 2" beach volleyball player from Hermosa Beach, California. J.J. was the product of a failed union between a gorgeous blonde surfer girl who never left Woodstock, and a pro beach volleyball player Dad who never quite made it past the beach bum stage. They were laid back to say the least, but they loved J.J. Unfortunately, they loved everybody else too, some physically and that ultimately led to the demise of the marriage. J.J. grew up playing beach volleyball with his Dad and surfing with him Mom and pretty much having a blast in Hermosa. His nights were pretty much unsupervised as Mom and Dad were invariably off somewhere partying or stoned or something.

J.J. became a great beach volleyball player, a great surfer and a prodigious party animal known far and wide in the beach towns. All the little California girls knew him and loved him—literally. But J.J. was no fool, and, despite the fact that he was such a prodigious party boy, he actually studied hard because he had come to a realization. J.J. saw what his parents had become, or, more precisely, what they had not become, and he had decided that he was going to make something of himself. He was not exactly sure what, but he knew that he would not stop until he had done something significant that was good for the world or good for the country or that made people look up to him and think him a hero. And so he set his plan in motion when he was only sixteen-years old.

J.J. was playing pro beach volleyball on the AVP pro beach volleyball tour right out of high school. J.J. was virtually un-blockable at the net, and his spikes were almost un-diggable. J.J. also had a jump serve that was virtually un-passable-- when it went in, which was only about half the time. It was more like an un-guided missile than anything. In beach volleyball games at Pensacola with his fellow student naval aviators, that jump serve earned him the call sign "Scud" after the notoriously inaccurate Iraqi missile of the same name.

J.J. Saleen was a eighteen-year old surfer and beach volleyball phenom, when the accident occurred. Twelve-foot surf was pounding that day as the result of high winds of a big storm sweeping in from the Northern Pacific.

J.J. was out body surfing with a couple of buddies when he caught a big wave late and rode it in about 50 yards when it started to disintegrate and he pearled out of the wave. The wave crashed down on him with such ferocity, it threw him into the relatively shallow bottom with such force that it knocked him out. Drifting underwater unconscious, he basically drowned.

His buddies had seen what had happened and, when he did not come up, they started searching for him frantically. They found him after four minutes underwater, and pulled him to the beach where they frantically waved the lifeguards over. J.J.'s heart had stopped, but his airway was sealed from laryngospasm so he did not have water in his lungs. Working frantically, with CPR and rescue breaths, they were able to get air into J.J.'s lungs, but his heart refused to start for a couple of minutes. Finally, the lifeguard truck arrived, and they were able to shock his heart back into a normal rhythm.

That was a close call for J.J., and he never went surfing again. J.J. developed a deathly fear of water as a result of this accident.

On the beach volleyball scene though, J.J was still a holy terror. He had worked hard at his beach game, and finally made it onto the AVP Pro Beach Volleyball tour after winning several qualifying events. At 20 years old, he won the Manhattan Beach Open, the Wimbledon of beach volleyball with his partner from UCLA's men's indoor volleyball team. UCLA's legendary men's volleyball coach had noticed him when J.J. finished second at an AVP event when he was only 18 years old, and recruited him for the UCLA men's indoor volleyball team.

J.J. tore Westwood up while attending UCLA. He had hot Bruin chicks all over him. But J.J. was no fool. He realized this was the chance of a lifetime, and he studied as hard as he partied. He did well at UCLA academically, and graduated *magna cum laude* with a Bachelor of Science in Aeronautical Engineering. He joined the Marine Corp while he was a sophomore in college and requested to go to OCS that summer, a request which was granted.

At Officer Candidate School, J.J. met Ricky, and they became fast friends when they found out they both wanted to be Marine fighter pilots. J.J. taught Ricky how to jump serve and hand set. When Ricky found out about J.J.'s near-death experience, that was all it took for Ricky to take J.J. under his wing and start working with him in the pool at the OCS complex. Ricky knew that underwater training was one of the first things they would encounter at Pensacola, and he knew that J.J. did not stand a chance of making it through that evolution if he arrived at Pensacola aqua phobic.

So J.J. and Ricky started working on overcoming J.J.'s fear of water in the pool at Quantico during their times on liberty on the weekends. They started with baby steps. Ricky and J.J. would get in the water together and just stand face-to-face for awhile and Ricky would just talk to J.J. about whatever came up. J.J.'s job was to control his fear and just make conversation with Ricky. Then they started having J.J. put his face in the water for a few seconds and holding his breath. When he brought his face up J.J. would be petrified, and Ricky would grab him by the shoulders and say, "You're OK buddy. Stay with me." They just kept working and working on it until J.J. could keep his face in the water for one minute. Then two, then finally three minutes without panic. Ultimately, it was J.J.'s ability to hold his breath and not pass out that was the limiting factor instead of his fear.

The fear overcome, they started worked on swimming underwater until J.J. could swim the entire length of the pool underwater without panic. Finally Ricky and J.J. worked on escape from ropes that Ricky had tied around J.J.

It had taken them the whole six weeks of OCS training to overcome J.J.'s phobia. But they had done it, and Ricky was proud as he could be of J.J.'s progress. In the process, Ricky and J.J. had become the best of friends. J.J. would die for Ricky and vice versa. That was the magic of the camaraderie that developed between men and between men and women undergoing stressful training together.

MARINE CORPS BIRTHDAY HIJINKS

After about the tenth toast of the evening, Ricky, Carmen and J.J. were all shit-faced. Ricky said with a wry smile, "Look at us, we look like the Jamaican bobsled team except white —and yellow."

"Blow me Ricky", Carmen said laughing at his lame, mock racism.

"Oh, OK", Ricky replied.

"How's your girlfriend Ricky?" Carmen slyly asked.

"Which one?"

"Ha – you scumbag." Carmen jabbed.

"She means your main girlfriend and not your backup girlfriend you knucklehead." J.J. said with a bemused smile.

"You have to forgive him Carmen. J.J. heard "The Dance of the Sugar Plum Fairies just one time, and he never turned back." Ricky jabbed back.

"Really? You are going to go there in front of my favorite girlfriend Carmen?" J.J. said.

"Imagine my enthusiasm J.J. Me competing with only two hundred other girls for you attention."

"I'm an acquired taste." J.J. said with a sly smile.

"Don't worry about me believing Ricky. He is just blowing smoke. Me thinks he doeth protest too much."

"Oh you little twerp." Ricky said laughing.

"You know, we have to do something about Sims", Carmen said referring to 2nd Lt. Adam Sims, a classmate of theirs.

"What are you talking about Carmen?", J.J. replied.

"Sims is pissing me off. I am not even sure he is a carbon-based life form." Carmen said. "He is such a horn-dog. The dude keeps hitting on me in class and making unwelcome sexual references in the most inappropriate settings. He comes and sits next to me in the lectures and makes lame comments while I am trying to concentrate and take notes. When we divide up into teams or sparring partners, he always wants to partner with me. At pugil sticks the other day, he wanted to fight me, so I let him. I knocked his dumb ass down and kicked him in the gonads." Carmen said with a sly smile. "He is a walking insult to the women of earth."

CARMEN'S BLACK BELTS

What 2nd Lt. Sims did not know was that 2nd Lt. Carmen Nicoise had two black belts, one in Wing Chun, and one in Mui Thai. It was her martial arts skills that later earned Carmen the call sign "SWAT" as in Special Weapons and Tactics at Naval Air Station Pensacola.

"Yeah, I know. The guy is a douche bag." Ricky said laughing. "He told me he was raised by wolves, but I don't believe him. I believe he is a bubble boy who spent his formative years living in a snow globe without any human contact."

It is not that Sims was a bad looking guy – he was just an arrogant prick. He was a blond, tan, handsome, cut, water polo guy from Stanford and he thought he was the bomb. Sims was, at that moment, a few tables over chatting up another female 2nd Lieutenant from Notre

Dame, the magnificent Victoria Chase – a repressed Catholic who Sims thought would be easy to score. He was right about that.

VERONICA CHASE INTRODUCED

Veronica Chase was a classic California beauty from Mill Valley. Her brown hair extended down to the middle or her back and framed a luscious, symmetrical face punctuated by deep-brown, bedroom eyes. Her face was crowned by full, pouty lips that a guy just wanted to lock onto and suck for awhile. It was hard to bring one's gaze up to her face though given the magnificence of her super-model figure punctuated by a pair of luscious breasts. She was used to it. It had been happening her whole life.

"I have an idea." J.J. said. "I snaked a smoke grenade the other day in the exercise on calling in airstrikes. I still have it in my room. Lets toss it in Sims' room in the middle of the night tonight."

"Excellent!" both Ricky and Carmen exclaimed. And so the nefarious plan was hatched.

It was only 11:45 PM when the dinner broke up and the crowd of drunken 2nd Lieutenants was dismissed for the evening. So Carmen suggested they go out and run the obstacle course using their car headlights for light. Ricky and J.J. thought that was a great idea, because Carmen was hot and they were so lit up that they would have agreed to anything she said.

So off they went to the obstacle course in their dress blues. Ricky brought his Vette and Carmen brought J.J. in her BMW convertible. They parked their cars so the headlights shined on the first obstacle – a thirty foot high wooden wall with a cargo net going up the side. Carmen said she would go first since it was her insane idea.

"Don't look up my skirt you scumbags. I am not wearing any panties." Carmen said suppressing a laugh.

"Excellent" both Ricky and J.J. exclaimed. "Don't worry Carmen, we can't she jack-shit out here." Ricky said.

"Carmen, it says in the Marine Corps Officer's Manual that all Second Lieutenants must wear panties at all times." J.J. said.

"It does not say that you nitwit. I actually read it." Carmen said with a laugh.

"Ouch. That is going to leave a mark." J.J. said with a smile.

It was 1:45 AM by the time they got done running the obstacle course. That was mainly because they were so wasted they had to rest and laugh between obstacles till their heart rates came down out of the 911 zone into the aerobic zone. They resolved that it was time to spring their plot.

They went back to their rooms and put on camouflage face paint and convened at the end of the second floor hallway into which Sims' door opened. It was pitch black and everybody was asleep. Except for Sims. He was in his room making love to the repressed Catholic 2nd Lt. Veronica Chase.

"Ready?" Carmen said. The plan was for Ricky to fling open the door and for Carmen to throw the smoke grenade in. J.J. was assigned the task of running down the hall and bang on doors and yell "Fire!" so everybody would come out in the hallway and see Sims when he ran out of his room naked to escape the smoke.

"Yes." they both replied.

They tiptoed down the hall and got to Sims room. They could hear the muffled sounds of 2nd Lt. Veronica Chase moaning and telling Sims not to stop. They waited awhile listening intently and perversely enjoying the show, whilst smirking and struggling mightily to suppress their laughter. "YES, YES." Veronica screamed. Just then, Carmen pulled the pin on the smoke grenade, and Ricky flung the door open. J.J. took off down hallway yelling "Fire, fire!" and pulled the fire alarm and flipped the light switches on in the hallway. Carmen tossed the grenade into Sims' room streaming huge volumes of red smoke.

Carmen and Ricky took off down the hallway running the opposite direction from J.J. and also screaming "Fire, Fire" at the top of their lungs.

Their plan would have worked, except only Veronica came out into the hall naked, and Hornsby, dumb ass that he was, jumped off the second floor balcony landing in the grass and breaking his ankle.

All the Second Lieutenants in that section of the Bachelor Officer's Quarters rushed out into the hallway in various states of disarray. And they were rewarded handsomely as they were afforded a full on frontal view of the magnificent, voluptuous Veronica Chase butt naked and sheepishly trying to cover her goodies. No dice. Not possible. They applauded, laughed and broke into a rousing chorus of "God Bless America". They were collectively grateful for the bounty this great land of ours could produce.

Ricky, J.J. and Carmen were laughing their heads off when they returned to Carmen's BOQ room. After they stopped laughing, Carmen looked at them both with a shit-eating grin on her face and said, "I'm still shit-faced and that Veronica babe's body made me horny as hell. What do you say boys?

Ricky and J.J. looked at each other in amazement, smiled and then broke out laughing and they both started ripping their clothes off and then ripping Carmen's clothes off. Off to the showers they went, and the rest is history. It was Carmen's and Ricky's first threesome, but for J.J., not so much.

The next day, Sims hobbled up to the trio on his crutches and said, "Very funny you retards."

Ricky, Carmen and J.J. broke into laughter and said, "Yeah, we thought so." They all looked at each other and smiled and winked.

Colonel Morris, Commander of The Basic School had less of a sense of humor about it. All three of them got letters of reprimand in their personnel files. But it was worth it. Sims left Carmen alone for the rest of the six month course at The Basic School.

They never spoke of the threesome again, and it never happened again. Whenever they saw each other, they just smiled, winked and gave each other a snappy salute. It was their secret, and nobody ever found out about it. All their classmates looked at each other quizzically and thought to themselves, "What the heck is going one? Why are these Second Louies saluting each other?"

CARMEN ALMOST LOSES IT IN THE SNOW

It was 3 AM on December 19th. Ricky, Carmen and J.J. were prone in the snow about 10 meters away from the side of a trail in an ambush position hidden deep in the forests of Quantico, Virginia. They were covered with stealth ponchos to hide their infrared heat signatures. In addition, their faces and hands were painted with special face paint containing cenospheres – tiny spheres of aluminum and silica that absorbed the body's heat and made their hands and faces invisible to infrared night vision scopes. The night was moonless. A blizzard was howling around them with 25 knot winds blowing snow and dropping the minus 5 degree F temperature to a wind chill factor of negative holy shit.

They had been suffering the freezing temperatures for three hours but could not move or take any steps to warm themselves. They were fully tactical. No light, no fires, no heat sources of any kind were allowed lest they be discovered and their ambush position be compromised. This ambush was critical to disrupting the Blue Force tactical plan, and the Red Force was depending upon Ricky's squad to carry it out without failure. It was the three day war, the final exercise before graduation from The Basic School and they had to do well or fail.

Ricky looked over at Carmen and could see her shivering uncontrollably. She only weighed 115 lbs buck-naked, dripping-wet and there simply was no fat on her body to insulate her body from the assault of the cold wind. He was suffering too, and he could see that

J.J. was also having a hard time staying still. Ricky felt compassion for his squad mates, but he knew they understood the situation and did not expect any sympathy or special favors from him. They just had to suck it up until their mission was completed.

"Holy Mother of God, I could die out here. I don't think I can take this much longer, but I can't quit now and let Ricky and J.J. down. And if I quit, I will never be able to smoke some Chinese Communist dirtbags. I just have to suck it up." Carmen thought to herself. They had already lost one second lieutenant to heat stroke in August on a run up the hill trail during Black Flag weather, so Carmen knew there was no guarantee that you absolutely, positively would not die while training at The Basic School.

She remembered that blazing hot, humid August day when they almost lost Ricky, and tried to distract herself to take her mind off the skull numbing pain. The wind was whipping the snow now, howling through the tree branches with a demonic fury. The blowing snow stung her exposed cheeks as the frozen crystals smashed into her face, stabbed her skin like little daggers and then melted.

It could not have gotten much hotter that day in August she remembered. China could be hot, but she had never experienced anything like the combination of heat and humidity of northern Virginia on a sweltering summer afternoon. The hill trail was a brutal 3-mile mostly uphill trail upon which the instructors loved take the young officers for a run when they were feeling particularly sadistic. It was about as much fun as Christmas with the Taliban. On that particular day, it was 95 degrees and 98% humidity, and the most sadistic instructor at The Basic School was setting the pace. At the two mile mark Carmen could feel her pulse in her eyeballs and the sweat was pouring off her forehead into her eyes blinding them with salt. She looked over at J.J., and he was straggling a little, but hanging in as one would expect from a professional athlete.

Then she looked at Ricky…. oh shit! Ricky was a much bigger guy that either Carmen or J.J., and he had a lot more muscle to be hauling up that hill. He was struggling. His veins were bulging in his neck, his face twisted in agony. He was still pouring out sweat so that was a good sign. Once a guy stops sweating and gets to the hot, dry skin stage, he is having a heat stroke and has to be immediately immersed in an ice bath or he will probably die.

"Ricky, Ricky listen to me. Can you do this for me dude? I need you to do this. I cannot lose you now. I need you badly. You are my rock here. I don't think I can do this without you." She lied for his benefit. "Can you hear me?" Carmen's voice was desperate now. She desperately wanted to help her friend make it, and would do anything to give him the courage to stick it out. It worked.

Ricky looked over at her, smiled a faint grin and then stopped momentarily, dropped to his knees, puked his guts out and then got up and started running again. He made it all the way to the end. Later he just gave her a hug and told her that if she had not said what she had said, he might have quit and been thrown out of TBS. It was a pivotal moment in his evolution. He learned then and there, as most officers do, that no matter how tired or uncomfortable you are and no matter how much you think you cannot go on, you always can and you always have more.

Carmen's thoughts drifted to thoughts about quitting. She knew what a huge let down that would be for Ricky and J.J.. They had become like the Three Musketeers, and her departure would leave a gaping hole in the team. He thoughts drifted back to the long, storied history of the Marine Corps and the incredible suffering of thousands of Marines before her. She thought about the First Marine Division and X Corp surrounded by 67,000 Chinese troops at the frigid Chosin Reservoir in the Korean War when a Siberian cold front swept through and dropped temperatures to −35 degrees F. It was so cold, the morphine syringes froze and had to be thawed out in the medics mouths before injection. Jeep and radio batteries all froze, throwing communication and transport into chaos. Even the springs on the firing pins of the Marine's rifles got so cold they would not strike the bullet's primers hard enough to fire the rounds. Those Marines endured unspeakable suffering, and fought their way out and into everlasting Marine Corps lore. Nope, quitting was out of the question.

The hypothermia Carmen was suffering started to get worse though and started to progress toward severe from merely moderate. Her thinking became muddled and her heart rate became very slow. She felt her shivering becoming so violent that she feared she would give her position away from the noise of the rustling of her poncho. Her muscle movements became very slow and labored, and her breathing became very shallow and labored. She knew she was on the verge of dying. She looked at Ricky with an expression of fear and no doubt some panic on her face, probably for the first time. It was a wonder he could see her expression through the thermo-masking camo paint, but he saw it.

Ricky studied her face for a minute silently. He had been observing Carmen closely for the six months they had been at basic school together. She was truly an outstanding individual. No bullshit, smart as a whip, tough as Kevlar yet fun to be around and easy going when she was not working and so hot she set off car alarms. She never blamed anybody else for her failures, never whined, never made excuses, always did her fair share of the work, never used anybody, never manipulated men and never lied. She could really haul the mail, this one. He had never in his life met anybody like her. But now he was worried by what he saw. He had seen Carmen come through the hellish physical training at The Basic School with flying colors. Fifty mile hikes, no problem. Ten mile timed runs, no sweat. Brutal obstacle course time trials and hill course runs in 95 degree heat and high humidity, piece of cake. Fifteen-mile orienteering races, easy. Hand-to-hand combat, easy. But this was different. She looked for the first time like she wanted to quit. He looked hard into her eyes, and mouthed the words, "Don't leave me now." and gave her the hand signals for "Friends for life." and "Be strong." Then he looked over at J.J. and gave him another hand signal. Silently they moved over to Carmen and crawled under her stealth poncho and put her into a body sandwich to warm her body with their body heat. They pulled their stealth ponchos over hers, and resumed their silent watch over the trail.

Slowly, they could feel her shivering subside as their body heat began to raise her core temperature. Eventually she actually began to purr slightly. After a few more minutes, she looked up and smiled at both of them. All you could see was her teeth. It was slightly comical. It was at that moment that they all knew they would be friends for life.

CHAPTER 2

DECEMBER 23: FOUR AND A HALF YEARS
BEFORE THE WAR WITH CHINA STARTS

Graduation from The Basic School was a great day. Ricky's parents showed up from Michigan and met Carmen's Mom for the first time. J.J.'s parents had split up several years earlier, but his Mom made the trip from Hermosa Beach to see her handsome son graduate into the ranks of real Marine officers.

The three friends had become inseparable at Quantico helping each other out through the tough spots. The Basic School was about teaching Marine officers the technical skills and leadership they would need to lead real Marines in combat situations. The syllabus included squad and platoon tactics, urban warfare, map reading, orienteering, emergency medical techniques to, for example, save a man with a sucking chest wound or to give a wounded Marine who has swallowed his tongue a tracheotomy with an ink pen, weapons training, hand-to-hand combat using Marine Martial Arts and many other things along with grueling physical training. It had been a tough six months, but they had made it.

Against all odds each of Ricky, J.J. and Carmen had all been accepted to Naval Aviation Training at Pensacola Naval Air Station to train with Navy and Marine Corp Instructors pilots and other Naval Aviation candidates.

To get an assignment to train as a Navy or Marine pilot, one had to be in outstanding physical condition, possess stamina and be intelligent and tough. Flying high performance aircraft and pulling G's was exhausting.

Perfect 20-20 vision without correction was required — no exceptions. PRK might be OK in some circumstances, but LASIK was an automatic disqualifier. Although one did not have to be a triathlete, it helped. If the Naval Aviation candidate could not do 42 pushups, they were toast. Any history of drug abuse, and you were out. If candidates first passed a battery of aptitude and suitability tests, they were allowed to endure the mother of all flight physicals. If they were too fat or too short or too tall to fit in a cockpit, or had certain chronic maladies, they were out. If a candidate was color blind or his or her eyes had any diseases or abnormality, they were out. A Naval Aviation candidate's hearing had to be good, and his or her nose, ears and throat were scrutinized. Any malformed or diseased ear canal was a killer. Even the teeth were examined. A battery of X-rays and cardiovascular tests are also conducted.

Ricky, J.J. and Carmen were all smart and in good shape though so they made it through this phalanx of tests and were given orders to report to Pensacola Naval Air Station to start pilot training.

"This calls for a celebration" Ricky announced to Carmen and J.J. when they received their orders. "To the O Club!" J.J. exclaimed. After the Tailhook Scandal, the Navy base O Clubs became ghost towns because the Brass had no sense of humor. But this was the Marines. "See you both in 45", Carmen said with a smile. Remember what the Gipper said. "Some people spend their entire lives wondering if they made a difference. The Marines don't have that problem." Ronald Reagan.

The officer's club at Quantico was an unimposing structure. Rather humble in outward appearance, but efficient. That was symbolic of the way of the Marines. The Marines, unlike any other organization operating at the pleasure of Congress, frequently gave budget money back at the end of the year. Go figure.

CBS STORY ON HUGE BUDGET CUTS

Ricky arrived first, and, as he walked in, the CBS evening news came on.

"Congress today finally faced up to the severe budget crunch caused by the loss of tax revenues of millions of workers laid off as the result of the recent wave of bankruptcies of large corporations caused by rising oil prices. Oil has risen to historic highs recently as supplies dipped resulting from the drying up of the Prudhoe Bay and North Sea oil fields. Faced with a national debt that is spiraling out of control and massive debt service payments to holders of U.S. bonds and other debt instruments, Congress passed a bill eliminating funding for the Center for Disease Control, the National Institute for Health, Fannie Mae, Freddie Mac, the National Park System and Medicaid" the pretty anchorwoman said with a grim face.

"Holy shit, things are going south fast. Better party hard while there is still time." Ricky thought to himself smiling but still very concerned about the direction the country was headed.

"In other news today, imaging satellites revealed the beginning of construction work to expand the massive, supposedly secret Chinese underground naval base at the southern end of Hainan Island. This huge facility was built by the Chinese in the late 90's to hide their development of aircraft carriers and ballistic missile submarines from the prying eyes of U.S. spy satellites. It is not known how many ships and submarines are based there" the anchorwoman stated in a matter-of-fact tone that was vaguely discomforting to hear.

"This was huge news and scary as hell." Ricky thought to himself. "She ought to be freaking out, but she isn't – very professional." he thought.

Just then, J.J. and Carmen walked in together. "Hola, comrades." Ricky said. "Did you hear the news?"

"No, what happened?" Carmen said.

"Our friends on the Hill just killed the CDC, NIH, HEW, Fannie Mae, Freddie Mac, Medicare and the National Park System to save budget money, and the DOW dropped 8500 points in one day." Ricky said. "And, furthermore, the Red Chinese are expanding their underground navy base on Hainan Island to make it even bigger than it already is. The world is going into the tank."

"Holy smokes." J.J. said with a wince. "We better hurry up and get our wings, because I have a feeling the caca is going to hit the compressor fairly soon if we keep going the way we are going."

"Don't get your panties in a bunch J.J.. Congress did not cut the military budget yet, and we have one of the strongest military forces in the world. If we have to, we will kick their yellow asses into the next hemisphere." Carmen said with the supreme confidence of a double black belt.

"Ooh-Rah!" (Jarhead version of Navy "Hoo-Yah", meaning Hell Yes) Ricky and J.J. exclaimed together and they ordered a couple of rounds for Attitude Adjustment Hour.

"I have been thinking it would be fun to drive down to Pensacola together. We can pack up my old '65 Thunderbird convertible and pull a small U-haul trailer and leave tomorrow night and drive straight through." Carmen said in her most persuasive voice. "What do you think?"

"Ooo-Rah." Ricky and J.J. exclaimed as the plan was born. There was no sense arguing with Carmen. When she wanted something, she was going to get it, and they knew it. Besides, they knew it would be a blast hanging together and meeting the salt of the earth people in the restaurants and bars along the route.

DRIVING TO PENSACOLA ALL NIGHT

The next night after a semi-relaxed day of packing and planning their route, they set off at dusk down I-95 southbound toward the Florida panhandle. Carmen took the first shift of driving. It was then the Ricky and J.J. realized for the first time that Carmen was a complete maniac behind the wheel. Pulling a trailer and 85 MPH did not seem like a very good idea to them, nor did it seem legal. Because it wasn't. To Carmen, it was another day at the office. But they were amused, so they stayed silent and looked at her.

"What?" she said with a sly smile.

After driving all night, the dawn broke clear and semi-chilly as they turned onto I-10 and started westward to Pensacola NAS. Ricky drove the final leg and pulled into the front gate of Pensacola in grand style with the classic old Thunderbird drawing admiring glances from the sentries at the gate. They snapped out a salute and said "Nice ride sir. How are you this fine morning?"

"I am doing well thanks. But it is still early, so things can still go FUBAR." The sentries laughed. Everybody in the military knows what FUBAR means.

And with that, the sentries gave the trio directions to the Bachelor Officers Quarters where they promptly headed and crashed for a few hours. It was the beginning of a long grind of training to be Marine pilots. They did not know it, but they were destined for the Advanced Strike pipeline which would take them four years to become qualified to fly the world's most advanced fighters. They don't give you a $40 million dollar jet to fly until they know you are not a yahoo.

"Oh there you are. " J.J. said to Carmen.

"Oh good. I was wondering where I was." Carmen joked.

DILBERT DUNKER

It was Dilbert dunker day at Aviation Preflight Indoctrination. When you fly off carriers, it is not impossible that you will one day wind up in the water, upside down, at night and strapped into your ejection seat. The instructors want to know if you can handle that or will lose it.

"What's up guys? You look like you are about to puke." Ricky said as he casually strolled up. The Dilbert Dunker was no fun and they knew it. They basically strap you into an ejection seat, drop you into a pool and turn you upside down. It is your job to get out without supplemental oxygen and without drowning.

"I am not exactly comfortable in the water." Carmen said. "I am more like a kitten than a dolphin if you know what I mean." she said apprehensively.

J.J. looked scared shitless. Ricky knew exactly why. "Even though I grew up at the beach, I have never been in the water upside down, blindfolded and sinking in a plane before.

"So you can imagine the source of my consternation," Carmen said apprehensively.

"Oh relax Carmen. Millions of Ensigns and 2d Lieutenants before you have passed this test, and nobody has drowned yet. There have been a few that are off in the VA hospitals on life support, but war is hell." Ricky tweaked her with a straight face.

"Screw you Ricky. If you weren't so big, I would kick your ass." Carmen said only mildly amused. Ricky loved to mess with people, and Carmen knew it. But she knew it was all in good fun. J.J. just gave a weak smile.

"You're up Nicoise. Strap in and no whining." the instructor said with a smirk.

"Hmmm. Imagine my enthusiasm." Carmen said with a straight face as she got in the wet, cold steel cage and strapped into the multi-point harness. She put on the blackout goggles and said a little prayer in the dark.

BANG went the release with a menacing metallic sound as she slid down the rails 10 feet into the cold pool with a splash. She pulled the simulated canopy release lever just before hitting the water. Over went the cage and she settled into her harness upside down and blind and cold. "So far, so good. At least it wasn't salt water." she thought to herself. She hated salt water.

Methodically she felt for the shoulder harness straps and lap belt straps and followed them to the latch apparatus. She worked carefully but fast. The plane would be sinking and every second counted because if it got too deep, she might not be able to escape. That would be the reality. Here there were Navy divers standing by only a couple of feet away making sure she did not drown – and grading her on her performance.

She found the release for the first shoulder strap, loosened it and slid her left arm through to free it from the strap. Then she did the same for her right arm. 48 seconds. She started looking for the release on the lap belt. There were not like seat belts in a car. More complicated and difficult to release, especially if you were in a state of panic. Finally she got the lap belt loose, and reached forward into the blackness to try to find the cage's front bar wrapped with tape that represented the front cockpit rail after the canopy was gone. She needed to grab that bar and and pull herself free of the cockpit and all the floating straps. 1 minute, 11 seconds. Found it. Not dead yet, but her lungs were screaming for air. "Hope I never have to do this for real." she thought to herself.

As she started to pull herself up out of the cockpit and further down into the pool, something caught. She was in a full flightsuit with a survival knife and other survival equipment strapped on, and she was floating in the middle of a bunch of loose straps. Something had snagged here and was keeping her from exiting. Panic started to set in, but she gathered her wits and worked her way through the problem. She felt around and found that a loose shoulder harness strap had snagged on her knife handle. She untangled it and found herself able to exit.

One minute, 30 seconds without a breath.

Now the problem was she did not know which way to swim. Being in a semi-weightless state and in black out goggles, she had a hard time knowing which way was up toward the surface. She started swimming hoping she would figure it out. Bang. She smashed her head on the side of the pool. "At least there is a reference point." she thought lungs screaming now with ever increasing urgency. The surface beckoned her, but she still did not know which way to swim. By trial and error and dumb luck and feeling the direction of boyancy, she deduced which way was up and swam to the surface. She broke the surface took a huge gasp and blurted out an expletive. She took off her blackout goggles just in time to see the Navy divers give the thumbs up sign. She had passed!

One test down and 10,000 more to go.

She hoisted herself up out of the pool and looking very much like a drowned rat, looked at J.J. and Ricky who were standing there with bemused smiles on their faces. "Well that was about as much fun as chewing tinfoil for an hour." she said, and they broke out into belly laughs.

HELO DUNKER

The helo dunker was worse. It is the most feared apparatus at NAS Pensacola. Each student aviator seeking the Wings of Gold and even pilots in the fleet had to pass four dunks of increasing difficulty. Helicopters had a tendency to crash violently into the water on occasion. If a pilot or passenger survived the crash itself, he or she still had to get out of the helo as it sank. Sometimes the windows were jammed and sometimes it was night. The Navy had found from hard won lessons that the helo dunker training increased the chances of survival by 50%. So every pilot had to do it every four years, and every student needed to pass the test a first time to be able to continue flight training.

The helo dunker was a metal box with windows on the side and 6 seat in the back and two seats up front separated by a bulkhead from the passenger compartment. Because lots of heavy machinery on a helo were at the roof level, helos all capsized when they went into the drink, because they were top heavy. So the helo dunker was turned over when it went into the water to better simulate the reality the crew and pilots would face.

The helo dunker was a large metal box-like structure that simulated the fuselage of a helicopter. The box had three windows on each side, a cockpit area up front with two seats which was separated from a rear compartment with six seats by a bulkhead having a hole in it simulating the entrance for the pilots to the passenger compartment.

McABLE INTRODUCED

Ricky was standing in a group with six other student aviators who were to go into the helo dunker with him when their turn came up.

"Hi there. 2nd Lt. Ricky Magnusson, United States Marine Corp." Ricky introduced himself to the tall, handsome Navy Ensign standing next to him.

"Hello. Ensign Neil McAble. Where are you from Ricky?" Ensign McAble inquired.

"Grand Rapids, Michigan." Ricky replied. "You? You scared?"

"Houston, Texas. Not a problem. I grew up bow-hunting wild boar, and playing volleyball at Penn State. No sweat." Neil drawled with a smile. "You're a long way from home there Lieutenant. Down there in Texas, we believe that you Yankees actually did not win the Civil War, and reports of victory by the Union were all a media hoax. Are you sure YOU can handle this little apparatus?" McAble said with a grin.

"Oh please. Are you serious? Of course we won the Civil War. If you would have had better logistics, the Confederacy probably would have won. And, I've been in worse situations. This thing will be a piece of cake." Ricky lied. He grew up with a lake behind his house, and had capsized his sailboat a couple of times and stayed under it breathing the resulting air bubble that rose to the bottom of the hull, but never had he been strapped-in, blindfolded and upside down. "Looks like fun to me." Ricky lied again as he watched the group before him being lowered into the water and the cable turn the dunker upside down.

Wow, this McAble guy was kind of a blowhard Ricky thought, but he decided to reserve judgment until after he had a chance to see what McAble could do under pressure. Fighter pilots have to be confident, aggressive and fearless. Or else they die in a fireball. But seriously, what did he expect. The dude was from Texas.

Ensign McAble was an athletic 6' 1", 185 pounds of solid muscle. He had dark brown hair and hazel eyes and beautiful white teeth which showed when he flashed his devilish smile. He had classic good looks and a twinkle in his eye which arose from his mischievous personality and his out-of-the box attitude. He was a little bit of a smart ass, but never in a mean way, always looking for a way to stick the needle in. Even though he himself was a bit of blowhard, he did not know it, and, ironically, he hated blowhards, show offs and arrogant people. In that way, he and Ricky were peas in a pod. He had grown up on a ranch doing hard physical labor during the summers working for his dad. He could take care of himself, and he had the quiet air of confidence that came from being tested numerous times in the past and knowing what he could do and what he could not. He was a guy you wanted on your side when the shit hit the fan. He was bank, and his word was as good as gold. Neil knew if he could handle a charging 400 lb. wild boar, the helo dunker things should be a piece of cake. He was wrong.

The first three dunks were not too bad. On the first ride, all they had to do was wait about 8 seconds before releasing their lap and shoulder harness belts, find the nearest exit and escape. The water rushing up your nose was annoying but not fatal. They made you wait 8 seconds to avoid being thrown around the inside of the dunker by the in-rushing water. After about 8 seconds, the dunker was completely submerged and filled with water and it was safe to unbuckle. "No swimming." Ricky reminded himself recalling the instructions from the Navy divers who were monitoring the test. You don't want to kick a fellow rider in the face swimming to get out. You pulled yourself out by handholds on the fuselage, so you had to memorize where they were because it might be pitch black at night when you went in. No jostling or pushing other riders either or jockeying for position at an exit. If the Navy divers saw any of that, you had to repeat the ride, something nobody wanted to do.

The second ride was tougher. On this ride, to simulate a very real possibility of jammed windows caused by distortion of the fuselage on impact with the water, everybody had to escape through the single escape port at the back of the passenger compartment. Neil and Ricky were strapped into the seats farthest forward toward the cockpit bulkhead. Ricky was in seat 6, the farthest seat from the single exit they all had to use. "Not good." Ricky thought to himself.

When the dunker went in and turned over, Neil and Ricky counted off 8 seconds and started to work on unbuckling their lap and shoulder harnesses as did the other 4 student aviators in the cabin. Something went wrong with Ricky's lap belt latch though and he could not get the lap belt off. Neil saw Ricky struggling with the lap belt and pulled himself over to help. He had heard the gouge that the lap belt latch on seat 6 would not release easily sometimes and he knew what to do to free Ricky. He waved Ricky off the belt and grabbed the latch and pulled it up and then gave the belt itself a mighty heave and it came open. Ricky looked at him in amazement, and Neil gave him the thumb jerk saying, "Lets get the fuck out of here." Ricky could not agree more. By this time, both of their lungs were screaming for air, but, fortunately, the other students had freed themselves without incident and already egressed the cabin so the coast was clear to pull themselves out of the fuselage without having to wait in a traffic jam. It had been about 65 seconds underwater for them, about three times the normal submersion time, but it felt like a year.

"Thanks Neil. I owe you one." Ricky said appreciatively.

"Nothing to it yankee boy. Buy me a beer tonight." Ensign McAble said with a grin.

The third ride was even tougher. Everybody had to wear black out goggles on the third ride and find their way to an exit and escape completely in pitch black. They were allowed to escape from the nearest window or exit though so it was not as bad as the fourth and final ride which was to come. Ricky and Neil both negotiated the blackness adeptly and escaped through the windows closest to them on the side of the dunker.

The fourth ride was a near death experience, or it at least seemed that way. This time they were simulating a night crash that jammed the windows. Everybody had to wear black out goggles and escape from the rear entrance one at a time. Luckily, Neil and Ricky drew seats 3 and 4 for this ride so they were across from each other and about midway in the fuselage. They each memorized the handholds they would use before donning their blackout goggles. The dunker went in and turned over, and they counted off 8 seconds and then started to work. Everything went according to plan except for the fact that the students in seats 1 and 2 had not memorized their handholds and were fumbling around in the darkness searching for handholds to use. In their panic, they blocked the exit and caused a traffic jam which caused the students in seats 5 and 6 to have to be rescued by the divers. Ricky and Neil knew approximately where the exit was and could feel the students in front of them struggling. They both grabbed one student with one hand and used their handholds with the other to gently guide the panicked students in seats 1 and 2 out the exit.

The students in seats 1 and 2 washed out of flight school on that ride. Neil and Ricky broke the surface of the water after about two minutes gasping for breath.

Ricky and Neil climbed out of the pool and were greeted by Carmen and J.J. who were in the group two rotations behind them. "Nice job guys." J.J. said to them both. "How was your ride?"

"About as much fun as Christmas with the Taliban." McAble cracked between heaving breaths.

J.J. and Carmen looked inquisitively at Ricky. "This is my new friend Ensign Neil McAble." Ricky said. "This is 2nd Lt. Carmen Nicoise and 2nd Lt. J.J. Saleen. We went to Basic School together." Ricky said as he introduced Neil.

"Join us at the O Club tonight about 8 Neil." Carmen said.

"Thanks. I will." Neil said.

RICKY AT O CLUB RECOUNTS NEIL SAVING HIM IN HELO DUNKER

Attitude Adjustment Hour was in full swing by the time Ricky, J.J., Carmen and Neil arrived. They sat down at a table for four and ordered a round. "So did I tell you what Neil did today in the helo dunker?" Ricky said.

"No." Carmen and J.J. both replied.

"He saved me big time. I was in seat 6 and was having trouble getting my lap belt off. The latch was open, but it was not coming loose for some reason, and I was starting to panic. It was the farthest seat from the cabin exit and there were 5 other guys in there with me all of whom had to get out that same exit. I was thinking if I have to wait for the traffic jam to clear plus have trouble with the belt, I was toast because I was going to run out of air and pass out. Neil saw me struggling and came over and gave me a hand signal to get my hands out of the way. Then he gave the lap belt a yank with the latch open and it gave way and opened up. I thought I was going to have to be saved and either wash out of the program or have to do the ride again. Thank God for Neil." Ricky explained.

"Good work Neil." Carmen said with an admiring gaze and a smile.

"It was nothing." Neil said. "I suspected Ricky was going to have trouble with that latch before we ever went in, because I talked to the Ensign in that seat that took the ride yesterday. He told me what he did to get it loose, so I just gave it a try and it worked. I did not tell Yankee boy here just for fun. I wanted to see if he panicked. To his credit, he didn't, but I did not want him to have to repeat the ride or wash out so I went over and helped him." Neil said refusing to blow his own horn. "You never know when you are going to need a favor." Neil drawled wisely.

Part of the grading and decisional process as to who is going to get jets and who is going to get prop planes and helos is how well people in your class and your instructors like and respect you. Neil knew this because his Dad was a Navy aviator during the Vietnam War. Competition for jets was fierce since almost everybody wanted to be a fighter pilot. These four certainly did.

THEY FIND OUT NEIL WAS AN OUTSIDE HITTER

Another round of drinks and chit chat with the four junior officers getting to know each other. After some questioning, they found out that Neil played men's volleyball for Penn State as an opposite and backup setter. This got their attention since now they had a fourth for the sand doubles games they liked to play on weekends when they were not flying. Although Carmen was not tall at 5' 6", she was very fast and played cagey defense and had huge vertical hops. She had played outside hitter at Mitty High School in Silicon Valley, the same program that launched Olympic Gold Medal winner Terry Walshe to beach legend status. She could put a good set down with the best of them, and now they found out that Neil was a setter and he could hit too. Sweet. A squadron sand doubles tournament was already set up for Saturday two weeks hence, and now Carmen had somebody to play with since J.J.

had already committed to play with Ricky. It was going to be epic since Penn State made regular appearances in the NCAA men's volleyball championship final four, so McAble had to be good.

DARTS TOURNAMENT-NAILGUN IS BORN

After another round of drinks, the foursome decided it was time for an impromptu darts tournament. After eight other aviators joined the fray, it was tied after four rounds between Neil and Ensign Smathers, an English born graduate of Florida State who had wasted his youth in the English pubs playing darts and drinking pints. How he ever graduated from Florida State and got a commission is still a mystery. On the final toss for Smathers, he threw a 9 putting Neil McAble under serious pressure. At this point, possibly because of the influence of one too many margaritas, Ensign McAble decided he had a better chance if he threw his utility knife. So he pulled out the knife, carefully unfolded it to its locked position and took up his position at the firing line. He briskly took aim and let the knife fly end-over-end from 20 feet. He hit the 9 ring and they lost, but the knife hit the board with a huge whack and stuck, pointy end in like it had been shot from a nailgun. There was a stunned silence for a second, and then the whole officers club erupted in cheers and laughter. And from that day forward, Ensign Neil McAble's call sign became "Nailgun".

Nobody screwed with Neil. Neil did not particularly like his call sign (being a longhorn from the University of Texas, he wanted Hook-Em as in "Hook-em Horns"), but once a call sign got spawned, it was yours forever whether you liked it or not. The more you fought it, the more it stuck.

ALTITUDE CHAMBER

The foursome now started to buckle down and tackle the tough classes in aerodynamics, aircraft engines and systems, meteorology, navigation, flight rules and regulations that were required subjects in Aviation Preflight Indoctrination. All tests on these subjects like all physical tests were graded by the instructors. They were looking for the best and the brightest with aggressive, no fear attitudes to fly the big expensive jets. There were also classes and field tests in survival tactics and aviation physiology. For the latter, they put them in a altitude chamber and took them up to 25,000 feet, well above the 10,000 feet one can safely ascend to without oxygen. Twenty five thousand feet is an altitude where, if you do not have an oxygen mask on you will experience hypoxia in a matter of a couple of minutes, a not unpleasant phenomenom which will kill you. Unless you recognize it and take corrective action immediately, you are toast. First you feel giddy and happy. Then you die.

Just for fun, the instructors have you play patty cake with a partner after your mask is off at 25,000 feet. You can bail at any time and put your mask on before the full 4 minutes, but nobody wants to be a loser. So they play on until they can no longer manage to clap their own hands, clap their partner's hands, touch their heads with both hands and start over. As the students get goofier and goofier in the pseudo-drunken state of hypoxia, the funnier it becomes – until it is no longer funny and somebody is about to suffer brain damage . The instructors have never let that happen though. At least not so far.

BEACH VOLLEYBALL TOURNAMENT

After four academic weeks, the final two weeks of physical training were over and the training squadron beach volleyball tournament was upon them. It was a fairly large tournament with quite a few doubles teams entered. Ricky and J.J. were on the opposite side of the bracket from Carmen and Neil "Nailgun" McAble.

After about five matches apiece, both Ricky and J.J. and Carmen and Neil had survived their semifinal matches and were scheduled to meet in the final at 5 PM. One game to 21, win by 2. It was a see saw battle all the way with the lead exchanging hands several times. Finally, as darkness approached, it was 35 to 34 in Ricky and J.J.'s favor with J.J. back to serve.

Carmen looked at Nailgun with a twinkle in her eye and said, "It is now or never dude. Let's light these guys up. Are you with me?"

"Hoo-Yah! Fly Navy." came the reply. They were ready.

"Bring it bitch." Carmen yelled across the net at J.J.. The crowd roared its approval at the bravado of this little 115 lb. wafer of a girl. She looked like the Tooth Fairy. J.J. smiled almost imperceptibly.

"Ooh, big mistake Carmen. I think your all hat and no cattle. If I were you, I would light the Bat signal." Ricky said with a crooked grin.

Just then J.J. started his approach run from behind the service line for his fearsome jump serve. About 3 feet before he reached the service line, he tossed the ball up in the air about 15 feet and about 3 feet into the court and leaped up into it as it accelerated downward. He made contact with heel of his hand slightly to the left of the center of the bottom of the ball and snapped his wrist over the top giving the ball top spin and side spin. It streaked over the net like a Scud missile, sinking and curving at it went. It started out heading straight for Carmen and she was tracking it with her eyes. "Mine, mine." she yelled. But then it started dipping and curving away from her, and Nailgun realized it was curving toward him and headed into the no man's land between Carmen and Neil. Carmen dived toward the streaking ball, arms outstretched to pass it, but Neil dived for it too. Carmen could see they were going to collide in midair in the middle, and that distracted her just enough that she broke concentration and shanked the ball off her fists into the crowd. 36-34. Game, Set and Match. The crowd roared its admiration for the huge jump serve J.J. had just unleashed on his hapless victims, and, after some deliberation later by the instructors, J.J.'s call sign became "Scud".

"Any questions?" J.J. said with a laugh.

Carmen and Nailgun, collapsed on the sand after their collision, looked up at J.J. and then rolled over laughing hysterically. They looked like sugar cookies.

"That will teach me not to be such a wise ass." Carmen said with a smile.

"No shit Sherlock." Nailgun said with a laugh. "How about a little heads up next time you plan to kick a sleeping giant in the teeth." Nailgun said.

They got up and walked under the net to congratulate Ricky and J.J., the new kings of Training Squadron 236. Pensacola and Aviation Preflight Indoctrination was over. For Ricky, J.J., Carmen and Neil, it was off NAS Corpus Christi for Primary Flight Training

CHAPTER 3

JANUARY: FOUR AND A HALF YEARS BEFORE THE WAR

Primary Flight Training taught the basics of flying for six months. Ricky, J.J., Carmen and Neil were sent off to NAS Corpus Christi, Texas for this phase of their training which included ground school, learning to take off and land, maneuvers and spins, instrument training, precision aerobatics, formation flying, radio instrument navigation, night flying and visual navigation.

Primary Flight Training was hugely important, because it ended with a selection by the instructors of who was going to fly jets and who was not. Everybody wanted to fly fighter jets for the most part. If they knew how difficult the training was, and the accident statistics, they probably would have reconsidered.

After Primary Flight Training, the instructors chose one of several different paths for each Student Naval Aviator and this selection put them into the Intermediate and Advanced Flight Training for the particular path selected.

The Tailhook pipeline was what all the aspiring fighter pilots wanted. The other paths were for helicopters, the E-6B which was a Boeing 707 jetliner modified for use as an airborne command and control platform and communications relay, and multi-engine prop planes such as the P-3 Orion sub hunter and some of the Marines were selected for MV-22 Osprey training. The Osprey was an airplane/helicopter mutant which could fly like a regular plane, deliver Marines to an objective and land vertically and take-off vertically.

PRIMARY FLIGHT TRAINING NAS CORPUS

Ricky, J.J., Carmen and Neil did well in Primary Flight Training, and all had been selected for the Tailhook Syllabus which meant each was going to be turned into fighter pilots to fly off carriers because all the Marines selected for Tailhook flew F/A-18's, E-6B's, the AV-8 Harrier (which was being retired) or the F-35 Lightning multi-role fighter. Tailhook was a highly sought after plum assignment in the world of Naval Aviation. It meant Uncle Sam going to let you fly one of his $50 million dollar jets, or, in the case of the F-35 Lightening, a $150 million dollar jet, and Uncle Sam was going to buy the gas.

The latter was no small point. An F/A-18C at mach 0.5 at sea level will burn all 11,560 pounds (about 1926 gallons) of its internal fuel in about 10.6 minutes. So at $17.80 per gallon in 2023 that works out to $3235 per minute. It was time for a celebration.

Ricky, J.J., Carmen and Neil invited a bunch of their friends to go out to celebrate the end of Primary Flight Training in one of the local bars in Corpus Christi. The drinks were flowing freely and spirits were high.

RE F35 AND RAND STUDY

"So what do you want to do in the Navy?" Ricky asked Neil.

"I want to fly F/A-18F two seater Super Hornet off the boat." Neil said without hesitation.

"Mazeltov! J.J. and I want to fly Super Hornets too." Ricky said. "We want to fly the F/A-18E single seater though because that is all the Corp has right now." Ricky and J.J. clinked glasses with Neil. "How about you Carmen?"

"I want to fly the F-35C Lightening carrier version fitted out for electronic warfare."

The F-35C was a new, almost stealth (low observability) fifth generation fighter with the new Northrop Grumman Electro-Optical Distributed Aperture System known colloquially as the DAS. The DAS was the world's coolest infrared search and track avionics system for a fighter, especially one that might have to dogfight with stealth fighters and other MIGs equipped with infra red search and track systems. The DAS formally known as the AN/AAQ-37, was comprised of six infrared sensors distributed around the plane which provided six views of the airspace and ground all around the plane in a 360 degree sphere. The data provided by the six sensors was all fed into a computer which integrated it into an infrared picture of the airspace all around the jet and the ground below it, in front of it and behind it. The image is fed to the pilot's helmet visor so wherever he or she looks, what the sensor see in that direction is projected.

"I love the DAS system in the F-35." Carmen continued. "I will be able to see what is out there in all directions projected on my visor even if I am actually trying to look down through the floor of the jet or behind and below me. I will be able to see stealth jets in range of the DAS even if they do not return radar echoes. I will be able to find and track multiple threats such as missiles and bogeys, and keep track of multiple jets in a dogfight including both friendly and hostiles, and provide launch point detection for surface-to-air missiles. I will be able to provide weapons support for smart bombs and missiles on the jet and provide day/night navigation capability. What I think is exceptionally cool about the DAS is that I will be able to see a fighter trying to sneak up for an attack in stealth mode without turning on its search radar even if he is down "in the weeds" flying in the radar ground clutter."

"That's all great Carmen, but are you aware of the controversy surrounding the F-35?" J.J. asked.

"No, I guess I was busy with studying or something. What is it about?"

"The essence of it is that experts who have looked at the F-35 say it is good in a long range fight beyond visual range, but useless in a visual range dogfight because of its high wing loading and dubious thrust-to-weight ratio. A big controversy erupted in 2008 after articles appeared in the Australian press that were uncomplimentary to the F-35 allegedly based upon conclusions in a RAND corporation report issued after a computer simulated war games exercise. The Australian newspaper articles claimed the RAND corporation report, I believe it was titled *Air Combat Past, Present and Future,* stated that the F-35 was almost useless in a close up visual range dogfight. I read it, and I can tell you that it did not actually say that. But it did give decidedly mixed reviews to the F-35. According to the Australians, in close in air combat against a Russian Su-30 "Flanker" MIG force, a mixed force of F-35s, F/A-18 Super Hornets and F-22s, the U.S. lost to the Flankers in a big way. It was not even close. The controversy caused RAND to issue a public statement indicating that their study drew no conclusions about the F-35's dog fighting capability nor did the study attempt a detailed adjudication of the air-to-air capabilities of the F-35 or the F-22 Raptor. But the beehive had been kicked, and the money interests forced the author to be fired. He was a PhD, and was RAND's top dogfighting expert. He gored the wrong ox by telling the truth to power.

"Very interesting. We will have to talk about that more later after training at the RAG to qualify in our specific jets when we know more."

"Done." J.J. said with a smile.

FIGHT WITH HELLS ANGELS

"Indeed. I look forward to further deliberations on this sobering subject. But for now, another round amigos." Carmen said with a smile and went up to the bar to fetch the round. "That J.J. dude is amazing" she thought to herself.

Just then a gang of six Hells Angels rode up and walked into the bar looking for trouble. One of them, admiring Carmen's shape, walked up to the bar and stood next to Carmen. She looked over at him. He looked back at her, was silent for a moment then slowly scanned her curvy body and said, "I have a dream that you and I will leave here together tonight."

"Some dreams must die."

"Ooh, I like a girl with spunk."

"Keep it up buddie and you will be taking your meals through a sippy cup."

He laughed. Then showing monumental lack of judgment, the huge, smelly biker put his hand on her shapely ass and squeezed.

Carmen's nostrils flared, and her right elbow instinctively flew up like a missile and smashed the biker right in the mouth. All of his front teeth went flying, some back into his mouth and into his wind pipe. The blow bent his nose back and sent blood spurting everywhere, and he started to choke on his own teeth. He staggered backwards stunned, and then doubled over choking. Moving slowly to his three o'clock position, Carmen did her version of a Heimlich maneuver and kicked him in the stomach. His two front teeth came flying out of his mouth like little yellow Sidewinders and skittered across the floor, and he collapsed in a stinking heap.

Turning to two of his dumbass friends who were standing about 6 paces away with their mouths agape, Carmen said, "Any questions?" Their faces then twisted up in rage and they charged Carmen. Ricky and J.J., recovering from their shock, shot out of their chairs like AMRAAMs off the rail, and they grabbed one of the Mexicans and pulled him off her and started beating him to a pulp.

Neil shot out of his chair and jumped on the other Mexican who had crashed into Carmen and was now engaged with her. Neil expertly kicked the biker in the back of the knees and he collapsed to the floor as Neil was pulling him backward in a horse collar tackle.

Carmen took two flying leaps, and kicked the biker Neil had downed right in the groin. He bellowed in pain. There were no rules. This was a bar fight.

And just like that, it was on – big time. The "fearsome foursome" young Naval Aviators engaged the bikers in a good old time bar brawl while the other Student Naval Aviators cheered them on and waited to see if they needed any help. The rest of the patrons in the bar backed up and cleared out of the combat zone.

Three other bikers came flying up to attack Carmen. She saw them in the bar mirror and spun around in a flying 360 degree arc and kicked one of them rushing up behind her in the head and knocked him out cold. Another one got behind her and started choking her from behind. She raked her combat boot down his shin and stomped on the small bones in the top of his foot breaking several of them and then grabbed the pinky on his left hand and dislocated it. He let go of his choke hold staring dumbly at the pinky of his hand and it pointed up toward ceiling at a sickening angle. While he was staring at his pinky, Carmen struck his forearm right in the middle of the bone with a mighty edge of hand blow, and broke his radius in half. The third biker of the original three got behind her and got her in a hammerlock with his arms under her armpits and his hands clasped behind her head while a seventh biker, arriving late to the fray from the outside, rushed her from the front. She used the floor as a trampoline and the chest of the biker holding her in a hammer lock as a pivot and leaped up and kicked out with both feet kicking the guy rushing her from the front right in the teeth with both heels sending his teeth and blood flying across the room. When she landed, she did a reverse head butt on the biker who had her in the hammerlock and broke his nose. He instinctively let her go and reached for his face. Big mistake. Carmen wheeled around and used her arm like a bull whip with a little clenched fist wrecking ball at the end and whipped it right into the bikers jaw breaking it and sending spurts of blood flying across the room. Splash four.

Every thing was almost under control, but then another biker came in from the outside, and charged in from Carmen's left and got an elbow right in the face which broke his nose and sent his teeth flying. Carmen followed up by a finger dart right to the Adam's Apple. As the finger dart connected, he gasped for breath and dropped his guard and Carmen connected with sweeping kick up under his chin which snapped his head back and stood him completely upright. Stunned, he just stood there in shock for a second. That was all it took. Carmen kicked him in the balls which bent him forward at the waist in agony. Then Carmen made a Tiger Claw with her nails and dragged it up his face to open up his skin with bleeding gouges and then launched her knee flying upward to smash him in the face knocking him completely unconscious. He collapsed to the floor in a 350 pound heap of stink.

Ricky, J.J. and Neil still had their two bikers down and were pounding their faces with their fists. They were crying *No Mas, No Mas.* Carmen walked over and said, "Let these pussies up. I think they have had enough."

The bikers that were still conscious got up and dragged their unconscious buddies out of the bar looking over their shoulders at Carmen. She just wagged her finger at them. They withdrew, fear in their eyes, tails between their legs.

Ricky, J.J. and Neil just looked at Carmen after it was all over with amazement in their eyes. "What the fuck Carmen? Who knew?" Ricky said with a smile.

"Yeah, I can be an unholy bitch sometimes. Especially when somebody really pisses me off." Carmen said with a twinkle in her eye.

Amazingly, none of the student naval aviators was hurt too badly. Looking at each other, they smiled, raised their glasses and joined in a loud chorus of Anchors Aweigh My Boys. Ricky, J.J. and Carmen sang along too with great gusto, because they loved the song and doubted these lunatics even knew the words to the Marine Corps Hymn.

In the multiple re-tellings of this story, Carmen's exploits grew in stature as things of this sort tended to do. On more than one occasion, she was referred to as a "One Woman SWAT team" and so it was that her call sign became simply "SWAT".

TAILHOOK SYLLABUS

The Tailhook Syllabus was hard work. In the Intermediate and Advanced Flight Training portion of the Syllabus, each of them had to prepare for and fly 58 graded flights over 27 weeks to learn instrument flying, flying in formation, night flying and airway navigation. Neil had about an 80% chance of being selected for the Advanced Strike Pipeline to train for fighters, but Ricky, J.J. and Carmen all were Marine Officers and that meant they all would automatically be selected to the Advanced Strike Pipeline for training that would eventually land them in an F/A-18 Hornet air superiority fighter, an EA-6B Prowler electronic warfare jet or the F-35 Lightning stealth fighter.

Neil made the cut, and was ecstatic. He always been sure he could do it, but neither his friends back home nor his frat brothers had never been as sanguine as he was. That is what buddies are for. They give you shit just so your head does not puff up and explode from unwarranted overconfidence. But Neil had worked hard and people liked him so his dream had come true. Now for the hard part.

ADVANCED STRIKE PIPELINE

Neil, Ricky, J.J. and Carmen were all ordered to Advanced Strike Pipeline training at NAS Kingsville, Texas next door to NAS Corpus Christi for another series of 67 graded flights. They were to be trained in bombing, air combat maneuvering otherwise known as dogfighting, advanced instrument flying, low-level navigation, tactical formation flying and carrier qualification flying the T-45C Goshawk training jet.

Landing a big, fast jet on an aircraft carrier is about the hardest thing a pilot can do, especially at night in bad weather. Landing on a carrier is not for the faint of heart. Many accidents happen during carrier landings and many pilots have been killed or dumped into the sea as their jets went over the side for one reason or another.

THE CORVETTE MAKEOVER

Ricky decided it was time to reward himself for making it this far. He found a nice 2008 6.2 liter Corvette C6 convertible that he could afford and bought it. He decided to make it into a supercharged Corvette ZR1, or at least as close as he could come with the resources he had, which were limited to a little bit of money and a lot of mechanical intellect and unlimited ambition – probably way more than his actual talent would support. He broke up with all his girlfriends to give himself enough money and time to do this project in ernest. New girlfriends were easy to find. Lack of confidence was never one of Ricky's shortcomings. Though new girlfriends were around every corner, a Corvette this fine was a rarity. Most used Vettes he could afford had been ridden hard and put away wet.

So Ricky set to work. He removed the quarter panels and hood and used them to make molds for layup of the carbon fiber composite parts he wanted to make to lighten the car. He picked the Edelbrock E-Force™ Supercharger because it would fit under the stock hood and give his engine 600 horsepower at the flywheel. This car was going to be a rocket sled more than a car, but it would be able to corner with any Ferrari or Masarati. Ricky bolted on the blower, upgraded the injectors and fuel pump, and added a water-to-air intercooler to keep the whole thing from overheating. Carbon-ceramic brakes gave the whole thing survivability. He thought about adding a drogue chute, but decided that was a little over-the-top even for him, a man who was not known as either conservative or even sane in some circles.

After weeks of weekend marathons, he was ready to test the monster. He asked Carmen to come along in case he blacked out from the G load on taking off from the line, and she happily agreed. She had a thing for muscle cars. No girlie BMWs for her. Sunday morning dawned clear and cool. It was a perfect day to die. They drove together to the field after having checked in advance with the base commander to see if they could use one of the 8,000 foot runways at NAS Kingsville. The base commander, being slightly amused by this adventure, granted permission and wished them luck. Carmen brought her handheld survival radio and they checked in with the ground controller in the tower to get permission to enter the taxiways. The reached the run up area and dialed up the tower frequency and inquired about inbound traffic. It was 6 AM and nobody was flying at the moment. The tower controller told them there was no incoming traffic on the radar anywhere and gave them permission to use the runway for 10 minutes. It was only going to take about two minutes according to Ricky's calculations figuring an average speed of 120 MPH in a drag race acceleration from 0 to 185 MPH. At 120 MPH, the car would be covering 10,560 feet in one minute and 176 feet per second. Ricky calculated they could hit top speed in one mile or 5280 feet, but needed to start slowing down at the 5500 foot mark to be safe and not fry the brakes.

Ricky rolled onto the runway and looked at Carmen with a smile. "Ready Carmen?"

"Do it you big stud." she said with a grin. She was about the coolest women Ricky had ever met. He hoped that: A) she did not know that he felt that way; and B) that he didn't kill her with this loopy stunt. Ricky punched it and smoked the tires. He actually had to let off the accelerator somewhat to keep the car going straight and to get more grip by the tires on the concrete runway. Carmen's head snapped back and then she recovered and started reading off the time, speed and distance on the runway. They had set up several traffic cones at various distances so she could know where they were on the runway.

"Two seconds elapsed, 1st to 2nd gear, 37 miles per hour, about 60 feet – 7 seconds elapsed, 2nd to 3rd gear, 96 miles per hour, about 550 feet – 11 seconds elapsed, 3rd to 4th gear, 128 miles per hour, about 1200 feet –16 seconds elapsed, 4th to 5th gear, 153 miles per hour, about 2200 feet – 28 seconds elapsed, 5th gear, 215 miles per hour, about 5200 feet. Plenty of time to stop dude. Looks like she is topped out." Carmen said silently calculating her chances of survival. They still had 2500 feet of runway left and the car had monster carbon-ceramic disk brakes.

"Well that was fun even though it probably is the dumbest thing I have ever done. This thing is going to get crappy gas mileage and gas just broke the $20 dollars per gallon barrier yesterday – for the first time ever. I have got to stop drinking the bong water." Ricky said with a wry smile.

RICKY AND CARMEN GO TO THE BEACH

Laughing hysterically, Carmen said, "Imagine my surprise. You crack me up dude. You know what I always say don't you? Live fast, die young and have a good looking corpse." She was only half joking. "Let's go to the beach." Carmen suggested.

"That is an excellent idea my friend. About going to the beach I mean." Ricky replied. Ricky flicked in his favorite mix CD into the Bose™ sound system and off they went in the monster Vette to the blasting sounds of LaRoux, *Bulletproof* and Tom Petty, *Running Down A Dream*.

RICKY GETS HIS CALL SIGN

Ricky almost got the callsign Merlin from this exploit. As word of this insane exploit spread around the squadron, some of his brethren suggested they start calling him Merlin after the supercharged Merlin Rolls Royce engine that made the Mustang P-51 the fighter that won WW II. But then everybody starting laughing about how Ricky loved to go to bed with his hair wet after taking a shower. He wore his hair slightly too long on the top for a Marine officer but somehow he got away with it. When he went to bed with his hair still wet, his habit of sleeping only on his sides and tossing back and forth caused his hair to stand straight up in the middle when he woke up. He looked like Woody Woodpecker. So his peers started calling him Woody and that is what stuck as his callsign.

RICKY AND CARMEN ON PADRE ISLAND

Their destination was Padre Island on the Golf Coast just south of Corpus Christie. It was about an hour's drive from Kingsville, but they made it in 40 minutes. Carmen looked down at the speedometer, and it read 120 MPH. It was early and there were no Texas State Troopers out yet. On the way, Ricky blew through a couple of stop signs and three traffic lights that were red going about 70 miles per hour. Carmen looked over at Ricky quizzically. Without removing his eyes from the road, he said, "It is not the first law I have broken, and it won't be the last." Ricky was a major-league scoff-law. Ricky went on to explain, "I only obey the rules and laws I agree with. I have a big thing about waste especially waste of energy. Braking for a stop sign or stop light when I can see in both directions and can see there is no traffic coming is a major waste of energy, so I have a tendency to view stop signs and stop lights in those situations as more suggestions than inviolate rules. They have taken my license away twice, but I got it back by doing community service. I am worried though. I am sweating making it through flight school, because you have to follow all the rules, even the ones that are bullshit. Everytime I run into a situation like that, I have to force myself to be a good doobie and just do it regardless of what I think of it. It is going to be my undoing someday probably. As long as we are talking about my faults, I have to add that I have a tendency to be critical of people sometimes. I don't suffer fools easily. I am working very hard on that, but sometimes, it just comes out before I can bite my tongue."

Carmen smiled. This dude was out-of-the- box she thought to herself. He intrigued her.

"Well as long as we are fessing up to our faults, I have to tell you mine." Carmen said sheepishly. "I am OCD. I just have a compulsion to just work and work and work on stuff that I want to accomplish and ignore my friends and family to my detriment. I have lost more than one friends that way. I just cannot relax and chill sometimes. I have been working on it, and hanging with you and J.J. and Neil have helped a lot. You crazy bastards crack me up."

"No problem Carmen. We will help you chill out and have some fun. We love you to death, and we don't want flakes around us. We want somebody who can really bring it when it is crunch time, and a workaholic is way better than a social butterfly. So relax, we are with you and we don't judge. Except for the flakes and chicken shits. We judge them. A bit harshly I would have to add." Ricky said smiling at Carmen.

It had been a big Saturday night for the Texas State Troopers. In Texas, not only can you drive with a loaded gun in the car, but you can also drive with an open container. Only in Texas would that be tolerated. That combination kept the troopers busy all night so they were sleeping in. As a result, Ricky and Carmen were able to fly down the flat, straight open Texas roads with little traffic to contend with. They probably could not have gotten there in their planes in less time. They only had to fill up the Vette twice.

They had a fun day together getting to know each other better and learning about their respective families, former lovers, their life's adventures so far and their hopes and dreams. As Ricky learned more and more about Carmen, his respect for her as a person grew greater.

She was not just another pretty face. This girl had substance. She was brainy, tough and talented in many areas but still was feminine and intriguing. He was starting to like her.

For Carmen, it was a great day. She too had a growing respect for Ricky as a person as she talked to him and learned about his personality. Sure he was a quirky, wise-ass, but that is not all he was. He had seriously thought it all through and was pretty much together as a dude. He disliked waste, corruption and lack of conviction, and especially hated the fact that the politicians regularly sold out their constituents in exchange for campaign contributions from big money interest groups. He was a Marine Officer, and did not understand why everybody could not just saddle up and be courageous and selfless and make sacrifices for their country even if they were civilian. Why should the military be the only ones who had to make the serious sacrifices for their country? Politicians seemed to him to only be interested in getting re-elected and not so much in doing what is right for the country. Carmen soon learned that this was his hot button when they discussed the problem of the growing national debt.

But what was most interesting to her is that he did not seem to be intimidated by her or in awe of her and was not sycophantic in any way. No false flattery, no over-attentiveness, nothing. He just was not like the other guys she had met so far. When she did something or said something that was genuinely impressive, he complimented her. When she tried to pull some shit, he called her on it. His attitude was, "Hey baby, you put your little panties on one leg at a time, just like me. So shut the fuck up and don't give me any of that bullshit." She was impressed.

RICKY AND CARMEN RETURN FROM THE BEACH

Back at NAS Kingsville on Monday morning, word of the monster Vette's run had already spread starting with the tower air traffic controllers. As the word spread, many of the SNAs in Ricky's training squadron congratulated Ricky and wanted to see his Vette's engine

"Hey Ricky, I heard about your speed run yesterday with Carmen. I am hurt. Why didn't you invite me?" J.J. said.

"Dude, we did it at 0600. I didn't think you would want to get up that early." Ricky explained.

"How did it go?" J.J. asked.

"185 miles per hour in a one mile run. I think she had more, but did not want to push it. The car is more of a rocket sled now than a car although it corners like a demon. We took it to Padre Island for the day afterwards. We had a really fun day." Ricky said with a smile.

"You dirtball! I would have loved to have gone to the beach with you and Carmen." J.J. ribbed.

"Sorry, only two seats my friend. Next time." Ricky sheepishly apologized.

"OK, I am going to hold you to that." J.J. said in good humor. "Are you ready for Air Combat Maneuver training this afternoon?" J.J. asked.

AIR COMBAT MANEUVER TRAINING

"Totally. It will be fun, although I have heard these instructors are good. I am expecting to die in an imaginary fireball not of my making on several occasions in the next few weeks." Ricky joked.

"No offense, but my money is on the instructors. In fact, we have a pool going so don't let me down." J.J. said with a smile.

Ricky laughed. "You bunch of dickheads."

At that, they went off to their first class on the classic art of dogfighting. In their first lecture, the learned some of the recent history of the art of dogfighting and some of the current tactical situation in fighter vs. fighter comparisons. This is what they heard. The instructor did not pull any punches.

The brass in the Pentagon thought, at least as late as the Vietnam War, that dogfighting with radar guided and heat-seeking air-to-air missiles would be a far cry from the historical dogfighting of the wars up to and through the Korean War. Their reasoning was that with modern sophisticated radars and fire control computers and long range missiles, it would be possible to get smoked by a missile fired from an enemy you never saw which was known as Beyond Visual Range or BVR . For example, the AIM-54 Phoenix missile comes at you at Mach 3.82 from as much as 100 miles away. The AWG-9 and the later APG-71 all-weather, pulse-doppler X-band fire control radars from the venerable F-14 Tomcat of TOPGUN fame was capable of detecting aircraft out to 100 and 230 miles, respectively, and tracking up to 24 targets in Track-While-Scan mode, and designating up to 6 of them as priority targets.

Further, to aid U.S. fighters and their allies, Airborne Warning And Control system (AWAC) planes such as the E-2C Hawkeye flying high above the fighters detect targets with powerful radars and feed data to the friendly fighters by data downlinks. The AWACs fly at 30,000 feet and radar scan the battle space and feed target data and the positions of other friendlies to the jets. This provides better situational awareness to all the fighter pilots and supplements the target detecting and tracking data their own fire control sytems generate. Likewise, the friendly fighters can link data from their radars up to the AWACs to be shared with other fighters through a data downlink.

The on-board, long-range radars of the fighters, AWACs planes and long range missiles were all designed for fleet defense of aircraft carriers. The idea was to develop a capability to destroy inbound enemy aircraft and anti-ship missiles while they were still a long way away from the carrier. These systems proved capable for long range dogfighting and enabled a fighter pilot to take out an enemy aircraft many miles away without ever seeing it. The brass thought that was all there was to it. No need to mix it up in close in dogfighting.

As a result of this flawed notion, fighters like the F-4 Phantom were procured without any guns. The problem was that the brass also set the Rules of Engagement so as to require visual identification of a target as being hostile before commencing hostilities. That virtually guaranteed a close in dogfight, and the long range missiles proved to be of little use, and the pilot was left with only shorter range heat seeking missiles like the Sidewinder. The "probability of kill" or PK performance factor of the Vietnam era missiles was also disappointing being less than 10%. The problems that the Rules of Engagement and low PKs caused in Vietnam became so severe, that the Air Force added an external pod carrying 20 mm canons to their F-4s, and the Navy required canons to be installed on the F-4s they ordered.

The brass never really gave up on the BVR kill notion though, and continued to spend big money on improved radars and missiles in the hopes that one day, they would be proven right. Inconsistently though, the brass was so afraid of friendly fire accidents, that they insisted on maintaining the positive identification Rules of Engagement that squelched BVR kills as a realistic possibility.

Newer planes like the F/A-18 of the Navy and the F-15 of the Air Force use the APG-73 and APG-63(V)2 AESA radars, respectively. An Actively Electronically Scanned Array (AESA) radar has an exceptionally agile beam which is electronically scanned to give nearly instantaneously tracking updates to the computer and enhanced multi-tracking capability. The APG-73 radar and its AESA upgrade, the APG-79, used on the F/A-18 are 8-12 Ghz I band pulse-Doppler radars used for air-to-air and air-to-surface missions. They had a variety of tracking, scanning and track-while-scan modes to give the fighter pilot a complete target search and track capability including look-down, shoot-down capability that allowed shooting down a fighter on the deck without the radar getting confused by ground clutter. Air-to-ground capabilities include Doppler beam sharpened sector, patch mapping, medium range synthetic aperture radar, fixed and moving ground target track and sea surface search capabilities. The Navy and Marine Corp F/A-18s still use the APG-65 and APG-73 radars which provide a velocity search mode for maximum range detection of head-on incoming nose aspect targets, range-while-search mode to detect all aspect targets, and track-while-scan mode which, when used with an autonomous missile like the AIM-120 AMRAAM "Slammer" (Advanced Medium Range Air-To-Air Missile), a high off bore-sight weapon, gave the fighter pilot a launch-and-leave capability.

The AMRAAM resulted as an improvement of the disappointing Vietnam era Sparrow air-to-air missile which required continuous radar illumination of the target by the launching plane until impact. That meant the launching plane had to keep the bogey in the view angle or aperture of the radar antenna in its nose and could not depart the fight. This inconvenient fact meant the attacker had to keep flying toward the target until missile impact so as to keep the attacker's radar beams painting the target.

ACEVAL/AIMVAL study at Nellis AFB and dev of AMRAAM

The Air Force did not conclude they needed a new missile though until the ACEVAL/AIMVAL mock air battle at Nellis AFB in the 70's. This mock air combat exercise proved that the Blue Force flying F-14s and F-15s armed with Sparrows flying against inferior Red Force F-5 jets armed only with all-aspect heat seeking Sidewinders were being mutually killed along with their F-5 targets most of the time. The reason was that the F-5s could get their heat seeking air-to-air missile shots off before being "killed" by the Sparrows because the jets launching the Sparrows had to keep the F-5s painted during the flights of their missiles. This resulted in the F-14s and F-15s flying into range of the heat seeking missiles of the F-5s before the Sparrows reached the F-5s. The reason this happened was because the Sparrows had a semi-active homing guidance system and had no radars of their own. That meant the Sparrow could only home on a target if the target was reflecting continuos wave radar signals from the attacking jet. Infrared homing missiles like the Sidewinder were fire and forget missiles. Once the pilot launching it confirmed the missile was locked onto a target, he or she could fire the heater and bug out.

The AIM-120 AMRAAM, or "Slammer" as it was affectionately called by its fans, solved that "mutual kill" problem. The Slammer guidance module has its own active radar target detection device. It is a long range, fire and forget missile that can home on its target all by itself in the terminal phase. The AIM-120 has an inertial guidance system which guides it to an intercept point with the target which is fed into it by the fire control system of the launching jet. Once it reaches that point, the AIM-120 turns on its own radar and homes on the target. The AMRAAM is an "off boresight" missile because it has a high-performance, directed-thrust rocket motor which is capable of making the missile do a U-turn. In other words, a Slammer can be launched while flying away from the target as long as the intercept point has been fed into the missile. To the delight of its users, an AMRAAM missile cannot be defeated by a jammer on the target. This is because every AMRAAM includes guidance electronics to detect jamming and switch over to a passive home-on-jammer mode to finish the intercept.

In short, a fighter pilot armed with these AMRAAM type missiles can come into a dogfight "merge" which is the intercept point with the target or targets, designate a target with his AESA radar and then radar lock the missile by sending it the location of the bogey and its course and speed. The fighter pilot can then launch the missile and fly right out of the fight. The missile will do a U-turn at Mach 4 and fly to an intercept point using its on-board inertial navigation system.

The intercept point is calculated using data received either from the launching fighter radar and fire control computer, or from data received from an Infrared Search and Track system such as the DAS on the F-35. The AMRAAM can also guide on from received from an AWACS plane or another fighter via the missile's data link.

When the AMRAAM gets within a short range of the target, it turns on its own active radar and completes the intercept.

If the bogey got off a missile shot of his own, the departing fighter theoretically can defeat the inbound missile with chaff, flares and suitable juking, although 4th generation air-to-air missiles are said to be impossible to defeat with decoys and maneuver. That assertion is yet to be proven in combat. Putting as much distance as possible between yourself as the target and the attacking jet helps.

Long range missile shots by AMRAAMs or any other missile are easier to defeat by chaff, flares and juking. A missile which has flown a long way has lost much of its kinetic energy, and any additional maneuvering it has to do to chase a maneuvering target or chase flares or radar scattering chaff further depletes its energy. When a missile loses its kinetic energy, or its rocket motor burns out, it loses its overtake speed, and can be defeated.

Conversely, if the missile is fired at close range from a high and fast fighter, it has a tremendous amount of energy and the chance of a successful kill is about 90%.

RULES OF ENGAGEMENT EFFECT AND F-35 DAS DEVELOPMENT

That is, among other reasons, why the Rules of Engagement requiring positive visual identification are dangerous. The AMRAAM was basically a beyond-visual-range missile, but that capability proved to be not as important as originally thought. In the Desert Storm and Operation Enduring Freedom, the Rules of Engagement were very strict and required positive visual identification as a bogey before a missile shot could be taken. This meant that U.S. fighter pilots had to be in visual range to see the target and identify it visually as an enemy plane before they could take a shot. These Rules of Engagement avoid friendly fire casualties, but they also drastically reduce the usefulness of beyond visual range weapons and radars to find targets far away.

Bogey pilots flying stealth fighters did not have to worry about all this though. Stealth fighters cannot be seen by any X-band AWACs or fighter radars or the AMRAAM missile guidance system radars except at very close range such as under 10 miles, and by then it is too late —the stealth jet will have already gotten its missile shot off. To satisfy the Rules of Engagement, a U.S. pilot has to actually see a stealth jet with his or her eyeballs or detect its presence with an Infra Red Search and Track system, and then make a visual sighting to positively identify the stealth jet as a bogey.

That simple fact led to the development for the F-35 of the infrared based AN/AAQ-37 Distributed Aperture System or DAS. This was an infrared search and tracking system which combined the views of six infrared sensors to give a 360 degree spherical view of the battlespace projected on the helmet visor of the pilot. If the pilot wants to see what is under the F-35, he or she need only look down toward the floor of the cockpit and what the sensors see is displayed on the helmet display. The same for the looking behind the plane. The pilot need only look over his shoulder.

The DAS provide three basic functions in all directions simultaneously: 1) it acts as a missile warning system to detect missile launches from the ground or other fighters including launch point detection and countermeasure cueing; 2) IRST aircraft detection for air-to-air threats and air-to-air weapons cueing; and 3) imagery for cockpit displays on the helmet mounted display, and pilot night vision. It is a shame the DAS system is installed on a fighter with such high wing loading and poor thrust-to-weight ratio. In terms of aerodynamic performance such as turn rate, climb rate and acceleration from a low kinetic energy state to a higher state, the F-35 is every Flanker's bitch.

The DAS IRST system augments the F-35 Joint Strike Fighter's AN/APG-81 AESA radar designed by Northrop Grumman Electronic

Systems. The F-35 fuses its radar target tracking and identification data with the infrared target tracking and identification data of the DAS and can share the combined data with an AMRAAM missile, an AWACS or other fighters via Multifunction Advanced Data Link. The AESA radar detects non stealth targets first which can then be tracked with the DAS. Stealth jets must be detected with the DAS.

Unfortunately, this modern infrared based DAS is not on the plain vanilla F/A-18 or the Super Hornet, so all Hornets are vulnerable to stealth jets sneaking up on them and even Flankers with their radars turned off who are sneaking up from behind or below. If you don't see them and the AWACs has been taken out or misses them, you are toast.

So there remains a need to learn how to dogfight the old fashioned way, that is, up close and personal, with a fourth generation fighter which visually identified as a bogey or a fifth generation stealth fighter that has been detected visually or with IRST. That is true even though your fighter may have serious performance deficiencies compared to the fighter of your adversary. Modern dogfights are likely to be visual range affairs because of the Rules of Engagement and the fact that fifth generation stealth fighters cannot be detected by radars. Many future dogfight victories will be jets that were shot down with cannon, heat seaking sidewinders or AMRAAMs used in visual range. You are going to have to be a better fighter pilot than your adversary, understand his plane's characteristics and weaknesses and know the strengths and weaknesses of your own plane.

The basic principle of classic dogfighting is information is king. There is no substitute for situational awareness. Fully 80% of all dogfight kills throughout the history of aerial combat have resulted when the victim never saw the attacker either because of inattention or because the attacker snuck up in a blind spot. Dismissed.

CARMEN DRESSES UP AND INVITES
RICKY AND J.J. TO THE O CLUB

Carmen had been studying all this stuff all afternoon. Her brain was swimming in a sea of highly technical details. She was not bewildered though since she was an electrical engineer from the very fine academic program at the Naval Academy. All the technical jargon actually made sense to her. But she needed a break so she called Ricky and J.J. and Neil and asked them to meet her at the O-club for a cocktail. She was feeling a little frisky, so she put on her tight black slacks that accentuated her magnificent derriere, a low-cut but classy blouse that showed some cleavage and makeup. This was something she did not do very often.

"Hey Woody, how are you?" Carmen greeted Ricky.

Taking a long look at Carmen in her nines, Ricky said, "Better now. But it is still early, and things could still get royally screwed up." She laughed. He loved her laugh. She had a quick wit and a great sense of humor, and, unlike some people, she got Ricky's sardonic, sometimes kinky wit.

"Wow Carmen, what got into you? You are looking very hot tonight. Not your usual bag lady look. I am telling you, you've got to get into the weight room and bulk up those sparrow legs so you can fill out that flight suit. The Navy is never going to make flight suits in size 0 or extra petite." Ricky ribbed. "I'm just saying."

"Oh blow me Ricky. I look better in that flight suit than you do." Carmen countered.

"You would look better than me in ANYTHING than I do." Ricky said with a smile.

Just then J.J. and Neil walked in, took one look at Carmen's slacks and whistled a low whistle and raised their eyebrows in unison in the universal sign language equivalent of "You're looking hot. Can I do you?"

Carmen just winked at them and waved them over.

They ordered a round and started talking shop about the upcoming Air Combat Maneuvering flights they were preparing for. The O-club was full of officers that night and was noisy with the boisterous chatter of men and women in the prime of their lives and doing jobs they loved.

PRESIDENT PARRY SPEECH ON TV AT O CLUB ABOUT BUDGET CUTS

A hush fell over the crowd as the President of the United States Richard Parry, former governor of Texas came on the big flat screen for a national address.

"My fellow Americans. Good evening to you all. My purpose this evening is to explain the situation the country is currently in so you can understand why I am about to ask you to make the sacrifices I am going to have to ask you to make for your country.

As you know, gasoline and diesel fuel prices have been rising dramatically recently. This has been caused by the dip in supply resulting from the drying up of the North Slope and North Sea oil fields under the pressure of unabated and rising demand for oil from the worlds economies. The Saudis, Libyans, other middle eastern countries, Venezuala and Mexico still have some oil left, but their oil reserves will be depleted in the next 5 to 6 years also.

The burgeoning middle classes in China and India have spawned millions of new drivers all of whom need gasoline and diesel fuel for their cars and trucks.

Rising gasoline prices is simply the result of the law of supply and demand in the free markets, and there is nothing I can do about it. The oil trapped in the Canadian oil sands, in shale deposits in the U.S. and the oil in the deep sea Tupi Field off the coast of Brazil is difficult and expensive to extract, and those costs are being passed on to you, the consumer. There is nothing I can do about that either. Synthetic fuels can be made from coal, but that industry has just barely begun and is years from production of commercial quantities of synthetic fuels.

The rising costs of fuel for transport of goods and people around the planet has led to price inflation caused by rising costs of good sold for almost every business. Rising gasoline prices have squeezed personal budgets and caused consumers to spend less to buy other goods so that they can afford gas for their cars. This fall in consumer spending has caused many companies to fail and has cost many lost jobs. The fall in consumer spending has caused major losses in the stock market.

Falling incomes of individuals and corporations and lack of capital gains for investments in the stock market has led to decreased tax revenues to the Federal Government and to almost every state and local government except in states which still have oil reserves.

While tax revenues have been falling, federal spending has been forced to increase to pay entitlement benefits for Social Security, Medicare, Medicaid, military pensions and interest on the National Debt. The National Debt has resulted from past borrowing by the Federal Government to finance past deficit spending to pay for wars, entitlement programs and many other government programs. The U.S. National Debt has risen from 14.71 trillion dollars in 2011 to 40 trillion dollars today, and this number does not count the unfunded liabilities of the social security system, medicare, medicaid and the military pension system. Those obligations already exceed tax revenues to the federal government, and have to be paid by borrowing by the federal government. If those obligations are included, it adds an additional 49.2 trillion dollars to the U.S. National Debt.

The ratio of public debt to Gross Domestic Product was 60% in 2010. This year the ratio of public debt to Gross Domestic Product will reach 90% according to the Congressional Budget Office.

The U.S. National Debt is not just a number on paper that doesn't really mean anything. The U.S. National Debt represents money that has been or will have to be borrowed in the future to pay the federal government's bills by the issuance of debt instruments like U.S.

government bonds and T-Bills that investors and foreign governments like China buy. Currently foreign governments including China, Japan, the UK and Brazil hold 65% of the U.S. National Debt held by the public. Interest will have to be paid on the entire U.S. National Debt or the United States will lapse into default which would be a cataclysmic event. The U.S. must continue to borrow money to pay the bills for Social Security, Medicare, Medicaid and the military and civil service pension programs. If interest is not paid on the currently existing outstanding debt instruments, no member of the public or foreign government will buy them, and the federal government will run out of money to pay for the entitlement programs I have mentioned.

These interest payments are currently 80 percent of all spending by the Federal Government and are rising every year. In the not too distant future, all spending by the Federal Government will be to service this debt and there will be nothing left for anything else including defense spending, Social Security, Medicare, Medicaid and the other entitlements let alone discretionary spending.

I do not tell you these things to alarm you. But if you are alarmed, you should be. These are the brutal facts we face today. The U.S. is on an unsustainable path, and unless major changes to the entitlement programs are made, the U.S. will eventually enter a death spiral from which there is no recovery.

As oil reserves are depleted, the situation will only get worse. Past administrations and Congresses have not done enough to get us ready for the day when the oil runs out. We are paying the price today.

In an attempt to avert disaster and a default on interest payments due on the U.S. National Debt, which would crash the stock markets around the world, I have today introduced a bill into Congress to authorize defunding Medicare completely and cutting the military budget by 45%. If this new level of military spending is not enough to effectively defend this nation, so be it. We have no choice.

All advanced weapon system research and development will be stopped. Large cuts in the active military force of the Army, Coast Guard and Air Force will be followed by lesser cuts in the standing forces of the Navy and Marine Corps. Cuts in Navy and Marine Corps aviation operations will not be made at this time so as to maintain the ability of this nation to project force where it is needed using our twelve active aircraft carriers strike groups. No new carriers will be built. Obsolete weapon systems will be retired, and no new weapon systems will be developed.

I have also proposed new tax hikes in the bill I introduced in Congress today.

I urge you not to panic and continue spending if you are able in order to prevent the situation from getting worse. However, you should all drive less and drive slower so as to conserve gasoline. I urge you all to not oppose the new tax hikes nor vote against Congressmen and Senators who support this measure. Your contributions in this regard should be considered sacrifices you are making for the sake of your country. The sacrifice needed to save this country should not be limited to our brave men and women in uniform.

Thank you and have a good night.

"Holy crap. Gutsiest speech I ever saw a politician make." J.J. said.

"Yeah, but what a buzzkill." Carmen said.

"We all know he is right. And it is about time a politician had the balls to tell the truth and take on the problem head on and try to deal with it. It is just too bad for these guys because they are going to have to pay politically for the deficit spending of Congresses going back many decades." Neil said.

"I cannot believe the Congresses of the past spent so irresponsibly. How can this have happened. Are you kidding me? They let the Federal Debt to get so large that the interest payments on it alone are now 80% of all spending by the Federal Government." Ricky said. "Congress only have one job up there, and that is to manage the spending. Shit even I could have done a better job."

"We are royally screwed. There is only one answer – party till you puke. Let's just all have another round." Carmen said.

"Fly Navy!" they all said as they clinked their glasses together.

CARMEN GETS PICKED UP AT O CLUB

Just then, a handsome young Navy Lieutenant walked up to their table and locked eyes with Carmen. "I have been admiring you from a distance this evening." Lieutenant Tommie "Slingshot" O'Leary said. "Lieutenant Tom O'Leary, United States Naval Aviator at your service." he said with a smile.

Carmen studied him for a minute. "Hmm, not bad looking, and you have to admire his gutsiness and confidence. It take big cohones to walk right up here and hit on me right in front of these three guys. I have to admire that." Carmen thought to herself. "Carmen Nicoise, 2nd Lieutenant, United States Marine Corps. Nice to meet you. What did you have in mind Lieutenant?" Carmen said with a warm smile.

"Dinner, a walk on the beach and a lullaby." Tommie said.

"Wow. This guy is cheeky." she thought to herself pausing before she answered. "But that sounds fun, and I have not been laid in awhile. Besides, Ricky has been busy with his car and has not paid any attention to me as a woman." she continued with her internal debate. She had developed a mild crush on Ricky over the weeks of training they had endured together, but nothing had come of it yet. She looked at Ricky and he smiled and winked at her. She looked at J.J. and Neil and they both grinned and raised their eyebrows twice in approval. "Besides, the world is falling apart, and if he tries anything I don't like, I can always kick his ass." she thought to herself. And she really could. One of the great advantages of having two black belts. "OK Lieutenant. Let's go." she finally said.

"Now?" Tommie said.

"Now." Carmen replied, and, with that, they were out the door into the Texas night. Ricky, J.J. and Neil all looked at each other and smiled.

Tommie and Carmen put the top down on Tommie's car, and drove to a local Caribbean theme restaurant that served good tropical rum drinks and sat at the bar while they waited for their table.

"So what's your story Lieutenant?" Carmen inquired.

"Just got here from TOPGUN to teach dogfighting. I was an instructor there. My call sign is "Slingshot". Before that I was deployed with the Black Knights of VFA-154 flying F/A-18F's for a couple of years. I have about 1000 hours in F/A-18's." Tommie replied.

"Where are you from?" Carmen continued.

"I grew up in Arizona. Played baseball at Arizona State on a full ride, and then joined the Navy and went to OCS." Tommie explained. "How about you?" Tommie asked.

"I grew up in Silicon Valley, Santa Clara to be exact. Went to Mitty High and played volleyball there, then off to the Naval Academy. I signed up for the Marines because I knew I wanted to go to flight school and, if I made jets, they would put me in an F/A-18 or an F-35. I want to fly the F-35." Carmen said. "So what is the secret of good dogfighting?" Carmen continued her cross-examination.

"Be aggressive, know what maneuver to use and when to use it and what to counter to his counter move. Situational awareness is paramount. Manage your airspeed and potential energy to gain the advantage. Know the weaknesses of your opponent's plane and how to take advantage of them. Know how to avoid an overshoot and how to cause one. If you are going to overshoot, pull up and bank your airspeed for altitude so you can turn tighter than your adversary. That is useful in for example in a high yo-yo when you have high airspeed and the enemy plane does a break turn across your flight path. The climb banks your airspeed as altitude and slows you down so you can turn more sharply than the bogey above his plane of maneuver. This cuts his corner, and then you dive down in behind him picking up airspeed and maneuverability for the pursuit and shot. Same concept as the outside barrel roll attack." Tommy said. "Thrust-to-weight ratio, wing loading and corner speed are all important in the real world, but not so much here."

"Why?"

"Because you and your instructor adversary will both be flying the same type of jet —the Goshawk, so your wing loading and thrust-to-weight ration will be the same. Turn radius, turn rate and specific energy of the aircraft are very important considerations, so pay attention when we teach you about that. Keep your potential energy, that is, altitude, in mind and trade it for kinetic energy, that is speed, when needed as in the high yo-yo I just told you about. And use your wingman effectively. Know where he is, use a loose deuce tactical formation so you can cover each other's sixes, and keep communicating with him." Slingshot was on a roll. "Sometimes your enemy will have a plane which can out-turn yours and out-climb you, but you can suck him right into a trap and your wingman can take him out." Tommy explained. "Use that technique if you are in a plane that does not turn as well as your enemy and cannot outrun or out climb his jet." he continued.

"HIS jet?" Carmen jabbed.

"Or hers. Sorry. I guess I have been a male chauvinist too long. Old habits die hard. You actually have an advantage in dogfighting since you weigh about 100 pounds less than your male adversary and every pound counts in terms of how many Gs you can take and still control your jet and how tight you can make it turn. Weight is everything. Danica Patrick could theoretically win every race she drives barring mechanical breakdown and team tactics blocking her out. If you can turn tighter than your enemy, that is always good." Tommie explained. "You need good eyesight and situational awareness. Lose sight of your enemy and you will lose the fight. In Vietnam, 85% of all kills came from a pilot spotting an enemy plane and taking him out before he was ever seen.

The historical average is 80% of all kills come when the victim does not see his attacker. Those are the basics. There is a lot more to learn which I and my colleagues will be teaching you all."

"Girlfriend?" Carmen continued her line of questioning.

"Hundreds. You want to know about the most recent one?" Tommie inquired.

"Yes." Carmen said with a smile.

"Beautiful girl. Brunette, skinny, big fakies, a real head turner. But her mind was tweaked. Huge temper problem and very self centered. She was always looking for what she could get out of a situation, and she never really understood that a relationship is a partnership and that she had to contribute. Or maybe she did and just did not care since things had always just been handed to her throughout her entire life and she never really had to work at anything. I have a theory that most beautiful women are that way. It is a real turn off for me, and that finally drove me crazy so I broke up with her. I am hoping you will turn out differently." Tommie said with a grin.

"Me too." Carmen said. "I hate it when that happens." she said with a sly smile. "I guess you will just have to wait and see how I am won't you?" not giving anything away about her personality. Carmen was aggressive and smart, beautiful but not spoiled, compassionate but deadly when she needed to be. And, above all else, confident." She had never had trouble with guys. "Guys were predictable and not too smart. Ha ha. But this one was intriguing. Too bad he is a white guy. Mom will be pissed if I marry this dude." she thought to herself.

They had a nice dinner and decided to drive to Padre Island for a walk on the beach. It was full moon that night and the air was balmy, not too hot with a nice sea breeze blowing. Carmen was feeling comfortable with Tommie and liked him.

They walked on the beach for about an hour and chatted. Then they were tired and still a little tipsy and decided to take a nap. Tommie said he had a couple of sleeping bags in the trunk so they went and got them. Tommie unzipped one and put it down on the white sand and then unzipped the other one to use for a comforter.

Carmen laid down on the beach and motioned for Tommie to join her. They reclined together holding each other in a relaxed embrace. They lay there face to face for about 10 minutes sort of half dozing and enjoying the warmth and softness of each others bodies. Then Carmen opened her eyes, looked at Tommie's handsome, dozing face and kissed him on the lips.

He woke up and kissed her back. He was a great kisser. She took his lower lip in her mouth and sucked and nibbled on it. He did the same to both of her full and luscious lips.

CARMEN GETS LAID BY SLINGSHOT

Carmen felt her excitement start to build. She snuggled in closer to him and ran her hand gently over the muscles of his arms and shoulders. They were very nice.

Tommie gently scratched her back over her blouse and moved his hand to her breast and gently caressed it and gave it a small squeeze.

Unable to contain herself she stood up and tugged on Tommie's hand to join her. She slowly started to unbutton his shirt. When she was finished, she pulled it down over his shoulders and what she saw took her breath away. She gasped slightly and her pupils dilated as she took in Tommie's magnificent chest. Nicely muscled with pecs of a bodybuilder and perfectly chiseled abs arranged in a perfect six pack. Tommie was no stranger to a weight room. His biceps were large but perfectly proportioned to his chest. Nothing was too big but nothing was small and puny.

"Yum Yum." she thought and she ran her hands over his shoulders and pectorals.

Tommie started to unbutton her blouse. A little tingle of anticipation went through her as she imagined this man running his hands over her naked body. She was starting to really get excited now and reached for his belt buckle and undid it as he slowly worked his way down the column of buttons. He pulled his shirt the rest of the way off and slowly removed her blouse revealing her bra straining to contain her full C cup breasts. He pulled her in for a hug and she nestled into his chest, her face buried in his neck, breathing in his enchanting cologne. He slowly undid and removed her bra, and she did not resist.

She could feel her full and soft breast pressed against his warm skin now and it was a wonderful feeling. She slowly slid down his body and ….

He could no longer resist her charms and reached to pull her up. He then laid her down on the sleeping bags ever so gently with his strong arms and lowered himself on top of her. A small purr came from her throat. Reaching for the clasp and zipper on the front of her pants he looked into her eyes as he slowly moved his body down gently kissing the skin of her chest with a hundred small kisses till his lips reached her breasts. He lingered there for a few minutes, kissing her breasts all over and taking her nipples into his mouth and gently massaging them with his tongue. As he continued his slow downward journey, he kissed the skin on her stomach and took little folds of it into his mouth and sucked it gently and then released it.

As he reached her waist line, he gently hooked the top of her slacks and panties with two fingers on either side just behind the points of her hips and gently pulled the garments downward ever so slowly until her secret garden came into view. She was excited now and he could hear her breathing increase in depth and volumn. As he dragged her slacks and panties past her ankles, he gently parted her legs and crawled back up until his lips were at her flower. He teased her trigger with his tongue and slowly parted her lips and flicked and sucked her with gently and slowly at first but with more speed later. He could hear her breaths shorten and increase in speed as the waves of pleasure rippled gently through her body. She tried to control herself and delay her arrival, but finally she could no longer control it as his tongue flicked her back and forth and a huge tsunami of pleasure crashed onto her beach and shook her.

She looked down at him and smiled and motioned for him to come up and join her. As he did, he entered her and they locked eyes as he held himself up in a pushup position above her. Finally he lowered himself down on her and kissed her gently. As each thrust grew more insistent, he could feel his own excitement start to build. She was making little noises now as her own excitement started to build again. Her noises started to get more primal now and that excited him greatly to know he was giving her so much pleasure. Finally in a crescendo of crashing symbols, they both came and it was over.

They lay there together in an embrace as their breathing slowly subsided. As they both calmed down, he gently stroked her jet black hair and sang her a lullaby in a tiny little voice. "Hush little baby, don't you cry. Tommie's gonna sing you a lullaby…" and they both drifted off to sleep in the soft warmth of the sleeping bags with the sound of the wave crashing on the beach a few yards away and the sounds of the wind rustling the trees. It was a perfect night.

They woke up just before dawn and had to hustle to get into Tommies car and get back to the base. They said little on the way back choosing to enjoy the coolness of the morning air and the colors of the sunrise lit landscape. Even though it was Texas, in a way it was still beautiful when lit by the pink morning light.

DOGFIGHT DAY FOR RICKY AND J.J.

It was dogfight day for Ricky and J.J.. After seeming endless classroom hours learning about all the basic fighter maneuvers in dogfighting, it was finally time to go out and each square off against an instructor and see what was what. Ricky's adversary was Navy Lieutenant Ron "Mad Dog" Miller, a former TOPGUN instructor and now an instructor of dogfighting in the Tailhook Advanced Strike Pipeline syllabus at NAS Kingsville. J.J.'s adversary was Marine Captain John "Luke" Lucas, a veteran F/A-18 pilot and former TOPGUN instructor with over 1000 hours of fighter time and a no shit ace who had taken out 5 Libyan MIGs in one sortie during the Iranian Oil War.

This day was to be a memorable one for both Ricky and J.J.. You never forget the first time, especially if you got "killed". Of course, they were not using real bullets or live missiles, but the news received over the radio that you had just been killed is probably worse than actually getting smoked.

"You ready Woody?" Mad Dog Miller asked as Ricky entered the squadron ready room.

"Darn straight. What's the plan?" Ricky replied.

"We are going to fly out to the Kingsville 1A MOA, do a G suit warmup left and right, then do a snap guns exercise from a neutral start at 15,000 feet, 250 knots. Whoever gets the advantage first, becomes the attacker. Hard deck is 8,000 feet. Copy?" Miller said.

The Kingsville 1A MOA was a large trapezoidal shaped piece of airspace south and west of Kingsville that was reserved for military operations when it was "hot" meaning military jets were in the airspace and operating. Civilian planes on instrument flight rules are cleared through a MOA only if Air Traffic Control can guarantee separation. Otherwise, they are re-routed around the MOA. VFR civilian pilots can enter a MOA, but they need to exercise extreme caution, and, when the MOA is "hot", as it would be today, civilian pilots are best advised to steer clear.

"Roger that." Ricky said. At that, they walked out to the flight line and did their pre-flight inspections and got into their T-45 Goshawks. They went through their pre-start checklists and started their jets. After taxiing out to the active runway, they did their take off checklists and called the tower for clearance for takeoff.

"Kingsville Tower, Echo Section 43 ready for takeoff, flight of two. Mad Dog and Woody. Left crosswind departure to Kingsville 1A." Miller said over the comm 1 UHF radio.

"Echo Section 43, left crosswind departure approved, climb and maintain 5,000, departure frequency will be 124.5, cleared for takeoff." the tower controller replied.

Mad Dog and Woody then applied full military power and started their takeoff rolls. At 700 feet on the upwind leg, they both raised their gear and flaps. Then the tower called, "Switch to departure frequency, left turn approved. Have a nice day."

Mad Dog and Ricky turned left and switched to 124.5 and started their climb to 5000 feet. "Kingsville Departure, Navy Echo Section 43, with you at angels 3.5, climbing 5, flight of two." Mad Dog called over the radio.

"Navy Echo Section 43, radar contact, climb and maintain angels 15. Cleared into the Kingsville 1A MOA. No observed traffic." the departure air traffic controller called after checking his radar scope.

"Kingsville departure, Echo Section 43 out of 4.5 for one five thousand."

Upon reaching the MOA, Mad Dog and Woody each did a G suit warmup maneuver first to the right and then to the left to make sure their G suit G sensors and the suits themselves were working.

"Mad Dog fenced in left. Speed and angels." Miller reported meaning he was in the MOA and as the pre-arranged speed and altitude for the start of the dogfight.

"Woody fenced right, speed and angels." Ricky replied over the radio. "Fight is on".

In the snap guns exercise the idea was that each would fly a Horizontal Scissors maneuver which is a series of turns toward the other jet, done by each jet in the fight, which starts after two jets are flying in the same direction and one makes a successful break turn in front of the other and forces the other to overshoot. The idea is to try to out turn the other jet, force an overshoot, and get on the other's six in a position for a guns kill. This may sound easy, but it is far from it. Timing of the reversals is critical, and it can turn into a stalemate, especially where each jet has the same wing loading and manueverability as is the case when both pilots are flying the same type of jet. It is called a snap guns exercise because the shooter would only have the interval involved in the snap of a finger, about 1/2 second, to get off the shot when the two jets are in the middle of their turns. Further, the "bullets" fall as they travel and the bogey travels too while the bullets are in the air so to make a guns kill, the shooter had to fly his plane so as to put the pipper on his heads up display in a position to lead the other jet by a suitable angle and shoot a suitable amount above the target given the range to the target and the speed of the target.

"Piece of cake." Ricky thought never having attempted to do it before. Ricky was to soon to find out that one does not become a jet ace if he does not know what he is doing.

Mad Dog Miller was to be the defender or target in the first dogfight and Ricky was to be the attacker. The two jets were about a mile away from each other, separated by about a mile, each travelling at 250 knots at 15,000 feet with Miller slightly ahead. At Woody's "fights on" call, Mad Dog made a hard break turn to the left right turn across Ricky's flight path forcing Ricky to overshoot and put him on the defensive.

Ricky countered by making a sharp left turn following Mad Dog. Mad Dog reversed his turn as soon as Ricky got close to crossing his flight path, and this caused Ricky to reverse his turn as soon as Mad Dog crossed his tail. The turning duel continued for three turns, when Mad Dog made a mistake. Ricky executed a nose-high rudder reversal with full power on, and Mad Dog did not notice it. The nose high attitude reduced Ricky's horizontal turning component and it reduced his velocity vector in the horizontal plane. That meant that Ricky was turning tighter than Mad Dog.

Ricky's move quickly put him above and about 1500 feet behind Mad Dog's tail, so Ricky quickly did a roll off down into Mad Dog's six and in range for a guns kill.

Mad Dog saw Ricky's position and realized he was in deep shit. Ricky was in position for a guns solution. Mad Dog needed to force an immediate overshoot by Ricky. "This nugget has me. Well let's see if he can handle this." Mad Dog thought to himself.

Mad Dog broke hard into a left, diving defensive turn, and Ricky followed suit. As soon as Mad Dog's airspeed climbed to 300 knots, he pulled hard back pressure on the elevator and loaded up the jet at a high angle of attack. That slowed him down very fast and caught Ricky by surprise. Mad Dog immediately applied rudder and aileron to start a High G Barrel Roll without releasing any Gs on the jet. Mad Dog released some aileron and applied more rudder as his angle of attack increased. As he rolled inverted over the top, Mad Dog maintained his back pressure and increased his roll rate. When he reached the 270 degree point in the roll, Mad Dog applied top rudder and looked back to see where Ricky was. It had worked. Mad Dog's airspeed decreased so rapidly, Ricky was forced to overshoot and was high and on the outside of the roll. Mad Dog maintain hard top rudder to keep his jet rolling until Ricky was forced to slide below and into Mad Dog's 12 o'clock in gun range. Mad Dog rolled into Ricky's six, put the pipper on him and called "Guns, guns, guns" over the radio. And just like that, in a matter of seconds, Ricky was "dead".

"Nice scissors Woody. Too bad about that last thing." Mad Dog called over the radio.

"What the heck was that?"

"I will teach you later at the O Club. Continue. Let me get ahead of you and we will start another furball."

"Roger that." Ricky retarded his throttle a little to slow down and let Mad Dog pass him and moved out to two miles to the right of Mad Dog.

As soon as Ricky was in position for a high angle off, high speed attack by Ricky, Mad Dog immediately broke hard right in a defensive turn into Ricky's attack.

Ricky saw he was going to overshoot again, and needed to reduce his airspeed to prevent the overshoot as well as reduce his angle off Mad Dog's tail. Ricky decided to do a Barrel Roll in the vertical plane combined with a High Speed Yo Yo to reduce his velocity vector along the axis of the roll which also reduced his velocity vector component that would otherwise have caused an overshoot, and simultaneously reduce his velocity vector component in the plane of Mad Dog's turn so he could turn tighter than Mad Dog. He started by diving below and inside Mad Dog's plane of turn, and then pulled up hard inside Mad Dog's turn and did an outside barrel roll away from the direction of Mad Dog's turn. The hard pull up killed off a lot of airspeed as did the barrel roll. This not only reduced his velocity vector in the vertical, but also in the horizontal which is exactly what he wanted to do to prevent the overshoot. As Ricky rolled nose-high through the inverted position, he applied back-pressure and kicked bottom rudder to obtain a nose-low, diving 270 degree change in direction to rapidly regain airspeed and point his jet in the same direction at Mad Dog's six. Ricky dove down into a six o'clock low position within Sidewinder range, got tone and called "Fox 2". Mad Dog was "dead".

"Nice shot nugget. Mad Dog is dead."

"I am bingo. Let's go back to base so I can lick these wounds. Woody out." Ricky called.

"Roger that. Join on me for return to base." Mad Dog replied.

"Roger. By the way Mad Dog, you probably ought not really be allowed to wander the streets unsupervised. That High G Barrel Roll could have pulled your wings off."

Mad Dog laughed. "That's funny dude. Listen nugget, you gotta die of something. I would rather it be quick. By the way, can you set me up with SWAT. She would benefit from more one on one instruction." Mad Dog said with a grin under his oxygen mask.

"Funny how everybody wants to teach Swat something. But I will pass that one along to her you pervert." Ricky said with a sly smile. "By the way, she told me she has a policy against dating clinically insane persons."

Ricky and Ron Miller landed at Kingsville about 6 PM. Walking back in from their jets, Miller congratulated Ricky on his good flying in the first fight. He explained how the High G Barrel Roll works to rapidly change direction and reduce the jet's velocity vector because of the high angle of attack and simultaneous conversion of the thrust vector from horizontal to much more vertical. Mad Dog explained how that almost always causes an overshoot that can be turned into a reversal of roles from defender to attacker. Mad Dog went on to explain that the thing that Ricky should have done as the attacker to counter the High G Barrel Roll by the defender was, not watch in amazement, but instead do either a Yo Yo out the top of the roll or a reverse High G Barrel Roll out of the top of the defender's roll. Either maneuver reduces the attacker's velocity vector along the axis of the roll which is exactly what the defender is also trying to do to cause an overshoot. This allows the defender to maintain his position on the defender's six even after the defender completes his roll.

Ricky said, "Got it. I was so amazed at your move, that I never thought of that. But I see your point. Where did you learn that move. They did not teach us that one."

"I read this book about Colonel John Boyd, the best dogfighter the Air Force had. He was called '40 second Boyd', among other things such as the Ghetto Colonel, because he had a standing bet that he could let anybody get on his six and defeat them within 40 seconds. Many tried, but nobody ever beat him. He invented the Energy Manueverability Theory that we have been teaching you since you started the Air Combat Manuevers Syllabus. He came up with one night in the 60's sitting around with his college friends from his thermodynamics class at Georgia Tech. He went there on the Air Force's dime to get an undergraduate engineering degree after he had been an instructor at their Fighter Weapons School at Nellis. He had done a lot of research on ACM at Nellis, and had initiated much of the Air Force documentation on how to dogfight. While he was shooting the bull with his thermodynamics student friends, he came to the realization that ACM is all about energy states of the two combatants, and that altitude is potential energy and airspeed is kinetic energy. He wrote the Aerial Attack Study in 1963, and it changed the way the Air Force conducted ACM. Eventually it changed the way the Navy and all the Air Forces of the world conducted ACM also. You should read it. It is unclassified now after the Air Force, inexplicably tried to classify it so the people who needed it the most could not have access to it. Some copies sneaked out, and they got copied and it went viral."

"Interesting. I will read that for sure. Let's go to the O Club for a beer Mad Dog."

Miller said he couldn't because he had a dinner date, but gave him a raincheck.

RICKY, CARMEN AND J.J. MEET AT O CLUB FOR DOGFIGHT DEBRIEFS

Ricky called Carmen's cell and asked her to call J.J. and ask him to meet them at the O Club. Ricky then called Neil to set up a "debrief" during happy hour at the O Club.

Carmen walked into the O Club and saw J.J. at the bar and snuck up to him and put her hands over his eyes. "How are you doing J.J.?" she asked.

"At this point, I am doing just about anybody who will let me." J.J. said with mock humility. J.J. was a stud and didn't have any trouble attracting pretty girls.

"Oh that's bullshit J.J.. I would do you if you weren't such a man-slut." Carmen laughed.

"Hmmm. Dubious. I don't know whether to be insulted or amused -- but that's pretty funny." J.J. said with a smile.

"Funny ha ha, or funny peculiar?" Carmen wisecracked.

"Both. But I suppose that it might even be true. Never really counted them all up. Too many." J.J. said with a devilish laugh.

"That's what I thought. There is no way I would ever believe you even if you told me your number. I can see you have not had any trouble with women in the past." Carmen said with a smile.

"Oh I don't. Not really. Too busy for women right now. One of these days though I will get busy and find a date. This dogfighting stuff is kind of fun except when you get killed. That ruins my whole day." J.J. said with a grin.

"Did you get killed this afternoon?" Carmen said with an inquisitive look on her face.

"Yeah, once. But I smoked my instructor once too." J.J. said.

"Tell me about it." Carmen said.

J.J. DESCRIBES HIS FIRST DOGFIGHT

"Ok. We were doing a level snap guns exercise on parallels paths about a mile apart, same speed and altitude but he was ahead of me a little. I was the attacker on the left and Luke was the defender on the right. He did a hard left break in front of me at 'fight's on', so I turned with him. But I was immediately in danger of overshooting him in his plane of maneuver because it was immediately apparent that I would not be able to stay inside his turn radius. I decided to do a High Speed Yo Yo attack to prevent the overshoot and maintain my nose-tail separation offensive position. So I rolled away from his turn a little and pulled the nose up through the horizon in a climb to store my speed as altitude. That diminished my turning component and vector velocity in the plane of his turn. As I climbed, I rolled away from his turn and toward the vertical plane just enough to provide me with an angle of bank less than his. I used rudder for directional change to turn in the vertical plane and maintained just enough back pressure to come over the top with my lift vector pointed at Luke's jet. I maintained the back pressure on the elevator while inverted with my lift vector on him to keep turning in the horizontal plane in same direction as him while simultaneously turning in the vertical plan back down toward him. I came over the top and dived down into his six. It worked well to reduce my turning component and vector velocity in the plane of Luke's turn and allowed me to stay inside his turn and maintain my nose-tail separation while turning. But I came down too close on his tail, so I did a barrel roll to reduce my forward velocity component to increase separation. I rolled out in guns range and called 'guns, guns, guns'.

"You got Luke on a guns kill first time out of the box?" Carmen was incredulous.

"Yeah, but he might have been sandbagging. I don't know. He said, 'Nice move Scud. Luke is dead. Now let me show you how an opponent would counter that move. Get back in trail a little bit on a parallel fight path and we will do the same fight, but I will show you something else'. So I got back to where we started from, and we did it again."

"What happened next?"

"He smoked me."

"Really. Do tell."

"Ok so Luke is on the right and slightly ahead again, and he makes a hard break turn to the left in front of me. I start to follow him and then roll away from his turn and pull my nose up through the horizon to start a High Speed Yo Yo. Luke sees me do this, and maintains his angle of bank but relaxes his back pressure to unload his jet and preserve airspeed. I saw his nose drop below the horizon and his greater turn radius, so I had a choice to make. I could either maintain the Yo Yo apex or commit to attack against a descending defender. I chose to drop my nose and set up for a Sidewinder shot. Luke saw me make this commitment, and immediately employed top rudder and back pressure to pull up into my attack. That put his nose high, and it put me nose low. That increased my airspeed and reduced my rate of turn relative to Luke's rate. That forced me to overshoot him and put me in front of him and below him. He rolled down into my six, got tone on his Sidewinder and called 'Fox 2'. And just like that, I was dead."

"Bummer. Don't you hate it when that happens? But I love the Yo Yo Attack combined with the Barrel Roll Attack. That was cool." Carmen said. "Luke is a smooth dude. He was a TOPGUN instructor before he came here, so don't feel too bad."

"Noted. Hmmm. I still feel bad."

RICKY DESCRIBES HIGH G BARREL ROLL

Just then, Ricky and Neil walked in and greetings were exchanged. The O Club was jumping that night as the four settled in for some more hanger flying and general conversation.

"How did you do in your dogfights this afternoon Ricky?" Carmen asked.

"Won a few and lost a few." but it was fun Ricky said.

"Who did you fly against?" Carmen asked.

"Mad Dog." Ricky said.

"Anything I should know about flying against him?" Carmen asked.

"Yeah, he has this cool move you need to watch out for called a High G Barrel Roll. He used it against me when I was on his six in guns range just as I was about to get off a burst. It turned the whole situation around in the blink of an eye, and all of a sudden, he was on my six and I was defensive. Smoked me with it. Coolest move I ever saw." Ricky said.

"What the heck is that move?" Neil asked.

"Its called a High G Barrel Roll. You never heard of it because it was invented by '40-second Boyd' who was a great Air Force pilot back in the 50s and 60s." Ricky said.

"Why do they call him '40-second Boyd'? Carmen asked.

"He had a standing bet when he was an instructor at the Air Force Fighter Weapons School at Nellis back in the 60s. The bet was he would let you get on his six, and in 40 seconds or less, he would be out of the situation and on your six. Nobody ever beat him."

"Holy mackeral. That is pretty arcane. How did you learn about him?" Carmen asked.

"I read books."

"Really?" Carmen asked with a sly smile on her face.

"Yes really."

"How does it work?" Neil asked.

"Well once I was on his six and very close, like guns range close that's when he did it. We were at 300 knots. He started with a maximum performance break turn that shed a lot of his airspeed and put me in a high angle off position. I followed, but then he caught me by surprise by doing a maximum performance barrel roll in the opposite direction from the break turn. That shed even more airspeed very fast. He started the barrel roll by not releasing any Gs from the break turn, and, then applied even more up elevator and then kicked in rudder with very little aileron to do the roll. When he was at 270 degrees through the roll, he looked where I was. I had tried to follow his barrel roll, but overshot because he shed so much airspeed so fast and reduced his vector velocity along the axis of the roll to much less than what mine was. So I was low and on the outside of his roll and had slid in front of him. He kicked in hard top rudder at the 270 point and kept adding more rudder to keep a nose up attitude and to keep his roll going. He rolled right into my six and called guns." Ricky explained.

"Cool move." Neil said. "Why have I never heard of it?"

"Because they have not taught us defensive manuevers yet, and this is a first class defensive move."

"How did your flight go this afternoon Carmen?" Ricky asked.

"I flew against Slingshot, and won both of them." Carmen said referring to her instructor Navy Lieutenant Tommie "Slingshot"

O'Leary, former TOPGUN instructor whom she had slept with a few days earlier.

Ricky, J.J. and Neil all looked at each other with twinkles in their eye and knowing smiles.

"Shut up you dickheads." Carmen snarled reading their expressions.

They wiped the smirks off their faces right away, because the last thing any of them wanted to do was piss off Carmen and lose their front teeth.

"How did you pull that off?" Neil asked.

"Well, we started off with a head-on pass, same speed and altitude. Slingshot was the attacker and I was the defender. He started a lead turn into my flight path early, and I countered by turning into him, but I cut the throttle and slowed down so I could turn sharper. He missed his high angle shot when he was abeam, because I pulled up sharply and did a hard break turn into him just as he was about to fire to slow down even further. That caused him to overshoot me on my six. I immediately reversed my turn and pitched up to shed airspeed. That gave me a sharper turning radius, so I turned inside his turn and got on his six and smoked him in a trailing guns solution."

The boys all looked at each other thinking he took a dive to lose that fight on purpose.

"Then we did a parallel flight path, guns only fight with me the attacker and him the defender. He was on my right. He did a left break turn in front of me, and my closure rate was very high and I did not have sufficient lead for a snapshot, which is exactly what he wanted to accomplish with the break turn. To slow my closure rate and get down to corner speed, I started a climb rolling right away from his turn as I climbed. As I rolled inverted, I pulled more back pressure to put my lift vector on his jet. When I looked up through the canopy and saw he was relatively straight up from me, I pulled the stick back into my lap, kicked in a little more rudder and pulled a max-G diving left turn toward his plane of maneuver, picked up my lost pursuit speed and got on his six. I got a trailing gun solution before he could juke and screw it up, let off a burst and smoked him. Ruined his whole day to get splashed by a nugget." Carmen explained with a smile on her face.

The boys looked at each other again. Same thought.

"Wow, nice." Neil drawled.

"I recommend you don't fly against Slingshot any longer." Ricky said.

"Why?"

"Because we don't think he is giving it his all and is patronizing you so you can win which short changes you on your training." Neil and J.J. nodded in agreement with Ricky.

"OK I see your point. I think I will take your advice. How about you Neil? What happened today in your dogfights?" Carmen asked.

"I decided to try a Low Speed Yo-Yo against Dingo. He got me once, and I got him once." Neil said referring to his adversary Marine Captain Larry "Dingo" Dingman, a Harrier ace with 1200 hours and 6 kills to his credit. "We started out in parallel with Dingo on my right. I was behind him, out of missile range and had insufficient rate of closure At 'fight's on' he did a break turn left in front of me and bled off a lot of airspeed hoping I would overshoot. I was turning left in his plane of maneuver but still had a low rate of closure. To gain airspeed, I dove hard till I was about 9000 feet below him and on his six, so I converted the airspeed to closure and pulled up into his six within missile range. I was in his blind spot, the first time I tried this because I started my dive when I could see he had his head in the cockpit, and he lost sight of me. When I was in heater range, I got tone, and nailed him with a Sidewinder shot."

"In the next fight," Neil continued "I decided to use a Vertical Rolling Scissors. That did not work out as well. We started out on parallel flight paths about a half mile apart, same airspeed, but I was 1000 feet higher with Dingo on my left. I dove down on him, but he saw me and pulled up into a zoom climb. I pulled up too, and as soon as he saw that, he did a rudder reversal 180 degrees in the vertical plane and dove back down toward me in a spiraling dive. I decided to do a cut off instead of zooming up through his turning circle to avoid an overhead attack with a negative delta mach. He saw my cut off, and knew that my 180 degree turn would be done at a higher airspeed and with a greater turning radius which was going to cause me to overshoot his descending flight path. He cut his power, and as soon as I overshot him, he put on back pressure and reverse rolled into me which gave him a lower vector velocity in the vertical axis. I rolled back into him, because I was descending more rapidly than him, but it was not enough to reduce my vertical axis vector velocity as low as his, so I slid below him, he rolled in on my six and smoked me. I learned that a rolling vertical scissors is not won by the fighter that can fly slower although it is the forward component of velocity that is still the deciding factor. The rolling vertical scissors is won by the pilot who can make steeper climbs and dives. He gets the position advantage, and that is what Dingo did to me. He made steeper climbs and dives than me with better slow speed sustained turn performance. But I didn't, and now I am dead—until tomorrow." Neil said with a smile. "Better here than in the Middle East somewhere."

GOLF OUTING ARRANGED

"Wow, what a day." Ricky said. Anybody want to go golfing tomorrow?" They all said yes.

"My Dad knows the manager of the Corpus Christie Golf and Racquet Club. I can get us a tee time tomorrow morning." Neil said.

"Super. Do it dude." Ricky said.

So Neil opened up his cell and called his Dad who conferenced in the manager of the Corpus Christie Golf and Racquet Club and arranged a tee time for 2 PM the next day for a foursome.

"We are on. It is a done deal. See you all tomorrow." Neil said as the group broke up.

It was a beautiful Sunday morning at the Corpus Christie Golf and Racquet Club. J.J. showed up in red plaid duffer pants and the loudest red, blue and yellow parrot infested shirt ever worn. He suffered a fusillade of mockery for his trouble from Carmen and Neil who had actually showed up on time and were waiting for J.J. and Ricky.

"OK, first of all, as for my shirt, I wear this because you can see it from space, and it is an important part of my survival gear which I wear under my flight suit when I am flying. You never know when you are going to go down in the mountains or the desert, and they are going to have to find you. This helps them." You of all people should understand that."

"Oh we understand it alright. We also understand the fact that it also helps the people who shot you down find you using their spy satellites." Neil wisecracked.

"OK, I will buy the shirt argument, but you know J.J., those pants don't show a sufficient amount of respect for this sport." Carmen said with a sly smile on her face.

"Sport! This is not a sport. You don't even sweat in this alleged sport, and it is perfectly acceptable to drink alcoholic drinks on the course and nobody even thinks twice about it. In fact, on practically every golf course I have ever been on, there is a hot chick driving a cart around the course selling cocktails and junk food to golfers. In fact, one of the pro golfers, I forgot his name, actually used to drink on the course while he was competing in tournaments. And he played better when he did. I rest my case." J.J. said. But he did not in fact rest. In a burst of brilliant punctuation to his argument, he added, "Try drinking on a gridiron or a beach volleyball court. You'd get hammered, literally in every sense of the word. Golf is not a sport, it is a bad habit. Actually, I look at as just a pleasant walk in the grass."

"Speaking thereof, I brought along a few supplies for those long, hot par 5 holes." Neil said bringing out three chilled Cocktails for Two cans of Pina Colada from a small ice chest he had brought. They each popped one and took a sip and started to feel the pent up pressures of Naval Aviation Training melting away.

"I know golf isn't a real sport." Carmen said. "I don't take it seriously either. I consider it a good round if I lose less than 10 balls. I just like walking around in the grass and trees and feeling the breeze on my face. I don't even bother to keep score." she continued.

Finally, Ricky showed up at 5 minutes to 2 in a white Tommy Bahama shirt with a beautifully embroidered golf scene on the back which said, "I golf, and therefore I swear".

"Nice Ricky. Criminy, we said 1:30 so it would not be such a Chinese firedrill to get all our shit together and get out to the first tee." Carmen jabbed.

"Sorry, I was indisposed." Ricky said sheepishly. "I had to break up with my dumb ass girlfriend from back home. She wanted to come down for a visit, but I am just not into her anymore. She would not get off the phone."

"Text her next time. It is easier to ignore her then." Carmen said with a laugh as she handed Ricky a chilled Pina Colada from Neil's stash.

On the first tee, Ricky teed off first. He put his Titleist 1 ball down on the tee and saddled up to it. Slowly he drew his club back and then whipped it downward. Crack! A beautiful drive, right down the middle of the fairway, 300 yards. The problem was it was only a par 4 hole and it was only 250 yards to the pin.

"Fucking steroids. I gotta knock that shit off." Ricky said laughing. Turning back to the group, Ricky noted they were rolling on the grass laughing. "Get up you nimrods. Worms live down there." Ricky said only half kidding.

Carmen teed off next and pulled out a Big Bertha™ driver with a club head that was bigger than her entire ass. Carefully assuming the position and with great concentration, she slowly drew the huge driver back into a menacing position over her head, whipped it downward and knocked her tee shot out a whole 50 yards with a wicked slice that caused the ball to actually sing as it flew into the next fairway over.

Peels of laughter from the group.

Neil said, "If you are gonna carry a club that big baby, you gotta be able to walk the walk." borrowing a phrase from the legendary Dallas Cowboys coach Jimmy Johnson. "I will call 911 to see if they can come out and help find your ball."

"Shut up wise ass."

Next up was Neil, but he could not stop laughing at Carmen's ridiculous tee shot, and, as a result, he topped his ball and sent it out 75 yards in three hops.

J.J. tee'd up last, and turned out to actually be a pretty good golfer – well, at least good with a driver, his tee shot putting him on the green in one. It was on the green that the group discovered why he did not consider golf a sport. He was bitter. It turned out that he could not sink a putt to save his life. He four-putted for a bogey.

"Drive for show, putt for dough. That's what I always say." Ricky said as he stuck the imaginary needle into J.J.'s derriere, a derriere hardened from years of playing volleyball on the beach and that many women had found difficult to resist.

Off the second tee, Ricky hit a good drive about half way down the fairway, and everybody else did a passable job on their drives except for J.J. who hooked his drive into a water hazard. "Damn it. I forgot my snorkel and fins." J.J. said with a laugh.

Out on the fairway, everybody drove their carts up to Ricky's ball which was the shortest of the group and watched as Ricky picked his driver out of his bag. Quizzical looks all around. Then Ricky walked up to his ball, pulled out a tee and tee'd up his ball right in the middle of the fairway. "What the fuck Ricky? You can't tee your ball up on the fairway." J.J. said.

"Yeah, what he said." Neil piped in.

"I am calling the course marshal Ricky. We have margaritas bet on this hole." piped Carmen.

"Oh shut up you whiners. This isn't really a sport anyway, and I look at the rules of golf as mere suggestions." Ricky retorted. Everybody laughed.

"Whatever you say Ricky." Carmen chuckled.

As the afternoon passed pleasantly, the group had many laughs and some great conversations. While they were waiting out a slow foursome in front of them, J.J. started trouble.

NEIL EXPOUNDING ON FEDS LACK OF ENERGY CONSERVATION EFFORTS

"Neil, what do you think about the federal deficit and the budget cuts the President is pushing?" J.J. asked Neil.

"I cannot believe it has come to this. You know, the real problem is the failure of the feds to impose energy conservation measures, lower speed limits and impose higher fleet gas mileage standards on the automakers. Excessive energy consumption has led to lower supplies with increasing demand. The result is higher costs which get passed along into the cost of everything. Big time inflation has resulted in people spending way less on stuff other than energy which has led to many bankruptcies and loss of jobs and loss of tax revenues. One thing that really pisses me off is the way people drive. It seems like it has gotten way worse since the rise of Starbucks. Now there a coffee vendor on every corner. Try driving 55 MPH for awhile to save on gas. Everybody on the freeway will fly by you at 85, and half of them will flip you off as they roar by. Did you know, you can save 33% on fuel consumption if you just drive 55 MPH instead of 70? People all over the world need a Big Government Nanny to tell them the maximum speed they can drive. Otherwise they would drive 95 MPH everywhere -- including in mall parking lots." Neil said with a grin. He was only half kidding. Anybody who had ever tried to drive the speed limit or lower on a freeway knew exactly what he was talking about.

"Nope, did not know that." Carmen said. I would probably be one of the one's flipping you off." she added with a smile. "Don't get your panties in a bunch Neil. There is nothing you can do about it. People are the way they are."

"Don't make me come over there and give you a wedgie." Neil said laughing. "I am trying to make a point here, and you are not taking me seriously."

"Sorry Neil. Just kidding. You are absolutely right as usual." Carmen said smoothing Neil's ruffled feathers.

Actually Carmen did know about the huge cost savings from driving slower, but she did not care. Carmen was always in a hurry. She was a little bundle of fast twitch muscle cells on speed and probably steroids. Often, the only evidence Carmen was at the scene was the vapor trail she left behind. She was basically the colorful, hard throwing heater queen of hot asian chicks —the Farrah Fawcett of flamethrowers --the one that packed the stadium with people with radar guns and cameras.

But the great thing about Carmen was that she did not think she was any big deal. She was humble and self-effacing and solid as a rock. When one or her friends needed help, she was right there doing whatever she could. She was the farthest thing there was from a fair weather friend.

"How is your relationship with Slingshot going?" J.J. asked Carmen.

"Well, it is more a series of booty calls than a relationship. We are both so busy that there is not a lot of time to just hang out together and build a real relationship. I wish there was more time, but there just isn't. Besides, he is not exactly my type. He's white." Carmen said with mischief in her eyes. All the boys looked at each other with puzzled expressions. Slingshot was a stud. "He is part of my super-stud catch-and-release program."

Everybody's game got slightly better as they negotiated the back nine late in the afternoon. Except for Carmen. True to form, she had lost 9 balls by the 17th hole, and she was running out. On the par 3 17th hole though, Carmen hit a beautiful drive, purely by accident and it landed on the green, rolled up to the pin – and dropped in.

A collective whoop went up from the boys and they all dropped down on the grass of the tee rolling over in hysterical laughter. "What the fuck was that Carmen?" Ricky said. "Where did that come from?" he laughed. "You know that this calls for a human sacrifice to the Gods of Golf don't you?" And they all looked at her.

"Fuck you guys. You can't sacrifice me. I am not a virgin." Carmen said laughing.

"Who said anything about needing to be a virgin?" Neil said. "If we needed a virgin, we would never be able to make any sacrifices at all to appease the Gods." But they let her off the hook and settled for picking her up bodily and throwing her into the water hazard in front of the 18th tee.

She came up spitting and yelling and pretty pissed off. "You bunch of retards. I am going to make you pay for ruining my hairdo and this tight little golf skirt. And the next one of you mofos that meets me in a dogfight is going to die in a fireball."

"You still look good baby." Neil said.

"Imagine my relief." Carmen said sarcastically. She already knew she looked good. Men had been telling her that her whole life. Every time some lame dude told her she was hot without really knowing her as a person, she thought to herself "You nimrod. Can't you think of something more intelligent and funny to say than that? You are not going to get very far with that start."

C'mon Carmen, we better get those wet clothes off you." Neil said only half kidding.

"You wish." Carmen said with a smile. And it was over. She wasn't pissed any more. One of the best things about Carmen is that she had a great sense of humor and did not hold a grudge.

On the 18th hole, Par 4, Ricky and J.J. both made good drives and put 9-iron shots on the green. Neil and Carmen both hit their 3rd iron shot up close to the green and Carmen pitched on, but Neil's chip went into a sand trap down below the level of the green surface.

NIKITA AND ALEXANDRA ENTER THE PICTURE

Ricky and J.J. were standing on the green waiting for Neil to hit his sand wedge, when they heard two girls laughing and jabbering in the distance. They looked behind them and saw a golf cart careening at a high rate of speed up the cart path that went past the 18th green, said golf cart bearing a beautiful blonde and an equally beautiful brunette.

"Hey look at those two hot dudes on the 18th green." the brunette Alexandra Bixby said to the driver of the cart, Nikita Novachev. Nikita and Alexandra were both stunning beauties. Both were tall and slender with magnificent figures, very short skirts and plunging necklines with lots of cleavage and long hair framing their pretty faces.

Alexandra was a native born Texan from Southern Methodist University who had joined the Dallas Cowboys front office doing PR after graduation and stayed there 2 years before going out into private practice. She was from Dallas, but found a job in Corpus Christie with the same Public Relations firm for which Nikita worked. She was a very hot brunette bombshell with shoulder length auburn hair, rich, dark brown eyes, full, pouty lips and a perfectly symmetrical face. She weighed 115 pounds dripping wet, 5'4" with 36 C cups and legs to die for. She could have been a Dallas Cowboys Cheerleader. She could control a man just by looking at him and smiling.

Despite her physical beauty, Alexandra was a very intelligent, mature woman with a quick wit and a great sense of humor and a delightful laugh. She came from rich Texas parents, Daddy being an oil executive and Mom being an OB-GYN doctor. They had raised Alexandra as her parents and not as her friends. There were rules, and there were punishments if she violated those rules. As a result, she and her younger sister were model citizens. They were both good students, active in student government and their church and participated in charity events whenever possible. Alex got top grades in her private high school, and graduated *magna cum laude* from Southern Methodist University with a degree in journalism with a minor in public relations.

Alex and Nikita had become best friends over the past year working together in the same firm, and spending lots of time together trading stories about the dumb things guys had done to get their attention over the years.

Alexandra was somebody you could talk to and have fun with and she was not stuck up at all. She was warm and friendly, and, despite being from Texas, she was not a blowhard at all. Quite the opposite. She always spoke the truth, and never pulled her punches no matter who her audience was. She was not intimidated by anybody no matter how rich or smart or accomplished there were. You had to earn Alex's respect, and that was not easy to do.

Alex always made it a point to be kind to the less fortunate and kind to her boyfriends of which there had been many much to her mother's chagrin. Alex was no slut though. These were quality men and she treated them well and with respect, and, as a result, she received the same treatment from them. Although Alex could have used her beauty to extract gifts and money from men, she did not do so. She considered herself an equal partner in every relationship she had ever had and carried her own weight. She loved being treated like a lady, but she was a smart and capable girl, and NOBODY ever treated her like a bimbo. If you ever did that, you were toast.

Nikita was quite different from Alex. She was a sexy, blonde, Russian bombshell with beautiful light blue eyes, hair down past her shoulders and a beautifully symmetrical face with pouty, very kissable lips. She looked like Gwen Stefanioso except her eyes were blue. She was 5' 6", had the body of a Dallas Cowboy cheerleader, 120 pounds naked, dripping wet with legs for miles.

Nikita was born in St. Petersburg and her parents had died young, victims of an excessive vodka habit. Nikita was sent into the foster care system of Moscow and had to scrap to survive. She was tough and smart and knew how to use men to get what she wanted. Which was money, status and U.S. citizenship. She had married an American guy who had come to Russia on a romance tour, and he had brought her to Chicago. It was a big mistake. He was a chauvanistic lout who did not lift a finger to help her around the house. She broke up with him after two years after she got her U.S. citizenship, and moved to Corpus Christie when her PR firm needed a person with her skills in the Corpus Christie office.

Nikita and Alex were semi-pissed and had been drinking heavily that afternoon, Nikita just having caught her boyfriend cheating on her with his secretary. They were both holding partially full martini glasses as they sped down the cart path. Nikita was driving with one hand and holding her martini glass in the other while looking away from the cart path and directly at Ricky. Alexandra had a martini glass in one hand and a full shaker of the concoction in the other and also was not watching the cart path as she checked out J.J..

"Wow what a couple of hunks." Nikita said as they sped past, both looking to their right, neither paying any attention to the path of their careening golf cart. As they stared to the right, the car also drifted right and the right front tire smashed into and ran up on a wedge shaped boulder just to the right of the cart path. That knocked the right front corner of the cart up in the air, and the steering wheel snapped full right causing the cart to swerve sharply right and then roll over left down the sloping terrain just off the green. Having spilled its contents and occupants all over the cart path and the grassy hillside, it looked kind of like a plane crash. There were martini glasses, shakers, balls, clubs, tees, Louis Vuitton purses, cell phones and chicks everywhere. Nikita and Alexandra lay sprawled on the grass. Nikita's crash was a face plant that pulled her low slung top off her shoulder and exposed one of her boobs. She had not been wearing a bra that day. Dazed and confused and slightly drunk, she rolled over on her back and looked up as the sky. "Shit, I guess I have to learn how to drive someday."

Ricky and J.J. watched in amused amazement. When the dust had settled, J.J. walked up to Alexandra and Ricky strolled up to Nikita. Nikita sat up groaning and was sitting on the grass leaned back on her arms like a blonde lawnchair. Carmen stayed on the green preferring to watch Ricky and J.J. work their magic from afar. Neil was still sand wedging and swearing in the sand trap on the far side of the green.

Ricky looked down at Nikita and said, "Nice boob. Maybe you should wear one of those orange traffic cones as a hat when you drive."

"Don't fuck with me cowboy. I have had a bad day." Nikita said somewhat indignantly and feeling a little foolish, and a more than a little drunk. She was in no mood to put up with a smart ass.

"Oh? Do tell." Ricky said in amusement.

"I caught my scum bag boyfriend cheating on me with his secretary last night. He told me he had to go on a business trip." Nikita sniffed.

"Don't you hate it when that happens." Ricky said. "Let's go to the clubhouse. You look like you could use another drink." and extended his hand to help her up. She tucked her boob back in, looked up at him and smiled and took his hand.

"Nikita Novachev." Nikita said with a smile.

"Nice to meet you Nikita. 1st Lieutenant Ricky Magnusson, United States Marine Corps." Ricky replied.

Meanwhile J.J., stunned by Alex's beauty, inquired if she was hurt.

"Just my pride. Can you help me up there stud." Alexandra said.

"Certainly. 1st Lieutenant J.J. Saleen, USMC at your service." J.J. said with a smile as he offered his hand.

Carmen watched in amazement as the two young officers picked up these stunning beauties. Neil finally got up on the green and saw what was happening and looked at Carmen and they both just rolled their eyes and laughed.

"Just putt out for us Carmen. J.J. and I have to nurse these ladies back to health." Ricky said with a crooked grin.

"Certainly Ricky. Anything else I can do for you?" Carmen said sticking in the needle as she laughed and flipped him off.

Ricky and J.J. lifted the cart upright and helped the girls pick up their stuff and get it all back in the cart. Ricky drove Nikita's golf cart to the clubhouse with Nikita. J.J. drove Ricky and J.J.'s golf cart to the clubhouse with Alexandra in it, but they were chit chatting and messing around and arrived about 5 minutes late to the party. Carmen and Neil were left to their own devices.

Ricky and Nikita settled at a table in the clubhouse bar overlooking the course and ordered a round of margaritas. Carmen and Neil joined them for a little while about ten minutes later to watch the show. It was the Golden Hour, the last hour of golden light before a beautiful sunset. That was Ricky's favorite time of every day.

AMBER BLACK WAITRESS

Shortly, Amber Black, the little high school girl who worked as a cocktail waitress at the clubhouse walked up to the table where Ricky, Nikita and Alexandra were sitting. "Ricky, I remembered how you like your margaritas – BIG." Amber said laughing.

"Ha, ha that's funny you little twerp. How did you know I was coming?

"There was a little black spot on the sun today." Amber said.

"Are you saying I am like a sunstorm?"

"No, more like a solar flare – big, magnificent and short in duration."

Nikita and Alexandra looked at each other momentarily and then burst out laughing.

Ricky looked back at Amber with a bemused expression and finally said. "Who knew. I had no idea you were a little science geek."

"There are a lot of things you don't know about me Ricky." Amber said with a flirtatious smile.

"Shouldn't you be home doing some homework or something?" Ricky said with a smile as he took a big gulp of his margarita. "Holy shit, that is strong. A couple more of these and I will probably start telling the truth." Ricky said with a laugh.

"Where's J.J.?" Amber said.

"Oh I don't know. Probably on trial somewhere." Just then J.J. and Alex walked in.

"Oh there he is. Would you mind bringing us four more margaritas please Amber?"

"OK but only because you are special."

"Yeah I know. That's what they told me in high school when they made me ride the short bus." Everybody burst out laughing.

Noting the extremely young and nubile but shapely appearance of Amber Black, Nikita and Alexandra looked at each other quizzically and then looked at Ricky with mirth in their eyes.

"No I absolutely did not. For God's sake, she's like 12 or something." Ricky took another big gulp of his margarita and suffered a brain freeze. "Fuck, I hate it when that happens." Ricky said squeezing his temples between his palms trying desperately to warm up his brain.

Nikita and Alexandra looked at each other with bemused expressions. "You are such a pervert Ricky." Nikita said.

"Thanks, I feel so much better now." Ricky retorted. "So how did you catch him?" Ricky asked Nikita.

"Catch who?" J.J. asked.

"Nikita caught her boyfriend cheating on her yesterday." Ricky said.

"Oh. That ought to be a good story." J.J. replied.

"It is." Alexandra said.

"By the way Ricky, this is Alexandra Bixby, my friend from work. And who is your handsome friend here?" Nikita said.

"Oh this stud is my best friend otherwise known in law enforcement circles as 1st Lieutenant J.J. Saleen, United States Marine Corps. He is in flight school with me. J.J., this is Nikita Novachev." Ricky replied.

"Nice to meet you Nikita. I cannot wait to hear your story. That was a big league crash out there. I don't think I have ever seen anybody roll a golf cart." J.J. said laughing.

"Yeah that thing is souped up. I had them put a blower on it."

Just then Carmen and Neil walked up and sat down with the group. "I ordered some margaritas for you guys." Ricky said looking at Carmen and Neil. "By the way Nikita and Alexandra, I would like to introduce you to 1st Lieutenant Carmen Nicoise, United States Marine Corps, call sign SWAT and Lieutenant Neil McAble, United States Navy, call sign Nailgun. They are both in flight school with me and J.J.."

"Nice to meet you all. My name is Alexandra Bixby, and my blonde friend here is Nikita Novachev." Alex drawled in her southern accent

"I called the Highway Patrol in case they wanted to issue a moving violation for that spectacular crash. What are we talking about?" Carmen inquired.

"Oh Nikita just found out her boyfriend was cheating on her yesterday, so Nikita and Alex were out pounding down martinis and taking it out on the golf carts today." Ricky said.

"Interesting. So what happened with your boyfriend?" Carmen said.

"We were just getting to that." said Alexandra.

"I sort of have been getting this feeling lately that he had something going on the side." Nikita said in her polished English with a Russian accent.

Ricky knew women could almost always tell things like that instinctively.

"So I went over to his house and staked him out for a few hours. I saw my boyfriend and his secretary arrive in his car about 10 PM last night and go into his house. I waited about 30 minutes and then used my key to walk into the front door. I walked into the bedroom unannounced, and caught them *in flagrante*. He had her wrists and ankles tied to the bed posts of his canopy bed with four of his neckties and she was blindfolded with a fifth. He was screwing her brains out and she was screaming in ecstasy. He never made me scream like that. That little prick." Nikita said in disgust.

"Ouch." J.J. said.

"Ditto. What did you do then?" Ricky asked.

"I picked up a heavy flower vase off the dresser and threw it at his head. Hit him right in the forehead and knocked him out cold." Nikita said with angry eyes and relishing the memory.

"Nice arm. J.J. can you pitch like that?" Ricky said.

"No. What now?"

"I am going to find a new boyfriend and forget all about that dirtbag. It won't take long." Nikita said with a smile. She knew it would not take long. This was not her first rodeo.

"Another round then." Ricky said.

"Tell us everything. We want to know you." Ricky said.

"I am a public relations account executive for a PR firm here in Corpus Christie. Alexandra and I work together." Nikita said. "How about you? What kind of pilot do you want to be?" Nikita inquired.

"A good one that is still alive four years from now. J.J. and I are training to be fighter pilots for the Marine Corps at NAS Kingsville." Ricky said.

"What are you guys doing tomorrow?" Alexandra asked J.J..

"We both have to fly training dogfights tomorrow morning early." J.J. said.

"If you have to fly tomorrow, should you be drinking tonight?" Alexandra asked.

"It is different in the Marines than in the airlines. In the airlines, the rule is no drinking within 24 hours of a flight. In the Marines, the rule is no drinking within 24 feet of the airplane." J.J. said with a shit eating grin on his face.

They all burst into laughter.

After about four rounds, they were all feeling no pain. It was getting late, and Nikita yawned.

"Well you have seen one of my boobs. Want to see the other one?" Nikita asked Ricky in her Russian accented English.

In sheer amazement and delight, Ricky said, "Oh yoooou betcha." in his best midwestern accent.

Alexandra smiled and winked at J.J. and gave him the come hither signal with her bent index finger. As he brought his face close to hers, she brushed his lips with her full, luscious lips and whispered in his ear. "Now is your chance big boy. Show me your stuff."

J.J. laughed and winked back and extended his hand which she took into the smooth skin of her palm and then slowly removed it, slowly and softly tracing a line down the length of his palm with her index finger.

Carmen and Neil just looked at each other and rolled their eyes. "Well, ladies, looks like you've got it from here. Nice to meet you." Carmen said as she got up and grabbed Neil's arm and pulled hard. She was a little pissed. "What a slut." she thought to herself as she looked at Nikita.

"Ditto. Are you sure you girls don't need any help, you know like a designated driver, butler to put away your clothes, threesome partner?" Neil said to Alex and Nikita.

"Ha ha funny boy. Another day perhaps." Nikita said winking at Neil.

Ricky escorted Nikita to his Vette and opened the door for her. He handed her the seat belt and she settled her shapely ass and long silky legs into the car sort of flashing him with her panties as she opened her legs slightly to get in the car. That excited him, but he closed the car door gently and walked around to the driver's side and got in. Nikita looked at him in the moonlight and he thought to himself what an extraordinarily beautiful creature she was. Only later was he to find out that looks are deceiving.

J.J. walked Alexandra to his tricked out Mustang Convertible. She wanted to drive herself home, but he would not let her as she was obviously in no condition to drive. Neither was he for that matter, but he was in better shape than her. She smiled at him as he opened the door for her and slowly dragged her hand across his ass as she walked around him to get into the car. He smiled at her.

J.J. fired up the Mustang and tuned his iPod™ to a playlist he thought she would like. The sounds of Armik, "Flamenco Tango" came on the sound system. She looked at him and smiled. "I love Armik. How did you know?" she said.

"Just a guess." J.J. said.

"Good one. I wonder what else you know about me from our brief encounter so far." she said with a flirtatious smile.

"I guess we will find out, won't we." J.J. smiled back.

"For sure dude." Alexandra said in her best guy voice imitation. She loved to talk to guys in mock guy voices..

J.J. AND ALEX HAVE GRAPHIC SEX

When J.J. and Alexandra arrived at her apartment, she opened the front door and pulled J.J. in by the front of his shirt. He did not resist. She closed the door gently behind him and they kissed a deep, wet kiss that lingered forever. Slowly she started unbuttoning his shirt as he sucked her lower lip into his mouth and played with it with his tongue. As his tanned and buff chest was exposed, she broke the kiss, looked down at his chest and rippling abs and she purred a little as she reached for his belt buckle. Looking into his eyes with a steady gaze, she unbuckled his belt and slowly undid the button and zipper on his red plaid duffer pants.

"Does your Mom still dress you?" she asked playfully.

"No. I am just color blind." J.J. said with a smile. He wasn't, but he fibbed. She giggled.

She hooked her index fingers around the waistbands of his pants and Calvin Klein tighty whities and slowly dragging them down to his ankles as she dropped slowly to her knees never losing the lock of her gaze on his eyes as she did so.

Finally she looked down and drank in the muscles of his thighs and calves. They were buff and tan from years of beach volleyball. She could feel the excitement rising in her loins…..

After enjoying her moist, warm lips for a few minutes, J.J. cupped her head in his palms and urged her upward. She stood back up and he kissed her again, this time running his tongue around her lips and the sucking both of her puckered lips into his mouth.

Slowly he started to unbutton her blouse while looking into her eyes. She gazed back unflinchingly and raised both arms above her head. He pulled her blouse up and off over her head and drank in the sight of her cleavage and magnificent breasts. He pulled her gently into his chest with one arm, and gently scratched her scalp with his other hand, running his fingernails gently across her scalp, then down to one ear and back across the back of her head to her other ear and back up to the top of her head. Not being able to contain himself any more, he undid her bra strap and let if fall to the floor. He cupped her breasts in both hands and bent down to lick and suck them gently until her nipples were aroused. As he came back up to her lovely face and opened his mouth to suck in her lips, he scratched her back gently, slowly dragging his fingernails up and down her skin. She purred a little and snuggled deeper into him. As he lowered her down onto her bed, he whispered, "Are you sure you want to get involved with a Navy pilot?"

"Yes, by all means." she whispered back. At that point, she could not have stopped even had she wanted to. And it was also at that point that her most recent civilian boyfriend of 6 months was officially toast.

CHAPTER 4

CARRIER QUALIFICATION – LANDING ON THE BOAT

JULY

One of great things about being a Navy pilot is that they teach you how to do one of the most insane things any pilot can ever do with an aircraft – land it on the pitching flight deck of an aircraft carrier regardless of how bad the weather is and regardless of whether it is day or night. It take balls of steel to do this, especially at night and in bad weather. Come in too low and you will fly into the unyielding fantail of a megaton supercarrier and become a fantail barbecue which is guaranteed to ruin your whole day.

Try to pull up at the last minute from a position that is too low, and the fantail will break your plane in half and you will slide across the flight deck at 120 knots un-arrested since you no longer have a tailhook and slide right off the front of the landing deck.

If you can eject, you might live even though you punched out from only about 50 feet above the water. The ejection seats are rocket propelled and are powerful enough to eject from the flight deck or below its level if your plane slides off the flight deck and still get you high enough that your parachute can deploy. If you come in off line with the centerline of the flight deck and try to correct at the last minute and catch a wire, the jet will fishtail and oscillate as it is slowed from 120 knots to 0 in about 2 seconds and 350 feet, possibly breaking the landing gear off or bending the wings.

If a sailor neglects to correctly set the "stopping power" for the hydraulic motor controlling the arresting wire you catch to the correct weight of your aircraft, you will be slowed down to a speed which is too fast to keep you on the flight deck, but too slow to fly, and you will be sliding off the front of the landing deck and punching out from 50 feet above the water.

Come in too high and you will miss all the wires and have to do a "bolter" – a full military power "go around" from a few feet above the deck and "dirty", i.e., with your gear and flaps down for landing. This configuration causes a lot of drag and you can stall the aircraft and spin into the sea.

Come in too "hot", i.e., too fast, and the wires may not be set with enough stopping power to keep you from cruising right off the boat at the forward end of the landing deck dragging the wire with you. All of this was enough to cause naval aviators to take carrier qualification training seriously and work hard at developing proficiency in this skill.

Ricky was in his room at Boca Chica Field at Naval Air Station Key West, Florida studying hard the night before his first landing on a carrier scheduled for the next day. His training squadron had been operating at Boca Chica and White Field for three weeks getting ready for carrier qualification. They had done many arrested landing at White Field both day and night, but that was landing on a concrete runway and not a real aircraft carrier.

VERONICA CALLS RICKY

A carrier landing is referred to by Navy and Marine pilots as a "trap". His cell phone rang and he popped it open and said hello.

"Ricky, it is Veronica. How are you?" Veronica's Chase's sexy voice inquired.

"Better now baby. What's shaking?" Ricky replied, pleased to hear Veronica's voice after not talking to her for a couple of years since The Basic School at Quantico. "Have you forgiven us for the stunt we pulled in TBS?"

"Oh yeah. That was pretty funny. One of the funniest things that has happened to me so far and kind of fun – all except that whole naked part. That wasn't as much fun. I still have guys from our TBS class call and ask me out. I just wanted to tell you that I made 1st Lieutenant and have been assigned to the National Reconnaissance Office at Area 58 as Marine Corps Liaison Officer." Veronica said with pride in her voice.

"Cool. What will you be doing out there wherever Area 58 is?" Ricky inquired.

Nobody except a very few people who worked in the spy satellite business even knew where Area 58 was. The National Reconnaissance Office or NRO is the ground control station for the U.S. spy satellites including the KH-11, the KH-12 Misty stealth satellite, the KH-13 and other U.S. spy satellites such as the Future Imagery Architecture SAR radar satellites. The Misty satellite was believed to have been adapted from a KH-11 so as to make it invisible to radar. The Future Imagery Architecture, unlike their name implies are actually Synthetic Aperture Radar spy satellites with no optical imaging capability, the program to develop their optical capabilities having been cancelled in 2005 for schedule and cost overruns. All these spy satellites are huge objects, kind of like a Hubble Telescopes turned toward earth, and there are about 14 of them in various orbits around the earth generally along north-south axes and east-west axes. The optical imaging satellites like the KH-11 and KH-12 and KH-13 use charge coupled device digital imaging and provide real time imaging capability of things on earth that can be seen from their orbits down to a resolution of about 6 inches. The later spy satellites also collect signals intelligence and have cameras that can detect infrared radiation and also have in-flight refueling capabilities to extend their useful lives. They orbit between 157 miles and 340 miles above earth. The NRO controls their orbits by controlling on-board rocket engines. The NRO also downloads signals intelligence information and images gathered by the satellites via the military's Satellite Data System relay network and distributes the gathered intelligence data to the CIA, NSA and various intelligence groups in the military.

"I will be working on monitoring intelligence data gathered by the spy satellites and relaying information important to the Marine Corps to the Commandant and the Joint Chiefs." Veronica said.

"So guys from our TBS class are calling you? Any boyfriends yet?" Ricky inquired.

"No, I am really picky, and currently geographically undesirable. There is nothing around here for miles." Veronica lied. "Besides, in this business, having a boyfriend, fiancee or husband is a liability because foreign intelligence services can extract information from you by threatening to torture or kill your loved ones. I probably should not have even told you what I do. Besides, who needs a boyfriend. I can get laid anytime I want just by snapping my fingers and pointing at a dude in any bar." Veronica said, this time telling the truth.

"Oh my God, you are such a mercenary. That is funny stuff. But to tell you the truth, I cannot think of any hole in that logic. And I won't tell anybody anything even if they torture me." Ricky said.

"You will never guess who called me the other day." Veronica went on. "Adam Sims. He got sent to the 2nd Marine Division at Camp Lejeune, North Carolina and made the cut and got into Force Recon. He is a MARSOC operator now."

"Hmmm. Strangely disturbing." Ricky said amused by this news. But he was impressed that Sims had made Force Recon. Force Recon marines were the Navy SEALs of the Marine Corps. The selection process was hellish and fully 80% of all applicants did not make it – most dropping on request. The training was brutal. They were the black-ops, snake-eaters of the Marine Corps. They were the ones who went deep into enemy territory to gather intelligence, make extractions of downed pilots or other people needing extraction and make hits on high value targets. It was highly risky stuff. You did not want to screw with them.

"I am impressed. I did not know he had it in him. But good for him." Ricky said.

"I agree. That is impressive. But enough about him. What is new with you?" Veronica asked.

"Well, I am about two thirds of the way through pilot training. I made the cut for tailhook and am down at NAS Kingsville in the Advanced Strike Pipeline trying to make the cut for F/A-18s. I am doing my first carrier landing tomorrow." Ricky said.

"Wow, way to go Ricky. Good luck with that. Don't crash into the fantail you big lug." Veronica needled. "Any girlfriends?"

"Girlfriends? Not really. I did meet a Russian chick named Nikita on the golf course the other day while I was playing golf with Carmen, J.J. and a Navy pilot trainee named Neil McAble. It is kind of a funny story." Ricky replied.

"What happened?" Veronica asked.

"Well she and her brunette girlfriend Alexandra were wasted on martinis and were careening up the cart path toward the clubhouse when they saw me and J.J. on the 18th green. They were staring at us and not watching where they were driving when they drove over a big boulder at the side of the cart path and rolled their cart.?"

"Is that even possible?"

"Apparently. There was stuff everywhere. It looked like a yard sale. And, to our delight and entertainment, Nikita had a wardrobe malfunction and one or her boobs popped out of her slinky little top." Ricky said.

"Noted. Bet you liked that." Veronica chided.

"Oh yooooou betcha. So J.J. and I picked them up and took them to the clubhouse for a drink or two. The rest, as they say, is history."

"You dogs." Veronica said laughing.

"Good to hear from you Veronica. Keep in touch. I have to finish my work to get ready for this trap tomorrow, so I have to get off the phone." Ricky begged off.

"Bye Ricky. I will talk to you later." Veronica said as she hung up.

FIRST GOSHAWK TRAP

The next morning dawned bright and clear. It was a great day for flying. Ricky made his way to the squadron conference room for a pre-flight briefing on the day's activities. The students were to make fly out to the carrier in groups of four, one instructor and three students. Ricky's group consisted of Ricky, Carmen and J.J. and their instructor was Tommy "Slingshot" O'Leary.

The group got their pre-flight briefing from Slingshot. The plan was that several groups, each consisting of four jets with an instructor pilot in the lead plane and three student naval aviators solo in the three other jets of each group would fly out together and enter a holding pattern circling at different altitudes. The lowest group would be called down first, make their landings and then be moved to the catapults for re-launch so as to do another trap. As the first group finished their traps, the next group would be called down to pattern altitude to begin their landings, and the whole stack of planes would descend to the next lower altitude in the stack.

All possible scenarios were discussed in the two and a half hour briefing. The jets had limited fuel and burned it at a voracious rate, 1800 pounds per hour at 300 knots airspeed. So fuel management was important, and if a student could not get down safely on the boat, extensive discussion about how the student was to set up the jet in fuel saving mode and fly back to the beach to land at the bingo field.

A bingo field is the airfield to which a jet which was having trouble landing on the carrier or which was too low on fuel, i.e., bingo, to make the attempt to land on the carrier safely taking into account the high fuel consumption that would occur in the military power burn in a bolter, i.e, missed landing attempt followed by a "go-around".

For most events in the training syllabus, the student pilot flew with an instructor in the back seat for the first time they performed a new thing. But not carrier landings. For traps, the students had to fly alone. Carrier landings are considered the most dangerous things the student pilots do, and the Navy and Marine Corps did not want to waste their instructors on some bonehead training accident. Furthermore, hardly any instructor could keep himself from grabbing the controls and flying the jet himself during the landing as a matter of self-preservation.

As they walked out to their T-45C Goshawk jets, Slingshot looked at the group of student naval aviators and said, "Showtime boys and girls. Everybody OK?"

"Define OK." Ricky said.

J.J. said, "I just pooped a little back there a ways."

"Dude, are you on acid. Of course I'm OK." Carmen said with false bravado. The truth was she was scared shitless.

They went through their pre-flight checklists, started their engines and went through their post-start checklists. After getting clearance from the tower, training division Tango-1 took off in pairs, joined on the lead jet flown by Slingshot and headed out to the carrier. When they arrived, Slingshot called, "Training Division Tango-1 overhead, flight of four, one instructor, O'Leary, and three chicks."

"Roger that Tango-1 lead. Assume your hold at marshall, angels two and wait for our call." the air traffic controllers answered. Marshall, in this case, was a left hand holding pattern, which happened to be above the carrier that day, and which served as an initial point from which the approach was started. Each group would be stacked at a different altitude. As luck would have it, Ricky's group was be the lowest in the stack that day and would be the first to be called down.

The group descended first to 2000 feet in a left hand racetrack pattern with the holding legs more or less aligned with the Base Recovery Course which was the heading of the carrier.

After about ten minutes of holding, the call came over the radio from the carrier's air traffic controllers, "Tango 1, Case 1 recovery, Charlie now." meaning Ricky's group was being called down into pattern altitude to make their landings. The carrier they would be landing on today was the USS John C. Stenis, a 100,000-ton, nuclear-powered supercarrier named after a dead Mississippi senator who formerly chaired the Armed Services Committee. As a group, all four jets then descended and flew past the right side of the carrier at 800 feet to prepare for their break turns to slow down to pattern speed. A break turn is a hard left 180 degree turn just in front of the bow to bleed off airspeed to pattern speed and put the jets one-by-one on the downwind leg separated by short intervals of about 17 seconds flying time.

"OK Tango flight, it is showtime. It is now or never. Make me proud." Slingshot said over the radio. The next few minutes could not only end their careers as naval aviators, it could also end their lives. A not insignicant percentage of Student Naval Aviators fail to carrier qualify, and are washed out of pilot training. Some died. It is the most difficult flying there is.

"Tango-1, roger that." Slingshot replied over the radio. On the air-to-air frequency by which Slingshot could talk to his "chicks" without ARTCC being able to hear him, Slingshot said, "Woody, you will be going first after me. You've got 350 feet and four wires. Don't fuck it up or you will be doing a high dive from 50 feet into the Gulf of Mexico. If that start to happen, say three Hail Mary's and punch out."

Slingshot flew to the initial point for a Case 1 (good weather) recovery at 800 feet, three miles astern the ship. He then flew his leg over the carrier deck at 800 feet, and made his break turn in front of the bow to slow down to pattern speed, and put his landing gear and hook down as he descended to 600 feet to fly the downwind leg and perform his landing checklist. About 17 second later, Ricky, Tango-2, followed and made his break turn by giving the kiss off signal to Tango-3, which in this instance was J.J.. Ricky put his gear, hook and flaps and slats down, deployed the speed brakes momentarily to bleed off a little more speed. About 17 second later, J.J. made his break turn kissing off Tango-4 which was Carmen. Slingshot flew the downwind leg and slowed to approach speed and made his base turn into the groove while descending to 500 feet. Slingshot flew down the groove like he was on rails, and made a perfect 3-wire trap for all to see.

Ricky was now in the #1 position for landing. It was time for Ricky to do it for real. Ricky established his jet on the downwind leg, about 1.25 nautical miles from the left side of the carrier and flying a heading which was 180 degrees opposite to the carrier's heading. Ricky descended to downwind leg altitude of 600 feet leg, and completed his landing checklist. When he was about 3/4 of a mile behind the ship, Ricky made a descending left base turn and rolled into the groove wings level on speed and at 500 feet altitude. Ricky established visual contact with the ball and called "Tango-2, ball, 9.2, Magnusson."

"Roger ball, 9.2." the Landing Signal Officer replied. A deal had been struck. The LSO was now in charge of the approach. Ricky started a 300 feet per minute descent flying at about 130 knots toward the landing area. Ricky's radio call had advised the LSO which plane he was, that he had visually acquired the ships Optical Landing System, affectionately called the "meatball" or "ball", given the LSO his landing weight and identified him as the pilot. The "ball" is a Fresnel lens and light which tells the pilot whether he is maintaining the proper glideslope which is a 3 degree descent.

The LSO is called "paddles" in the vernacular of Naval Aviation, because in the early days of carrier aviation, he held a paddle in each hand which he manipulates to give hand signals to the incoming pilot how to correct his line up and altitude to make a good landing and to give him the "wave off" if he or she screws it up, the hapless pilot then having to do a "bolter" to go around and try it again. The sailors manning each arresting wire heard the call from Ricky, and reacted by setting the hydraulic stopping power of the arresting wire they were in charge of to stop an aircraft weighing 9,200 lbs and traveling at 124 knots. Each reported in on the Arresting Gear Officer's intercom when they had done so. The Arresting Gear Officer is responsible to make sure the deck is clear for each landing and for supervising the sailors who set the hydraulic engines which control the stopping power of the arresting gear wires.

From that point until touchdown, Ricky focused only on three things: meatball, lineup, angle of attack, meaning maintaining proper descent or glideslope tracking, maintaining his alignment with the centerline of the landing deck and maintaining proper angle of attack which is techno-speak for maintaining the proper airspeed for landing which is 132 miles per hour (124 knots) in a Goshawk at 11,000 pounds gross with half flaps. If he got too fast, he would have to raise the nose, i.e., increase your angle of attack, to decrease airspeed and lower the power setting to keep from ascending up off the glideslope. Screw any of that up and he would be too high and miss all the wires or be too hot on the landing and be given the go around by paddles.

It all went by in a blur. His laser focus on the ball and tiny little adjustments in throttle and stick as the ball started to drift too high or too low paid off. Just at touchdown, Ricky slammed the throttle to full military power as he was trained to do so the engine could spool up and be developing full power just in case he missed all the wires and had to do a "bolter". At touchdown, there was a huge thud as the jet slammed down on the deck and caught the number 2 wire. A carrier landing is more like a controlled crash than an actual landing. Ricky and his jet decelerated from 124 knots to zero in less than 2 seconds and about 300 feet. His first trap was over. "Hail Mary, full of grace." Ricky said to himself and then let his pride well up. He was a carrier pilot.

Well not quite. There were still a lot of other traps to be made on carrier-controlled, radar-guided approaches and instrument landing system approaches to learn for landing in bad weather and at night. But he had done one of the hardest things a pilot can do and he was rightfully proud of himself.

Under direction of the flight deck crewmen on the deck, Ricky taxied clear of the landing area and taxied up to the ready area near the catapults for his first cat shot. Behind him, J.J. made his first trap. A three wire OK pass. Each pass a carrier pilot makes is graded by the LSO. OK is the highest grade a pilot could get from an LSO. J.J. sailed through his carrier qualification landings like it was no sweat.

Carmen had problems flying the ball on her first approach. She was waved off when the ball went low and turned red just before touchdown and the LSO lit the two vertical columns of red lights flanking the central column of lights on the Fresnel lens optical landing system. If she had continued the approach, she would have been turned into a molten blob of protoplasm on the fantail. "Don't spot the deck Swat. Fly the ball all the way down, and make smaller adjustments of throttle and stick. Airspeed and angle of attack have to be controlled within a couple of knots and your lineup has to be near perfect. Glideslope has to be maintained all the way down." the LSO advised. An off-center engagement with the wires if lineup is not near perfect can damage the jet or its gear. Carmen had been making adjustments that were too big and caused the ball to first slide up above the datum lights, and then sink below it as her adjustments in power and angle of attack conspired with the pitching of the ship to move her jet first above and then below the proper glide path.

"Shit, now I am embarrassed. This is hard." Carmen said to herself.

"OK Swat, on this next pass, fly the ball with the throttle and don't yank the nose up and down. That screws up your angle of attack and destabilizes your approach airspeed. Maintain airspeed and lineup and fly the ball, fly the ball, fly the ball. Don't spot the deck."

"Roger paddles." Carmen went around the pattern and rolled wings level in the groove with good lineup about 3/4 of a mile behind the ship, on airspeed, on altitude and with a centered ball. It was a good start. "Fly the ball Carmen. Hail Mary full of grace." Carmen said to herself. She wanted a three wire to make up for her first pass fuck up. The next 17 seconds would be the most intense flying she would do since she started training.

Carmen started out in the groove, but started to sink and added too much power. That took her too high on the glidepath, so she reduced the power, but she reduced it too much, and sank below the glidepath, which is not where one wants to be. Fortunately, she was still far enough away and had time to correct. "Power, power, now!" came the call from paddles. She added a little power and then took it off right away. The jet floated up onto the glidepath and stayed there nicely for awhile.

"Oh, I see how this works. You have to just think about adding power and then dismiss the power right away. That is all it takes. Just a little bit then stop." Carmen thought to herself. She was on glidepath, but her alignment had drifted right and her airspeed had gotten too fast. Too correct she banked ever so slightly to the left and pulled her nose up to reduce airspeed and simultaneously reduced just a touch of power to keep from flying above the glidepath. That worked. She was getting pretty close to the deck now, and she could see the deck was pitching up and down which started to worry her. Just as she was 5 seconds away from touchdown, the deck started its upswing, and the ball went low and went red. Not good. She only had 5 seconds to live unless she did something fast.

"Wave off, Wave off, power now!" paddles screamed into the radio.

"Shit. I almost had it. I guess I will anticipate the deck movement on this next pass." Carmen thought. "Paddles, can you watch the deck swing and give me a little more heads up on the next pass." Carmen transmitted.

"Roger that Swat. I should have done that on that last pass." came the reply. Lets get it right this time."

The third time was the charm. Carmen came off the ninety in the groove and sitting pretty. She managed the power, angle of attack and lineup nicely with small control movements, and paddles warned her that the deck was starting its upswing again on short final, and she added just a touch of power which turned out to be almost enough but not quite perfect. She caught the one wire and got a taxi grade meaning she was too low on deck impact and had effectively taxied her jet to the one wire, although that is a gross misrepresentation of hitting the deck at 124 knots and applying full power instantly and then being jerked to a full stop in about 2.5 seconds. "Whew, that was a bitch." Carmen thought to herself as she watched the yellow shirt deck crewman give her the hook up hand signal instructing her to raise her tailhook and the hand signal instructing her to taxi straight ahead.

Ricky taxied to the re-fueling area near the cats, shut down his engine, and took on a couple thousand pounds of fuel. He then restarted, went through his post-start checklist: throttle: advance to 70%; HYD 2: reset, all hydraulics at 3000; fuel control: manual, less than 5% Dec/M Fuel Light; throttle: idle; menu/BIT/Mant: no exceeds or overflows; menu/Data/Acft: GPS 4 SATs/align countdown, verify waypoint zero correct when heading info displayed; paddle switch: press; C Aug Lt: check on; C Aug Sw: reset, verify light out; check rudder trim at 12 o'clock; flight controls: full throw; NWS: disengaged; down: hook, bar, flaps, boards – check operable; up: flaps to half; canopy: down; nav equipment: check and verify waypoints; VOR/Tacan: set/lock; cockpit lights: set; airspeed/VSI: check prim/stby; altimeter: set; wet compass: free; Heads Up Display/Horizontal Situation Indicator/ADI: check headings; turn needle ball: check on and working during taxi.

When he had gone through his post start checklist, Ricky made a radio call, "Boss, 310 up and ready, gross 11.2, Magnusson." calling the air boss of the carrier and telling him that he was ready to taxi and his gross weight was 11,200 pounds. The air boss relayed the report to the flight deck crew, and a yellow jersey sailor, called a flight deck director, ran up to about 20 feet of Ricky's jet and held both fists clenched over his head meaning "hold your brakes." He then wiped his sleeves which was the "clean-off" signal telling the plane captain or PC to go to the tie down chains and remove them.

Ricky then went through his takeoff checklist: Control Aug: all, lights out; anti-skid: on, lights on; flaps/slats: half, slats out; trim: set to 0, 0, 2-3 nose up; canopy: check closed and locked, light out; harness: connected at 8 points, pins removed, ready to go hot in the front; ejection seats: arm to hot in the front; check nav instruments and switch to tower frequency; pitot heat: on; IFF normal; taxi lights and strobe lights: on; VCR: on; bit page: check; bingo set at 3.5. "Ready" Ricky thought to himself.

A sailor ran up to the jet and made eye contact with Ricky. He was holding up a box with changeable numbers, the number showing being 11,200. That was the weight of Ricky's jet. Ricky confirmed the displayed gross weight with a thumbs up, and the sailor ran over the steam cat operator and confirmed that the cat should be set for sufficient power to launch an aircraft of 11,200 pounds gross weight. Ricky then confirmed visually that his flaps and slats were set to takeoff setting, double checked the items on his takeoff checklist, did a wipeout to verify his elevator and ailerons and rudder controls were free, and set his #2 radio to the departure frequency and gave a thumbs up to the yellow jersey.

The yellow jersey then signaled Ricky to release the brakes and gave him hand signals directing him to taxi up to the Jet Blast Deflector behind the starboard catapult. Slingshot was on the cat waiting for launch. After Slingshot launched, the JBD was lowered and a yellow shirt gave Ricky hand signals to taxi up to the catapult and told him when to stop. Once there, the deck sailors hooked up the hold back bar to the nose gear of his jet and signaled him to lower his launch bar.

Ricky was then directed to taxi a few feet forward to drop his launch bar into the catapult shuttle to establish a connection with the carrier and ready the jet for a cat shot. Ricky saw the catapult officer put his jet into tension as the shuttle moved forward several inches to take out the slack. Ricky felt a thud when the cat shuttle took tension and reached its position ready for launch. A sailor ran up to inspect the cat hookup and then retreated to his station, and gave a thumbs up. The yellow jersey then passed Ricky off to the shooter who signaled for Ricky to advance the throttle to full military power. Ricky did so and inspected his engine instruments as the jet engine spooled up to full power. "Good, no over speeds, over temps, caution lights or warning lights. Batteries look good and three good hydraulic indications are displayed. I think I am ready to get out of town." He then did another full control wipeout with his stick and rudder pedals to make one last check to make sure all his control surfaces were moving fully throughout their ranges without restrictions. Ricky looked outside to ensure his ailerons, rudder, and elevators were moving and the flaps appeared to be in the right place. Sailors on the deck also confirmed the control wipeout with thumbs up signs. "Good to go" Ricky thought to himself. He then saluted the shooter who responded by kneeling down and pointing toward the water off the bow with his right arm and two fingers extended. Showtime. Zero to 120 knots in two seconds. It was a gut-wrenching, rough ride – like a roller coaster on steroids doing the first big dive into oblivion. "Holy shit, what a blast this job is." Ricky thought to himself.

Back in the pattern, Ricky did 3 more traps that day and was done. He was now an official member of the tailhook club. J.J. and Carmen joined him that day having performed their traps, J.J. to perfection and Carmen with some difficulty but finally making the cut. They flew back to the beach for landing at Boca Chica Field in Key West Florida. It was time to party.

Not everything went without a hitch that day though. Four student naval aviators in the detachment had "helmet fires" or full on mental meltdowns, and could not reliably execute their carrier landings. They were washed out of flight school that day and their Naval Aviation careers were over. One unfortunate Ensign died. He had failed fasten his koch fittings. The koch fittings are fittings which fasten the aviator's torso harness to the ejection seat. Fail to fasten them, and, in the event of an ejection, the unfortunate aviator becomes a rocket-launched hockey puck sailing through the air without the benefit of the parachute which is packed into the back of the ejection seat. On short final, the Ensign in question had let his jet sink so low on the glide path that he was about to impact the fantail. He reached for and pulled the ejection handle, and the rocket-powered ejection seat shattered the canopy as it rocketed upward through the hole. The Ensign stayed with the seat during the rocket-powered portion of the flight having been pressed into it by the 12 g ejection forces, but as soon as the rockets flamed out, the Ensign continued to travel upward in a ballistic arc as the seat fell away with its parachute. He hurtled through space for what seemed like an eternity until he crashed into the seat right in front of the carrier and was run over by the ship. His body was never recovered.

Flying high performance jets off aircraft carriers is an inherently risky business.

PARTY TIME AT BOCA CHICA AFTER CQ

Back at the beach, the detachment of SNAs at Boca Chica from NAS Kingsville were given a two day liberty pass as a reward for completing their carrier qualifications. It was Friday afternoon, and a large contingent of the group decided to go to the beach and have a bonfire and camp out Friday and Saturday nights. Ricky called Nikita and J.J. called Alexandra. They asked the girls to fly over to Key West and join them for the weekend, and they agreed. Nikita and Alexandra flew in about 10 PM that evening and Ricky and J.J. picked them up at the airport and took them to the beach encampment.

When Ricky, J.J., Nikita and Alexandra arrived at the beach party in Key West, the partying was well underway. Carmen came up to them with Slingshot carrying four margaritas for them. Some of the guys had brought their four wheel drive Jeep Sahara's and one had an inverter to power the boom box. There was a portable generator generating electricity for the blenders and lights. A bonfire was cooking along nicely in the middle of the encampment. Ricky and J.J. set up their tents while they were drinking their margaritas. The more margaritas they had, the harder it was to set up the tents. Nikita and Alexandra were parked on a blanket drinking with Carmen and Slingshot completely ignoring the colorful language being emitted by Ricky and J.J. as they struggled with the tents in the semi-blackness of the night.

Slingshot was having a hard time keeping his eyes at eye level while gazing at Nikita and Alexandra since both were wearing their bikinis as was Carmen and all of their magnificent cleavages were on public display. Slingshot knew it was not cool, so he tried to do it on the sly, but got busted on more than one occasion. Sheepishly, he apologized for his lack of attention span and blamed it on the long, tough day he had worrying about his students killing themselves in a flaming wreck. The truth was these girls were exceptionally hot, and he was toasted.

Slingshot did care whether his students killed themselves, but he had developed a hardness over the years after too many no casket or closed casket funerals of his friends and students. It was awful developing a close personal relationship with a student or another pilot only to lose them to a training accident or in a crash in combat. He had lost several of his best buddies that way. What they did for a living was highly dangerous, and pilots did get killed on a regular basis. So he tried to keep a cool professional detachment without being cold. He had done his level best to teach his students everything he knew, but it was up to them to absorb it and execute correctly.

CARMEN SIZES UP NIKITA

Carmen, in a very relaxed and mellow state induced by more than one margarita working on her 115 pound frame, looked at Nikita with curiosity. She was sizing Nikita up but did not want Nikita to know it. Carmen was curious as to what kind of a woman attracted Ricky. She was also curious about Alexandra, but she wanted to know about Nikita first.

"So how was your flight?" Carmen said to Nikita.

"Oh it was OK. I had this fat guy sitting next to me kind of invading my space and wanting to talk to me. I just wanted to be quiet and sleep after a tough week." Nikita said. "So I was kind of rude to him and blew him off and went to sleep."

"That's reasonable." Carmen said. "Don't you just hate it when guys hit on you when you just want to be left alone."

Nikita replied, "Yeah, it's a bummer. It happens to me all the time. I have gotten to the point where I don't even look at men for fear they will try to engage me. I have my own stuff to think about, and I don't really want to hear their lines and BS."

"So what kinds of things have you been thinking about lately?" Carmen inquired.

"Well I am kind of sick of my job, and would like to find a rich guy to just take care of me." Nikita admitted under the influence of too many margaritas for her 115 pound package.

"So you are dating Ricky?" Carmen said incredulously.

"Yeah, he's fun, but pilots don't make much money and they do a dangerous job so you can find yourself a widow with nothing in the way of support in the blink of an eye. But for now, he is OK and the sex is mind blowing." Nikita said abandoning all caution to the winds. If she knew how close Carmen and Ricky were, she did not seem to care.

"Nikita, what the fuck? Are you crazy?" Alexandra broke in. She did not approve of Nikita's gold digger attitude, and showed her displeasure visibly. Carmen just looked at Alexandra and smiled with approval.

Carmen did not approve of Nikita's viewpoint either, but did not say much because she did not know Nikita well. But in Carmen's world, women were strong and capable and competent and could take care of themselves and did not need men to support them. At least Nikita was up front about it. You had to give her point for honesty and ballsiness.

At this point, Slingshot spoke up. "Jesus Nikita how can you just admit to being a gold digger like that with a straight face?"

"At lot of women are like me." Nikita replied not defensively at all. "I am just admitting it, and I don't care what you think. I am what I am, so just deal with it. If you looked like me, you probably would do the same thing."

"No, I could never just sit in somebody's trophy case." Slingshot replied. "I need to get out and tackle tough challenges and conquer them. That makes me feel happy with a sense of accomplishment— you know when I take something on that is tough to do and kick its ass."

Carmen looked at him and smiled. She was exactly the same way. She liked this guy. But she did not think she loved him. And then there was the fact that he was white. Her Mom would kill her if she brought home a white ghost. Her mother was not a racist. She just did not want mixed race grandchildren of which she was expecting several from Carmen, and did not hesitate to tell her so. As far as love goes, there was just something missing, and she could not exactly put her finger on it. He was good looking and a major stud, but that alone was not enough for her. She had lots of fun with Ricky when they were together, and she was thinking maybe that was the x factor. Or maybe it was just Ricky's attitude and bearing. She really did not know, but she knew that there was something missing when she was with Slingshot. It was all percolating around in her mind, and she was sure that eventually she would figure it out.

Alexandra changed the subject. "You know, I saw a fascinating documentary last night on the Science Channel about what caused the collapse of the Egyptian civilization." Alexandra said taking another sip of her margarita.

"That's sounds interesting. What happened to them?" Carmen said.

Alexandra explained, "Well about three scientists working independently on different theories collaborated and came up with a theory that combined all their findings. One analyzed the hieroglypics in the tomb of the last Pharaoh who died just before the collapse of the civilization at about 4000 BC. But there was no mention made of any calamity. So he concluded whatever it was, it came upon the civilization suddenly. Another scientist analyzed satellite photographs of the Nile delta region that showed the positions and sizes of ancient settlements. I forgot how the satellites distinguished them from modern settlements. That researcher analyzed the photographs over a time sequence and it showed a pattern of abandonment of settlements on the marginal branches of the Nile in the delta region with the remaining settlements on the major branches of the river in the delta region growing larger. Apparently, the Egyptians in the smaller marginal settlements were moving to the larger more mainstream settlements to share resources with those people. So a theory emerged that climate change had caused a failure of the monsoons in Ethiopia for about 200 years. Ethiopian tributaries are the source of the Nile. Those monsoons caused annual flooding in the Nile delta, and these floods brought a large amount of dark rich topsoil to the Nile delta which supported crops nicely and the river itself supported a vibrant fishing industry. When the monsoons stopped happening according to the theory, the Nile did not flood every year and there were massive crop failures in Egypt and starvation set in. Then this same scientist went to the tomb of an Egyptian governor in the Nile Delta region that had died about the time of the supposed failure of the monsoons. She analyzed the hieroglyphics in that tomb, and there was mention of massive starvation and people being like a plague of locusts throughout the land. Massive lawlessness and complete collapse of the civilization ensued. The hieroglyphics in that tomb even mentioned that people were throwing their children against walls to kill them and were eating them."

"Oh Alex you are such a brainiac." Nikita said slurring her speech slightly. "I don't want to have any children."

Carmen and Slingshot just looked at her quizzically for the spacey *non sequitur* she had just emitted.

Ricky and J.J. had come up by then, and had been listening to Alexandra's story with rapt attention, even if they were fairly well inebriated. Ricky just looked at Nikita in amazement and rolled his eyes. Luckily she could not see him do that because he was standing in J.J.'s tall, muscular shadow and his face was darkened.

In utter amazement after Nikita's *non sequitur*, Carmen thought to herself, "Oh my God Nikita. First, we are not talking about you right now. Second, Ricky is clearly thinking with his dick again."

Alexandra paused briefly, and then gave Nikita a quizzical look and went on. "Anyway, to prove their theory, the first scientist started excavating sites in the Nile Delta region. The sediment layers are a historical record of what the climate was in the past. The clay content of sediment layers versus the level of sand indicate how much moisture was present. He found that starting in the sediment layers dating back to about 4000 BC, the level of clay dropped drastically and the sediment layers were comprised primarily of blowing sand. So that suggested that in at least the Nile Delta there was a very dry period starting about then. Then these two scientists contacted a paleoclimatologist who had access to a vast collection of drilled core samples from all over the world. He checked the core samples in the archive for verification of the theory for the general region. The paleoclimatologist found that the core samples from the Sahara, the Nile Delta region, the middle east in general all showed layers of primarily blowing sand starting in the layers representing about 4000 BC. So basically, the entire Egyptian civilization, or at least most of them, starved to death."

"Well we now have a new call sign for you Alexandra – buzzkill." Ricky said with a smile. Everybody cracked up.

After the laughter died down, J.J. found himself looking at Alexandra with admiring eyes. He was starting to love her. "Nice Alex. Got any other uplifting stories for us tonight?" J.J. said sticking the needle in.

"What? I am just saying." Alex said with a smile and a shrug. "Shit happens. You just have to deal with it as best you can."

"I have been saying something similar for a couple of years. When the world starts to run low on oil, there are going to be wars. The cost to grow crops and livestock and get them to market will skyrocket and finally there won't be any oil to get the crops and livestock grown and to market at any price. The strong nations will then try to take what they need from the weaker nations and eventually the whole thing is going to blow up in our faces." Ricky said. "But enough of that apocalyptic talk. Lets party. We are *bona fide* naval aviators as of today."

Carmen pulled Ricky aside. "What the fuck Ricky, this Nikita girl is a gold digger and kind of a strange mix of a bimbo but with some brains. And she is a slut too. She slept with you about two hours after she first met you. What do you see in her?"

"All fair points my friend. Normally I look at how beautiful a woman is inside. Her outward appearance is not that important. I like women who are generous, compassionate, smart, funny and intelligent. If I respect their intelligence and respect their persona and their outlook on life, it is game on. And if I like them as a person and enjoy hanging around with them and can laugh with them, it is a done deal. I am friends with them for life. At that point, I don't care if they sleep with me on the first date or the tenth. It just does not matter. I respect a person based upon their inner qualities and whether or not they go for a little trim early or not just does not matter. Of course there are always exceptions like Nikita where the woman is so hot that you just want to do her and will overlook her obvious character flaws." Ricky said with a laugh.

"Oh my God, you are such an asshole Ricky." Carmen said laughing. "But I understand now, and I have to say, I really respect that outlook on life. Except for that whole man-slut part. But, in general, I am impressed."

"Oh good. Imagine my relief." Ricky said smiling sinking the needle into Carmen all the way. But the truth was he really did care what she or anybody else thought about him when it came to matters of the heart. Ricky was Ricky and so be it. If she liked his program, then good. If not, she could just go fuck off.

Carmen and Ricky walked back to the group. "Lets go over to the bonfire and see what shaking." Ricky said.

SQUADRON DANCE TO BULLETPROOF

At that, the group got up and went over the bonfire. When they got there, the blenders were buzzing up a storm and the boom box was blasting out rock. When the Ting Tings came on the boom box singing *That's Not My Name*, everybody spontaneously broke into dancing. The party raged. Then, *Bulletproof* by La Roux came on the boom box, and the party spun into orbit. It was just the perfect song for the occasion, and it was one of those songs you just could not sit still for. J.J., Ricky, Carmen and Neil, looked at each other, gave the secret hand signal, and got into their tight diamond formation and broke into the dance routine they had been working on throughout flight school for just such an occasion. Ricky danced in the slot by his choice so he could get a good look at Carmen's ass while she was dancing. OK he was kind of a pervert, but at least he admitted it.

The dance routine was kind of a combination of some rock routines J.J. saw in a Lady GaGa concert, some Salsa spins Ricky learned when he was taking Salsa lessons, some break dancing moves Neil knew with the move known in pro beach volleyball circles as the Sand Worm as the big finish. J.J. had learned the Sand Worm from the Geeter-Man, a legendary pro beach volleyball announcer who used to perform it for the crowds at the AVP tournaments. Nobody really knew why they called it a Sand Worm, because they it looked more like a Sand Dolfin than a worm. The crowd went wild when they finished, and another round of margaritas was blended.

DRAG RACES ON THE BEACH

It was a blast. Soon a battle cry arose from some of the lit up Lieutenants and Marine Corp Lieutenants for drag races on the beach. The Lieutenants making the call to action had brought their four wheel drive Jeeps out onto the sand, and had unwisely decided they were going to let their drunken colleagues race them in the sand. Hastily, a beach drag race tournament was arranged. Ricky tried to bring his monster Corvette out onto the sand for the festivities, but got stuck and had to be dragged back to the pavement by a slew of party-goers.

The drag races went on into the wee hours of the morning with the party-goers dancing to the boom box tunes and drinking between races. Carmen blew through her match races till she reached the semifinals and faced off against Ricky.

"May the wind be with you grasshopper. Prepare to be schooled." Ricky said with a smile to Carmen.

"Bring it Master. Grasshopper is about to kick your ass." Carmen said with a laugh.

After Carmen totally blew Ricky out of the water, she came up to him and said, "Your kung fu is not strong Master."

"You lit me up baby. Where did that come from?" Ricky said.

"Never send a boy to do a man's job." Carmen said with a grin kicking sand on Ricky's shoes in the process. "Oh, by the way, did I not tell you I used to date a NASCAR driver in high school. So sorry."

Ricky laughed and grabbed her and flipped her to the ground and followed her down in the only jujitsu move he knew. She played along even though her Wing Chun could have taken Ricky out in one quick blow and he knew it.

"Nice move dude. Did you learn that from Nikita?" Carmen said.

"Oh don't get me started on Nikita." Ricky said lying on top of her but supporting his weight so he did not crush her petite little frame. "I know she is a gold digging airhead, but she is a good lay, so I don't really care."

"Oh my God. I did not heretofore know you were a gigantic, flaming dickhead. I don't know whether to rat you out to Nikita or admire you." Carmen said sticking the needle in but silently celebrating Ricky's low opinion of Nikita.

Ricky laughed and helped her up.

Amazingly, Carmen won the tournament facing off in the finals against Alexandra. It helped greatly to only weigh 115 pounds when all other competitors except Alexandra weighed 75 to 100 pounds more. Alex was a cupcake and a tiny little girl, albeit a fierce competitor. Nevertheless, Carmen still took her out by about 800 feet and became the Key West Beach Drag Queen. Further, as a result of the evenings activities, she gained another call sign to all those present: Leadfoot. There was some grousing about the lack of a handicapping system based upon driver weight, but the malcontents got over it.

CHAPTER 5

CHINA RUMBLES

THERE ARE TWO WAYS TO CONQUER AND ENSLAVE A NATION. ONE IS BY THE SWORD. THE OTHER IS BY DEBT. JOHN ADAMS, SECOND PRESIDENT OF THE UNITED STATES

July 1, Three Years Before the War: Meeting of the State Central Military Commission of the Peoples Liberation Army at the Xichang Satellite Launch Center 64km northwest of Xichang City, Liangshan Yi Autonomous Prefecture in Sichuan Province (Translated from the Chinese)

SIZE OF THE CHINESE MILITARY

Lo Binxiao was a Shang Jiang (Senior General) and General of the Army. He was a small and wiry man with a flinty gaze and the gravitas of Abraham Lincoln, but not as noble. He was not a man to be trifled with. Both his subordinates and his peers were afraid of him, because he wielded the full military power of the state in his hand —the largest standing military force in the world. Lo Binxiao was about to call a meeting and lay out a war strategy designed to save China from collapse. China had become a no shit super power in the decades since

Richard Nixon orchestrated the opening of China for trade with the western world.

At the time Lo Binxiao arrived in Xichang City, the Peoples Liberation Army or PLA was a unified military force comprised of 3.3 million uniformed men and women. It was comprised of a Ground Force, a world class Navy called, inexplicably, the Peoples Liberation Army Navy or PLAN, and a world class Air Force called the Peoples Liberation Army Air Force or PLAAF. China also had a nuclear and conventionally tipped missile force called the Second Artillery.

The PLA had 2.3 million soldiers organized into 35 Group Armies comprised of 65,000 soldiers apiece. The Peoples Liberation Army Navy had 9 supercarrier battle groups either completed or in various stages of construction, and amphibious assault forces. The Second Artillery maintained and operated a large force of PLA ICBMs, other medium and short range nuclear tipped missiles, the PLAs anti-satellite missiles and a significant force of anti-ship ballistic missiles (ASBMs).

The Peoples Liberation Army Air Force, or PLAAF, was the third largest air force in the world. It had hundreds of Sukhoi Su-27 and Su-30 Russian-designed Flanker air superiority fighters built in China under a manufacturing agreement with the Russians. The PLAAF also had a host of Chinese designed and manufactured Chengdu J-10 and Shenyang J-11 air superiority and multi-role fighters. It also had hundreds of Chinese built fourth generation JF-17 fighters.

Significantly, the PLAAF also had unknown number of fifth generation Chengdu J-20 stealth fighters that were virtually invisible to radar. They were huge 80,000 pound jets designed to kill tankers and AWACS, and were no match in a close-in, turning dogfight for the much lighter U.S. air superiority fighters such as the F-22 Raptor stealth fighter and the low observability F-35 Lightening Joint Strike Fighter, or, for that matter, the aging 66,000 pound F/A-18 Super Hornet.

One advantage the Chinese Flankers have always had over the U.S. F-35s and F/A-18s is the fact that the war loadout of air-to-air missiles on the Flankers is up to three times as high as for the U.S. jets, and the Russian missiles have a greater kinematic range which means they can be fired from further away. The latest Russian designed Flankers also have modern DRFM monopulse jammers which U.S. AIM-120 AMRAAMs, the principle U.S. BVR air combat air-to-air missile, have not yet faced in combat. The fact that the Flankers carry more missiles allows the Chinese pilots flying them to fire 2 or 3 or 4 missile salvos of different types of missiles with different seeker heads at a single U.S. jet. This puts the U.S. jet in the unenviable position of having to detect, jam, outmanuever and cripple with countermeasures a group of closely spaced, mach 3 inbound missiles—a difficult task indeed. Tests have proven that the probability of a kill increases exponentially with the number of missiles in the salvo, reaching 75% in a 4 missile salvo even assuming a per round kill probability of only 30%.

But a J-20 was a dangerous adversary if it could sneak up on a U.S. fighter without being detected and fire a fourth generation radar guided or heat seeking missile at it. The fourth generation air-to-air missiles are very difficult to defeat by jamming, maneuver and countermeasures. To make matters worse, if the Chinese pilot follows the typical Russian Beyond Visual Range tactic of firing 3 to 4 air-to-air missiles in a salvo with different types of seeker heads, some radar guided and some heat seekers, the probability of a kill is very high even against a target that can outmaneuver the J-20 in any close-in dogfight.

A J-20 could be most easily detected using an infrared detection system such as the AN/AAQ-37 Distributed Aperture System (DAS) 360 degree infrared detection system of the F-35. Unfortunately, that infrared DAS system was not put on the Super Hornets, and they had only forward looking infrared targeting systems which could not see above, below or behind the aircraft.

The PLAAF also had hundreds of bombers, tankers and transport aircraft. All these PLAAF aircraft were organized into 38 fighter, bomber, attack and transport divisions in the 7 military regions of the

PLA. Purchase of a large number of IL-76 transport planes and II-78 tankers from the Russians in 2005 greatly increased the troop airlift capability of the PLAAF.

THE ECONOMIC SITUATION AT THE TIME OF XICHANG MEETING

All the big guns were at the meeting at Xichang, because this was an immensely significant gathering the outcome of which could determine the survival of China as a viable entity. As the world's oil supplied dwindled and the price of a barrel of oil had risen to $400 U.S., the cost of transport, manufacturing and everything else had risen drastically as the cost of almost everything in a modern economy is linked in one way or another to the cost of oil. China's meteoric rise as a modern super power started with the opening of China by Richard S. Nixon for trade with the West. Massive out sourcing of manufacturing jobs from the U.S. and other industrial powers followed and China grew in wealth and significance greatly. However, the arc of China eventually followed the arc of the U.S., and around 2010, labor unrest began rearing its head in the ranks of China's working class. Workers started jumping off buildings, and the Chinese Communist Party tried hard to order its people to be happy, but it did not work. The middle class grew as China's prosperity grew, but with the rise in wealth of the middle class so also arose a massive gulf between the rich and the poor.

The reality of unintended consequences also played a role in bringing China to its current state of crisis. As the middle class grew in number and wealth, so did the number of automobiles and trucks on China's highways. The massive rise in the number of drivers in China and India, which was following a similar historical arc to that of China, spiked demand for oil. That, coupled with the short sighted policies of western governments and the failure of first world denizens to conserve energy or become more efficient in any meaningful way led to massive shortages of oil as the world's oil fields started to dry up and new discoveries tailed off. The law of supply and demand did what it did, and the rise of oil rose and rose and rose. With it rose the cost of food and the cost of just about everything.

As the cost of food and housing and gasoline rose inexorably, but wages in China's manufacturing plants did not keep pace, hardships of unimaginable proportion bore down on the working class. As a result, unrest started and the workers started attempts to organize against management much as had happened in the earlier decades in the West. But the Chinese Communist Party was merciless and brutal, and it ordered labor protests crushed with force. As a result millions of worker/protestors were murdered by the PLA under orders of their own government as the world watched in horror. Nobody dared intervene however since it was an internal Chinese matter and China was by now a genuine superpower. For now the protests had been quelled and the working class was working away slavishly and suffering in silence, and most of the goods in the world continued to be made in China. But sporadic food riots had occurred all over China, and the central government realized that if nothing was done, eventually the Chinese economy would melt down. The cost of sending a shipping container from China to the U.S. had risen drastically and had many manufacturers were on the verge of pulling their manufacturing operations back to the U.S. Any rising labor costs would definitely tip the balance and cost China many of it manufacturing jobs. China had to find a way to supply its energy needs and keep the cost of labor down. China also had to find a way to keep the cost of shipping from China to the rest of the world down to prevent the flow of manufacturing jobs back to the U.S. and other countries of the world.

CHINA LAYS OUT ITS STRATEGY TO SAVE ITSELF

And so it was that a meeting of the State Central Military Commission, the leaders of the Chinese Communist Party and the leaders of the

Ground Force, Navy, PLAAF and the Secondary Artillery was assembled to discuss a strategy for the survival of China.

General of the Army Lo Binxiao opened the meeting.

"Gentlemen we are assembled here today to discuss a strategy worked out in advance in closed door meeting between myself, select leaders of the Peoples Liberation Army Air Force, the PLA Ground Force, the Peoples Liberation Army Navy, the Second Artillery missile command and leaders of the Central Committee of the Communist Party to ensure the survival of China. We have worked out this strategy within the bounds and in accordance with the dictates of the 13th Five Year Plan.

We have come to a crossroads where it will no longer be possible to meet the energy needs of China purchasing oil and liquefied natural gas on the open market. Costs have risen so much in recent years that the cost of food has become prohibitive to the average worker and the cost of shipping the goods made here in our factories has become so high that we are starting to lose manufacturing jobs back to the U.S. and other countries. We cannot afford to go back to the stone age times before China was opened to the West for trade. Massive unemployment and starvation would result if we lose our manufacturing base

In order to ensure our survival, we have devised a strategy to invade Brazil and crush them and then take over the Tupi oil and gas fields off the coast of Rio De Janeiro and divert the product of those fields to our uses. We expect the U.S. to intervene and possibly some of its allies to try and stop us, so the main part of our strategy is designed to defeat them.

The operation, code named Canary, will be a surprise attack scheduled for April 1 three years from now. The Second Artillery will begin the attack by shooting down the American's KH-11, KH-12, KH-13 spy satellites and their Milstar military communication satellite constellation as well as their Advanced Extremely High Frequency and Enhanced Polar Satcom communications satellites. The Second Artillery will also shoot down their Defense Satellite Communication System and their Wideband Global SATCOM broadband data networking satellite constellations. This will be done using our SC-19 class kinetic kill vehicle anti-satellite missiles. Simultaneously, Wicked Rose, the Evil Security Team, the Honker Union of hackers and the hacker force of the Sichuan Military Command Communication Department will conduct cyber-warfare to attempt to disrupt and disable the American DOD communication and fire control networks. Attacks will be carried out by opening the back doors created in the American DOD computer by the Wicked Rose GinWui rootkit and taking control of their computers to find and destroy files, create our own files, manipulate services and start and kill processes, get information about the computer and its user, access and alter the registry, and lock, restart or shut down the operating systems, etc. These back doors have been distributed throughout the American networks by the distribution from one DOD computer to another of Microsoft Word word processing documents. We have, through infiltration of their networks over the past few years, installed back doors on DoD computers throughout their headquarters, bases and ships. External drone bot armies will also be used to externally attack their networks and servers with barrages of empty packets.

We expect to defeat the Brazilians in a matter of two to three weeks. We will crush the Brazilian Air Force with our fourth generation carrier based Flanker fighters and our J-20 stealth fighters. Their surface to air missile defense network and the air-to-air search radars in their fighters will not even be able to see our stealth fighters before they knock out the Brazilian SAM sites and radar-guided anti-aircraft guns. Our fourth generation J-11 and Su-30MKK Flanker fighters will then engage and decimate their older generation fighters with ease. After establishing air superiority, we will then make a blitzkrieg style attack on their air bases and navy bases with carrier-based fighters and marines of the Peoples Liberation Army Navy and paratroopers of the Ground Force to gain control of the sea, their airfields and ports and their petroleum and gas refining and shipping facilities.

We expect the Americans to arrive in the area of the Tupi Field with multiple supercarrier strike groups by May 1. The American technology is, in some cases, superior to ours except for their fighters, so we will use deception and overwhelming force to overcome their Aegis missile cruiser defenses and their carrier-based fighters. A large force of Kilo-class diesel-electric mini subs will lie in wait for the American ships to arrive at the Tupi fields and fire torpedoes and supersonic anti-ship cruise missiles at them. Drone fighters will then attack their carriers. This will deplete their supply of ship-based Terminal High Altitude Area Defense missiles and air-to-air anti-aircraft missiles. Then we will attack their carrier with our Flankers and J-20 Stealth jets to further deplete their missile supply and shoot down many of their F/A-18 and F-35s. Finally, in the crowning blow, our newly developed nuclear-tipped, anti-ship ballistic missiles will be used to sink the American supercarriers. They have no effective defensive systems to counter our ASBMs. They will be fired from both truck mounted launchers and from two Jin-class nuclear ballistic missile submarines we will send with the fleet. The truck-mounted ASBMs will be fired from camouflaged sites in Porto Alegre in southern Brazil that will be seized and secured by Marines of the Peoples Liberation Army Navy in an amphibious assault. We do not expect much resistance at Porto Alegre as the Brazilians will not be ready for an amphibious assault there. After we sink the American supercarriers, their carrier-based fighters will have to crash into the sea when they run out of fuel. We will control the Brazilian airfields and shoot down their tankers with our J-20, so the American fighters will have no place to land and no place to refuel. While all this is going on, special forces teams of the People's Liberation Army Special Operations Forces will seize the oil and gas drilling and pumping platforms to keep the Brazilians from sabotaging them and seize control of pipelines and any supertankers that offload oil and gas from the platforms. After we have defeated the Brazilians and Americans, we will start pumping oil and gas into our tankers and LNG liquification and transport ships and ship it back to China for sole use in our economy. Questions?"

"Yes, Supreme General of the Army. What about China's previous promises not to engage in the militarization of space and not to make a first strike nuclear attack on any country?" General Xin Baowing commander of the Second Artillery asked.

"Fuck all of that. We are talking about our very survival here. History is rife with examples of countries saying one thing and then doing another when economic interests were at stake. For example, soybean farmers and cattle ranchers are now conducting deforestation of the Amazon rainforest at a rate six times higher than they were at the time Brazil promised to slow the rate of deforestation. The U.S. participated in the Kyoto talks and supported slowing the rate of global warming but then refused to sign the Kyoto Protocol. We ourselves endorsed the Missile Technology Control Regime in support of suppression of proliferation of missile technology for missiles capable of delivering weapons of mass destruction and then secretly shared long range ballistic missile technology with Pakistan and helped them develop a long range ballistic missile very similar to our own, for money of course. The dollar always trumps moral or ethical or environment concerns, and this situation is no exception. We are going to do what we need to do, and nobody can stop us or shame us into stopping. Anybody who gets in our way will be annihilated." General of the Army Lo Binxiao stated without remorse or apology.

"Any other questions?" Lo Binxiao continued. There were none.

"Good then. You will be distributed packets with further information with which to begin making your battle plans and preparations. Use face-to-face meetings and couriers as much as possible in your communications in case the National Security Agency and CIA cryptographers have broken our codes. Our cryptographers are working on a new code set called Yellow Dragon which the Americans have never seen before, and which we will put into use as soon as we have knocked down their satellites and are about to launch our ships. The Americans will be playing catch-up from that point forward and we will have the tactical advantage. Go and start your planning and preparation." General of the Army Lo Binxiao concluded.

And with that, the meeting was adjourned.

CHAPTER 6

WASHINGTON D.C.

JANUARY, TWO AND ONE HALF YEARS BEFORE THE WAR WITH CHINA—JOINT CHIEFS OF STAFF MEETING WITH POTUS, SECRETARY OF DEFENSE, HEADS OF THE NSA AND NATIONAL SECURITY COUNCIL, HEADS OF THE CIA AND DEFENSE INTELLIGENCE AGENCY

"**G**ood afternoon Mr. President." Admiral Roger Picket, Chairman of the Joint Chiefs of Staff said to President Richard Parry. "There have been some important developments in China we thought you should know about. Let me turn the chair over to Mr. Rogers and the other intelligence chiefs to brief you up to speed on what our intelligence sources have found out."

Richard Rogers, Director of the Central Intelligence Agency took the podium along with Tom Wilmont, Head of the NSA and William Headman, Director of the National Reconnaissance Office. Rogers spoke first.

WASHINGTON SPECULATES ON WHAT THE CHINESE ARE UP TO

"Mr. President, our human intelligence sources report that last week a major meeting of the military leaders of the State Central Military

Commission of the Peoples Liberation Army at the Xichang Satellite Launch Center took place. They were not able to penetrate the meeting to report on the subject matter. NSA reports that there has been increased encrypted chatter referring to Operation Canary, but we have not been able to make any sense of that chatter. We have broken their codes, but they are only using their electronic communications channels to arrange face-to-face meetings to discuss the operation. We suspect they know we have broken their encryption codes at Fort Meade, so they are being very tight lipped about what they say in their military communications over e-channels. I will turn the podium over to Mr. Headman to discuss imagery intelligence we have gathered in the last week."

William Headman took the podium and hit the button to display his first slide. It was a reconnaissance satellite photo of the secret Sanya underground navy base on the southern tip of Hainan Island.

"Mr. President, over the period from 2009 to 2011, the Peoples Liberation Army, Navy built a huge underground naval base on Hainan Island which is large enough to house a fairly large number of nuclear ballistic missile submarines and at least 9 super carriers. Lately, there has been an accelerated pace of activity at the base suggesting preparation for a major military campaign involving sea power. This satellite photograph shows numerous warships moored to long jettys and a network of roads leading into tunnels which penetrate hillsides around the base. There has been unusually high truck traffic on these roads.

The Hainan Island base has two 950 meter piers shown here and here, and has three smaller piers which are capable of mooring two carrier strike groups and amphibious assult ships. One gigantic opening was dug into a mountainside that comes down to meet the sea and is big enough to sail a super carrier through into what we presume is a very large interior chamber inside the mountain where construction is carried out safely from the view of our satellites.

Mr. President, this photograph taken earlier this morning shows increased transport of raw steel into the Sanya underground navy base on Hainan Island. We believe the Chinese are constructing more super carriers inside the mountain. Here, here and here you can see massive tunnel entrances we estimate to be 370 feet high. The main entrance is here. It is 500 feet high by our estimates and about 500 feet wide. It is big enough to sail a super carrier through. We do not know how big the caverns behind these tunnel entrances are, but we think up to 12 nuclear ballistic missile submarines could be hidden in the caverns to which these tunnels lead. We are pretty sure the Chinese have already completed four super carriers, and we believe they have five more in various stages of completion.

We have noted a massive increase in activity at the base since the meeting last week of the State Central Military Commission. A large number of trucks have been observed delivering raw steel, hydraulic and steam equipment, wire, rivets and what we think are nuclear reactor components. Those deliveries have taken place over the last two weeks. Many busloads of construction workers have also arrived at the base in the last week. We think they are accelerating the construction of super carriers based upon the increased delivery activity and the large increase in the number of workers on the island. The Chinese have offered no explanation for their construction of this base and the increased level of activity there recently."

Headman continued shifting the subject slightly.

"We think they have eight 094 nuclear submarines operational now, each capable of carrying 12 JL-2 nuclear tipped missiles. We also know they have successfully tested their anti-ship ballistic missile, but we don't know if they have adapted it for deployment on their nuclear ballistic missile submarines. We do know that they have truck mounted launchers for these ASBMs. This next slide is a KH-13 Misty satellite shot showing arrival of 12 truck mounted anti-ship ballistic missiles two days ago. The next slides shows these trucks being driven onto an amphibious assault ship. That ship disappeared into one of the tunnels after the trucks were loaded, and we have not seen it since."

"What are the ASBMs capable of, and what is their range?" President Richard Parry asked.

General Tim Steadman, Director of the Defense Intelligence Agency replied.

"They are carrier killers, and they have three versions. The DF-15 has a range of about 620 nautical miles. The DF-21 has a range of about 1500 nautical miles, and the DF-25, has a range of about 1900 nautical miles. We think the ASBMs that arrived on the trucks were DF-21's."

"Why do the Chinese need ASBMs, and when did they start working on them?" the President asked.

ASBM OPERATION EXPLAINED TO THE PRESIDENT

General Steadman elaborated further on the ASBMs.

"We know they developed their ASBMs to keep our carriers at bay if and when mainland China decides to invade Taiwan and we decide to come to Taiwan's aid. Their purpose is to prevent us from using our carrier based planes to assist the Taiwanese in defending the island." They started research in 1986 on the "863" program. It took the Chinese a long time to perfect their ASBMs, because they first had to develop or steal the technology for very high speed integrated circuits and advanced digital signal processors as systems-on-a-chip. They also needed to develop compact power amplifiers to power the on-board synthetic aperture radars that search for and find the target ship when the missile is in cruise mode looking down at the ocean. The Chinese also had to develop or steal the Synthetic Aperture Radar, also called SAR, the ASBMs use to look down at the ocean and develop radar images of the ships these missile see while they cruise parallel to the earth's surface at the edge of space. The Chinese also had to write automated target recognition software to recognize the target ship from the SAR returns to make the missile a fire-and-forget weapons system. The missiles also needed special heat shielding to protect the re-entry vehicle bearing the warhead and the guidance module from the intense heat of re-entry as the missile makes its vertical death dive down onto the target ship. The Chinese had to develop that special heat shielding as well.

The way these ASBMs are used is this. First, the missile is launched from a truck launcher, missile pad or a possibly a boomer after its guidance system has been loaded with an approximate or last known position for the target ship and an SAR image of the ship. The missile then goes ballistic riding its booster and secondary stages up to the edge of space. It then turns to a trajectory parallel to the surface of the ocean and cruises horizontally at the edge of space while looking down at the ocean with its Synthetic Aperture Radar in an attempt to find its target. As the missile cruises in this mode, it compares the SAR images it gleans from its SAR returns to the SAR image of its target stored in memory. When the ASBM finds the ship it is programmed to recognize, it starts a death dive straight down toward the ship, and crashes into a specific place on the ship it is programmed to recognize. It makes this death dive using a maneuverable reentry vehicle and some kind of terminal guidance system. The tests of these ASBMs we observed used kinetic kill vehicles, but we believe they may have added nuclear warheads since the first tests in 2006.

The Chinese also had to develop optimized antennas and placement for these antennas to overcome the RF blackout caused by the plasma sheath of super heated ionized gas that builds up around the re-entry vehicle when it plunges back into the thicker part of the atmosphere. We believe they also developed millimeter wave radar and infrared "hit-to-kill" terminal guidance systems so they can guide the missile to a specific point on the ship for impact. We are not sure if they still need that if the missiles are nuclear-tipped.

We know that they also developed missile defense countermeasures to protect the re-entry vehicle from our anti-ballistic missile missiles. We do not have an airtight defense against these ASBMs right now. The best we can do is use terminal phase interceptors like the SM-2 Block IV missile which was originally designed to shoot down different kinds of missiles than the ASBM. Specifically, the Chinese ASBM warhead re-entry vehicle can maneuver during its death dive toward its target, and that represents a gap in our current defensive technology. The problem is that the ASBM terminal phase is less than a minute, and the warhead is traveling at mach 12 and is capable of maneuvering to defeat interceptor missiles. That makes it a very tough intercept indeed.

Our RIM-161 SM-3 Block II surface-to-air missiles currently cruising on our AEGIS cruisers have successfully shot down intermediate range ballistic missiles. The problem is they are designed to intercept inbound ballistic missiles which do not maneuver in their terminal phase. The ASBM's cruise at mach 10 horizontally 79 miles up at the edge of space for most of their tragectory, and then dive vertically down at mach 12. The SM-3s use a kinetic warhead which crashes into the missile instead of a warhead which explodes upon impact or when a proximity fuse senses the target is near. The problem is therefore literally one of how does one hit a mach 12 bullet that is very far away and manuevering with another bullet traveling at mach 8. Although the SM-3s have had a number of successful missile intercepts during development, they have never been tested against a Chinese ASBM, so a successful result is certainly not guaranteed.

In the earlier versions, the Chinese ASBMs used over-the-horizon radars, and unmanned aerial vehicles to get an initial fix on the target ship. More recently since the launch of the Jianbing-5/YaoGan-1 and Jianbing-6/YoaGan-2 ocean scanning Synthetic Aperture Radar satellites, the Chinese can get a position fix for the target ship using SAR radar images and visual imagery for verification which has been downloaded from these ocean-scanning satellites. The missiles' guidance system then autonomously takes the ASBM to the general area of the target ship, and then turns on the missiles own SAR radar and target recognition software. This is the way the missile finds the current location of its target ship. It does this without the need for any guidance transmissions from the launch vehicle.

The Chinese successfully tested a DF-21D ASBM with a 1500 kilometer range in 2010. Our spy satellite imagery also showed the arrival at the Hainan Island underground naval base of several over-the-horizon radar trucks which were also loaded on the same ship on which the truck launchers were loaded."

"But if they want to use these ASBMs in support of an invasion of Taiwan, why would they load them on boats? Couldn't they just launch them from the Chinese mainland?" the President asked.

"Yes, they could and why the loaded them on boats is the 64,000 dollar question." General Steadman replied. "Our spy satellite imagery also showed them loading several large truck-mounted VHF radar arrays on the ships too."

"So what do you think they are up to?" the President asked.

"We think they are going to invade someplace other than Taiwan and use the ASBMs to keep our carriers at bay while they do it. We have no idea where that would be." General Steadman opined. "Quite possibly, their target may be someplace in Africa since they have been heavily investing in Africa since 2010 to guarantee access to its natural resources.

The others present in the meeting nodded their heads in agreement.

"Africa? Holy Mary, Mother of Jesus!" the President said.

The fact that the Chinese had loaded truck-mounted, Russian-designed VHF radar arrays onto ships that have only one purpose – to detect stealth aircraft – was overlooked in the confusion and consternation that General Steadman's caused.

CHAPTER 7

MAY, ONE YEAR BEFORE THE WAR WITH CHINA STARTS

GOODBYES AT THE WINGING CEREMONY

It was a great beach party, but now it was time to go back and get their Wings of Gold and receive their "community selections" and orders to the RAGs. Naval aviators get sent to Replacement Air Groups or RAGs after they get their wings to train for about a year in the aircraft type to which they have been assigned in the "community selections". These squadrons are now called Fleet Replacement Squadrons, but, like call signs, RAG stuck and that is what everybody called them. Naval aviators get their "soft wings" after their final training flight and their Wings of Gold at a winging ceremony later.

The winging ceremony was actually a tearful occasion. Not only was there a huge release of emotion after 4 years of hard work and struggles, but now they were also to be separated from the people with whom they had forged close bonds through the trials and tribulations of their training. All the challenges, the successes, the failures, and the tragedies came flooding back into their minds. The love and friendship relationships they had formed over the years at the parties and just by hanging out with each other and hoisting cocktail from time to time were strong bonds that would last a lifetime. It would be a bittersweet goodbye as they all scattered about the country to their next duty stations. But that was the nature of military life, and they knew that this would happen when they signed up.

Nikita and Alexandra came in for the winging ceremony to say goodbye to Ricky and J.J. and Slingshot came for a final weekend with Carmen. He was still assigned as a flight instructor and could not go with her. Although she liked and respected the guy greatly, she was not in love with him at the level she needed to be for that kind of a commitment. She was actually somewhat relieved that the Navy had ripped the relationship asunder, because she did not want to hurt him. Long distance relationships rarely worked. The need for closeness and intimacy usually overwhelmed the moral rectitude needed to stay faithful. It was just a fact of life that everybody knew. They worked when the relationship was exceptionally strong and meaningful, but not otherwise most of the time.

"I will miss you Ricky. We had some great times together that I will always remember. Will it be OK if I come out to visit you in California once in awhile?" Nikita asked.

"Of course. You are a great girl, and I will never forget you. Some guy is going to be very lucky to land you as his wife." Ricky said graciously. He was just relieved it wasn't going to be him. And he would in fact never forget her. She was a piece of work that one. "Give me a couple of months to settle in, and then come out. I will show you San Diego. It is a great town and you will love it."

"Don't you want to marry me Ricky?" Nikita teased.

"No not really. I cannot afford you." Ricky said laughing, and Nikita burst out laughing too.

"J.J., you are the coolest guy I have ever met, and I have met a lot of guys." Alexandra said. "I am sad that you are leaving me, and I will miss you."

"Oh I am not leaving you baby. You are very cool, and I am sure that there are no California girls who can turn my head. Besides, I have pretty much slept with them all by now anyway and they aren't speaking to me anymore." J.J. said with a smile.

Alexandra laughed. She was an exquisite creature and had a great personality. Mature, funny, friendly, generous, compassionate, considerate and smart as hell. You just couldn't really beat Alexandra as a woman, wife or girlfriend material or otherwise. J.J. had met and bedded down many women, and he was very impressed by Alex. No, she was a keeper, and he wanted this one as his girlfriend and he told her so. J.J. did not play games. His word was as good as gold. Despite his beach boy appearance and his high-flying, hard-partying past on the pro beach volleyball tour, J.J. was solid.

"Great J.J., I am glad to hear it. I love you and you know that. Maybe I will even move out to California to be with you to make sure you don't forget me." Alex said.

"Not a chance I am going to forget you. If you can swing that, I am in." J.J. said, and this time he was serious, and Alex knew it. She smiled and kissed him and said goodbye.

Ricky, J.J., Neil and Carmen were all stoked. They had gotten assigned to exactly the types of planes they wanted to fly. F/A-18 Hornets for Ricky, J.J. and Neil and F-35B Lightening stealth fighters for Carmen. The only bad part about their community selections were that they would be on opposite ends of the country and would not see each other as much. Ricky and J.J. were ordered to report to the Marine Fleet Replacement Squadron VMFAT-101, the Sharpshooters, at Marine Corps Air Station, Miramar, California (Fightertown). The FRS squadron was still referred to as the RAG which was short for Replacement Air Group, and it was a place where for 5-6 months of very intense training, the newly winged carrier pilot learned to fly a front line fighter and use its weapons systems with deadly efficiency. Carmen was ordered to report to the Warlords of VMFAT-501 at Eglin

Air Force Base in Florida. Neil was ordered to report to the Navy RAG VFA-122, the Flying Eagles based as NAS Lemoore, California for training in the F/A-18E Super Hornet.

RICKY AND CARMEN SAY GOODBYE

"Well Ricky, I guess this is it. I won't be seeing you for awhile. It was a great ride wasn't it?" Carmen said.

"Oh you betcha baby. It was the most fun I have ever had with my clothes on. Friends for life. You are the wierdest but coolest chick I have ever met. Definitely the only chick I know that can kick the crap out of a 300 pound Hells Angel. I am sure we will be seeing more of each other." Ricky said. He was very impressed by Carmen. Despite the fact that he had always wanted to jump her, he had never tried. Ricky respected Carmen too much and was actually a little intimidated by her. If he had known how she felt about him, her dress would have been on his bedroom floor in a New York minute. "I will come to see you when I can and you should come to San Diego to enjoy the good life. Honest to God, I don't know why anybody lives in Florida. It is so hot and muggy in the summer."

"OK deal." Carmen said. "See you on the flip side." Turning her gaze to J.J., a slight smile crept over her face. "And you Mr. J.J.. I am going to miss you dude. I think I might have to come out to California and supervise your activities, because you are a danger to women the world over."

"My CO has already alerted the California Press to warn the women of California, so they are already preparing their bomb shelters pending my arrival. Take care of yourself Swat. And remember if you get jumped by an Su-27 or Su-30MK2 Flanker, you are not going to be able to out-turn, out-climb or out-run him so bend over and kiss your ass goodbye." J.J. said with a smile.

"Noted. And you are to remember what I told you. If we get in a dogfight and a Flanker is on my six, when I call 'Thatch' start your magic show and do whatever the fuck you guys figure out is the best way to save my little ass." Carmen said.

"And a shapely one it is." J.J. said admiring her charms openly.

"Stop thinking about my ass and start thinking about how you are going to save me." Carmen scolded lightly. She was serious. "Remember our discussion at the Officer's Club about the Flankers versus the F-35? I certainly do, so I am expecting you hot shots in your Super Hornets to save me." She smiled and winked, and Ricky and J.J. smiled back at her.

Carmen knew that in an F-35 she was going to need some help if in a visual range dogfight with any Flanker. But with good energy management, tactical superiority, and a mistake by the Flanker pilot, she could use of the F-35 advantages over the Flankers such as stealth and better situational awareness in the F-35 to possibly save herself if she was alone. But it was unlikely all those things would coalesce at the same time. The F-35 was overweight and under-powered, and designed for beyond visual range fights using missiles. It was not designed to dogfight up close. The F-35 was doubly inferior to any Flanker, because of the lower wing loading of the Flankers and the higher thrust-to-weight ratio of the Flanker.

"OK roger that." J.J. said. "Hmmm, thinking, thinking …. Nope, there will be no premature Carmen terminations on my watch. The world needs more Carmen and not less." J.J. continued with a smile. But he was still looking at her ass. So was Ricky.

Carmen just laughed. "Get out of here you scalawags. I will see you guys in California sometime soon. You are such a wise ass J.J.. A little bit of you goes a long way, but I am still going to miss you." Carmen said laughing at J.J.'s comical attitude.

About 15 yards away, Neil McAble walked up to Patty Pushkin, his latest girlfriend from Kingsville, Texas. "I will miss you Patty. We had a lot of fun together." Neil said. Neil had had a string of girlfriends while in flight school. Neil, being a long tall Texan with a magnetic charm had no problem attracting the ladies. He was like catnip to them. "Not so fast mister. This is not goodbye yet. This relationship will end when I say it ends and not before." Patty drawled with a mock stern tone of voice. She loved Neil, but it might have been too early for her to commit to a new relationship having just gotten out badly from a prior long term relationship when she met Neil at an O-Club function at NAS Kingsville. She wasn't really sure yet about him, but she unwisely said, "I have a dream that someday you will marry me Lt. McAble."

"Really? I have a dream that I will live through to the end of my training." Neil said grinning.

"Don't be such a smart ass Neil. I will come out to California to see you from time to time. If you don't have a new girlfriend by then, we can go to the wine country and visit Yosemite. I have always wanted to do that." Patty said with a hopeful tone.

"That's a deal Patty. You are a terrific girl and I am glad I met you." Neil said graciously. He liked Patty just fine, but he was too young to settle down with one girl. There were many fine young women to explore and now he had a good job and Wings of Gold and an itch for a life of adventure. He had been working hard all his life, getting good grades in high school and college and working hard to start on the men's volleyball team for Penn State, a team which regularly appeared in the NCAA national tournament final four. It was time to relax a little and have some fun.

Just then, Ricky, J.J. and Carmen walked up to him and Patty. "Well Neil it has been an honor training with you. And you little Miss Patty Pushkin, you are a hoot." Ricky said.

"I concur." J.J. said. "Your not bad for a couple of crackers from Texas. You have raised my opinion about that whole state. Before you guys came along, I thought that whole state was populated by loud mouth, blowhards with egos the size of Alaska. Now I know for sure it is. Just kidding. I will miss you Pushkin. Don't be a stranger. And you

McAble, we are going to smoke you as soon as we meet you in a mock dogfight somewhere over the deserts of California." J.J. said with a smile.

"You know where I will be." Patty said.

"And you Miss Pushkin. I have enjoyed hanging with you. I can see why you like this handsome dude. Call me sometime. You have my cell number." Carmen said to Patty.

"I will do that Carmen. You are an awesome woman. Go out there and kick some Commie bastards in the nuts." Patty said laughing.

Neil piped up just then. "I will miss you guys even though you are a bunch of crazy jarheads. It has been a fun ride which I will never forget. Who knew a little asian chick could fly like a she-devil and kick the crap out of a bunch of Hell's Angels. I would fly wing for any one of you anytime." Neil meant it too. He had never had friends this good before, and he appreciated them.

"Well Nailgun, NAS Lemoore is not all that far from Miramar. Maybe you can scam your boss into bringing your wingman down to San Diego and dogfighting us." J.J. said.

"I will try. I don't really know how those RAG squadrons work and how much flexibility they have in their training schedules for hijinks. But that sounds like fun if I can scam my CO."

And with that they left for the airport to catch their respective flights.

Ricky and J.J. visit Michigan

Ricky and J.J. decided to visit Ricky's home in Michigan following their winging ceremony and reporting for duty at the RAG squadron in Miramar. Ricky's friends and parents threw him a welcome home party upon his arrival. J.J. came with him and drank it all in. Michigan is a far cry from southern California and the beaches of LA, but J.J. kind of liked how everybody was so down to earth, honest and spoke their truths. No vegans, very few BMWs. It was like being on a different planet. The Michigan girls really liked J.J.. They would come up to him and feel his biceps and look up into his blue eyes and black hair and you could almost hear them sigh. J.J. just laughed. He had seen it all before. Besides, he loved Alex, and surprised himself by not taking advantage of the situation. "Wow, I must really love that girl I guess. Who knew." J.J. thought to himself.

Ricky saw his old girlfriend Mini and spent hours talking to his parents and friends about his experiences at The Basic School and in Primary Flight Training. Everybody loved the smoke grenade story, and wanted to know if he and J.J. had looked up Carmen's skirt on the obstacle course. They both swore they hadn't. Fucking liars. They didn't see diddly though because it was pitch black, and they could not even see past the ends of their noses.

MCAS Miramar – the RAG takes on Ricky and J.J.

Ricky and J.J. reported in at the RAG and started the familiarization phase of their training.

"Lieutenant Ricky Magnusson reporting for duty sir." Ricky said to the Sharpshooters Commanding Officer, Captain Jerry "Tiptoe" Thomas.

"Lieutenant J.J. Saleen reporting for duty as ordered sir." J.J. followed.

"Welcome to the Sharpshooters. Woody and Scud your reputations have preceded you. No fucking around here boys. We are not going to give you a $67,000,000 jet to fly just to fuck it up. You get me?" Captain Patterson, Commanding Officer of the VMFAT-101 Sharpshooters at MCAS Miramar said.

"Yes sir." They replied in unison.

"Training command tells me you are both good sticks and you did very well in your courses, so you are welcome here. We like to party just as much as the best of them, but we are all business when it is time for business. Woody, you will be the S1 and legal officer. Scud, you are the Recreation Officer responsible for setting up rec activities for the troopers, you know, baseball and flag football leagues, picnics and field days. We study hard and fly a lot too. Here are your course manuals." Captain Patterson handing them each a 50 pound bag of NATOPS manuals on the F/A-18E Super Hornet and its systems. "Memorize these and you will have a good start. Dismissed."

"Whew, that was about as much fun as chewing tinfoil for an hour." Ricky said to J.J..

"No shit. I hope he lightens up a little so we can have some fun around here sometime soon." J.J. said.

The course load in the RAG squadrons was crushing. In a little over a year, the newbie pilots who had just come off carrier quals in Goshawks with a fresh, shiny new set of wings had to be turned into a systems manager of a very complex, very expensive jet. They had to be able to fly it, navigate it, drop bombs with it, dogfight with it and land on a carrier in all sorts of bad weather and at night. It was no picnic.

They both dug in and started working.

Endless hours of lectures and computer-guided, interactive study of systems was the first order of business as is the case for each new plane in which a pilot qualifies.

The F/A-18E Super Hornet is an incredible plane. Ricky and J.J. were stunned by the incredible capability of it and a little awed by its complexity. It is a beautiful bird too. It made you want to jump in it, select zone 5 burner and fly straight up out of sight. And they did that more than once, wasting a whole bunch of the government's gas. But what a ride.

At the RAG, all the nugget pilots would learn the planes systems, how to fly formation, perform low level navigation, make instrument approaches, strafe and bomb ground targets, shoot rockets at ground targets, launch air-to-air missiles at airborne targets, refuel in flight, use the jet's onboard radar as well as ground controlled approach and

EWACs instructions to intercept bogeys. In the final phases, they would learn how to dogfight with bandits and how to land their 67 million dollar jets on the carrier as well as fly instrument flying approaches to the carrier. Carmen would be learning how to do the same things in her 200 million dollar F-35.

RAG training for Ricky and J.J. started with extensive study of the Super Hornet's fly-by-wire and other systems, HOTAS, HUD, weapons systems, and the mission computer and its modes. HOTAS stands for Hands On Throttle and Stick, a modern system which provides switches, buttons and controllers on the throttle and stick the pilot can control to do most of the things he needed to do. HUD stands for Heads Up Display which, in its various modes, displays all the information the pilot needs to fly the jet and dogfight without having to put his eyes down in the cockpit and possibly lose sight of his enemy which is usually a fatal error in a dogfight. They had to learn how to use these system to bomb ground targets and to fight dogfights. They also had to learn the properties of U.S. and Russian and Chinese air-to-air missiles and how to defeat them, the various kinds of precision and non precision weapons they would use as well as dogfighting tactics in the Super Hornet. They learned that the fourth generation missiles of both sides were almost impossible to defeat by maneuver though, especially the ones with focal plane array sensors, so information was king because whoever got the first missile shot, usually won.

The F/A-18E Super Hornet jets Ricky and J.J. would fly were single pilot jets meaning the sole pilot had to do all the flying, radio communications, systems management, navigation, radar and weapons systems operations to fly a mission without any assistance. Neil would be learning how to fly the F/A-18F, two place Super Hornet up at NAS Lemoore in the central valley of California so he would have a back seater to assist in running the radar, setting up and controlling the weapons systems, carrying out some of the communications and doing various other tasks to ease the workload on the pilot.

Ricky and J.J. dug into the NATOPs manuals and attended numerous lectures on the F/A-18E systems and capabilities. They learned many interesting things.

In the single pilot, F/A-18E, as in all other versions of the Super Hornet, there was a powerful mission computer, top notch AESA radar and weapons systems and a glass cockpit with three digital display indicators known as DDIs including three large flat LCD displays to display all the information the pilot needed for all aspects of operation. The pilot can, by pushing switches in the right order, get to all the information he needs about any subject on a maze of pages displayed by the jet's software. But it is very easy to get lost in the menus and submenus and not know how to get out or get the information needed. Getting lost in a maelstrom of confusion is a common phenomenon known in jet fighter circles as a "helmet fire", and in single seat Hornets, it happened to the best of them.

A Hornet pilot never has to take his hands off the throttle and stick to do everything necessary to fly the jet. The F/A-18 has a Hands On Throttle and Stick control system with a multitude of switches and buttons that the pilot can manipulate with the various fingers on the pilot's left and right hands. There were over 60 combinations of button and switch commands the pilot can use to control almost everything he needs to control while flying a mission. For example, the pilot can issue commands using the throttle and stick switches to: transmit on the radio; steer the nose wheel; select radar search and track modes; designate a target on the radar; select a radar-guided or heat seeking missile; fire the missile; select guns; fire the gun; select the correct weapon to drop; drop the weapon; engage the autopilot; deploy the speed brakes; turn his lights on, etc. In the heat of combat, it is easy to get confused and press the wrong button or switch leading to a frenzy of button pushing called a "finger fire".

F/A-18 HUD

All the information the pilot needs to look at to fly, navigate, bomb or dogfight was on the heads up display called the HUD. With the HUD displaying all the information needed for every mode of flight, the pilot never has to look down in the cockpit during critical phases of flight such as dogfighting or bombing. Looking down into the cockpit for even an instant can cause the pilot in a dogfight to lose sight of his adversary, a fatal error. The fighter pilot adage is "Lose sight, lose the fight." Key to a fighter pilot's survival are situational awareness, encyclopedic knowledge of dogfighting maneuvers, radar and weapons systems characteristics, modes and launch parameters as well excellent knowledge of the energy-maneuverability theory, and quick thinking embodied in rapid transitions between maneuvers. In other words, the pilot has to have his or her shit together to stay alive in a modern fighter encounter. Either your own airplane or the enemy will kill you in the blink of an eye.

The HOTAS system was critical to allowing one pilot to fly the jet. The pilot's left hand rests on split throttles which control the thrust of the two engines but also does much, much more. The left pinkie finger controls the jet's radar by a first switch to turn it on or off.

The left ring finger engages the autopilot by manipulating a second switch on the throttle. The Super Hornet autopilot is very capable and is necessary because there were so many other things going on simultaneously. If the pilot tries to fly the jet all the time while trying to manage the radar, the weapons systems, the navigation system, the fuel system and the communication system, he will probably find what is left of himself in a smoldering crater on the desert floor.

F/A-18 HOTAS AND SPREAD SPECTRUM AESA RADAR ADVANTAGES-RWR CANNOT DETECT SPREAD PULSES

The pilots left middle finger manipulates a joy stick like control to slew the jets AESA radar beam up and down or left and right to search for intercept targets. The F/A-18E/F Super Hornet APG-79 AESA radar has an electronically steered beam steered by several hundred gallium arsenide transmit-receive –phase-shifter modules driven by the system software. It is capable of nearly instantaneous track updates and has multi-target tracking capability. The Super Hornet AESA radar can find non-stealth jets many miles away. Further, AESA radars have the advantage of being programmable to perform pseudo-random scan patterns as opposed to the repetitive scan behavior of mechanically scanned radar antennas of prior generation radars. The scan behavior is an important factor radar warning receivers use to determine what type of radar has been detected painting a jet. The fact that the Super Hornet AESA radar can scan pseudo-randomly and use spread spectrum modulation techniques on each radar pulse makes most radar warning receivers unable to detect the fact that the Super Hornet AESA radar is painting the adversary's jet.

RWR DISCUSSED

Radar warning receivers, which are a principal electronic warfare countermeasure in a modern jet, depend upon pulse repetition patterns to identify radar types. The RWR must be able to integrate enough received pulse energy over a fixed, short amount of time in each of the bands of frequencies the integrator is monitoring so as to be able to see the radar. Spread spectrum modulation spreads the pulse's energy over a large bandwidth, so the amount of energy in any particular band of frequencies is usually not enough to be detected by a radar warning receiver. These factors also foil the guidance systems of enemy air-to-air missiles that home on the radar emissions of their targets.

But the Super Hornet radar works in X-band so it cannot find stealth jets unless it is right on top of them. Stealth jets are designed to be almost invisible to X-band radars.

SUPER HORNET FLIR AND STEALTH JET DETECTION-LINK 16

Further, the current Super Hornets only have a forward looking Infrared sensor, so it cannot detect a stealth jet on its heat signature if the adversary is directly above, directly below or behind or to the sides of the Super Hornet or anywhere else out of the field of view of the infrared sensor. Future Super Hornets will have an Infrared Search and Track system which is mounted in a modified centerline fuel tank and will be able to see infrared heat signatures in directions other than forward.

The Super Hornet does have a Link 16 data link however, so it can receive target information on stealth jets detected by other more capable planes such as an F-35 with 360 degree DAS Infrared Search and Track system.

The pilots left index finger manipulates a designator mouse on the throttle that moves a target designator visible on the radar target display in the HUD to select a target and lock the jet's weapons systems on it.

HOTAS SWITCHES, FOCAL PLANE ARRAYS, ANTI MISSILE MOVES

The pilot's left thumb can move to and manipulate several switches. One deploys the jet's speed brakes, another switch changes frequencies on the radio between frequencies the pilot had dialed into his VHF/UHF radios.

The last switch he/she can manipulate with his left thumb selects the jets air-to-air missiles to ready them for firing. A switch on the stick actually fires the missile once lock has been achieved.

ANTIMISSILE COUNTERMEASURES, FOURTH GEN MISSILES

Another switch the pilot can manipulate with his left hand activates the countermeasures to dispense radar chaff and flares while under missile attack. Chaff and flares are important last ditch countermeasures to counter missile attacks. Chaff dispensed as a missile countermeasure is like a bundle of small strips of tinfoil that are thrown out of the back of the plane. These strips of metallized material have a very high radar cross-section and give a very strong radar return, a return which is much stronger than the target jet's pulse doppler return.

However fourth generation heat seeking air-to-air missiles with digital focal plane arrays and modern AMRAAM radar-guided missiles are improved so much that chaff and flare countermeasures often do not fool them. For example, chaff immediately stops in the air and have very little velocity relative to the missile. This can be filtered out by signal processing software in the missile seeker head. Other factors are more important in defeating modern air-to-air missiles.

AMRAMM Pk KILL FACTORS AND COUNTERMEASURES

With earlier generation heat seeking missiles like the first generation Sidewinder and early radar guided missiles such as a Sparrow, if a pilot saw the missile soon enough, it was possible that he could defeat it. To defeat the older missiles, the pilot did a hard turn to put the missile at his 9 o'clock or 3 o'clock, known as a beam turn, and dispenses chaff and flares to distract the missile's guidance system. Then he would make a hard break turn at the last second to outturn the missile by exceeding the capability of its smaller control surfaces to turn the missile sharply while travelling at mach 3.

The beam turn was effective against the older radar-guided missiles, because they used pulse doppler radars which depend upon the doppler shift in reflected pulses which occurs when the target is moving relative to the motion of the missile. When a target suddenly turns to put the missile on his beam, the relative motion between the missile and the target goes to zero. This is because the only relative motion is the missile's own motion toward the target which is filtered out by the software. In other words, the missiles have a doppler notch. The beam turn significantly reduces the strength of the target's radar return when a pulse doppler radar is being used in the missile's guidance system. This coupled with the strong return from the chaff frequently confused the missile's guidance system and caused it to home on the chaff instead of the target.

However, a modern AIM-120D AMRAAM type missile can defeat the beam turn tactic. The modern AMRAAM does not turn on its own terminal guidance pulse doppler radar until the very last part of the flight which is at very close range. This means the target's return is going to be strong, because reflected radar energy from an interrogation pulse dies off in intensity with the square of the distance. So a short range to the target means stronger reflected radar pulses. Further, the AMRAAM's guidance system software includes algorithms to defeat the beam turn tactic.

Because the AMRAAM is at close range when it turns its terminal guidance radar on and is travelling at mach 4, the target gets little warning, and may never even see the missile after the radar warning receiver goes off. The fact that the terminal guidance radar is not turned on in an AMRAAM until close range also means that the terminal guidance radar is highly likely to burn through any electronic warfare countermeasure transmissions emitted in an attempt to fool it.

The AMRAAMs own terminal guidance radar is also very capable with the ability to operate in look-down, shoot-down mode and filter out the return of the target from the ground clutter of radar waves scattered back toward the radar's receiver by the earth's surface. Evading an AMRAAM by diving down and flying low "in the weeds" is unlikely to defeat the missile.

Further, the AMRAAM can receive its initial point to which it flies before turning on its terminal guidance radar from any one of several sources including an AWACs radar fix relayed to the launching jet by a data link, or from an Infrared Search and Track System (IRST). IRST systems do not paint the target with radar but detect it from its heat. The target jet may never be painted by the search radar of the launching jet in a mode which can be detected by the target's radar warning receiver. The AMRAAM has a mode where it flies to an initial point supplied to it by the radar of the launching aircraft, with the radar operating in Track While Scan mode. This mode is not a mode which indicates to the radar warning receiver that the target has been locked by a hostile radar. In other words, TWS mode gives the AMRAAM its initial point to which it must fly and simultaneously does not give the target notice that it has been "spiked" or locked by a hostile radar.

The whole point to the development of the AMRAAM was to avoid the need to continuously paint the target with radar while the missile was in flight thereby causing the launching jet to have to keep flying toward the target and flying into range of the target's own missiles and being "mutually killed". This was the problem with Sparrows discovered at the ACEVAL/AIMVAL mock dogfights back in the 70's at Nellis AFB. Once the initial point or last known target position is loaded into the AMRAAM guidance system, the missile flies autonomously to that point before it turns on its terminal guidance radar to find the target's current location. The fact that the target does not have to be continuously painted by radar complicates detection of the fact that a missile has been launched.

Seeing such a missile in the air before it hits you without any notice a missile has been launched is very difficult indeed. The AMRAAM is small, being only 4 inches in diameter and only a few feet long and is painted dull gray and propelled by a smokeless rocket motor at mach 4. Seeing one coming without any forewarning that a missile is in the air takes extremely good eyesight and a huge dollop of luck.

HOW TO DEFEAT AN AMRAAM

Even if the pilot of the target sees the AMRAAM coming, the modern AMRAAM is difficult to defeat. A beam turn is not likely to defeat it. Further, a last minute break might also not defeat the modern AMRAAM or the Chinese and Russian equivalents: the Vympel R-77 (Nato code name Adder also referred to as the AMRAAM-ski); and the Chinese PL-12 Sino-AMRAAM. These missiles can withstand 14 Gs in a turn and outturn any jet in a 12 G turn, a turn most pilots cannot physically withstand and almost all jets are not stressed for. Even the king of the dog fighters, the Air Force F-16 Viper can only withstand a 9 G turn before it is in danger of airframe failure. These missiles can also filter out the returns of chaff and older generation decoys.

Success in defeating a modern AMRAAM and soviet-bloc air-to-air missiles depends upon several factors including aspect (head-on, tail-chase or side-on interception) and energy factors such as altitude and speed of the firing jet and range and speed of the target jet as well. The Pk or probability of a kill also depends very much on whether the target jet is aware of the incoming AMRAAM, and, if so, how hard the target jet can turn and how far the missile has flown to get to the target and how much kinetic energy the missile still has.

SIDEWINDER CAPABILITY AND Pk FACTORS

If the incoming missile is a heat seeker like the Sidewinder, the missile sometimes can be confused into tracking and hitting the flare rather than the jet's hot exhaust, because the flare is much hotter than the jet's exhaust. That often confused the missiles into missing.

However, the modern AIM-9X is very difficult to defeat. It has an agile thrust-vectoring, reduced-smoke, Mk-36 rocket motor. The seeker head includes 3-gimbal, a high-performance, staring focal plane array passive heat sensor feeding a digital image processor for guidance which tracks on the target jet's hot exhaust. It has a range of more than ten miles, and is immune to electronic countermeasures since transmitted signals cannot jam its infrared sensors. The Sidewinder can be incorporated into a helmet-mounted sight system and is a high off-boresight missile, meaning the jet firing it does not have to be pointed at the target jet.

The pilots right hand is just as productive in an F/A-18E/F Super Hornet. The right hand controls the stick to give control inputs to manipulate the elevators, ailerons to control pitch and roll, but that was just a vote in a system actually controlled by a computer. The F/A-18 is a fly-by-wire jet, where the pilot merely suggests with the stick what he wants the jet to do and the actual controls are manipulated by the computer and a servo system so that the jet's G limits are not exceeded. In other words, the computer won't let the pilot break the jet. Moving the stick is accomplished only by the right ring and middle fingers since control forces are light.

The pilot's right pinkie finger controls the nose wheel steering of the jet or unlocks the jet's air-to-air missile system when it is time to go hot.

The pilot's right index finger is used to squeeze the red trigger button for the jet's guns for a gun kill. A gun kill was still the most reliable way to bring down an enemy jet. Guns cannot be confused by chaff or flares. If the pilot has the jet lined up properly with the pipper on the computerized gunsight set up with a suitable lead when that trigger is squeezed, the other guy was going down in flames.

The right thumb controls the positions of four switches: one to drop a bomb; a sensor control switch to detect enemy planes; a trim switch to move a trim system to trim away control forces acting on the jet's control surfaces; and a weapons select switch. The guns, heat-seeking Sidewinder missiles and radar-guided Sparrow and AMRAAM missiles all have different ranges and can only be used effectively if the target was within the range parameter of the selected weapon system.

The computer system in the F/A-18 is a "glass cockpit" with three Digital Data Information displays which can display many pages of information including stores management, radar, HUD repeater, GPS and waypoint data and an Horizontal Situation Indicator, fuel status, checklist pages, engine status, autopilot and artificial horizon as well as Flight Plan Advisory System with fuel estimates to bingo. Associated with each display is a set of switches that controls which page of information the pilot will see on that display. There is a DDI display on the top left, another DDI display on the top right, and one DDI display in the center between the pilot's legs. Above the middle display, there is another set of smaller displays, and a keypad to enter information to program the autopilot and enter information into the nav system for waypoints, destinations, identify approach procedures to use and set frequencies on the radios.

J.J. and RICKY CALL CARMEN

Carmen's cell phone rang with a sonar pinging sound. She just loved the sound of sonar, ever since "The Hunt for Red October" hit the theatres. "Hello. This is Carmen."

"I know nitwit that is why I called you." J.J. said. How is it going down there at Eglin. Are the Air Force pilots leaving you alone?" Ricky and Neil were on the line too. They had convened that Friday night in the BOQ at Fightertown and had started happy hour and decided they missed Carmen's shapely little ass to distract them from thinking about weightier matters.

"J.J. you reprobate. I would have thought you would be in jail or on trial by now. Yes, unfortunately the Air Force boy are leaving me alone. I am bored out of my mind at the same time as being scared out of my wits." Carmen said. "The F-35 is a great jet, but there is so much to learn."

"Tell me about it. We are up to our necks in Super Hornet systems out here too. Ricky and Neil are with me."

"So how is life out in Fightertown?"

"Miramar is a cool place and San Diego is awesome." J.J said.

"We have been learning about the F/A-18E Super Hornet in a big way." Ricky said.

RICKY AND J.J. EXPLAIN HOW THEY WILL SAVE CARMEN

"We have also been studying the RAND Corporation war games report, and we think we have it figured out." J.J. said.

"Figured what out?" Carmen inquired.

"How we are going to save your shapely little ass if we are ever in the area when you get jumped by a Flanker. We are so smart we scare ourselves sometimes." J.J. said.

"You scare me too, you silly bastards." Carmen said laughing. "Pray tell."

"OK, if you get jumped by a Flanker, their IRST on the nose and tail can only see 15 degrees down and 60 degrees up in addition to straight ahead and straight behind the jet. So if you get jumped by a Flanker, call 'pucksniper' on the radio and start jinking like crazy toward us and then back away from us to keep him from getting a snap gun kill. Keep your eyes open and watch your IRST for missile shots and break hard and late and deploy chaff and flares to defeat the missiles. Keep doing that until one of us gets there. Keep him working hard concentrating on you. We will run a sucker fight. While he is trying to kill you, one or more of us will hit zone 5 burner and sneak up on him from below and behind in the IRST blind spots of him and his wingman if we can. If we are higher than you, we will stay in the sun and get over them vertically so they cannot see us on their IRST. Once we get in their blind spots, if we are in their high blind spot, we will do a swoop right down on top of them and take them both out with Sidewinders and/or guns. If we are lower than you, we will hit zone 5 and go ballistic right up under them until their bellies fill our windscreens and take them both out with guns or a Sidewinder. If there are two of us, one above and one below, we will run a double sucker fight, one in their blind spot under their belly and one in the sun and in their upward IRST blind spot. The guy on top will be most likely to be seen visually, but while they are trying to kill you and deal with the one of us on top of them, the other of us will come up from below like a Great White on a seal and smoke them both." J.J. explained, quite proud of himself for the brilliant plan he had devised. "But stay close to us, about a mile or so off our wing, so if you get jumped, we can weave toward you and you toward us so one of us can be in the Flanker's blind spot within about 20 seconds. You are only going to have 45 seconds to live unless one of us gets him very quickly."

"I should set you to thinking more often. You do good things when you are not chasing women." Carmen said sticking in the needle all the way. "I always thought you were just a pretty face, but now I can see you are an evil genius. Do Woody and Nailgun like this plan?"

"Fucking-A. They thought of the double sucker fight part of it which is pure black inspiration." J.J. said.

"I wonder if they will let us fly together as a unit? I mean mixing F-35s and Super Hornets as flight elements is not standard. Usually they will send the F-35s in for the ground attack with Super Hornets for Combat Air Patrol."

"Yeah, we know. We are going to have to convince the brass that our idea is better."

"Good luck with that."

"Yeah I know." J.J. said resignedly. He had been in the Corps long enough to know the brass were not all that flexible.

Woody piped up. "If it is a Chinese J-20 Stealth, there is a different plan. The Chengdu J-20 may have an IRST just like yours, but maybe not as good. It is a twin engine with a canard so it might have better thrust loading and better maneuverability than your F-35, but we think not because it weighs 80,000 pounds and is designed for long range. It has bad wing loading and a bad thrust-to-weight ratio, probably quite a bit worse than yours. It is much larger and heavier than the F-22 Raptor. A J-20 Chinese stealth jet definitely will not have the instantaneous and sustained turn rates of the F-22 Raptor, which, by the way, are better than an F-15. Your maximum takeoff weight is 70,000 pounds. The J-20 is believed to have a takeoff weight of 80,000 pounds so he is heavier than you. The problem is the J-20 has two engines with 29,000 pounds of vectored thrust each. Your single engine puts out 28,000 pounds of vectored thrust dry and 43,000 pounds in burner. So even though the J-20 is heavier than you, it will be able to out-climb you and accelerate faster. Even if you go into burner, he has more thrust than you – by a lot. So don't get in a vertical energy fight with him, because we think you will probably do better jinking in a turning fight and taking off-boresight missile shots at him to keep him defensive. If we are with you, we are going to run a sucker fight on him, so just jink long enough to stay alive till we save your ass. A Super Hornet will be able to outturn him, outclimb him and out accelerate him, so he is toast if we are with you. Got it?" Ricky said.

"Roger that Sir Ricky. Doesn't sound like you have much of a plan yet." Carmen said.

"Ouch. That is going to leave a mark." J.J. said.

RICKY'S PLAN TO GO UP AGAINST
THE FLANKERS AND J-20

"Shut up wise ass. I am getting to it." Ricky said with mock derision. "One possible strategy is our hope they will use the J-20 as a long range AWACs and tanker killer and you will never see one. That is what it is designed for more than as an air superiority fighter. Another possible strategy is our hope is that his Chinese engines will fail catastrophically. They have in tests. If they put the Russian 32,000 pound thrust engines in, the situation only gets worse for you. They might be developing a 37,000 pound thrust turbofan for it, but that only makes it worse for you if that is true."

"Great Ricky, we are depending upon your hopes? I'm screwed." Carmen said only half kidding.

"Relax Carmen, I haven't finished yet." Ricky said a little impatiently. Carmen interrupted sometimes because her mind was going so fast and was far ahead of the speaker. "We know that the Chinese stole a lot of the information used in the development of the J-20 via cyberespionage on the contractors Lockheed used in the F-35 project. Therefore, they probably didn't come up with any better ideas than are in the F-35. The J-20 has an AESA radar, but probably not better than the F-22 AESA which the F-35 can track and jam. So if he turns on his radar, you will know where he is and can track him outside your IRST system's range and possibly take him out with an AMRAAM beyond visual range. The problem arises if he defeats the AMRAAM and then comes in for the intercept and a visual range fight. According to the Aussies, neither the F-35 nor the F/A-18 Super Hornet has any chance against a J-20. For some reason, the Aussies believe the J-20 will be operating with a 10,000 foot and 700 knot advantage. That is a lot of energy. I don't really believe that because the J-20 is a huge, heavy plane, and I know we can at least take one out working as a team. Our F/A-18C Hornets only weigh 29,852 pounds in fighter configuration with half internal fuel and a missile load of 4 sidewinders and 2 AMRAAMS.

The F/A-18c has a dry thrust of 22,000 pounds which gives us a weight-to-thrust ratio of 1.35. A J-20 80,000 pounds takeoff weight and with two Chinese WS-10 turbofans in the production model generating 60,000 pounds of thrust total gives him a weight-to-thrust ratio of 1.33. Our J-20 weight data is sketchy and it may be as little as 66,000 lbs which would give him a weight-to-thrust ratio of 1.1. An F/A-18C, with a weight-to-thrust ratio of 1.35, should be able to run, climb and accelerate right with him and shoot him from his six with either Sidewinders or AMRAAM missiles here because the J-20 is not stealthy from the rear and assuming a J-20 weight of 88,000 pounds. At 66,000 pounds, the J-20 has a weight-to-thrust ratio of 1.1 so the F/A-18C should avoid trying to out-run or out-climb this lighter J-20 and take him out using teamwork.

As you can see from my graph, the J-20 is off the chart high in wing loading with a wing loading of 126 based upon a weight of 80,000 pounds. We do not have good data on this weight, but even at 66,000 pounds, the J-20 has a wing loading of 104 which makes it way less capable than even an F-35B in a turning fight. The J-20 is operating deep in the double inferior region and should avoid a dogfight with either an F-35B or an F/A-18C. Either an F/A-18C or an F-35B should be able to take him out in a turning fight, but avoid an energy fight if possible since his weight-to-thrust ratio is 1.1 at 66,000 lbs with the 60,000 pounds of thrust the WS-10 engine. If he has the 72,000 pounds of thrust of the WS-15 engine, the situation is even worse at 60,000 lbs gross and the same at 80,000 pounds gross. Neither an F-35 nor an F/A-18 will be able to out-run or out-climb him but both should be able to out-turn him. Avoid an energy fight with a J-20 because you just don't know which engine he has or how much his plane weighs, but you do know that, even in the best case scenario, he has the same weight-to-thrust ratio as you do and, in the worst case scenario, he has a much better weight-to-thrust ratio than you.

The Chinese, if they have a single brain cell, will not be putting the J-20 into visual range dogfights, because it will be like shooting clays for us.

Where we might be wrong is in how much he weighs in fighter configuration and in the thrust to weight ratio. If we are right, we should be able to out-turn him and out-accelerate him. If we are wrong, we should still be able to get him if we outnumber him and work as a team. With IRST and AESA radar, his avionics are better than the F/A-18's avionics, but not yours. But we can link our AMRAAM missiles to your IRST infrared DAS or your AESA radar via the data link and shoot him using your plane's data to program our AAMRAM missiles to the intercept point. The J-20 is not stealthy to the rear, but it is to the front. That means, if he jumps you, and we are behind him, we can lock onto him with our radars and smoke him with an AMRAAM or, if we are close, take him out with a sidewinder. What we want to do is put him into a sucker fight and bleed off his energy chasing you so we can use an energy fight on him. If he sees us and turns to engage us, we will sucker him into hard turns to deplete his energy by faking an angles fight while preserving our energy. You jump on his tail when he turns to engage us. We will jink to spoil a guns solution, if they put guns on the J-20, and we will dodge his missiles until he has depleted his energy advantage and we can convert our energy into a swoop kill or until you kill him by firing a Sidewinder up his ass."

"Sounds reasonable. Meet me at the O-club." Carmen joshed.

"Pay attention. This is serious shit." Ricky scolded. "Air Power Australia, the Aussie's RAND corporation, looked at the situation and did not mince words. They said, even after the 2011 redesign, the F-35 is 'toast' against a J-20 which makes the F/A-18 Super Horner 'cinders'. They concluded that with the fancy cockpits of the F-35 and F/A-18E/F, the American pilots would be able to see with great clarity and resolution the precise moment they would die. The Aussies took an unbiased view of the situation and concluded the American designers have made the faulty assumption that the missiles would do the turning and maneuver was irrelevant because all kills would be Beyond Visual Range.

As a side note, the American designers made the same mistake before the Vietnam War when we had the Sparrow and Sidewinder. Those missiles did not work much of the time, and the result what they had to retrofit the F-4 with a gun.

But getting back to the Aussie analysis, they reasoned that the introduction of significant stealth capabilities in the J-20 and PAK-FA Russian stealth MIG, erased the temporary sensor advantage the F-35 and F/A-18 Super Hornets had. The stealth of the Russian and Chinese Fifth Generation jets has reduced our sensor advantage from detection at 82 miles for the F-35 and 111 miles for the Super Hornet to best case 35 miles for the F-35 and 47 miles for the Super Hornet with worst case scenarious of 11 and 15 miles, respectively. That reduces air combat from BVR where maneuver is irrelevant to close visual range combat where maneuver and pilot skill is everything. Real nice. But it is what we have to work with, so we are going to have to outfly the Commie bastards. So in our thinking, we fell back on what the RAND study found and which has been a proven historical fact. Numbers win. The Chinese will have to have a kill ratio equal to the square of the ratio by which they are outnumbered to prevail. We will be four on two assuming the J-20 has a wingman and you have a wingman."

"Holy Shit. Our military industrial complex is not going to like what the Aussies have to say one bit. The Aussies should go to charm school." Carmen said, stating the obvious.

Ricky continued.

"So, in short, what we want you to do if you get jumped by a J-20 is call for help, fire a multiple missile salvo at him, off bore sight if necessary, roll inverted and dive into his doppler notch and light your burner to extend out of the fight. Try to preserve your kinetic energy if that is possible. The missile shots should force him to make hard turns and deplete his energy till we can get there and jump him. But lead him toward us if possible. We will maneuver in behind him for an AMRAAM missile shot at his non stealthy rear or come in close for a Sidewinder or guns kill. When he sees us take a shot at him, he may turn on us. We think we have a greater thrust to weight ratio and greater climb rate so we will take him into hard turns and try to extend horizontally to get separation. You jump him from the rear then. If we get horizontal separation with a speed advantage, we will then convert speed to energy by climbing and turning back and diving in on his tail. If we do it right, his energy will have been depleted and he won't be able to get up in our plane of maneuver, so we can get an energy advantage on him. All the while this is happening, you are tracking and locking onto him with your IRST and AESA radar aimed at his non stealthy rear quarter and can take a missile shot. While he is busy evading your missiles or guns, we will then dive down on his tail in a swoop maneuver and take him out with a snapgun shot or a sidewinder or both. Make a radio call when you fire your missile and we will set up a lead pursuit angle in our swoop anticipating his break and get him with a snap gun shot. If there are two of us, one of us will set up for each possible break left or right so one of us will get him. One of us may have to fend off his wingman though, but you can designate both him and his wingman on your IRST DAS fire control system and loose both your air-to-air missiles to keep them both busy while we move in for the kill. If we get jumped by a J-20 while you are in the area, the whole process is slightly different. We will take him into turns to spoil his guns solution and try to get angles on him and take an off bore-sight Sidewinder shot and try to lock him up with our AMRAAMs. I am not confident we can lock him up from anywhere but the rear quarter because of his stealth airframe. The turns while we lead him toward you will deplete his energy. You bank your speed as altitude then do an Immelmen energy attack. That is, you dive down on him in a guns pass, and, if you miss him do a zoom climb and a rudder reversal at the top and dive down on him again. That will keep him busy long enough that we can take him out. If he does not engage you, and continues after us, take a Sidewinder shot at him, get on his tail, lock your radar on him, and take him out with an AMRAAM missile. All this is unlikely because we think the Chinese will use the J-20 to make stealth attacks on our tankers and AWACs. Capiche?"

"Got it Ricky. Good thinking. Scary stuff, but if we work together, we can do it." Carmen said. "I am exhausted. Good night boys. Don't do anything I would'nt do out there."

"Well that kind of leaves it wide open doesn't it." Neil said laughing, and they hung up.

NIGHT CARRIER QUALS INSTRUMENT LANDING

Every Navy fighter pilot has to do night carrier qualification. Landing on a boat in the pitch black of night or, worse, at night and in bad weather, is just about the scariest thing a pilot can do. The Air Force doesn't have to do it, and of that, they are glad.

Ricky and J.J. had been practicing traps at night on a ground strip at MCAS Miramar for a couple of weeks. Easy. But now it was showtime. CVN-70, the USS Carl Vinson, one of the Navy's finest super carriers had departed Naval Air Station North Island that fine October morning, and was waiting for them on this moonless night 70 miles offshore from San Diego. A front had moved in that day, and it was overcast, ceiling 1000 feet, visibility 2 miles. It was a crappy night to fly, but Ricky and J.J. were out there, and Marine officer or not, they were scared shitless.

"San Diego Departure, Silverlight 201, Navy flight of two, 600, climbing 5000." Ricky said as Ricky and J.J. reported into San Diego departure control. "Silverlight 201, San Diego departure, fly heading 280 degrees, climb and maintain angels 5 to marshal fix, hold on heading 180, 6 minute legs, left hand turns, report to Carl Vinson air traffic control on 279.6 upon reaching marshal." the San Diego departure air traffic controller radioed as Ricky and J.J. were vectored to the marshal fix. The marshal fix is a unique position in space typically about 180 degrees from the carrier's base recovery course and at a fixed distance, typically about 20 to 25 miles away from the carrier and at stacked altitudes if there was more than one plane in the pattern.

Ricky and J.J. climbed up through the overcast layer in formation, setting up their heading and leveling off at 5000 feet. They had both set the marshal fix into their nav systems and were watching their progress on the moving map display. When they reached the marshal fix, they turned to a heading of 180 degrees and started their timers and set up their autopilots to fly the holding pattern and set up their navigation receivers to fly an instrument landing system approach and an automatic carrier landing system approach through the clouds down to the carrier should that become necessary. Both set waypoints to their bingo field, MCAS Miramar, in case they could not get aboard the carrier safely. Both checked their fuel levels and set their bingo fuel level into their system so the plane's system would warn them audibly when they had hit bingo fuel and needed to head for shore, and both set their radar altimeters to the altitude at which they wanted to hear an audible warning that they were too close to the ocean.

"Yogi control, Silverlight 201, flight of two, established angels five at marshal." Ricky called the air traffic controllers on the USS Carl Vinson.

"Silverlight 201, Yogi Approach. Have dash two establish at angels six. You are first. Left to heading zero niner five for final approach course three five niner." The Carl Vinson, like all Navy carriers had rooms full of mainframes, radar systems, communication systems, Instrument Carrier Landing System radio equipment and Automatic Carrier Landing System radio equipment. The Instrument Carrier Landing System is used on all Class III instrument flight rules recoveries and on all night landings. It is like the civilian ILS that airliners and general aviation aircraft use for precision IFR approaches to land runways. It displays a bullseye to the pilot on his heads up display showing the aircraft's position relative to the desired glideslope and final approach course lineup. The Automatic Carrier Landing System displays needles on the pilot's HUD, the needles showing the aircraft's position relative to the final approach course and glideslope. The pilot can couple his autopilot to this system and let it fly the approach, but most pilots don't trust the system totally, because the link to the autopilot can fail if reception of the navigation signals on the data link from the carrier hits a dropout. Still, for a freaked out pilot, it can be a lifesaver. Regardless of the approach type, the final 3/4 of a mile on the approach is flown using the optical landing system, otherwise knows as the meatball.

"Silverlight 201, Yogi approach, descend 2000 feet per minute to angels 2, maintain angels 2, heading zero niner five. Establish landing configuration at 10 nautical miles. Fly mode two alpha when established on the final approach course." the approach controller told Ricky. A mode two alpha approach was a coupled approach down to about 3/4 of a mile off the fantail. Ricky was to couple his autopilot to the needles of the Automatic Carrier Landing System when he was established on the final approach course and let the autopilot fly him down through the clouds to a point 3/4 of a mile short of the fantail. At that point, Ricky would take over flying the jet manually using the meatball and make the trap without the aid of any computers. Ricky was slightly relieved that the computers would be doing the flying. It was black as pitch and he was in the soup. All he could see was his strobes flashing in the clouds.

"Silverlight 201, 20 miles, come left to three five niner final approach course. Maintain angels 2." the controller called.

"201, left to three niner five, maintain 2000." Ricky responded.

"201, 10 miles, descend and maintain 1200." the Vinson controller ordered.

"201 out of 2000 for 1200, three down and locked." Ricky responded after he had set up his landing configuration by putting his gear down and slats and flaps out and tailhook and checked his cockpit displays to confirm his gear were down and flaps out.

"Silverlight 201, six miles, lock on and say needles." the final approach controller said indicating he wanted Ricky to lock his autopilot onto the glideslope and final approach course needles of the ACLS and report when he was locked on.

'201, needles." Ricky reported after he had punched the appropriate buttons on his up front control panel to lock the Super Hornet autopilot to the ACLS and confirmed he was locked on. When the jet was properly locked on, a little display icon called the spermie displayed in his HUD and showed the correct heading and altitude he should be flying and, if the icon representing his jet's actual heading and altitude overlapped the spermie, all was well with the world. If the spermie disappeared, the computers had lost lock and he was on his own. The spermie had a nasty habit of disappearing.

And sure enough, it did disappear. "201 has lost lock." Ricky reported.

"201, fly bullseye." the final approach controller ordered.

"201, fly bullseye." Ricky confirmed.

The bullseye was slang for the horizontal and vertical lines on his HUD that the carriers instrument landing system displayed on the pilot's HUD when a jet was on the final approach course, had its nav receivers properly tuned to receive the navigations signals of the system and was generally in the ballpark in terms of altitude relative to the glideslope and the final approach course bearing. If the pilot could fly the jet to maintain the aircraft position icon in the HUD at the intersection of the horizontal and vertical lines, he was on the final approach course and on the glideslope. It was sometimes hard to do, especially in bad weather and gusty conditions like those prevailing this evening.

Ricky bounced around in the gusts, and struggled to keep his plane on the bullseye. Concentrating on the bullseye, he occasionally glanced outside, but he was still in the soup. At a mile and a half, he started to be able to see some glimmers of lights from the carrier in the soup. He was descending at about 700 feet per minute which worked out to be about a 3 degree angle. Finally he broke out at a mile and could see the lights of the ship. At 3/4 of a mile, he could see the meatball. "Silverlight 201, ball, 7.5, Magnusson." Ricky reported indicating he now had the optical landing system in sight and his jet had 7,500 pounds of fuel remaining. The carrier's arresting gear operators would use that figure to set the stopping power of the cables. Ricky double checked his angle of attack by looking at the HUD and confirming the aircraft symbol was centered in on an "E" symbol at the side of the HUD display. The center of the E represented the proper angle of attack so his hook could catch a wire.

"201 Roger ball, 7.5, slightly below and slightly left." the final approach controller confirmed and gave Ricky some final correction advice before turning him over to the Landing Signal Officer.

"201, power, come right." the LSO radioed. Ricky corrected ever so slightly. The key to successful carrier landing was tiny corrections. Over control and you would bolter — or worse. Ten seconds later, BOOM. Touchdown. He caught the number 2 wire. He had cheated death one more time.

J.J. followed a couple of minutes later, and caught the three wire. They had now done the hardest thing any aviator can do.

They followed with a few more cat shots and traps, but once you had done it once, the rest were not quite as nerve wracking. A night trap is never easy, but at least they had not killed themselves or anybody else on the first one.

CARMEN AT THE RAG IN EGLIN

Carmen was loving the F-35 although she had doubts why anybody lives in Florida at al. She was from the temperate and pleasant San

Francisco bay area, and Florida was so hot in the summer it could actually melt you. Eglin Air Force Base was a nice place in the Florida panhandle at Valparaiso, but it was still hot and humid in the summer. Better than Miami though. What were those people thinking? Well that is not fair. Miami is beautiful, no argument there.

But Eglin was not a Marine base, and she missed the comraderie and smack talking of the Leathernecks. She did like the Green Berets that were moved there from Fort Bragg as part of the 2005 base re-alignment and closure program. They had a certain something about them, an air of confidence more than anything she guessed, which she found attractive. That comes from going through hell and coming out the other side alive. Green Beret selection and training was no day at the beach. They were there to conduct operations in Latin America should the need arise.

But most of all, she missed Ricky, J.J. and Neil with whom she had grown very tight over the four years of intense training that they had endured together. She had seen them at their best and possibly at their worst, but that remained to be seen she said to herself.

The F-35B was a jump jet, and that is why the Marines loved it. It could land and takeoff vertically from any hard surface or grass by vectoring its jet exhaust downward. What made it unique was the when landing vertically or taking off vertically, it had a thrust fan that was driven by the shaft of the jet turbine and blew air straight down to provide lift. The airplane's computers controlled the fan and thrust vectoring so all the pilot had to do was just tell it where to land and it did it practically all by itself. It created a lot of turbulence though, so the landing surface had to be hard enough that the engine exhaust and thrust fan would not blow dirt and sand up into the jet's air intakes and wipe out the engine.

The Marine Corps had loved the Harrier jump jet before, but it was notoriously hard to fly and many pilots were killed just trying to learn how to fly it.

The F-35 jump jet version was much easier to land vertically. To land the F-35 vertically, all the pilot had to do was push a button in the cockpit which caused the lift fan doors to open and the jet's exhaust nozzle to swivel downward so as to start generating vertical lift. The pilot checks the aircraft weight on the glass cockpit display and, if the plane is too heavy to hover, just touches a magenta area representing a fuel tank from which he wishes to dump fuel and the dumping starts automatically. A display also shows up on the pilot's visor showing the angle of the thrust vector to the vertical and how much of the engine's thrust is being demanded to generate vertical lift. When the vertical lift get generated, the lift vector slowly moves toward vertical and that slows the airplane down to well below the stall speed. However, the plane does not stall because of the vertical lift. While all this is happening, the stick and rudder pedals work just like a regular airplane with the computers and fly-by-wire system doing all the calculations to make the plane fly as the pilot has commanded. When the pilot gets close to the place he or she wants to land, he presses a button on the throttle called decel which vectors the thrust vector forward of vertical to slow the plane down and bring it to a hover. The computer and fly-by-wire system generates all the control inputs to cause this to happen. The helmet visor display shows the airspeed decreasing to zero, the radar altimeter reading of the height above the ground and the angle of the thrust vector changes to 90 degrees as the plane reaches the hover state. At this point, pulling back on the stick causes more vertical thrust to be generated and the plane to ascend, and conversely when the stick is pushed forward. The rudder pedals in the hover state just control in which direction the nose is pointing. It is so easy, new pilots can get in the cockpit and learn how to land vertically in just a couple of minutes. Pushing the vertical takeoff and landing button again, closes the thrust fan doors and vectors the exhaust to the rear and converts the plane into a supersonic fighter again.

F-35 DAS

The F-35 also had a distributed aperture infrared sensor system called the DAS with six sensors that provided infrared image data from a spherical space around the jet. The image data from all these sensors was fed to a computer which put it all together in one integrated image and displayed it on the pilot's helmet visor along with the altitude, speed, missile state and the positions of all hostile and friendly aircraft and missiles in the battle space. The pilot could see the entire space around his or her jet using this system including the space directly underneath it. All the pilot had to do was look down, and what was below the jet would be displayed in the face shield of her helmet. If the pilot wanted to see what was behind him or directly above him, he or she just looked that way and the computer did the rest selecting and displaying the proper image data. It was virtual reality to the max, but there was nothing virtual about it. Because it was infrared, the pilot could see surface-to-air, aka SAM, missile launches as they happened from the intense heat plume the missile threw off. Same for air-to-air missiles. In fact, the pilot could even tell what type of air-to-air missile was launched from its heat signature. An AMRAAM looked different to the DAS than a Sidewinder, because each missile had its own unique heat signature. That helped the pilot decide what type of evasive action to take and what type of countermeasures to launch at the break turn.

The F-35 really could not be called an air superiority fighter, because it would gets its ass kicked in a fight with a Su-30 Flanker or a J-20 Chinese stealth fighter, as the Rand Corporation had pointed out in an afterthought to their study of a mock engagement between U.S. forces and the Chinese over Taiwan. But you could not beat the F-35 for close air support and that is what the Marines liked – bombing the shit out of stuff on the ground that was pissing them off. Besides, the Marines had plenty of F/A-18E Super Hornets to help out in the air superiority department, although their effectiveness alone against a J-20 Stealth or Su-30 Flanker was open to question.

CARMEN GOES BOMBING AT THE RAG

It was a beautiful morning in January, and Carmen was scheduled for a hop to practice bombing that day. Bombing targets on the ground required flying a precise pattern in the sky, diving at a very precise angle and releasing the bomb at a very specific point in the sky. At least that is the way it was taught for dumb bombs. With the laser guided and GPS guided smart bombs that existed at the time, Carmen wondered why bother with this shit, but she found out that even if the bomb was smart, it still had to be put in the right ballpark to do its job, and that was her job, putting it in the right ballpark.

It was a flight of four Marine pilots this morning, all in F-35's, and she was the flight leader. Heading southwest toward the Eglin AFB bombing range in the Gulf of Mexico she wondered what Ricky and J.J. were doing that day. They were practicing dogfighting, but she did not know that. Looking down at her navigation display, Carmen spoke into her helmet headset, "Cracker Lead shows 12 miles northeast of Control Point Alpha."

"Dash 1 concurs." her right wingman confirmed.

"2."

"3."

"Dash 1, detach and climb to angels 8 and hold at Alpha, Dash 2 detach and climb to angels 9 and hold at Alpha, Dash 3 detach and climb to angel 10 and hold at Alpha. Cracker lead will go first flying mission ten tac 1, followed by the rest of you in order at 1 minute intervals." Carmen ordered. Her flight confirmed and detached and climbed to their assigned altitudes to wait their turns to make the bombing run. "ten tac 1" was the designation of the bombing mission specifying the target, and the initial point.

"Friendlies in the north side of the target. Standby for TOT" the forward air controller radioed to Carmen indicating the imaginary troops she was providing close air support for were on the north side of the target. TOT was short for Time on Target which was the time to hit the target.

Carmen set up her autopilot to fly to the initial point and from there to the target and designated the target on her DAS. The cockpit navigation display now displayed the course lines to the initial point and from there to the target. The target had to be bombed within a very small window of time from the time the forward air controller designated that it be hit. That required a very precise calculations and adjustments in airspeed to avoid arriving too early and being hit by your own artillery or too late to help the Marines on the ground such as if the target was an enemy tank or a missile launcher.

"Cracker 1, TOT is plus 24." the forward air controller said to Carmen. Carmen filled in +24 in the times she had written on her charts that showed the target, the IP and the control point. She had already entered the latitude and longitude of the control point, the IP and the target and a second control point where all the jets would meet after their bombing runs. Now she needed to make some quick calculations in her head to arrive at a "push" time to leave the control point so that her time on route and the free fall time of the bomb would put the bomb on the target at exactly 24 minutes after the hour which happened to be 10 AM. She calculated how long it would take to fly from the initial point to the target at a constant ground speed of 350 knots from a chart – 2 minutes, 10 seconds -- and subtracted that from the TOT of 10:24 AM to arrive at 10:21:50 AM. Then she calculated the distance from Alpha to the initial point and calculated how long it would take to fly that distance at a constant ground speed of 350 knots – two minutes, 45 seconds. She subtracted that time from the time she had calculated previously to arrive at a "push" time of 10:19:05 AM. She checked her watch. Thirty-five seconds to push. Carmen entered the ground speed she wanted to fly and the time on target value into the computer and entered the sequence of the waypoints she had previously entered to tell the computer the sequence which was the numbers of the waypoints she had previously entered and the order in which she wanted the computer to fly to them in. She then watched the computer adjust the throttle to get a ground speed of 350 knots and watched the seconds tick away. At precisely 10:19:05, she pressed the autopilot engage button to tell the autopilot to fly the sequence she had told it to fly. "Cracker 1 is pushing." she radioed. The autopilot turned the jet to her inbound heading to the IP and started her run. She monitored the time and tracking of the course line as the autopilot did all the heavy lifting. At the IP, she watched the autopilot, bring the jet to her new heading to take her from the IP to the target and double checked the time. Right on time she smiled.

NIKITA AND ALEXANDRA VISIT SAN DIEGO

It was Friday night in San Diego, and Nikita and Alexandra had just arrived at Lindbergh Field. Ricky and J.J. were waiting for them after a long day practice dogfighting over the Pacific.

"Hi there you big stud." Alexandra said to J.J. with a glowing smile.

"Holy crap, I thought I would never say this to a woman, but it is nice to see you Alex." J.J. said with a crooked grin. That was the nature of their relationship. A lot of screwing around with good natured ribbing and smack talk. But underneath all the kidding, there flowed a strong current of respect and admiration for the other one as a person. They loved each other.

"Nikita, you came! I thought you were kidding." Ricky said to the lovely Ms. Novachev.

"Of course I did Ricky. I have never been to San Diego before." Nikita said. "Did you miss me?"

"Too busy." Ricky said with a smile. "Just kidding. Of course I missed you. We have been working our asses off out here and J.J. just isn't as much fun as you." At that she smiled a broad smile, knowing that Ricky was just kidding. Of course he missed her. How could he not?

"Its happy hour. Lets go get a cocktail." J.J. said. The girls readily agreed, and they all proceeded to the rooftop bar down by the Convention Center overlooking all of San Diego and Mission Bay. It was a beautiful clear night, the golden hour just before sunset. San Diego, as it almost always is, was accommodating to their outdoor adventure -- a just right 71 degrees with a refreshing ocean breeze. The lights of the city sparkled and spirits were high. And as a bonus, the Padres were playing a night game in the stadium below the rooftop bar so they had the best seat in the house.

After several rounds of rum drinks were downed, the girls were feeling no pain. Ricky and J.J. had the weekend off with no flying, so they let if fly also.

"So my handsome friend, what do you have planned for us this weekend?" Alex asked J.J..

"Ricky and I thought it would be fun to take you golfing tomorrow morning and see if you have learned how to drive a golf cart yet. Then some time at the beach and a sunset sail on a retired America's cub yacht and dinner late tomorrow night and a late night beach party and camp out. Then brunch on Sunday morning and off you go to the airport to return to reality." J.J. said.

"Excellent!" they both exclaimed. "How romantic." Alex added.

RICKY PONTIFICATES ON THE DEBT CEILING AND CUTS AND DEMOCRATS

"So what do you think about the latest news out of Washington, D.C." Alex asked Ricky.

"What particular news are you referring to?" Ricky asked.

"The posturing and puffing over raising the debt ceiling again to 34 trillion dollars to avoid defaulting on all those Chinese bonds and forcing further cuts in social security payments coming due and further cuts in the Medicare and Medicaid systems." Alex the brainiac said.

"Oh, that news." Ricky said. "I just cannot believe how out to lunch those guys are. The democrats want to tax and spend and save everybody. The Republicans think that all jobs arise from tax cuts despite the fact that trickle down, supply-side economics is a proven failure. Economic growth will come from government policies that favor innovation and creation of new industries and protection of our industries from foreign competition. And the labor unions have to back off on the wages and benefits or we will lose all our jobs to China, India, Vietnam and elsewhere. The whole situation is royally fucked up. Jiminy Cricket, do I have to do all the thinking around here?"

J.J., being a liberal, kept quiet. Ricky had his opinions and he was not afraid to let them fly. Nor was Nikita.

"You know the Vikings from Iceland, when they settled Greenland in the 980s, started a colony that lasted 500 years. But they had a rough time of it caused by the Little Ice Age climate change and crop failures. I have heard stories that the Vikings would push their old people and non-productive people off the cliffs into the ocean. I saw it on Nova. I am not making this up. That sounds pretty screwed up, but I think that is what you Americans have to do here. Medicare spends 80% of its money on medical care for old people in the last two years of their lives. Medicare pays huge money to the hospitals and doctors for the doctors to torture these poor bastards with surgeries and chemotherapy and radiation. It make their lives miserable and then they die anyway. I know. I watched them do that to my Mom. That sucks and is stupid. Let them die with dignity. I am in favor of physician assisted suicide. Besides these people have had their whole lives to prepare for their retirements and their final illnesses. If they get to 65 an are unprepared for retirement and they get to 80 and are unprepared for the final illness, too bad. The constitution does not say anywhere in the government is going to be responsible for their security cradle to grave. Right now, the government is having to borrow 67 cents of every dollar it pays in foreign aid, entitlements programs, farm subsidies, tax breaks for the wealthiest corporations. And it is getting worse. The baby boomers are retiring and paying less taxes and sucking huge amounts of money out of the government. These people are dead wood. They are not inventing anything, not working and not paying taxes. If they cannot take care of themselves, then screw them. They are going to take us all down. The debt service on the national debt is eventually going to take up the entire budget and there will be no money for defense. None. When that happens, we are fucked. We already have the Chinese spending huge amounts on defense, stem cell research and research of all types. Their Flanker jets and stealth jets can kick the shit out of our Joint Strike Fighters and we cannot afford to build enough Raptors or design a new jet than can take on the PAK-FA fifth generation jet Russia has built or the Chinese J-20 stealth fifth generation jet. When they have billions of starving people on their hands, they will just take what they want, and then it will be us who are starving. They have already had food riots, and the national debt here is such that we now have to borrow 60% of every dollar we spend because the idiots in Congress flew us right into the ground with bloated entitlements, an overly large and overly brassed Pentagon, unnecessary and expensive wars and other massive stupidity. So we are toast unless we do something drastic and mean. You just can't save all the sick people and poor people. There are too many of them and not enough money." Nikita said in her best Russian accented English obviously feeling no pain.

"What the fuck Nikita, where did that come from." J.J. said. "Maybe a couple more of these and I will start telling the truth too."

"I read a lot. I am not as big a bimbo as you probably think I am. I also am not hung up on the 'nice guy, lets save everybody mindset of your feeble-minded, spineless, anything-to-get re-elected' legislators and your ill-informed public."

"Holy shit Nikita, you are never going to get elected President with a Nazi outlook like that." Ricky said. And he was right. Even if she had been a U.S. citizen, which she was not, she could never get elected as soon as those views came out. There were just too many old people and poor people, and they all could vote.

"You nimrod. I can't be President anyway. I only have a green card. I will be lucky if they don't throw me out of this country on my ass if somebody outs me." Nikita laughed.

"And a fine little ass it is I must say." J.J. said thereby pissing Alex off a little bit. But Alex was a mature woman and confident in her own charms and she shrugged it off after a few seconds. J.J. was a ladies man and incorrigible. She had to live with that, and because she was confident and smart, she knew that she had J.J. if she wanted him and to make a big deal about a dumb crack like that would only make her look insecure and immature. So she glared at J.J. and then ordered another round.

RICKY HAS HOT SEX WITH NIKITA

Around 2 AM, they were all tired and ready for bed. Ricky and Nikita kind of weaved down to his Corvette, and although Ricky knew he should not be driving, they only had to go to a hotel a few blocks away so he took the chance. J.J. did the same. But first he had to lend a hand to Alex who was having difficulty negotiating with the elevator to get it to go in the right direction even though the only direction it could go was down.

Ricky pulled into the driveway of the hotel and tossed the keys to the valet. He came around to the passenger side and opened the door for Nikita and offered her his hand to help her get up and out of the thing. Any woman who has ever tried to get out of a Corvette in a tight miniskirt and 6 inch "chase-me, catch-me, fuck me" heels knows what a difficult task this can be without a helping hand. She did fairly well, only showing Ricky her lacy little panties once for a brief second. "Here we go." he thought to himself with a smile.

"Take me to bed my Lord." Nikita said with a come hither look in her eyes and a smolding wetness in her lacies.

"If you insist Madam. I have been Headmaster in this nunnery with these shriveled up old shrews for far too long." Ricky said. He already had a party in his pants.

Ricky fished around in his pockets for the key card after they got to the right floor and he let Nikita in with a big, wet kiss, sucking both or her lips into his mouth and sucking them. "Ooh peach flavored lipstick. Nice." he thought to himself as he drank in her Giorgio™ perfume and tasted her lips. Her sumptuous breasts were pressed against his chiseled chest now and he felt like he just wanted to rub her chest against his like a hot little matchstick and start a big fire.

Ricky took her hand and led her to the balcony. Her lovely face was bathed in moonlight. Ever so slowly, Ricky removed her blouse, one agonizing button at a time, all the while gazing into her eyes. Her breathing started to deepen ever so slightly and he could feel her excitement.

Slowly he unhooked her bra and dropped it to the floor. Then he led her to the side of the bed and pulled two pillows off and had her kneel on one and rest her chest and head on the down comforter. He kneeled on the other pillow beside her and slowly dragged his fingernails ever so lightly up and down the skin of her back. She purred with the sensation of it. Then he did it again, but this time leaving a tiny space between his nails and her skin and touching down ever so lightly from time to time and his hand slowly caressed her skin. Just enough to cause her to half turn on and half shiver and raise the goose bumps which were lovely in the moonlight streaming in from the open patio door with the cool ocean breeze. He gently pulled the silk scarf from around her neck pulling one end only so that it slithered off her neck and into his hand and, with one motion, swept it across her back lightly just to tickle her. She giggled a little then purred. He slid the scarf between her face and the down comforter and tied it around her head to turn it into a blindfold. He slid his hand slowly down to the small of her back and then over her gently curved derriere and caressed her bottom and her thighs gently.

He gently grasped her shoulders and pulled her up and turned her around and raised her up gently to her feet and then he sat her down on the bed and pulled the comforter up over and around her shoulders and asked her to sit still and be patient. "Yes my Lord." she said.

Ricky silently walked over to the mini bar refrigerator and removed some food items he had prepared for her pleasure and put them on a tray. He turned on the CD player to play a CD of the most romantic classical music in the world: Clair De Lune; Abendied; Chopin's Ballade No. 1; Argonaise from Carmen; Catalonian Folk Song; Chopin Etude #3; Fur Elise; Eine Kleine Nachtmusik; Gymnopedies No. 1; Pachelbel; Beethoven's Moonlight Sonata and Liszt's Lieberstraumme.

Ricky removed a rose from its vase and put that on the tray and walked back over to Nikita and knelt on a pillow at the edge of the bed and put the tray down beside her. He slipped his hands between her knees and gently separated her legs and moved his pillow so he was now kneeling before her and between her legs. He took a spoonful of whipped cream and put a raspberry in it and brought the rose up to her nose. She smelled it gently and smiled. He brought the spoon up and gently touched the space between her lips with it. She obediently opened her mouth and he slipped the spoon and whipped cream into it. She closed her lips on it and removed the whipped cream and raspberry with her tongue and savored the taste. Then Ricky dipped a strawberry into melted chocolate and brought it to her lips and asked her to bite off half the strawberry. She murmured something that sounded like yum. Ricky was not done yet. He dipped a slice of a ripe peach in brown sugar and caramel and brought that to her lips. Obediently, she sucked the peach slice into her mouth and savored it slowly. As she enjoyed the tastes, Ricky ran his fingers through her hair. He gently dragged his fingernails across her scalp, starting at the top and slowly moving down each side of her head and around to the nape of her neck. He gently stroked down from her neck out across the top of her shoulders and down her arms to her hands and then to her thighs and down the outsides of her legs to her ankles. He slowly and gently cupped each foot and gently massaged her feet.

Gently he lowered her shoulders down onto the top of the comforter, lifted her ankles and moved her legs onto the bed. He then gently turned her over so she was lying on her tummy. Gently he massaged her scalp with his left hand and then moved his right hand with the lightest of touch down her back, down her derriere to the top of her thighs. He walked around to the foot of the bed and gently spread her legs and laid down with his chest on her derriere and took his hands up to her shoulders and dragged them down the sides of her chest with the lightest of touches, feeling the sides of her breasts bulging out to the sides of her chest. He gently massaged her derriere and moved his hands down to the tops of her feet. He stood up at the foot of the bed and cupped one foot at a time in one hand and used the other hand to massage it. Then he dragged his hand slowly up the inside of her thigh to her wetness and gently parted her lips and teased her flower.

Ricky gently took the point of her hip and turned Nikita over on her back. He gently spread her legs and cupped her secret garden in one palm and took her lips into his mouth and ran his tongue over them and gently sucked on them bringing one then the other into his mouth further with a gentle suction. Moving his face downward, he nuzzled into her neck and smelled her perfume while he kissed and nuzzled her neck while he moved his hand up to her breast and gently cupped it and then played with her nipple.

Slowly he moved his face down to her breasts and nuzzled them and then down to her flat tummy, kissing and nibbling lightly at each station of delight. Reaching her hips he stood up and grabbed her ankles and gently dragged her hips down to the foot of the bed. Putting two pillow under her curvaceous derriere, and putting his legs over his shoulders, he teased her flower with his tongue until her breathing increased in frequency and became more shallow. Finally, she expelled a big breath and turned her head to one side. His work was done here. He laid down beside her, wrapped the comforter around them both and fell asleep with her nestled in his arms.

GOLF OUTING IN SAN DIEGO

At 8 AM the next morning, the suite phone rang. "Dude, get your snaggletooth ass out of bed. Tee time is in an hour." J.J. said.

"Roger that dude. I am on it. Meet you in the lobby in 30." Ricky said. "Nikita, wake up baby. Time to go golfing."

"Oh Ricky, that was so wonderful. I think I love you." Nikita said.

"Yeah, I know. But it is time to go golfing. And furthermore, my Lady, we only have an hour to get there so go shower up and I will go get a muffin and coffee for you." Ricky said in his usual nonchalant way. Ricky was a great guy and treated his women well, but he was not at all mushy and it kind of annoyed him when all women wanted to talk about was their relationship with him. He would rather go golfing.

Showered and caffeinated, they were both ready to go. They met J.J. and Alex in the lobby and walked out to their cars which the valets had retrieved and had ready with the engines running. Ricky opened Nikita's door for her, and got in with a "Follow me dude." to J.J.. J.J. had the clubs in his Mustang, and gave Ricky the same salute they gave the launch officer when they were ready for a cat shot.

Ricky pulled out onto the surface streets and made his way to the Highway 5 Northbound on ramp and got on the freeway heading north toward La Jolla and the Torrey Pines Golf Course. The morning traffic was light and when they got a little north of the downtown area and the landscape opened up, Ricky floored it. The big, blown 5.7 liter ZR 1 wanna-be engine roared with delight. In a blink of the eye, they were going 130 MPH. J.J.'s Saleen Mustang was right on their tail.

Unfortunately so was Officer Lopez of the California Highway Patrol, and he pulled them both over.

"So dude, where's the fire?" Office Lopez said as he walked up to the Corvette convertible.

"Sorry officer, we are headed up to Torrey Pines for a 9 AM tee time and we are running a little late. Plus, I had a tailgater back there. I hate that." Ricky said sheepishly, lying just a little bit about the tailgater. Nobody on the freeway had been able to keep up with him since he got on it.

Noticing Ricky's leather flight jacket with his squadron patch on the sleeve, Officer Lopez said, "You a Sharpshooter up at Miramar?"

"Yup. That's my wingman, 1st Lieutenant J.J. Saleen back there in the Mustang." Ricky said.

"Jack Jarvis, Gunnery Sargeant, 3/7, 1st Marine Division. Good morning sir. Just finished a tour on Okinawa for two years a couple years back. Slow down please sir. Have a nice day." And with that, he snapped a salute, did an about face and saluted J.J. followed by a wave indicating J.J. was free to go with a "Have a good round sir." send off with a big smile. "Thank you both for your service."

The day was looking up already. It did a great deal to ease the pounding in their heads. Thank God it was only rum.

Ricky picked up his cell phone while he was driving and hit speed dial to connect with Neil's cell.

"Woody, what is happening dude?" Neil answered entirely too cheerfully.

"We are partying in San Diego and we need you down here to party with us tonight. Can you make it? J.J. and Alexandra and Nikita are down here with me. We are going golfing right now, but we are going to the beach this afternoon and then on a sunset sail." Ricky asked.

"You know, I think I can." Neil answered. "I have to take a cross country in my Super Hornet so I might as well go to San Diego. Even though it will only take me about 20 minutes to get there from NAS Lemoore. I am there dude. I think I can get there by about 2 PM."

"Perfect. See you this afternoon and the beach on North Island in front of the Hotel Del Coronado." Ricky said.

BEACH PARTY AT THE HOTEL DEL CORONADO

"Adios amigo. See you this afternoon." Neil replied, hiding his excitement to see his best friends again. He hung up and immediately dialed his latest girlfriend Dr. Tina Thompkins. "Tina, good morning baby. Can you hop on Southwest to San Diego, rent a car and meet me at NAS North Island at 2 this afternoon?" Neil inquired hopefully.

"Sure baby, what is the occasion?

"Woody and Scud are down there partying with their girlfriends and just called and wanted me to come down. I want to introduce you to them." Neil explained.

"OK sounds fun. See you at two. I gotta get a move on then. Ciao." Tina said as she hung up.

Neil called his training officer and told him the plan and got the OK to log the time in his F/A-18, planned his flight and went to breakfast.

On the first tee, J.J. took the lead and tee'd off first. He hit a terrible drive which shanked off to the right and into the rough. "Rough night." he said sheepishly.

Nikita went next and sent one sailing right down the middle of the fairway for a whole 50 yards give or take a couple of feet.

"Criminy, you could have thrown it farther than that." Ricky said sinking the needle in with devilish delight.

"Blow me Ricky. I don't take steroids like you lunatics." Nikita said with a smile.

"Those aren't steroids. They are pure testosterone." J.J. said. The truth was that neither took steroids or testosterone having no lack of the natural substance in their well trained bodies. They lifted weights regularly and played beach volleyball to stay in shape to fly. You had to be strong to fly the jets when you started pulling Gs. They played beach volleyball just to screw around and bond with their buddies. It was great fun even though it was actually more fun to sit in the shade and smack talk their buddies who were playing. Which they did on a regular basis.

Alexandra smacked her ball right down the middle of the fairway for 200 yards.

"Holy shit. Bixby came to play." J.J. said. "We are going to have to get serious Woody."

"Roger that. I bet you $50 bucks she can't do that again." Ricky said sinking the needle into Alex too.

"OK wise ass you are on." Alex said with a smile. She was hustling Ricky. He did not know she played college golf at SMU.

Alex, not suffering as much as the other three from the excesses of the night before, went on to relieve Ricky of his money and win the round by 15 strokes. "Show off." Ricky said as he handed over the money. It was 12 PM now so they stopped in the clubhouse and had a quick lunch.

"So how is the training going Ricky?" Nikita asked.

"Oh its going. J.J. and I both did night carrier quals and have a round of dogfight training coming up. About 3 more months and we are done. The night carrier quals were scary as hell. We did them in bad weather. But after a few of them, it got a little better. You having fun down there in Kingsville?" Ricky said.

"Yes, but the boys are boring. Not nearly as much fun as you and J.J.. That is why we are here besides the fact that Alex is head over heels in love with J.J.." Nikita said.

Alex glared at her. She did not want J.J. to know he had her wrapped around his finger, but now she was outed. "Nikita needed to get laid by a real man. That is why we are here." Alex retaliated. "You know any?" she ribbed and the boys cracked up.

They got to the beach on Coronado about 1:30 and set up their campsite in front of the Hotel Del. They did some body surfing, while the girls sunbathed and napped. About 2:15, Neil rolled up plus 1.

"Holy crap Neil, why didn't you tell us you were bringing a super model. We would have showered." J.J. said.

"Gentlemen and Ladies. This is Dr. Tina Thompkins, my current GF."

"Current girlfriend? You asshole. How many more are there?" Tina laughed. She actually did not care that much. She liked Neil, but knew she could get another boyfriend just by pointing at him and crooking her index finger in the universal come hither sign.

"Just a couple." Neil said and he wasn't kidding. But she did not know that. He looked like he was kidding.

"Doctor Thompkins? What are you a surgeon or something?" Ricky asked.

"No, I am a plant geneticist. Doctorate in plant biology from Cal. We are working on Round Up resistant soy beans and wheat up in the valley and I am the chief scientist on the project. I work for Monsanto." Tina replied. Round Up was a widely used weed killer. Round Up resistant corn had been a smash hit for Monsanto and increased corn yields worldwide.

"Well welcome my dear. Any friend of Neil's is part of the family. This lovely creature is Nikita Novachev, she is from Russia and has a Bachelor of Arts from Moscow University. And this brunette bombshell is my love, Alexandra Bixby, BS English Literature from SMU." J.J. said. He knew she played golf at SMU, but did not tell Ricky just to fuck with him. "And this handsome stud is Ricky Magnusson, aka Woody, BSEE from Northwestern University. I am J.J. Saleen, also known as Scud, Bachelor of Arts, Political Science, UCLA."

"Scud also was formerly a pro beach volleyball player on the pro tour before he decided he needed a real job." Ricky added.

"How interesting. What a delightful group." Tina said.

They sat around and chit chatted for a bit and then Ricky saw some guys playing beach volleyball and got J.J. and Neil to join him and go over and ask them if they wanted to play. They did, and the group and three great games. The guys Ricky had seen were pretty good and played every weekend. Scud toyed with them to let them stay in the game but put the hammer down on them when it was time to win. He let them win one time just in the spirit of diplomacy and to maintain good relations between the civilian population and the Navy and Marine Corp.

About 5 P.M. the group picked up their stuff and headed over to Harbor Island Drive to board an 80 foot America's Cup class racing yacht owned by a former America's Cup skipper for a sunset cruise out of San Diego harbor. She had been retired several years earlier and was now enjoying her golden years cruising beautiful San Diego bay. The wind was fresh and it made for a great sail. As they sailed out onto the open ocean past Point Loma, the dolphins started racing the boat. They were "porpoising" in and out of the water just in front of the bow. Some of them were getting major air and spinning as they leaped out of the water like they were bullets. "It is either dolphin happy hour somewhere, or they are working for tips." Ricky said and everybody laughed.

TINA AND NIKITA SPECULATING ON FUTURE ENERGY WARS

"So Tina, what will your research do to help ease the food riot situation in China and the countries of the developing world?" Alexandra asked.

"Well our research, if it is successful, and I am confident that it will be, will increase the yields of soybeans and wheat because farmers will be able to spray Round Up directly on their fields and kill the weeds without killing the crops. That means bigger supply and it should ease prices. The bigger yields will not solve the problem though because the majority of the cost of harvesting a ton of wheat or soybeans and getting it to the market are the energy costs. It's the costs to run the tractors to plow the fields, plant them, run the ag sprayer planes, run the combines to harvest the product, ship it to markets around the world and distribute it to grocery stores all over the countries by truck. So we can help, but the solution is much more complex than we alone can provide." Tina explained. "I fully expect an energy war in the future as oil reserves continue to dwindle. There are promising developments in harvesting natural gas from shale, and in recovery of oil from the oil sands in Canada. They are also making progress in lessening the expense of deep water drilling and exploration. There are tradeoffs though and the environment is going to get hurt as are some people. But the downside of not having enough energy is catastrophic economic cataclysm, so countries are going to fight over oil unless something major happens in the near future to avert the crisis."

"I agree." Ricky said.

"Me too." J.J. added.

"I think your are right also." Alexandra said. "I think it is going to be China that starts it too."

"I agree. They are big and powerful and have been growing like a weed, pardon that horrible pun, since their economy was opened to trade with the free world by Richard Nixon. They have been building their military power steadily, and the countries in the region are all They have been building their military power steadily, and the countries in the region are all scared of the CCP, because they are ruthless and immoral and do not tolerate protests by their people. and immoral and do not tolerate protest by their people. So even if the people did not want a war, the Chinese government, which is controlled by the Communist Party, and which controls the military, will start one anyway." Nikita added. "I fully expect you boys to see some big time action in the not too distant future." Nikita said presciently.

They got back from the sunset cruise after dark and decided to go to dinner and then camp out on the beach overnight on North Island. They all went to Tradewinds, a wonderful little restaurant on the water with a Polynesian theme and wonderful tropical rum drinks. Alexandra and Nikita had been plotting something and they took Tina aside and filled her in. She burst out laughing and said she was in. Then they took Ricky and Neil aside and filled them in and they said "Cool" and laughed.

JJ GETS CROSS DRESSED ON THE BEACH BY THE GIRLS

They had a round of tropical drinks and dinner arrived. They had not eaten much all day so they were fairly hungry and had little trouble with eating dinner and dessert too. A final round of drinks arrived and the plot sprang into action. Alexandra suggested they go out to the beach and set up their campsite because she and Nikita and Tina were tired and a little toasted. The boys all readily agreed since they were even more tired than the girls since they had been playing volleyball all afternoon. The truth was the girls weren't tired at all since they had lounged around all day sun tanning and cat napping. So off they went to the beach.

Blankets were spread out, a campfire built, a tent was pitched and a round of Daiquiris was mixed in a shaker. Alexandra poured a couple of glasses of Daiquiri in the tent and dropped a roofie into the glass destined for J.J.. She carefully kept it in her right hand and winked at Nikita and Tina who poured another set of drinks for themselves and their boyfriends. Alex handed the spiked drink to J.J. with a twisted little smile and said "I love you you big stud. Do you love me?"

"You will do." J.J. said with a smile and he took a big gulp, got a brain freeze and said, "Fuck, I hate it when that happens".

Alex cupped his head between her palms and rubbed it back and forth to generate friction like she was trying to start a fire.

"Hey you know that actually helps." J.J. said as he took another gulp and got another brain freeze. Slowly recovering, he got up on his knees, raised his glass and said, "A toast comrades to our goofy little friends of the female persuasion." He took another big gulp and 10 seconds later did a face plant into the sand.

Ricky and Neil just laughed and crashed on their blankets next to the fire and dozed off.

The girls sprang into action. First they stripped J.J.s board shorts off and shaved his legs until they were smooth as a baby's butt. Then they gave him a Brazilian bikini wax and tucked and taped him and put a specially made bikini bottom on him that Alexandra's tailor had ginned up for them.

Turning their attention to his upper body, they stripped off his shirt and shaved his chest and arms until he was completely hairless except for his beautiful black hair. That they covered up with a long brunette wig. They put a specially tailored bikini top on him that Alex had had made for the occasion and stuffed it with falsies so J.J. wound up a 36 C. Nice. Then, they started on his face. It was the mother of all makeovers. They did his face in a nice beige foundation, and put blush and glitter on his cheeks. Then they put mascara on him, and attached a set of long, curly fake eye lashes. They put a beautiful shade of pink lipstick on him and adorned him with a beautiful set of diamond earrings which they had to glue on since J.J. did not have pierced ears. Finally, a nice set of acrylic fake nails and their masterpiece was done. He was very hot.

Then they stood back, giggled, put on the Kinks, *Lola* on the boom box and danced around him in a circle in the firelight like a coven of witches. Ricky and Neil were rolling in the sand laughing and sloshing down margaritas. Finally, exhausted, they propped him up and posed with him for pictures, each of them taking their turn putting their smiling faces right next to his stoned countenance. Those pictures were destined for his scrap book, and they stayed in there forever with captions which cannot be repeated here.

The morning light broke slowly, sweeping majestically across the beach at 6 AM. Ricky and Neil were first up. They took one look at J.J. and started laughing again. Then Ricky put on Jesse Cook, *Closer to Madness* on the boom box, and that woke J.J. up. He rose to his feet in a wobbly fashion, saying "Holy crap, what kind of rum was that anyway?"

Ricky got up off the sand from his prone position, and walked up to J.J. slowly, a smile slowly growing on his face. Ricky put both of his hands on J.J. well muscled, bronze shoulders, more to stabilize him than anything else and looked into his eyes. Then Ricky said quietly, "Dude, you are one hot chick. I would do you in a New York minute if I did not already know the truth about you."

J.J. looked at him quizzically and then looked over at Neil who was laughing his ass off. He looked back over at Ricky and saw that Ricky was holding a mirror up in front of his face. J.J. took one look in the mirror and said, "What the fuck happened here last night?" That cracked the girls up who by now were up and enjoying the fun.

"Hey not bad." J.J. said. "Did I get any action last night?" He looked at Alex, and she laughed and just said "No." "Crap, all this work for nothing." J.J. said in good humor. Then he looked down at his legs and arms and saw that they had been shaved, and said, "You little twits. How am I going to explain this in the shower at the gym?"

They just shrugged and laughed. Then Alex composed herself and said, "Just tell your locker room buddies that you have been moonlighting as a trannie in a gay bar."

"Not helping." J.J. said, less amused now.

"If you want, we can replace it. We brought some fake leg hair and arm hair too." Tina said.

"Really not helping."

"You can fly my wing anytime there stud muffin." Neil said with a smile.

"So you two rats let these little smurfs do this to me without any heads up?"

"Yup, pretty much." Ricky said laughing.

"OK I get it. Nice." J.J. said as he realized he was getting morning wood and his dick was hurting from being taped between his legs. "Holy crap Alex, you let Tina and Nikita see my junk?"

"Yup, pretty much." Alex said mimicking Ricky's deep voice. "Besides, this isn't their first rodeo if you know what I mean." she said in her normal, breathy, very sexy voice.

Digging around in his bikini bottom, J.J. was able to free his member with an "Oh that is so much better." proclamation.

Having had their fun, the girls set to work removing the pancake makeup, the false eyelashes, the blush and lipstick and mascara. They gave him his clothes back with a giggle. On his way to the tent to change, Nikita could not resist one more, "Hey J.J., you really were pretty hot. I would have done you had you been awake."

"Very funny wise ass. I may make you do me just to pay me back for this little stunt." J.J. said in good humor.

Later that afternoon, Ricky and J.J. took the girls to the airport and Neil got back into his F/A-18F and flew back to NAS Lemoore. What a great weekend it had been.

ADVANCED RAG DOGFIGHT TRAINING AT MIRAMAR

Regrettably, they had to get back to work. They were in advanced dogfight training now in the F/A-18E Super Hornet, and it was time to learn 2 v 2 and 2 v unknown tactics.

Ricky's cell rang on Monday morning, and it was Neil. "Dude, I convinced our training officer to let me and my wingman come down to Miramar and smoke you boys in a 2 v 2 as soon as you can arrange something."

"On it. I will get back to you as to when you sissy boys can show your faces down here. This is jarhead country." Ricky said laughing.

"Oh your on now buddy." Neil said with a chuckle.

Ricky went over to the squadron HQ and walked into the training officer's office came to attention and saluted Major Johnson. "Good morning sir. I have a request. One of my buddies from Pensacola is in the Navy RAG up at LeMoore and he wants to bring his wingman down here to do a 2 v 2 against myself and J.J.. We all went through the Avanced Strike Pipeline together and it would be fun to show them how we do it in the Corps."

"Granted Lieutenant Magnusson. You can do it Thursday afternoon as we have a hole in our training schedule at that time." Major Johnson said with a slight smile.

CHINESE DISCUSS PLAN TO SHOOT DOWN SATELLITES

"Good morning General Baowing." General of the Army Lo Binxiao said with a smile. General Baowing was an important part of the Chinese plan to attack the Tupi Field since he commanded the Second Artillery Corp, the strategic missile force of the People's Liberation Army of China. General Baowing reported to the Chinese Central Military Commission, and commanded six missile brigades spread across China. It was September, and the two distinguished generals were meeting at the Xichang Satellite Launch Center where the Chinese had anti-satellite missiles garrisoned. Although General Baowing had nuclear-tipped Dongfeng-5 intercontinental ballistic missiles that could hit targets in the United States at his command, that was not the plan.

"How are your preparations going General Baowing? Your mission is critical to the operation, and we are planning the launch the operation is less than 6 months." General Binxiao said.

"The kinetic kill vehicles have all been tested with their delivery systems, and the Alpha Weapon is in the final testing stages." General Baowing replied.

"Good. Do not disappoint me." General Binxiao replied.

RICKY, JJ AND NEIL DOGFIGHT AT YUMA TACTS RANGE

Thursday morning dawned clear and cool at MCAS Miramar. It was a perfect autumn day in southern California. Ceiling and visibility unlimited. Ricky and J.J. had been huddling all week going over 2 v 2 tactics between their regular training assignments. Takeoff was scheduled for 2 PM with a join up with Neil and his wingman at Telegraph Pass at the corner of the TACTS range over the desert east of Yuma, Arizona. The TACTS range was otherwise known as Restricted Area R-2301 and was a vast expanse of desert devoted to military training. Civilian pilots were forbidden to enter this airspace. The TACTS range (Tactical Aircrew Combat Training System) was the range used exclusively for dogfight training and was made famous in the movie TOPGUN during the debriefs using video graphic representations of the dogfights. Each fighter carried a pod that communicated data to the TACTS system about the aircraft's altitude, speed, heading, fuel state, weapons state, simulated missile launches, simulated guns use, range to target, etc. The TACTS system could display multiple aircraft and their maneuvers in real time and was a useful tool for debriefs and learning about what worked and what did not.

Ricky and J.J. took off in formation from Miramar exactly at 2 PM, and headed east toward Yuma climbing to 22,000 feet. It took about 20 minutes to fly out to Yuma in their F/A-18 Super Hornets. Both pilots switched their radios to tactical frequency for the TACTS range. "TACTS control, Bagman One and Two on station at Telegraph Pass and holding. Ready for weapons check." Ricky called over the radio.

"Bagman One and Two, TACTS pod is working. Bogeys on station, reporting ready." the TACTS range controller replied. Neil and his wingman had arrived and were ready.

"Fighters ready." Ricky replied.

"Recorders on, fight's on. Bogeys 185 degrees, 27 miles, angels 20 heading 015 degrees." the controller said.

Ricky and J.J. both confirmed the bogeys on their APG-79 AESA radars. Ricky looked over and gave J.J. hand signals to maintain radio silence. The message spelled out by the hand signals was, "Scud, fighters steady 172, take angels 26."

"Roger that." J.J. replied with a single hand signal. Both fighters turned to an intercept heading of 172 degrees and started climbing to 26,000 feet.

"Woody and Scud are 25 miles, bearing 005, angels 24 climbing." Neil said to his wingman Lieutenant Tommie "Taco" Thomas on the radio.

Lieutenant Thomas confirmed that contact on his Super Hornet radar. "Roger that Nailgun, suggest an intercept heading of 005, and take angels 28."

"Nailgun turning to 005, climbing to angels 28." Neil replied.

"I concur. Let's go make these guys our bitches." Taco said uncharacteristically. He usually didn't use prison lingo, but this was a simulated "fight to the death" so he was talking himself into it as much as he was trying to inspire Neil to fly his best. They knew Ricky and J.J. were good. They had to be better today. The two F/A-18s started their turn to a heading of 005 degrees and began their climb.

Ricky and J.J. had their radio tuned to the tactical frequency and heard Nailgun talking to Taco. Ricky gave J.J. several more hand signals to confirm that J.J. had heard what he heard and that the bogeys would be coming into the merge on a heading of 005. That information assisted both of them in directing their gazes so as to make visual contact as early as possible. "The guy you don't see will kill you."

legendary Air Force ace Robin Olds was fond of saying. Both Ricky and J.J. checked over their shoulders looking for a wild card bogey just to make sure this wasn't a sucker fight and Nailgun and Taco did not bring a friend or two. Nothing. Back to scanning the sky in front of them looking for the bogeys. The rate of closure was about 800 knots, so the 27 miles separation between the fighters would only take about 2 minutes to eat up.

Both Ricky and J.J. designated the bogeys on their radars using their cursor control switches, and switched into auto-track mode to track the bogeys while scanning for new threats. Within about 55 seconds, the bogeys were 2 miles away. Ricky and J.J. had spotted them at about 5 miles and Ricky, who had seen them first gave J.J. hand signals for "two bogeys, line abreast, combat spread, 5 miles." J.J. gave his confirmation by a thumbs up sign. Ricky then gave J.J. several more hand signals for "Bracket attack. Go to combat spread, line abreast" and pointing in the direction of the two jets flown by Neil "Nailgun" McAble and Tommie "Taco" Thomas. J.J. acknowledged the call for a pincer attack plan and flew his jet out to combat spread position about a mile from Ricky and 1500 feet above him on the "perch". This position allowed J.J. to defend Ricky if the bogeys attacked Ricky in a 2 v 1 move.

Both Ricky and J.J. looked back over their shoulders checking for wild cards. Nothing.

Section 2 v 2 dogfighting is hairy because each pilot has a huge workload including keeping track of the positions and maneuvers of three other aircraft for starters, and providing visual protection for a wingman as well as looking out for new bogeys entering the fray. Ricky and J.J. had previously discussed the problem and decided to handle it by division of labor. Ricky was to engage the trailing bogey and keep track of J.J. and provide visual cover for him. J.J. was to keep track of the other bogey and keep him off Ricky by engaging him if necessary, and also look for new bogeys entering the fight. There are many tasks for each pilot engaged in a 2 v 2 section dogfight, and so each pilot devotes less time to each task and may prioritize them in his head. Eventually the workload gets so high and the tasks are so difficult, the pilot fixates on one task and that is usually the end of him. He gets shot down by another fighter he does not have in sight. Ricky and J.J.'s plan was to cause pilot overload in Neil's section by extending the engagement until fixation occurred and Neil or Taco made a mistake and "died" because of it. Neil and Taco had the same plan. There were no differences between the capabilities or weapon systems of the four F/A-18 Super Hornets in the fight. It would all be mental. All that was to go out the window now. The pincer attack was an attack on both bogeys simultaneously, with J.J. attacking the jet farthest from him in the line abreast formation of the bogey and Ricky doing the same.

Just then, Ricky and J.J., flying toward the merge in combat spread, heard Nailgun and Taco each call "Fox-3" indicating they had each just simulated firing a radar guided AMRAAM missile at Ricky and J.J.. Per their pre-arranged plan, Ricky and J.J. broke hard, each in opposite directions before the merge, and each launched flares and chaff countermeasures. This defeated the missiles and the TACTS controller called "Good break. Continue." indicating the missiles had not scored kills and the fight was still on.

Now Ricky and J.J. turned back in toward Neil "Nailgun" McAble and Tommie "Taco" Thomas in their bracket or pincer attack maneuver. Ricky thought to himself, "Dudes, you just wasted those missiles. You were inside minimum firing range for those AMRAAMs." J.J. was thinking the same thing. Even though AMRAAMs can be fired in visual range, you can still be too close when you fire them such that their terminal guidance systems don't have time to lock on or they just lock on when the defender does a break and launches countermeasure flares and chaff to confuse the missile's on-board radar. That is exactly what Ricky and J.J. had done, and the missiles were defeated easily.

By now Ricky and J.J. had achieved some lateral separation and were in good position to turn in behind Nailgun and Taco to get in their cone of control, i.e., their rear quadrants. The bracket maneuver was a good move, because now each of Ricky and J.J. had a full view of both bogeys and their wingmen out of one side of their planes while Nailgun and Taco each had to look both ways to get the full picture of what was happening in the engagement.

Seeing the bracket move, Neil and Tommie, perceiving the nearest jet to be the biggest threat, made defensive breaks away from each other and toward Ricky and J.J.'s jets to spoil a guns solution. This move played right into the hands of Ricky and J.J. because they were not attacking the bogey closest to them but instead were attacking the bogey farthest from them. That bogey had just turned away from each of them thereby putting each of Ricky and J.J. in the cone of control behind Neil and Tommie's jets, respectively. Ricky got tone on his Sidewinder indicating the infrared heat seeking missile had acquired and was tracking its target, so Ricky radioed "Fox-2" indicating a simulated AIM-9 Sidewinder missile shot against Taco's jet. J.J. did the same thing launching a simulated Sidewinder toward Neil's jet. Narrowly averting a midair as Ricky and J.J. closed on each other in their bracket pincer attack, they each breathed a sigh of relief to the extent one could do that while pulling 6 Gs in their turns.

Hearing the Fox- 2 radio calls, Neil and Tommie each did a hard break turn at the last second and launched flares and chaff countermeasures. It worked. The simulated Sidewinders were defeated and flew off into oblivion.

"Good break. Continue." the TACTS controller radioed. The fight was still raging on.

Nailgun and Taco now realized they each had a different jet on their tail than they thought was going to be the case. Each did a hard defensive break turn to spoil a guns solution and try to reverse the situation. Taco did a hard break turn to the left. Neil did a hard break turn to the right. That hard break turn by each of Neil and Tommie depleted their specific energy by bleeding off airspeed.

Ricky's airspeed was now higher than Taco's, and Ricky was now in danger of overshooting Taco as a result. Ricky chose to avoid the overrun and bank his airspeed as potential energy with a high Yo Yo maneuver. He pulled the nose up hard, rolled left to put his lift vector on Taco's jet in a pure pursuit angle to attempt to get another missile lock on Taco. The high Yo Yo allowed Ricky to turn inside of Taco's turn, because the sharp climb had drastically slowed Ricky's airspeed down to corner speed, the speed at which his maximum turn rate could be achieved. This also put him in Taco's bubble between Taco's post and his flight path. Since Taco was already at his maximum G load, he could not turn any tighter and Ricky was, for the moment, safe. The climb phase of the high Yo Yo's maneuver also put Ricky's jet above Taco's jet and in the sun making it harder for Taco to see him. The sudden decrease in Ricky's airspeed caused by the high Yo Yo's climb component also slowed the closure rate so Ricky could stay in missile range. Ricky checked his HUD and saw that he was still in range for a Sidewinder shot and switched to AIM-9 Sidewinder. He immediately heard the Sidewinder growl in his headset indicating it had acquired the target and was tracking. Ricky called "Fox-2" on the radio to simulate the Sidewinder launch but did not actually mash the fire button.

Hearing the radio call, Taco reversed his turn in a hard break to the right and launched flares and chaff countermeasures. It worked again, defeating the simulated Sidewinder missile.

"Good break. Continue." the TACTS controller called indicating the missile had been defeated and the fight was still on.

"Shit, this guy is good." Ricky thought to himself. But then he realized that Taco had to have depleted much of his airspeed in the two hard break turns. Ricky was higher than Taco and therefore had much potential energy in the altitude bank and he was still in the sun so Taco may not even have spotted him yet. He decided to do a "Swoop" move otherwise known as a high side guns pass. Ricky rolled inverted and pulled back on the stick to start a powered dive toward Taco's rear quadrant and put his nose in lead pursuit for a guns pass. Ricky selected zone 5 burner and was instantly screaming down on Taco. Not yet seeing him, he kept flying his left turn. Ricky put his guns pipper on him and called "Guns, guns." on the radio. Anticipating that Taco would hear the guns call and make a reversal into a right break turn, Ricky put his pipper where he thought Taco would be when he made is break turn to the right and called "Guns, guns." again two seconds later after his first burst. Taco, who was late seeing Ricky coming out the sun, did in fact make a break turn to the right when he heard the first guns call and flew right into the second "fusilade" of imaginary cannon shells.

"Good shot Woody. Sorry Taco, but the computer says you are dead. Continue." the TACTS range controller called. Taco rolled out of the fight, and Ricky then turned his attention to Neil and J.J.'s dogfight. Ricky zoom climbed to bank his excessive airspeed as potential energy and turned toward Neil and J.J. who were locked in a horizontal scissors stalemate.

Just as Ricky found them, he saw Neil throw his speed brakes, flaps and gear out suddenly and pitched his nose up violently. That was all the drag Neil had available to him. Throwing out all those drag inducing elements plus the rapid pitch up caused an extremely rapid deceleration of Neils's jet and caught J.J. by surprise. As a result, J.J. overshot Neil on the next criss-cross. Throwing the jet's landing gear out at 400 knots is not recommended, and, as a result, Neil's landing gear doors ripped off both the nose and main gear wells and flew clear of the plane. However, the beefy landing gear designed for controlled crashes on carriers came down into the 400 knot slipstream without even a hiccup.

After J.J. overshot him, Neil slammed the gear and flaps handles into the retract positions and pulled his speed breaks in while simultaneously turning in on J.J.'s tail. Neil now had J.J. right where he wanted him. The much slower airspeed for Neil's jet as a result of the maneuver caused Neil's jet to have sharply higher turn rate than J.J.'s jet. The slower fighter always wins the horizontal scissors because of its ability to turn tighter than the faster fighter. This gave Neil an immediate angular advantage allowing him to turn tighter than J.J. in the horizontal scissors and get behind him. Neil now had a choice of either a lead pursuit position for a guns snapshot or for a Sidewinder shot.

It all happened so fast, J.J. was not able to copy Neil's move and, the "fatal" result was a drastic overshoot putting Neil on his six, exactly where you don't want to see a bogey. J.J. unloaded the G forces on his jet and tried to dive straight down in a desperate move to extend, gain some separation and get out of guns range. Unfortunately for J.J., it was too little, too late. Before Ricky could get to them and put Neil on the defensive, Neil had caught up with J.J.'s diving jet and had a guns solution on him and called "Guns, guns."

And just like that, J.J. was "dead".

"Good shot Nailgun. Scud is dead. Knock it off." the TACTS range controller called. That was fighter lingo for announcing the fight was over.

"Hoo-Ya! Nothin' but net." Nailgun crowed into his radio to nobody in particular. Neil was not normally an arrogant or boastful guy, but the thrill of the victory just kind of welled up in his chest and he let out an uncharacteristic burst of enthusiasm. "I love this job." he said, also to nobody in particular.

"Well I am glad you are on our side at least. Mazeltov." Ricky said congratulating Neil on a fight well fought. Ricky was crushed that he had let his wingman get killed on his watch. But it was a good lesson for all.

All jets were bingo and needed to land to refuel. They all joined up in echelon formation and headed for NAS Yuma to land, refuel and debrief.

After they taxied in and shut down, the crew members chocked them as they climbed down their ladders into the 110 degree blast furnace of summer in Yuma, Arizona. They walked into the debriefing TACTS room together. They were quiet for the walk.

They all grabbed a tall glass of ice water. They were drenched in sweat from the heat and the constant exertion of pulling Gs and having to do their flex and clench maneuver to assist their G suits from keeping them from blacking out.

"Congratulations Woody. You really snookered me. I did not expect that second burst out in front of my reverse break turn. How did you know I was going to break right when you were on my left side and I was breaking left in front of you?" Taco said.

"Just lucky. The gouge on you is that you do the unexpected so I just guessed and happened to be right." Ricky replied humbly.

"Nicely done my friend. Good to know." Taco said extending his hand.

J.J. walked up to Neil smiling and said, "I knew you were reckless, but I did not know you were crazy. That was so MacGuyver."

"What does that mean? Neil asked.

"Crazy? Its an adjective."

"No dipshit. MacGuyver." Neil said smiling.

"Oh. It means completely, insanely unbelievable. Who throws their gear and flaps out at 400 knots. Speed brakes maybe, but 400 knots is about 220 knots above your max flap and gear extension speeds." J.J. said with a smile.

"Yeah, my squadron maintenance officer is going to be really pissed at me. Oh wait, I am the squadron maintenance officer. I think there was a malfunction in my systems, and the gear got accidently deployed." Neil smiled.

"Duly noted." J.J. said. "I will watch for that malfunction."

NAILGUN EXPLAINS HIS MOVE USING KOBAYASHI MARU ANALOGY

"In my defense, Captain Kirk taught me that move, well indirectly that is. *Kobayashi Maru.* It was a test of cadet ingenuity at the Starfleet Academy in dealing with a no-win situation. Kirk got himself out by thinking outside the box and re-defining the problem. Actually, on his third attempt at the problem, he surreptitiously re-programmed the simulator to make the Klingon ships "afraid of **the** *Captain Kirk.*" In other words, he cheated but was given a commendation for original thinking. More pertinent, it was actually a Cunningham move. Commander Randall Cunningham, United State Navy pulled that move in his F-4 to take out one of North Vietnam's best MIG-17 pilots after a three minute dogfight. That was an eternity in dogfight years. Cunningham was the Navy's biggest fighter ace in Vietnam. He actually first used that move at TOPGUN to defeat his instructor. Cunningham and the MIG pilot were locked in a vertical rolling scissors then went over the top and turned it into a horizontal scissors. The MIG pilot had achieved an angular advantage in the horizontal scissor because of the better maneuverability of the smaller MIG 17 airframe compared to the heavy, overpowered F-4. Just as he was about to die, Commander Cunningham threw his speed brakes and flaps out, pitched his nose up, rapidly decelerated and the MIG pilot flew right by him, no doubt with a surprised look in his slanted little eyes. Kind of like the look you had on your face when you flew by me. Anyway, Commander Cunningham smoked the little commie bastard with a Sidewinder. Hoo-Yah. God bless America." Neil said smiling.

"Fuck. I didn't get the memo. Nicely done." J.J. said with a laugh extending his hand in congratulation. "I will add that one to my scrap book of major fuck ups of which there have been more than a few. Would not want to be on your ramp when your crew chief sees how badly you ripped up his bird."

"Ah yes, that is going to be a problem. But I would rather be in the doghouse than dead." Neil said. In fact, Neil got a letter of reprimand in his file for pulling that stunt and ripping the gear doors off a perfectly good F/A-18F Super Hornet just to win a practice dogfight. But his commanding officer also recommended he be sent to TOPGUN in the same letter .

The TACTS debrief was more or less an afterthought. Everybody knew what had happened and what they had done wrong and what they had done right.

HAPPY HOUR AT YUMA O CLUB

Ricky looked over at J.J. and Neil and Taco and said "Lets go dudes. It is happy hour somewhere. They went to the O Club and got a cold one and sat down to chat for awhile. They had to hold it down to one because they all had to fly home later that afternoon.

About 4 PM, J.J.'s cell phone rang. It was Carmen. "How are you doing J.J.? It's Carmen."

"Better now baby. What's shaking with you Carmen?" J.J. said looking at Ricky and Neil and Taco and winking at them.

RICKY, JJ, CARMEN AND NEIL GET THEIR SQUADRON ASSIGNMENTS AFTER RAG TRAINING

"Oh I just called to find out you little boys were doing out there without any adult supervision. Finished my RAG training. They are sending me to the Moon Dogs at MCAS Cherry Point. How about you boys?" Carmen inquired.

"We have not received our orders yet, but we think they are going to send me and Ricky to the Black Knights out of MCAS Miramar and Neil to the Navy's Black Knights at NAS LeMoore. Neil just smoked me in a practice dogfight this afternoon in a classic out-of-the-box move you would have been proud of. We are all sitting at Yuma in the O club having a beer and shooting the shit right now. I am glad you called." J.J. said.

"Seriously? Never send a boy to do a woman's job. What did he pull on you." Carmen asked.

"I had him in a guns solution out of a horizontal scissors, then the crazy bastard did a Cunningham – he pulled his nose up, chopped the throttle, threw out his speed brakes and flaps and went even beyond Cunningham by dropping his gear at 400 knots. I flew right by him and he blew me away with guns. Blew the gear doors right off his plane. His crew chief and CO are going to be really pissed." J.J. said winking at Neil. J.J. was right about that. They were very pissed.

"Where was Ricky during all this? Oh he had just blown up Taco in a classic Ricky move and was late getting to my aid." J.J. said glaring with mock disgust at Ricky." Ricky just smiled sheepishly.

"Interesting. Stick the needle in Ricky for me. That was kind of a big fuck up." Carmen said laughing.

"Oh he knows and he knows he owes me big. I will make him pay later when I get him out on the sand for some volleyball." J.J. said.

"Who is Taco and how did Ricky smoke him?" Carmen asked.

"Taco is Neil's wingman. Handsome dude from Nebraska. He's a Husker." J.J. said winking at Taco. "Ricky snookered him by loosing a cannon burst on him while in lead pursuit on a left break turn, and then, anticipating he would reverse his turn and break right, Ricky set up another burst where he thought Taco would be if he did what Ricky thought he would do, and he did. Flew right into the second barrage according to the TACTS computer." J.J. explained.

"Nice. That Ricky is a clever boy, boy being the operative word there." Carmen said.

"You coming out to visit us?" J.J. inquired.

"Can't right now. Too busy, but soon I hope." Carmen said with disappointment. "I miss you boys big time."

"We miss you too gorgeous. We will call you later sometime soon and make a plan. Right now we gotta fly these jets home. Ciao." J.J. said hanging up.

"How did she sound?" Ricky said.

"She said she misses us big time." J.J. replied.

"I miss that silly little shit too. How about you guys?"

"Yeah, I miss her." J.J. said.

"Me too." Neil said. You would love her Taco.

"I am sure I would. If you boys like her that much, I am sure I would too." Taco said.

RICKY AND JJ TO VMFA(AW)-314 Black Knights at MCAS Miramar- They would deploy with U.S. Carrier Strike Group One, CVN-70, on the USS Carl Vinson based at NAS North Island. Neil and Taco to the VFA-154 Black Knights based at NAS Lemoore and CVN-76, USS Ronald Regan.

Ricky and J.J. finished their RAG training and, as J.J. had predicted, they got orders to report to the Marine Fighter Attack Squadron (All Weather) VMFA(AW)-314 Black Knights at MCAS Miramar of the 3rd Marine Air Wing. They would deploy with U.S. Carrier Strike Group One, CVN-70, on the USS Carl Vinson based at NAS North Island. Neil finished his RAG training at NAS LeMoore and he and Taco got orders to report to the VFA-154 Black Knights based at NAS Lemoore. They would deploy on CVN-76, USS Ronald Regan with Carrier Strike Group Seven, and also based at NAS North Island in San Diego.

Carmen finished her RAG training and received orders to report to the Marine Tactical Electronic Warfare Squadron MMAQ-3 Moon Dogs flying the F-35B STOL Lightning Joint Strike Fighter out of MCAS Cherry Point, North Carolina of the 2nd Marine Air Wing. Although primarily land based, if she needed to go to sea to support the 2nd Marine Division operations out of Camp Lejeune, she would deploy with U.S. Carrier Strike Group 12, on CVN-65, the USS Enterprise out of Norfolk, Virginia. It was May, two years before the war with China would start, but they did not know that.

CHAPTER 8

TOP GUN - FALLON, NEVADA AND STRIKE FIGHTER TACTICS INSTRUCTION

NOVEMBER 15, ONE YEAR BEFORE THE WAR

Ricky, J.J., Neil and Carmen had all excelled in the squadrons in their first year of flying, and had rapidly moved to the top of their respective fighter pilot wolfpack ladders. Being duly impressed by the newbies skill and panache, their commanding officers had ordered them to report to the Naval Strike and Air Warfare Center at NAS Fallon, Nevada to attend the Strike Fighter Tactic Instructor (SFTI) program. The SFTI program was the modern day equivalent of what was, until 1996, the TOPGUN Navy Fighter Weapons School. The school used to be based at NAS Miramar which is now MCAS Miramar, but was moved to Fallon in the base re-alignment and closure program.

Carrier Air Wing level training, of which SFTI is a part, is conducted at NAS Fallon with the adversary forces flying F-16s, F/A-18s and F-5s. Carrier Air Wing level training is analagous to the Air Force Red Flag program and involves Fleet Squadrons conducting mock combat against dissimilar airplanes. Navy and Marine Corp adversary squadrons were formed at NAS Fallon, NAS Oceana, NAS Lemoore, MCAS Yuma and NAS Key West to provide adversary forces for fleet pilots to train against. The adversaries initially flew the A-4 Skyhawk and later added the F-5E/F. Later, specially built F-16Ns were added as were F-14s and F/A-18s.

VIETNAM KILL RATIO

During the Vietnam War, the exact kill ratio between the F-4 Phantom and the lighter, smaller MIG-21 remains classified. However, one report from Robin Old's autobiography indicates U.S. pilots were achieving only a 2:1 kill ratio against the MIGs. The MIG-21 turned out to be a fearsome adversary against the F-4 Phantoms and F-105 Thunderchiefs flown by Air Force, Navy and Marine Corps pilots during Vietnam. Another report by Annie Jacobsen, a journalist for the LA Times, historian and author of *Area 51: The Uncensored History* indicates that the kill ratio was actually 9:1 in favor of the MIG-21.

The Pentagon brass deemed this unacceptably low and ordered the Navy and Air Force to do something about it. The Air Force chose to focus on technical issues and retrofitted their jets with radar jamming pods and machine gun pods mounted on the belly. Inexplicably, the designers of the F-4 Phantom originally left out a gun and depended solely upon missiles. The assumption was that future dogfights would all take place at long range and supersonic speeds. This turned out to be a mistake, and it was found by the Air Force that dogfights almost never occurred at supersonic speeds and long range and that most were subsonic and at close range. To succeed in such a dogfight, a jet needed a gun. So that is what the Air Force focussed upon.

Unfortunately, this was the wrong focus, and the Air Force kill ratio actually dropped from 2:1 to 1:1 and never really improved that much even after the Pentagon ordered an improvement.

In stark contrast, the Navy chose to focus on training, and in 1969 established the Fighter Weapons School popularly known at TOPGUN at NAS Miramar.

ESTABLISHMENT OF TOPGUN

Establishment of TOPGUN turned out to be an outstanding move and improved the Navy's Vietnam kill ratio first to 13:1 and, subsequently, to 22:1. According to Annie Jacobsen's book on the history of Area 51, the establishment of TOPGUN and the syllabus taught there was greatly aided by the reverse engineering at Area 51 of a MIG-21 obtained by Israel from an Iranian defector. The engineers did not learn the secret of the MIG-21's stunning success against the bigger, more powerful, more sophisticated F-4 by taking it apart and re-assembling it. The vast majority of the progress was made in actually flying the MIG-21 in mock combat missions against the F-4 and other American fighters of the time. It was learned that the way to fight a MIG-21 was to sneak up on it and smoke it before it had a chance to react to your presence. Once the MIG pilot knew you were there, you were toast. There were no second chances against a MIG-21. The MIG-21 was highly maneuverable, because it was very light compared to the F-4. The F-4 weighed 38% more than a MIG-21. The communists built their fighters for close-in dogfighting, a concept that the Pentagon and American aircraft designers had declared dead at the end of World War II and had been proven wrong in each war since. The Pentagon and American aircraft designers were sure that all air-to-air combat in the future would be beyond visual range combat using missiles. How else can one explain the lack of guns in the original F-4 design. But visual range dogfights have been a part of every war since World War II. As a result, lighter, more maneuverable fighters excel in these situations. What the TOPGUN instructors learned in their mock dogfights against the MIG-21 at Area 51 became a part of the TOPGUN syllabus and increased the effectiveness of Navy and Marine fighter pilots in Vietnam greatly.

In response to their dismal performance in Vietnam, the Air Force, eyeing the success of the Navy and Marine Corps in Vietnam with envy after the formation of the TOPGUN school, decided in 1975 that they would do the same thing. The Red Flag mock air battle conducted four times per year at Nellis Air Force Base outside Nevada was the result.

It was 0700 on Monday morning, first class of the day in week four of the TOPGUN program at NAS Fallon, Nevada. Van Halen's *Jump* was blasting on the boom box. That was how all the TOPGUN classes were structured. Rock was played before the class started and during the breaks. Ricky thought it was odd for such a serious business, but that was how it had always been at TOPGUN. Who was he to question tradition. Fighter pilots were a hot-blooded bunch of young studs, and that is what they liked.

TOPGUN CLASS ABOUT THE FLANKERS AND J-20

The class was about Chinese and Russian adversary jet capabilities today. The planes of the day were the Russian Sukhoi Su-27 Flanker, the Su-30 MKK Chinese version called the Flanker-G and the Su-30MK2 navalized Flanker-G of which the Chinese had purchased a large number. Also on the menu were the Chinese J-11 copycat Flankers and the new Chinese J-20 Stealth fighter first flown in 2011.

Su-30MKK Flanker-G is a version of its Russian ancestor the Su-27 Flanker which Russia sold to the Chinese and several other countries. The Su-30MK2 is a navalized Flanker-G which is capable of flying off aircraft carriers, and which has had its avionics upgraded to support anti-ship missiles. The MK2 has an entirely new command, control, communications, computers, intelligence, surveillance, target acquisition and reconnaissance system. It also has a new N001VEP fire-control radar specifically modified to launch the NATO designated

Kh-17A Kryption-A long-range, supersonic anti-ship missile. Both Su-30 versions can deliver a range of precision guided munitions such as the Kh-29 and Kh-59 air-to-surface missiles, the Kh-31P anti-radiation missile to take out radar sites and TV-guided bombs. Both aircraft carry the NATO designated AA-12 Adder (Vympel R-77) active radar-homing medium range air-to-air missile affectionately called the AMRAAMski. Both airplanes have sophisticated electronic countermeasures systems and C4ISR suites for target acquisition and weapon guidance.

The Su-27 Flanker is considered one of the most capable 4th generation fighters in the world. The Su-30MKK and MK2 Flankers inherited the superior aerodynamic performance from its ancestor Su-27, outperforming most Western designed fighter aircraft in close-in air combat. This makes the Su-30MKK and MK2 formidable foes with a combat radius of 1,600 kilometers, and 2,600 kilometers with one air-to-air refueling. Both the Su-27 Flanker and the Su-30 Flanker, when combined with AWACs aircraft, are comparable to the American F-15 air superiority fighter, but are superior in many respects. Both are much less expensive costing only about 33-53 million dollars per copy. They are tough Russian fighters designed to operate in adverse conditions.

Both Chinese Su-30MKK and MK2 Flankers are twin-engine, two-seat, dual-role fighters for all-weather, air-to-air and air-to-surface engagements on deep interdiction missions and fleet defense. The ancestor Su-27 Flanker is a single-seat, twin-engine Mach-2 class fourth generation fighter.

Marine Captain Jack "Icepick" Jacoby strode briskly into the room and shut off the boom box. "Icepick" got his callsign from his fondness for a happy hour challenge game of pulling out an icepick from his backpack and spreading out the fingers of his left handing and stabbing between them with the icepick in his right hand as fast as he could without stabbing his fingers. The challenge was to see who could stab the fastest without injuring themselves. The class snapped to attention. Captain Jacoby began his lecture.

TOP GUN LECTURE BY ICEPICK

"As you were. I am Captain Jack Jacoby, USMC, call sign Icepick. Today were are going to talk about the Su-27, SU-30MKK and Su-30MK2 Flankers, the Chinese copies of them, and the Chinese J-20 Stealth jet. Pay attention. What you learn here today could save your life later for reasons I will explain. I have sourced much of the information I will present to you today from the RAND Corporation report entitled *Air Combat, Past, Present and Future* and from various Air Power Australia papers and Wikipedia articles.

As some of you may know, there has been a raging controversy over the suitability of the F-35 Lightening and our F/A-18s as air superiority fighters versus Russian-made Flankers. This controversy is based upon a couple of studies by think tanks. The F-35 flap is based upon a Rand Corporation white paper predicting the outcome of a battle between the U.S. and China over the fate of Taiwan. In this fictional battle, 5 regiments of Flankers were pitted against a smaller number of F-22s and F-35s. The F/A-18 flap is based upon an Air Power Australia white paper comparing the F/A-18E/F Super Hornets to the Flankers. This paper concluded the Flankers were much better planes. Air Power Australia is Australia's RAND think tank.

The reason that there were a smaller number of F-22s and F-35s in the RAND scenario was that the closest bases the U.S. had were Kadena on Okinawa and Anderson AFB on Guam, so only a smaller number of U.S. sorties could be generated. U.S. carriers were assumed to be held at bay outside the battle by the threat of Chinese Anti Ship Ballistic Missiles. In contrast, the People's Liberation Army Air Force, aka, the PLAAF, has 27 bases within 500 nautical miles of Taiwan.

You will learn today that the RAND study said an F-35 could not out-run, out-turn or out-climb a Flanker, and that the Super Hornet is in all ways aerodynamically inferior to the Flanker. I am here to tell you that the situation is not nearly as bad as the experts make it out to be. But if I am wrong, you need to heed the advice of the experts at RAND and Air Power Australia and assume it is correct and fly accordingly. Regardless of who is right, if you fly intelligently, you have a good chance at survival in a furball with Flankers.

In the Air Power Australia white paper comparing the F/A-18E/F Super Hornet against the Flankers, the following conclusion was drawn:

> "the Flanker in all current variants kinematically outclasses the Super Hornet in all high performance flight regimes. The only near term advantage the latest Super Hornets have over legacy Flanker variants is in the APG-79 AESA and radar signature reduction features, and that advantage that will not last long given highly active ongoing Russian development effort in these areas. The supercruising AF-41F engine upgrade to the Flankers will further widen the performance gap in favour of the Flanker. What this means is that post-2010, the Super Hornet is uncompetitive against advanced Flankers in beyond visual range combat, as it is now uncompetitive in close combat."

The Aussies give the Flanker the edge in firepower, speed, raw agility, range and maneuver over the Super Hornet.

The Su-27 through Su-30 Flankers sit roughly in the same class as the Air Force's premier dogfighter, the F-15 Eagle in terms of thrust/weight ratio and weight. Flanker variants weight between 37,240 – 40,800 pounds with internal fuel capacities of 20,750 – 22,600 pounds. With the thrust of the AL-31F engine in the earlier Flankers, the Aussies conclude the Super Hornet cannot compete with any Flanker variant. Some Flankers still have the AL-31F engine which delivers 27,000 to 32,000 pounds of thrust each at sea level. This AL-31F engine outperforms the F414 engine of the Super Hornet which only delievers 20,700 pounds of sea level thrust in afterburner. In terms of supersonic speed, supersonic and subsonic acceleration and climb performance the Super Hornet cannot compete with any Flanker variant. High speed turning performance, where thrust is limited, also goes to the Flanker as does supersonic maneuver ability according to the Aussies. The Super Hornet is severely handicapped by its lower combat thrust to weight ratio and hybrid wing planform which is not optimized for dog fighting but for a multi-role air combat and ground attack platform.

One area where the Super Hornet may be competitive with the Flanker is near-stall, low-speed, high-alpha flight. The Super Hornet's strakes and wing work well and its advanced fly-by-wire flight controls perform superbly in this low speed arena. This is not a regime favored by combat pilots and is thus not considered pertinent by the Aussies. I think you should sit up and take notice of this small advantage.

Unfortunately, most Flankers today have the newer AL-41F engine. Each AL-41F produces 40,000 pounds of sea level static thrust. Obviously this magnifies our disadvantage in the speed, acceleration and climb performance arenas.

With the AL-41F engine, the Flanker can supercruise, and, as you know, speed is life. With the AL-41F, the Flanker's superiority in kinematic performance against the Super Hornet grows considerably in all flight regimes.

The wing loading of the Super Hornet is actually only slightly higher than the Flanker, but the lower thrust/weight ratio of the Super Hornet means it will bleed energy faster in a turning fight than the Flanker. The Super Hornet does not have the thrust to make up the energy lost in the turn whereas the Flanker does.

The lower thrust/weight ratio of the Super Hornet pretty much dooms the Hornet in a dogfight started with no energy advantage to either jet. Further, the canard sporting Flankers like the Su-30MKI and the Su-30MKK and MK2 variants sold to India and China will have even better high alpha trim drag and pitch rates.

Fuel load is also critical. The Flanker's huge airframe allows it to carry much more internal fuel than the Super Hornet. This gives the Flanker a larger combat radius than the Super Hornet even when the Hornet is carrying external tanks. There is significant drag advantage to having aerodynamically clean internal fuel tanks as compared to the external fuel tanks the Super Hornet has to use for similar fuel load.

The Su-30 and Su-30MK2 Flankers also have thrust vectoring, so they can turn on a dime like the F-22 Raptor. Here, however, is your single advantage in the aerodynamics arena over the Flankers. The Su-30 and Su-30MK2 Flanker thrust vectoring has the tail nozzles moving on two slanted axes forming a V configuration when looked at from the tail of the airplane. This means when an Su-30 or Su-30MK2 Flanker is in a turning fight and is in a banked turn, if the pilot get greedy and uses thrust vectoring to increase his rate of turn, there is a major down thrust force vector pushing down the rear of his jet. That shoves his tail toward the ground and pushes the entire planform of the airframe into the wind like a gigantic speed brake. This dissipates most of his kinetic energy and give you a brief moment of advantage.

Therefore, if you are caught by a Su-30 and Su-30MK2 Flanker at the same altitude, engage him in a one circle fight, two circle fight or horizontal scissors turning fight. Once so engaged, watch his plane carefully. As soon as you see water vapor condense over the top of his wings or his tail drop from use of thrust vectoring, pull up immediately into a ballistic climb. He will not have sufficient kinetic energy to follow you up. As soon as you get enough vertical separation, do a rudder reversal or go over the top in a loop, dive down and gun him or give him a heater shot since he almost certainly will have his burner on. This move will blow him out of the sky. If you do not get this opportunity, you are toast unless you have a buddy with you in another jet to take him out while he tries to take you out.

My calculations at least as to wing loading and weight-to-thrust ratio lead me to believe that the situation is not as bad as Air Power

Australia makes it out to be at least in terms of close combat. But since it is your lives on the line out there, I am going to just call it as I see it and tell you what other experts are saying. We will tell you what we think you should do based upon our mock air battles with Flankers at Area 51 and against Indian Su-30MKI Flankers at Red Flag. Feel free to develop your own tactics.

It won't be the first time pilots in the fleet have developed their own tactics, nor will it be the first time U.S. planes were aerodynamically inferior to the enemy's planes. At Guadalcanal in World War II, Marine pilot Joe Foss and his Cactus Air Force operating out of Henderson field in F4Fs were getting hammered by the more maneuverable Japanese Zeroes. In response, he adopted the thach weave tactic invented by a Navy Lieutenant named John Thach. In the Thach weave, a fighter and his wingman fly an interleaved weaving pattern, each turning toward the other and reversing the turn after the pass. Any fighter on the tail of one of them eventually winds up in the sights of the other. This adaptation of their tactics turned the tide. After adopting the Thach weave, Foss went on to shoot down 26 zeroes and maintained air superiority over the island so the Marines below were safe from air attack. Foss won the Medal of Honor for his exploits there.

With regard to the controversy over the F-35 versus the Flanker, I am biased toward believing the conclusions of the Air Power Australia and RAND studies with some reservations. A great deal of money and many careers have been pinned on the success of the F-35. When RAND called it like they saw it and gored the F-35, RAND fired the chief author of the study, probably under pressure from the Pentagon. He was their top analyst, and had a PhD in aerodynamics, I will leave it to you to decide whether that was a knucklehead move.

Everyone believes the Air Force F-22 Raptors can dominate the Flankers because of their stealth and aerodynamic superiority. Unfortunately, they carry fewer missiles than the Flankers and will be outnumbered since we only have 185 of these birds total. The clear answer is to build more F-22s and add Infrared Search and Track to them. However, F-22s cost 150 million dollars apiece, and the state of the federal budget deficit is such that building more is not possible.

To be perfectly honest, it is my belief that the U.S. should buy a manufacturing license for Flankers from the Russians and build them in the U.S. for 37 million dollars per plane like the Chinese did.

China has been investing heavily in defense. They have built ten super carriers, and have acquired about 400 Su-30MKK and Su-30MK2 Flankers from the Russians. China has also built many Flankers based upon a manufacturing license to build Su-27s in China. The Chinese have also developed their own Shenyang J-11 single-seat Sino Flanker based upon plans for the Su-27 Flanker and unlicensed technology which the Chinese stole from the Russians.

Unfortunately, as a result of the U.S. national debt situation, there will not be any more than 183 F-22 Raptors that have already been built. All the F-22s built will be flown by the Air Force and cannot land on carriers. Since that is how we project power into remote theatres, there will be no Raptors in the fight unless there are friendly bases that have not had their runways cratered near the theatre of operations.

The following slide is a quote from the Air Power Australia white paper entitled, *Will the U.S. Air Force be Annihilated in the Next War.* Let me put a slide up on the projector that projects the fate of a superior force of 450 F-35As taking on a force of 400 SU-35BM Flankers. This slide also makes a projection in the case where the Blue force is flying F-22s. No projection was made in the case the Blue force is flying Super Hornets, but assume it would be total destruction of the Super Hornet force. This conclusion follows directly from the Air Power Australia conclusions re the superiority of the Flankers over the Super Hornets in aerodynamic performance, avionics and number of air-to-air missiles carried.

> 'Suppose the U.S. Air Force deploys 450 F-35A to counter the 400 Su-35BMs. Notwithstanding the claims that the F-35 enjoys a 6:1 advantage over the Flanker,

slightly superior JSF numbers have been assigned 'just to be sure'.…The outcome is devastating for the U.S. Air Force. After only 44 missions, the U.S. Air Force's F-35A force is annihilated, with some 401 F-35As being destroyed and presumably most of the pilots killed.…How does the F-22A Raptor fare? Well, much better, as we would expect, and also as the RAND modeling predicts. Deploying fewer aircraft, 350 in this case, the Raptors quickly establish dominance of the airspace. After 31 missions of 16 aircraft flights, some 354 Su-35BMs are destroyed, and the 'Red Force' is the one annihilated.…These are truly scary results. Clearly, opting for the currently planned mix of F-22A and F-35A aircraft has serious long term strategic implications for America's future.'

Do I have your attention now?

It gets worse.

In addition, the Chinese have developed a home grown navalized Flanker designated the J-15s are believed to have been derived from stolen technology from an unfinished Russian Su-33 navalized Flanker prototype. The Chinese outfitted the J-15 with Chinese engines and weapons systems.

The Chinese Chengdu J-20 Stealth fighter is more original, but it too has an airframe that is based upon stolen F-35 technology. The J-20 is very large and heavy, and is not really designed to dogfight. It is an AWACs killer. But if a J-20 does enter a dogfight, you may never see it on your X-band radars while it is approaching. However, if you are still alive after its visit, you may see it as it leaves the area, because it is not stealthy from the rear. At least that is what experts who studied pictures of the prototype have said. We do not have a captured J-20 to test or fly against.

The J-20 is designed to make stealth approaches to AWACs airborne early warning radar planes and our aerial refueling tankers and take them out without warning using long range BVR missiles. As you know, aerial refueling tankers are the critical enabling technology for our fighters, and without them, we lose the battle. Without a sufficient number of tankers flying in support of air superiority operations, our jets run out of gas and crash into the sea or the jungle before they get back to base. Thus, we lose our assets necessary to maintain air superiority, and we lose the battle.

In the battle space, information is king. The AWACs radar planes provide our pilots with early warning of approaching bogeys and big picture radar information about the combat arena. This information is critical to our success in maintaining air superiority. Unfortunately, it does not look good for our AWACs and tankers either as you will see when we discuss the relative numbers of missiles the Flankers carry versus the number of missiles the Hornets, F-35s and F-22s can carry.

Air superiority is critical. Without it, our forces on the ground will be decimated. It is up to you to achieve air superiority to protect the fleet and any Marine divisions engaged in ground operations on the beachhead and beyond. The key advantage of air superiority was proven by the Luftwaffe in World War II blitzkriegs. The Nazis achieved air superiority over Poland, Holland, Belgium, Luxembourg, Norway and France. Defenders from those countries were crushed by the German Army in a matter of days in each case. During the Battle of Britain, neither side was able to achieve air superiority, and, as a result, the English still speak English as do we.

How do you achieve air superiority? We must destroy enemy aircraft in the sky and on the ground. We must destroy their radars and their airbases. We must defend our critical assets.

Dogfighting is critical to achieving air superiority. That is why you are here today – to learn the weaknesses and strengths of the jets you are likely to face and how to exploit them to your advantage.

Dogfighting will primarily be the province of the F/A-18 pilots among you. Destroying their radars and ground assets, and carrying out electronic countermeasures such as jamming their radars will be the job of the F-35s. In addition, protecting our AWACs and aerial refueling tankers from being shot down will primarily be the job of the F-35 pilots among you with assistance from the Hornets. However, dogfighting using the F-35 electronic countermeasure planes in support of F/A-18 operations is not unlikely. In fact, it is desirable if an F/A-18 force encounters an equal strength Flanker force. Dogfighting in an F-35 is a very bad idea if the opponent is a Flanker or J-11 unless you can get a BVR missile shot off undetected and then beat a hasty exit. If you go into a visual range furball with a Flanker in an F-35, you might as well bend over and kiss your ass goodbye. More on that later.

Three major technological developments since the 1980s have changed the air superiority calculus.

First, is the growth in sensor capabilities. These sensors include AESA radars which are hard to detect and jam, Infrared Search and Track Systems which provide all weather and night time visibility of targets on the ground and in the air, and Synthetic Aperture Radars which can provide detailed ground maps and images of targets on the ground or sea from their returns.

Second, is the development of smart munitions such as smart bombs and missiles which have many times the lethality of prior dumb munitions. Unfortunately for you, these weapons are not just the province of the U.S. any longer. Smart munitions are being exported to countries worldwide by the U.S., the EU, Israel and Russia. Russian smart munitions are equivalent to their U.S. counterparts, and China and many other countries are buying them as well as making their own.

Third, is the development of stealth technology and drones. Stealth fighters are not invisible. They are just hard to detect at certain radar frequencies such as X-band which is the 7 – 11 Ghz frequency range used by most fighter airborne radars because the dish antenna is small enough to fit in the nose.

Stealth fighters are designed to minimize reflections from X-band engagement radars. Stealth fighters are not stealthy against VHF radars having wavelengths from 1-3 meters. The dimensions and angles of the component surfaces of stealth fighters and the radar absorbing coatings on them are designed to deflect and absorb the much shorter wavelengths of X-band radars not the much longer wavelengths of VHF radars. Key fighter dimensions of our F-35 Joint Strike Fighter and F-22 Raptor are 4 to 10 times the VHF radar wavelengths which is in the heart of the Raleigh scattering regions. In simple terms, that means they can be seen. The F-35 and F-22 and Russian and Chinese stealth fighters, which are designed for low observability to X-band radars, are easily visible to VHF radars. Do not think you are invisible if you are an F-35 pilot –Carmen are you listening? VHF radars are huge antenna arrays though, so they can only be mounted on trucks, ships and fixed radar stations on the ground.

Drones are rapidly emerging as weapons of choice. The US has used Predator drones to effectively to spy on and take out adversaries. The U.S. has used the Global Hawk for theatre surveillance, more detailed surveillance of specific targets and painting targets for weapons launched from other vehicles. Global Hawks can also be used for communication relays.

Other countries have sat up and taken notice of this trend. China has developed a large array of their own drones, and their developmental work in ongoing. The Russians too have developed a variety of drones.

Many so called experts believe that manned aircraft dogfighting is a thing of the past. But they also thought the BVR was the aerial combat of the future, and they were wrong about that in a big way. The F-4 Phantom was originally released without a gun, and was only modified to add one after it became apparent in the Vietnam war that the missiles were not as reliable as the experts thought they would be.

ADVANCED INFRARED SENSORS

Advanced Infrared Sensors are also a rising concern for F-35 and other stealth jet pilots as well as Hornet pilots. Even if your plane is invisible to X-band radars, you can be seen on infrared search and track systems. The Flankers and probably the J-20 Chinese stealth jets have Infrared Search and Track systems. The J-20 is thought to have a 360 degree IRST. This, like in the F-35, gives spherical coverage of the entire battle space around the jet. We do not know for sure if the J-20 has 360 IRST yet.

The Flanker's IRST system has a blind spots directly above them and directly below the jet. A Flanker's radar also has blind spots above and below the plane. The Zhuk-MS/MSE Flanker radar has a forward scan of 170 degrees and elevation scan from −40 degrees to +56 degrees. That is important. Flanker IRST systems such as the M400 reconnaissance pod mounted between the engines and its nose mounted OL-27 IRST can see forward and back and up and down to a limited degree.

With regard to smart bombs and missiles, we will teach you F/A-18E/F and F-35 pilots how to use them to take out ground targets, and we will teach the F-35 and F/A-18 Growler pilots how to use the HARM anti-radiation missiles to home in on and destroy ground-based air defense radar arrays. Critical ground based radars that need to be destroyed will be Chinese ground controlled intercept VHF and X-band radars and Chinese VHF over-the-horizon radars. The Chicoms sometimes use over-the-horizon radars to get an initial targeting fix on aircraft carriers and other ships against which they wish to fire their anti-ship ballistic missiles.

F-35 DAS AND FLANKER BLINDSPOTS BY ICEPICK

I am going to dig a little deeper on IRST systems. All Flankers carry an Infrared Search and Track System whereas existing U.S. fighters, except for the F-35, do not. The Flanker's IRST does not however present the pilot with a 360 degree spherical view all around the aircraft like the F-35 IRST does. The latest OLS-35 Flanker IRST version is capable of tracking a typical fighter target head-on at 27 nautical miles and tail-on at 50 nautical miles. That is much farther than your eyes can see in both tail-on and head-on modes. That means the Flanker pilot will see you on his IRST before you see him visually. That is bad news for you. A Flanker will be able to see Hornets and F-35's even if you are in the clouds. That is unless you are in one of his blind spots.

IRST systems are passive so you will not be able to detect the Flanker from the operation of his IRST like you would be able to detect him when he lights off his airborne radar.

In contrast, you F/A-18 pilots won't be able to see the Flanker even if you have a FLIR infrared pod. A FLIR pod is used to identify ground targets and paint targets for laser guided bombs. It is not designed for air-to-air combat.

More importantly, a Flanker will be able to see your BVR missiles on his IRST if they are not in a blind spot. The Flanker pilot will possibly be able to defeat a missile by a last second break and deployment of flares and chaff. I say maybe because the fourth generation missiles like the AIM-9X Sidewinder with Focal Plane Array and the newest AMRAAMs are very difficult to defeat by manuever.

I cannot over emphasize the importance of the Flanker's IRST system to its combat effectiveness. You need to know its performance characteristics and its weaknesses.

The Flanker IRST has a smallish blind spot directly above the plane and a much bigger blind spot below the plane. Specifically, a Flanker OLS-37 IRST system has a plus/minus 90 degrees azimuth coverage but only +60 degrees and −15 degrees elevation coverage. You can use these blind spots to your advantage. The Su-30MK2 Flanker the Chinese have purchased has an airborne radar with a 170 degree wide view forward, but it can only scan its radar −40 degrees and + 56 degrees. So its radar also has a blind spot directly above and directly below the jet.

The moral of this part of the story is try to jump a Flanker from directly above him or, more preferably, from directly below him, and hope his AWACs has been shot down and has not warned him you are there.

You should be able to see the Flankers coming on the F/A-18 X-band radar before he sees you. The Flanker is a huge jet, and is not stealthy in the slightest. The Flanker has a radar cross section which is twice as big as that of the Super Hornet But the F/A-18 X-band radar cannot see above, below or behind the jet so you also have blind spots. Further, use of the radar also has the unintended consequence of announcing your presence to the Flankers. In addition, your X-band radar can be jammed just like you can use your superior AESA airborne radar to jam the Flanker's radar.

F-35 DAS DESCRIBED BY ICEPICK

The F-35 has a top shelf Infrared Search and Track system called the Distributed Aperture System or DAS. The DAS gives the pilot a 360 degree spherical view of the battle space around the plane. The F/A-18 Super Hornet does not have IRST. The Flanker IRST is not as good as the F-35's DAS.

The Flanker even has a slight advantage over the F-22 Raptor in that the Raptor can be seen on the Flanker's IRST. Unfortunately, the IRST system on the F-22 Raptor was deleted as the plane's weight and cost rose to unacceptable levels. That was a big mistake in my opinion.

The AWAC in your battlespace will be able to warn you about where the Flankers are if the AWAC is still operational. The Chinese love to use their stealth jets to shoot down our AWACS and re-fueling tankers. So if you have an AWAC feeding you big picture and intercept vectors, consider yourself lucky. Shooting down of the AWAC must not be allowed to happen. Information is king in modern aerial warfare. And by now, I am sure you are all familiar with the gas guzzling nature of jets. You simply must have sufficient tankers in the air to survive. So the tankers must be protected vigorously.

BVR MYTH AND LAST MOVE ADVANTAGE TO DEFEAT MISSILES

Lets talk about the notion that dogfighting is dead and all bandits will be shot down beyond visual range. With regard to BVR, consider this. Missiles, even infrared homing ones, can be defeated if the pilot is aware of them and knows what to do. Experience in Desert Storm with air-to-air missiles and infrared homing Sidewinders in particular has taught us much. The AIM-9M Sidewinder has an all aspect capability seeker head, infrared tracking to target and flare rejection countermeasure electronics. Even with all that, there is a significant last move advantage to the jet which is its prey.

The Advanced Medium Range Air to Air Missile or AMRAAM is a radar-guided missile which was developed in 1988 to replace the relatively ineffective radar guided Sparrow which failed in epic fashion in Vietnam. The intent of the AMRAAM program was to provide a higher speed missile with greater range, increased maneuverability, better resistance to electronic countermeasures such as jamming and an active radar terminal seeker head. The missile flies to an initial point sent to it by the fire control system of the launching jet and then takes over tracking with its own Doppler radar. It is a fire and forget missile, meaning you can fire it and then start evasion of any counter attacks without babysitting the missile all the way to the target with your radar -- which was a major flaw with the Sparrow and caused more than one pilot to be killed. With your fire control computer programming multiple initial points into the guidance systems of multiple AMRAAMs, you can launch multiple missiles agains multiple bandits simultaneously and then immediately start defending against the inevitable counterattacks.

The AMRAAM may also be launched at close range such that it immediately goes into terminal guidance mode with its own seeker head. This gives it greater capability to burn through defender's jamming signals without getting confused. Close range firing of a Slammer is therefore a desirable situation. The Chinese and Russians have copied these missiles, and we affectionately call them AMRAAMskis.

Air-to-air missiles can be defeated and there is a "last move advantage." But the proliferation of extremely agile heat seeking missiles for close combat coupled with the growth in Helmet Mounted Displays makes close combat with a situationally aware opponent a risky game. The effectiveness and lethality of the new fourth generation heat seeking missiles with exceptional G capability aided by thrust vectoring control makes these heaters almost impossible to defeat by maneuver. More and more, these missiles are being built with Focal Plane Array imaging seekers instead of the older scanning seekers. This makes them virtually immune to flares and jammers developed to defeat scanning seekers. Whoever takes the first shot in a close in engagement is likely to win. Still there can be a last move advantage.

Inbound missiles are a big challenge to you seeing your next birthday. This is especially true of the fourth generation heaters with focal plane arrays and the newer radar guided missiles with the active phase array antenna such as the Russian K-77M. Lets talk about how to defeat them. According to the Russians, it is impossible to defeat the K-77M, so just hope the inbound missile is not one of those. The good news is that these missiles are extremely expensive and Russia has decided to keep the technology to themselves. The Russians have decided to put them on their new T-50 stealth jet, and they refuse to sell them to the Chinese or anybody else. Lets talk about how to defeat inbound missiles.

According to Dr. Carlo Kopp of Air Power Australia, the following weaknesses in air-to-air missile design can be exploited to defeat them.

First there is propellant exhaustion. A typical air-to-air missile has a high thrust-to-weight ratio with a solid propellant giving a high impulse burn to get to cruise speed followed by a slower sustainer burn. Once the propellant burns out, the drag of the airframe rapidly slows the missile down. The missile's ability to turn very much depends on its speed. If you are lucky enough to be at max range of the missile, increase your distance and do a hard break turn into the missile at the last minute. If the rocket fuel is gone, the missile will not have the energy and speed to make a large enough course correct to hit you.

Two, there are altitude limitations on a missile's range. The missile's range at say 25,000 feet is about twice that at sea level. A missile's smoke trail will give you important clues as to its type, at what range was it launched and its flight path.

Third, there are aerodynamic performance limitations imposed by the airframe and controls. A missile will use a combination of body lift and wing lift to turn with minimum energy bleed. Rotating control surfaces on the missile's tail change the missile's attitude relative to the airflow past it. This causes wing and body lift and turn the missile. This turn rate is proportional to speed, and there will be basic turn limits at every missile speed. If you can maneuver to exceed these turn limits, the missile will miss, so break hard into a missile at the last second if you cannot defeat its lock.

Fourth, there is an inability to maneuver of thrust vectored missiles after propellant burnout. If you are lucky enough to get outside the range of a thrust vectoring missile and it burns out before it reaches you, break hard into the missile and it will miss you.

Fifth, there are three categories of guidance for missiles: command link, beam riding and homing missiles. Both command line and beam riders require exceptionally high turn rates of the missile. They can be defeated by beating the radar that is illuminating your jet and by exceeding the turn rate of the missile by a last minute break into the missile.

Homing missiles can be passive which home on infrared radiation or emissions from the target, semi-active which home on radar reflections from the target from an illuminating source or active homers which use their own on-board radar to paint the target. You can defeat many of the passive and semi-active missiles by flare countermeasures, flying up into the sun, confusing the ground-based radar with chaff or disappearing into the Doppler notch or flying into brightly lit clouds. You defeat an active radar homing missile by disappearing into its Doppler notch breaking its lock, or making a break into the missile to get out of its field of view. You can also exceed the slew rate of its seeker head or exceed the turn rate of the missile for its current speed.

Fifth, ground clutter can be used to defeat active radar homing missiles. One way to do that is to disappear using a vertical dive into the Doppler notch and into ground clutter.

Sixth, infrared noise can defeat heat seekers such as diving toward hot terrain, going ballistic toward the sun or flying behind, into or in front of brightly lit clouds.

Seventh, seeker head have motion limits or field of view limits on homing missiles. There is a maximum angle off the axis of the missile which the seeker head can slew to on any azimuth. If you can get outside the cone defined by this angle before the missile adjusts its course, you can break the lock. You would do this by a suden hard break turn into the oncoming missile. Seeker heads can only slew at a certain rate to a new azimuth. Exceed this slew rate by a sudden hard break turn into the missile and you can break its lock. If you are facing one of the Russian R-77M missiles, this will not work, and you are probably going to die. A hard break into a flight path which is orthogonal to the axis of the missile will put you in the Doppler notch and your return may get filtered out by the missile's software. Changing your aspect to a radar seeker head varies your radar cross-section and varies the strength of return the seeker sees. This can cause line of sight jitter and return scintillation which can each break lock.

Finally, missile warheads have lethal radii limitations – which are typically 20-30 feet for an air-to-air missile. The effectiveness of the warhead depends upon the performance of the fuse. The most common fuses are radio-proximity and active laser fuses. They detonate the warhead when something enters the volume of space around the missile. If you can get down to the deck right over the tree tops or buildings, etc., the vertical structures such as trees you fly over may trigger the warhead before it gets to you.

A "last move advantage" means making a hard break turn at the last minute to get outside the field of view limits of the missile's seeker head. The field of view is an imaginary cone terminating at the seeker head. If a pilot can maneuver suddenly to get outside this cone, the missile's lock is defeated and it will miss.

Lock can be broken earlier if the pilot can maneuver to exceed the seeker head's rate limit on how fast it can slew to track the target. A seeker head slews inside the nose cone to maintain a line of sight to its target. Its slew rate has limits.

The performance of your radar warning receiver and your visual awareness are important. If the pilot sees the missile coming or is warned of its approach, he immediately makes a hard break turn to put the missile on his beam. This is called flying into the Doppler notch. This causes his relative velocity to the missile to appear to the missile's guidance system to match the missile's speed. Doppler returns with relative velocity matching the missile's speed are assumed to be stationary objects and are filtered out. This is referred to as getting into the missile's Doppler notch. For a radar guided inbound missile, the break turn should be a descending turn to force the missile's radar seeker head to look down into ground clutter. For a heat seeker inbound, breaking hard upward into the sun or diving toward hot terrain or into brightly lit clouds can saturate the infrared seeker head with background IR. Finally, the defender makes a hard break turn at the last second into the missile, and deploys flares and chaff countermeasures. This can overwhelm and defeat the missile's maneuverability limit, especially if it is at maximum speed and minimum mass which it will be just before the rocket motor burns out. Once the rocket motor burns out, the missile's kinetic energy rapidly bleeds off and it may not have the capability to follow a fighter up in a ballistic break turn or in a hard break turn into the missile. Using proper tactics, the missiles can be defeated about 75% of the time. The newer heaters with focal plane arrays or radar homers with active phase arrays substantially decrease your chance of survival.

Break turns, chaff and flares are much more effective than anticipated according to the RAND study. We believe that to be the case for AMRAAMs also, especially if the target sees them coming from far away on an IRST.

Our newest generation Sidewinders and AMRAAMs have not been tested in combat against highly capable foes like the Flankers with advanced countermeasures systems. The shots against the Iraqi and Libyan MIGs in the desert wars were mostly against much less capable jets many of which did not even have operative electronic warfare suites and countermeasures systems.

That raises the question of the Flanker's IRST capability to defeat inbound missiles. One of the major disadvantages to us resulting from the presence of the M400 reconnaissance pod on the Su-30MK2 Flankers the Chinese use is the IR visibility to of our inbound BVR missiles like the AMRAAM. The Flanker M400 reconnaissance pod can see our AMRAAM missile launches 70 or more kilometers away, and the Chinese pilot may know it is an AMRAAM from its launch plume heat signature. The Chinese pilot will therefore know how the incoming missile's initial guidance and terminal guidance active radar homing systems work and from how far away it was launched. This gives him information on how much propellant will be left by the time the missile reaches him and how long it will be before his radar warning receiver will goes off when the Slammer goes into terminal guidance mode. AMRAAM 's have a large, unique thermal signature which lights up an IRST display. An AMRAAM at Mach 4 generates a 1200 degree F shock cone that can be tracked from 45 nautical miles or more away on an Su-30MK2 M400 reconnaissance pod. Modern IRST systems with integrated Quantum Well Infrared Photodetectors will greatly increase IRST performance and be able to track our AMRAAM missiles from even farther away.

All this negates the surprise factor of the AMRAAM thereby drastically reducing its effectiveness. The Chinese pilot can immediately break turn into the Doppler notch when the missile goes into terminal guidance mode and possibly break its lock. Normally, an AMRAAM is not detected by the target's radar warning receivers until the missile enters the terminal homing phase and turns its own radar on. By then, it is often too late. With his or her IRST system, the Su-30MK2 Flanker pilot can see the AMRAAM coming from far away and be ready to make a last-move break turn into the Doppler notch of the missile while simultaneously deploy flares and radar scattering chaff just as the missile enters terminal guidance phase. This will often defeat the missile. Such defensive measure will work about 75% of the time although our missiles are getting better at defeating countermeasures.

Not giving the Flanker pilot much time to defeat the missile is important. A Sidewinder shot or AMRAAM shot from within visual range will be more effective.

So much for beyond visual range kills. Don't rely on them. It is good to try to sneak up on a Su-30MK2 Flanker in his blind spotw and gun him or use a Sidewinder from short range. The M400 reconnaissance pod is mounted between the engines, has TV and thermographic cameras, an optical camera and side looking airborne radar with a range in excess of 100 kilometers. Max range for the TV and Infrared cameras is in excess of 70 kilometers. The M400 reconnaissance pod can also be used to detect targets in the blind spot behind the jet and provide targeting information for rearward firing air-to-air missiles.

The M400 reconnaissance pod on the Su-30MK2 is in addition to the OLS-27 IRST system mounted in front of the canopy on the aircraft nose. This IRST system feeds information to the Shchel-3UM helmet-mounted target designator and is controlled by the Ts-100 mission computer.

The helmet-based target designation system can be used by the Flanker pilot to designate targets just by looking at them which is similar to our F-35 helmet DAS-based synthetic vision and target designation system.

That still leaves blind spots above and below the Flanker. I cannot emphasize this enough. Attacking from directly above or directly below is your best plan other than trade your jet in for a Flanker.

FLANKER RADARS AND BVR FANTASY

A BVR kill on an Su-30MK2 is probably a fantasy. Flanker radar performance has doubled in recent years, and is continuing to improve as new and better Russian and Chinese AESA radar designs are introduced.

The Flanker is a huge airplane. It has a big airframe, so its radar antenna and radar aperture are substantially larger than the Super Hornet. This gives it longer range. The only good news on the avionics front is the Flankers do not yet have the highly sophisticated AESA radar the Super Hornet has although the Russians and Chinese are working on that. Unconfirmed sources indicate the Chinese ordered 20 Sokol AESA radars which were delivered in 2004 and installed on the Su-30MK2 Flankers. By now they probably all have these AESA radars. The range of this radar is 150 kilometers and it can track 20 targets simultaneously and engage 6. It is possible the Chinese Flankers will use the J-11B's radar which has a range of up to 350 kilometers.

Right now, even very stealthy targets like the F-35 and F-22 with radar cross sections of .0001 square meters are detectable by Flanker radars up to 10 nautical miles away. If you are a F/A-18E/F with a substantially larger radar cross-section, of, for example, 1 square meter, the Su-35 Flanker AESA radar will be able to see you up to 175 nautical miles away. You might as well call him on his cell phone and tell him you are coming.

The only good news on the avionics front is the Su-33 carrier-based Flankers have no tail warning radar. The bad news is the Chinese did not buy any of these. Only the Su-27 Flankers and Su-30 and MK variant Flankers have rearward looking radar, and the Su-35 Super Flanker has it also. Therefore, you will not be able to sneak up on a Flanker from the rear unless you are sufficiently lower or higher than him as to be in his radar blind spot.

The Su-35 Super Flanker, an improved version of the Flankers we have been talking about, has a search and acquisition air-to-air intercept radar that can search and track mainly off its nose. It does this using an AESA phased array antenna set on a 2-axis hydraulic actuator to extend its coverage angles. The Su-35 Flanker radars cannot search directly above or below or behind the plane because of limitations on movement of the antenna, but they do have a fairly extensive search sphere off the nose. China has not purchased any Su-35 Super Flankers yet.

In summary, beyond visible range kills are not to be relied upon, and it is highly likely that most of your kills will result from close in dogfights, possibly using guns or sidewinders much of the time. This puts you at a disadvantage because of the aerodynamic superiority of the Flankers in wing loading and thrust-to-weight ratio.

Experience over the years has shown that most air-to-air kills resulted when the victim never saw his attacker. As you can see that is becoming more difficult all the time in the modern optronics and avionics environment

FLANKER MISSILE TYPES AND NUMBER ADVANTAGE

It gets worse. We have a major problem with the large number of missiles it can carry compared to how many our jets can carry. A

24-aircraft Flanker regiment can lift 304 air-to-air missiles. The missile battery carried aloft by a Flanker regiments will be comprised of 240 PL-12s Sino AMRAAMs or Vympell R-77/AA-12 Adders which are equivalent to our AIM-120 AMRAAMs.

The Flanker regiment may also carry Vympel R-27/AA-10 Alamo long range BVR missiles comparable to our Sparrow. Some models of the R-27 missile require terminal guidance illumination of the target by the launching fighter. Some models have infrared seeker heads. Other models have X-band radar passive seekers and work like our HARM missiles but are air-to-air missiles. This forces the target jet to either go nose cold or turn off its radar.

The Flanker regiment will also carry 48 R-73/AA-11 Archer infrared-seeker head, short-range, air-to-air missiles equivalent to our Sidewinders. These R-73 missiles are high off-boresight weapons that have cryogenically cooled IR seeker heads. These missiles that can see targets up to 60 degrees off the boresight and turn after launch to take them out.

FLANKER HELMET MOUNTED TARGET DESIGNATION SYSTEM

A Flanker regiment can also lift 16 anti-LD/HD missiles which they will use to take out our AWACs and tankers from very long range.

In contrast, a regiment of 24 F-35s or 24 Super Hornets can only lift 96 total air-to-air missiles. Specifically, a regiment of 24 F/A-18 Hornets can only lift 96 Sidewinders or 96 AMRAAMs or a combination of Sidewinders and AMRAAMs that totals 96. That gives the Flanker regiment a 3:1 advantage in the number of missiles.

With regard to the "last move" advantage we previously discussed, there is a offensive ploy the Russians and Chinese like to use. Their typical tactic is to fire multiple missile salvos each with a different type of sensor. So you could be facing an inbound missile with an infrared seeker and another missile such as an AMRAAMski with active radar homing. Defeating multiple inbound missiles with different types of seekers is more difficult.

So by extension, if they have more Flankers than we have missiles to kill them, we lose the fight because the surviving Flankers shoot down our tankers and AWACs and we crash into the sea when we run out of gas or get jumped by other bandits the destroyed AWACs could have warned us about.

Lets see how this would work in, say a battle for Taiwan.

RAND SIMULATED BATTLE OVER TAIWAN

The RAND study supposed a battle over Taiwan between the U.S. and China assumed three Flanker regiments of 24 planes apiece attacking against 6 stealthy F-22s. The Chinese were able to put together this three regiment attack because they have many airbases on the coast of Chinese close to Taiwan, and our only bases are Guam and Japan. No F-22 is navalized so they need land bases.

It was a no win scenario from the outset even assuming a kill ratio of 100% for our beyond visual range air-to-air missiles. That is simply because the number of Chinese Flankers and the number of missiles they carried were so large compared to the number of our planes and missiles resisting them. Specifically, even if our missiles are 100% effective, which has never proven to be the case in previous air combat, and assuming we get as many of the Flankers as we have missiles, they will still have Flankers and missiles left over after we are Winchester. They will use their remaining jets and air-to-air missiles to take out our tankers, AWACS, Global Hawk surveillance drones and P3 Orion sub hunters. Our jets will then run out of gas and have to ditch or divert to a bingo field if one is available. If no bingo field is available, we lose our jets to ditching and many skilled pilots are taken out of the fight.

Note in this scenario that stealth was a non-factor. The Chinese used VHF radars and ground controlled intercepts to vector the

Flankers to the F-22s and IRST systems on the Flankers were used to close on the F-22s. So it actually may not make a lot of sense to build a lot of expensive F-22s and F-35s if the Chinese and Russians perfect the VHF radar techniques to assist Surface to Air Missile installations. Such VHF radar systems already exist and can be used to program initial points to which ground launched SAMs fly before turning on their own onboard homing radar.

VHF RADARS TO DETECT STEALTH DISCUSSED

Let me expand on the use of VHF anti-stealth radar. Stealth only works if the emitting radar is relatively far away and is X-band or some frequency the airframe was designed to defeat. The Russians have developed 14 different VHF radar systems many of which are mobile by virtue of being mounted on a truck. Another anti-stealth radar is a passive radar system. A passive radar system uses existing radio and TV and cell tower emissions to determine disturbances or shadows in the electromagnetic spectrum caused by a stealth plane flying through these emissions. Such a passive radar systems can triangulate radio and TV signals bouncing off a stealth plane and get an approximate position and use doppler shift to determine a heading and speed.

What the Russians have done is use old school VHF radars and digitized the front end to improve range and resolution. These VHF radars operate at frequencies the stealth airframe is not designed to defeat. The VHF radar is steered toward the approximate position found by the passive radar to get a fairly good approximation of the location of the stealth plane. An example of such a VHF radar is the 1L119 Nebo SVU. The location derived from the VHF radar is fed to a truck mounted phased array engagement radar such as the Russian 30N6E to illuminate the target and give mid-course guidance to a truck launched surface-to-air missile such as the S-300PMU-2 which carries its own active radar seeker. The ground radar gets the missile close enough that the missile's own terminal guidance X-band radar can get enough return off the stealth airframe to home in and destroy the plane.

China has a CETC Y-27 VHF radar which is very similar to the Russian Nebo SVU VHF digital AESA acquisition radar. Therefore, you F-35 pilots will not necessarily be as invisible to the Chinese as you may think. Their ground controllers might see you with VHF ground radars even if their pilots cannot see you with their ship's onboard X-band intercept radars.

VHF radars are huge antenna arrays, and they cannot be put on AWACs. It therefore is a good idea to find and take out any ground-based VHF radars.

Because of this development of anti-stealth VHF radars, we might actually be better off saving the money needed to build more F-35s and F-22s, and buying a manufacturing license for Flankers from Russia and build them in the U.S. We could add the F-35 DAS to them and the excellent F-35 AESA radar. That would create millions of jobs. But that is all for the politicians to decide, so don't hold your breath that they will do the intelligent thing.

FLANKER AERODYNAMIC SUPERIORITY
HOW TO FLY SMART AGAINST THE FLANKERS

Lets focus now on how to fly smartly against the Su-27, Su-30MKK and Su-30MK2 Flankers and their Chinese copies, the J-11 Sino Flanker. First, as I have previously emphasized, don't count on beyond visual range kills using missiles. Maybe you get him with a BVR shot, and maybe you don't.

Current concepts for air superiority count on having close, secure bases to generate sufficient sorties, and domination from beyond visual range using missiles and superior stealth, sensors and BVR missiles that are lethal and work. History teaches that you should not count on these concepts and assumptions as workable. Never underestimate the power of large numbers of smart people to get it wrong. Large groups of smart people can royally fuck it up in group-think unison. I point to the federal government deregulating derivatives thereby causing the huge financial meltdown of 2008 as Exhibit A. . Count on a close-in, visual range dogfight.

The keys to surviving a close-in dogfight with Chinese Flankers is numbers and teamwork and/or starting the fight with a substantial energy advantage. The Lanchester Equation teaches that to stalemate a force three times as numerous, our forces must be nine times as effective. Not likely. We should put the same number or preferably more planes in the sky than the opponent and everybody must fly smartly.

As I mentioned, the Su-30 Flanker and variants have thrust vectoring, so do not get into a turning fight with a Flanker. The thing to remember about thrust vectoring is that if you can sucker the Flanker into using vectoring to get angles on you, he will have squandered much of his kinetic energy because he just turned his entire airframe into a speed brake. I cannot overemphasize the significance of the V-shaped track the Flanker engines move on when the thrust is vectored. It was a huge fuckup by the Russian designers, so use it to your advantage if you cannot avoid a close in fight. If you can preserve your energy and get the Flanker to use his thrust vectoring, go vertical right away and get vertical separation and potential energy in the bank, and then do a rudder reversal at the top when he runs out of energy and come diving back down on him. A German pilot made this attack famous. It is sometimes called a Boom and Zoom. He would dive down out of the sun and make a guns pass, and if he missed, he would zoom climb to bank his high airspeed at potential energy and then dive down again for another pass. You might be able to get away with an iteration of this until the Flanker's higher thrust allows him to rebuild his energy sufficiently to go vertical with you and prevent you from obtaining separation. Kill him before he does that.

In any close-in dogfight, certain factors regarding the airplanes themselves loom large. Dogfighting is an energy game, and the pilot who manages his or her energy best, has the upper hand. Wing loading, body lift, thrust-to-weight ratio and the weight of the aircraft are critical parameters, because these factors directly affect the turning capability of the jet and its climbing and accelerating capabilities. The jet that turns the best and accelerates best and climbs best usually wins a dogfight started from a neutral position given two pilots who see each other and are trained in air combat maneuvering. Keep in mind though that throughout history, most dogfight kills happened because the victim never saw his attacker. That is much harder to do these days with airborne radar and AWACs. In today's battlespace, information is king.

The Su-27SK Flanker B was designed to defeat the F-15C and F-15E. That is the jet from which the Su-30MKK and Su-30MK2 inherited their aerodynamic characteristics. The F-15C is considered to be a premier air superiority fighter with wing loading and weight-to-thrust ratio far superior to the F/A-18C and F-35B.

WHAT IF YOU ARE FIGHTING BVR: ASSUMPTIONS DEBUNKED

I think all this means our air superiority assumption #1 of close, secure bases in the form of our aircraft carriers is dubious at best.

Air superiority pundits are counting on the fact that our stealth will work. I think that assumption is also dubious. First, the Navy and Marine Corps only have one stealth fighter, the F-35. If the Chinese use VHF radars, which they have, and ground controlled intercept vectors, which we know they use. Even at 0.0001 square meters radar cross section, which you F/A-18 pilots do not enjoy, the VHF radars will be able to see you F-35 pilots out at 25 nautical miles which is plenty of time to vector their Flankers in for the merge.

AMRAAM PK ***

Assumption #3 is that our beyond visual range missiles like the AMRAAM will work to kill the bandits far away. Vietnam proved that to be a bogus assumption. The pre-war estimated kill efficiency in Vietnam was 0.7. What was actually found to be the case was 0.08 which means the MIGs were 100 times more likely to make it to gun range in Vietnam than was expected. The current versions of the AMRAAM have a demonstrated kill ratio of 0.59 which is much better. But that is a deceptive number if one looks at the underlying facts. Since the introduction of beyond visual range missiles, there have been 588 air-to-air kills. Only 24 have been from beyond visual range. Since 1991, 20 of 61 kills have been BVR. The U.S. has recorded 10 AMRAAM kills, 4 of which were not BVR. The remaining kills were against Iraqi MIGs that were fleeing and not maneuvering, or against a Serb J-21 with no radar or ECM. One was one of our own helicopters which was not expecting the attack from a friendly jet. The six Serb MIG-29's that were shot down all had inoperative radars.

BVR NOT LIKELY BECAUSE OF RULES OF ENGAGEMENT

Furthermore, depending upon BVR kills is not likely to happen simply because the brass won't allow it in the Rules of Engagement. In Desert Storm, the brass was so skittish about friendly fire casualties, they set tight Rules of Engagement that required a visual identification of a target as a bandit before any engagement was allowed. So the BVR missiles are effectively useless for an actual BVR engagement since they are not likely to be allowed because of the Rules of Engagement. Go figure.

SIDEWINDER PK

The Sidewinders, especially after their evolution to all-aspect seeker heads, have been much more effective. They have a kill ratio of 0.73 in actual visual range combat situations. But many nations have developed countermeasures in the form of IR decoy flares. Even though the U.S. sidewinders now have flare rejection circuits, the flares have proven to be much more effective than anticipated. In Desert Storm, 48 Sidewinders were fired resulting in only 11 kills. That is why I said earlier, there is a significant "last move" advantage. If you see the missile and make a good break and launch your countermeasures, you have a good chance of defeating the missile.

In summary, BVR kills with AMRAAMs are not to be relied upon. You must know how to dogfight in a visual range fight with Sidewinders and guns and be good at it. So lets turn to that topic.

CLOSE IN DOGFIGHTING WITH FLANKERS

Wing loading is a measure of a jet's agility meanings it ability to turn. The lower the better. Thrust-to-weight ratio or T/W is a measure of how much the jet's thrust exceeds its weight, and is a measure of the jets ability to accelerate. It is simply F=MA where F is the jet's thrust and M is the jet's weight at 50% fuel and 2000 pounds of air-to-air missiles. But beware of the fact that some authors use military power and others use full afterburner power and some authors divide the weight by the thrust and others divide the thrust by the weight. Unless the author states his assumptions, it is easy to get confused.

BOOK WING LOADING AND T/W OF F18, F35 AND FLANKERS

The Flanker was designed to defeat the F-15. An F-15 outclasses the F/A-18 and the F-35. The F-15C has thrust-to-weight ratio of from 0.93 to 1.07 depending upon your assumptions. The F-15C wing loading of 73 pounds per square foot is less than either of the F/A-18E at 94 pounds per square foot or the F-35B at 89.2. The F/A-18E/F Super Hornet has a thrust-to-weight ratio of 0.93, and the F-35 has a thrust-to-weight ratio of 1.04 at 50% fuel and 0.90 at full fuel. Neither the F/A-18E nor the F-35 has thrust vectoring which can be useful in a dogfight, if used judiciously. The F-35 can thrust vector for a vertical landing but not a dogfight. An F-15C has a thrust-to-weight ratio of 1.08, and also has no thrust vectoring.

The Su-27 and Su-30 Flankers and derivatives were designed to kill all three of these airplanes. Consider the following salient facts. Assuming half fuel and 2000 pounds of air-to-air missiles, an Su-30MKK has a thrust-to-weight ratio of 1.00 with the AL-31F engine, and this will rise with the adoption of the AL-41F. The Su-30MKK has a wing loading of 85 pounds per square foot. All Su-30 variants have thrust vectoring and canards.

All this means any Su-30 variant with thrust vectoring and canards will be able to outturn either a Super Hornet or a Lightening or an F-15C and get to a firing solution faster. An SU-27 Flanker, the predecessor to the Su-30, has a T/W ratio of 0.98 and 82.3 pounds per square foot wing loading.

The SU-27SK Flanker-B supposedly can match the speed, acceleration and climb performance of the F-15, exceed the instantaneous and sustained transonic turn performance of the F-15, exceed the radar detection range of the baseline APG-63 radar in the F-15 and exceed the number of externally carried air-to-air missiles. The Flanker also has a forward looking IRST Infra Red Search and Track system that the F-15 and F/A-18 lack which allows it to get early warning of missile launches from their heat signatures. Since the heat signatures of the AMRAAM and Sidewinder are unique, the Flanker can even know what kind of missile was launched.

The Flankers have mutually competitive visual range air-to-air missiles and helmet mounted sights. The survival of any Super Hornet, F-35 or F-15 pilot in a close-in combat knife fight with a flanker is going to depend upon pilot ability and good or bad luck, unless you have superior numbers on your side. You could also win such a fight possibly if you have superior information such as you have an AWACS and the Flankers do not, or their radars do not detect you as far out as you detect them. If you detect them before they become aware of you, it might be possible to sneak up on them in a blind spot above them or below them, or use a doppler notch attack. That is the subject of another lecture.

China's air force is known to have purchased and operate 72 of the export version Su-30MKK Flanker G and they obtained a license to build 250 more. The Chinese naval forces are known to have purchased 24 Su-30MK2s. I repeat. Each of these Chinese Flankers has thrust vectoring and fly-by-wire so they can control it down to zero airspeed in extreme high alpha maneuvers. This means each one of these Flankers can do hard turns with almost no radius and incorporate vertical somersaults into level motion and do high alpha maneuvers such as the Pugachev Cobra or the Somersault to put the brakes on and cause you to overshoot. These maneuvers cause the whole airframe to act as a speed brake, and the jet rapidly sheds airspeed. This will cause you to overshoot. If you see a Flanker do one of these, and you have vertical maneuver flying speed, immediately pull up and go ballistic to obtain vertical separation using your energy advantage. When you have obtained vertical separation, roll down on him or do a rudder reversal and point your nose at him, get a lock and fire a missile and then close for a guns kill.

The Flankers high alpha maneuverability coupled with excellent thrust-to-weight ratio allows them to rapidly recover kinetic energy lost in a high alpha maneuver. So use your energy advantage to gain an offensive position and kill him fast before he regains his energy lost in either using his thrust vectoring or performing a high alpha manuever such as a Cobra or Somersault.

Do not go into a turning fight with a Flanker unless you are trying to sucker him into using his thrust vectoring. Are you hearing me? If you go into a straight turning fight without an energy advantage, you are going to die a violent death.

You should not engage a Flanker unless you have an energy advantage and use it to gain an offensive position on him quickly before he can build up energy.

A good plan for a Super Hornet would be to go into a high aspect merge with an Su-30MK2 Flanker at a higher airspeed and with a 1000 foot altitude advantage. At the merge, take him into a two circle turning fight and watch his energy state closely. He will be bleeding energy but not as fast as you because his thrust at military power is higher than yours. His wing loading is lower than yours, so he will be outturning you slightly but may be impatient and use his thrust vectoring to tighten his turn. As soon as you see him do that, pull up into the vertical and use your energy advantage to obtain vertical separation. He won't have the energy to follow you all the way up because he just squandered a lot of it using his thrust vectoring. Watch him as you climb. As soon as he runs out of airspeed in his climb, assuming he is foolish enough to follow you up, his nose will drop and he will start to dive away to rebuild his energy. Do a rudder reversal at that point and bring your nose back down and point your jet at him and hit full burner. You will close the gap on him quickly. If you have a missile shot as soon as you do the rudder reversal, take it, but keep closing for a guns kill in case he evades the missile. As soon as you get into guns range, hose him with 20 mm cannon shells.

Everything I just said is the conventional wisdom on the Flanker from the publicly available sources. It would be conservative and wise to believe it.

But the situation may not be as grim as it appears. I did some research and calculations based upon data which I found on Wikipedia and other public sources, and I come to a slightly different conclusion.

ICE PICK'S CALCULATION

There seems to be some confusion as to whether to use full military power thrust or full thrust with afterburner in the calculations and whether to divide the weight by the thrust or vice versa in the wing loading and thrust loading numbers which are published. There are also assumptions about the weight of the missile load and the empty weight of the aircraft and whether to use 50% fuel. The sources I consulted use full thrust on afterburner and divide that into weight of the airplane with 50% internal fuel and 2000 pounds of air-to-air missiles. That does not make much sense to me since you cannot be in burner all the time and weight divided by thrust is not acceleration but the reciprocal of acceleration so a smaller number is better. My point is, make your own calculations based upon reasonable assumptions on fuel and missile load, and don't get freaked out by the thrust-to-weight ratios and wing loading numbers published by others. My calculations for the F/A-18E, F-35, Su-30MK2 and the F-15 all came out somewhat differently than published sources. Sometimes they were substantially different from numbers published in public sources and books and the RAND report. It could be disinformation, and it could be different assumptions. My point is, make your own calculations. We will give you tactics to use even in inferior jets when compared to the Flankers and the Chinese J-20 stealth jet.

It is best though to heed the advice of the experts at RAND and Air Power Australia: the Flankers are aerodynamically superior to your jets in most areas and have comparable and in some cases better avionics and missiles. So fly your jets accordingly. Don't go into a turning fight with a Flanker. Do get an energy advantage and use it. Try to sucker the Flanker pilot into squandering his energy. For example, you can sucker him into squandering his kinetic energy by shooting a missile at him and forcing him to do a Pugachev Cobra or somersault to defeat the missile. Alternatively, you can make him think you are stupid and go into a turning fight with him, but do, by all means, marshal your kinetic energy wisely. In other words, don't pull maximum Gs and squander your own energy. Then watch him closely. If he uses his thrust vectoring to outturn you, go vertical to get separation and then do a rudder reversal or some other maneuver to turn back in on him below you when he runs out of airspeed.

So there you have it. Go figure. I think, aerodynamically speaking, we can stand and fight Flankers with our F/A-18E/F Super Hornets if we have an energy advantage going into the fight. Maybe not after the Flankers get the AF-41 engine which is more powerful. I think it is not a good idea to fight the Flankers with F-35s unless you have F/A-18s with you, or you have a substantial energy advantage, or, for some reason, the Flanker is not aware you are there, which is extremely unlikely.

The take-home lesson here is that, if you want to survive a fight with an Su-27 or Su-30MKK Flanker in an F-35, you are going to need help from your friends, preferably in F/A-18E/Fs who are more on par with the Su-30MKK and Su-30MK2 Flankers in terms of wing loading and thrust-to-weight ratio. Engagement tactics should be adjusted accordingly.

We recommend engaging Flankers with a team of at least one F/A-18E/F and one F-35 so that the strengths of each jet complement each other. The F-35 has a great sensor system with a 360 degree IRST and a great radar that can even see a stealth jet such as the F-22 Raptor. But it is not good in close in knife fights. That is where the Super Hornet comes in. The F/A-18E can provide turn and burn capability in close in dogfighting to protect the F-35. We recommend using the F-35 to spot the Flankers and any inbound stealth fighters or air-to-air missile sites or SAMs. That data should be sent to the Super Hornets on the Link 16 data link. The Super Hornets can use their fire control systems to launch AMRAAMs and Sidewinders to complement your own salvo of missiles against the fighters. The Super Hornets can vector to intercept the inbound fighters, and the F-35 can keep them covered and apprised of the situation in the 360 degree sphere around them. The F-35 may also be able to get a shot off against a Flanker pilot distracted by the Super Hornets.

The F-35s can also designate and shoot down any inbound SAMs with AMRAAMs and jam any SAM radar sites and destroy them with anti-radiation HARM missiles. The F-35 can also jam the search radars of any Flanker's or stealth fighters in the area and shoot anti-radiation HARMs at hostile fighters with their radars lit up. Be careful to clear the area of friendlies before firing a HARM or AMRAAM, so check your HUD or Helmet Mounted Display.

Then we recommend using two F/A-18s to engage the Flankers and keep them busy and on the defensive. While the Flankers are engaged with the Super Hornets, use two F-35s as sucker fight trailers to sneak up on the Flankers. Sneak up in their blind spots either below or above the Flanker. Flankers do not have 360 degree IRST, so they cannot see beneath them, and neither their radars nor their IRSTs can see directly above them. The can however look out their canopies and see you if you are above them.

Flankers have an IRST that can see forward and backward as well as somewhat above and somewhat below their altitudes in both directions. They can see more above their altitude than below, so the blind spot below them is bigger. Thus, if the trailers don't sneak up on them properly in their blind spots, the Flankers will be able to see the trailer F-35s if they come in from behind and anywhere in the cone of their rearward looking radar or IRST systems.

The Flankers will also be able to see any long range missile shot heat signatures from the F-35s or Super Hornets and dodge the missiles using flare and chaff countermeasures, so think twice about giving your position away by firing an ARAAM at a Flanker if you are in an F-35 and outside 15 miles. At that distance, he probably will not be able to see you either with his radar or his IRST. If you do fire a missile, the Flanker will probably be able to dodge it, and then he will know you are out there. A guns kill of the Flanker by an F-35 sneaking up on the Flanker from below is the preferred *modus operandi*.

As I said, a vertical attack by the F-35s from above or below is recommended so the Flanker pilot never sees you. Once he sees you, your chances of a kill drop significantly.

If the Chinese or some other enemy are using VHF radars on the ground which can see stealth aircraft, your element of surprise is gone. With VHF search radars, the enemy ground controllers may see the F-35 sucker fight trailers coming in even though the F-35 has low front quarter visibility to X-band airborne and ground target acquisition and tracking radars. So a good plan if the enemy is known to be using VHF search radars would be to find their VHF radar arrays on the ground or on their ships and take them out with HARM anti-radiation missiles as job one in any fight.

FLANKERS AS MOTHERSHIPS GUIDING DRONE ARMY

Another thing you need to know is that each Chinese Su-27MKK or other Su-27 Flanker is equipped with the TKS-2 C3 airborne two-way command and control system which can simultaneously command and control up to 15 other aircraft including providing initial target fixes to their R-77 AMRAAM type radar-guided missile shots. So you cannot just take out their command and control on the ground and think they are out of the command and control business. They are not. Their jets can be controlled and their R-77s armed with initial intercept point data computed by another Flanker's computers.

R77 CAN SHOOT DOWN AMRAAM AND PHOENIX IN FLIGHT

Of significance is the fact that their R-77 missiles can be fired against our AMRAAMs and AIM-54 Phoenix missiles and take them out in flight. Their R-77s can also take out our Patriot surface-to-air missiles in flight. Since their IRST systems can see these AMRAAM and Phoenix missile signatures, the chances of making a long range kill against a Flanker using one of these radar guided missiles is small. Last move advantage remember?

The Chinese MKK Flankers have an Su-27 radar with a mode allowing it to use the R-77 AMRAAMSKI missiles. The Chinese also have their own home-grown radar guided air-to-air missile called variously the PL-12 or SD-10. It is a Mach 4 missile with a range of 80 kilometers, proximity fuse and an inertial/data link midcourse guidance system with an active radar homing terminal phase mode just like our AMRAAM AIM-120. It may not be as good, because it is, well, made in China, but don't bet your life on it. They use this PL-12 AMRAAM type missile on their J-11 copycat Flankers.

These Chinese J-11 copycat Flankers built with the Chinese WS-10 engines instead of the Russian AF-31 Lyulka engines may be a problem. The WS-10 engines put out 20,050 lbs of thrust each as compared with the 16,910 pounds each of the Flanker AF-31 Lyulka Russian engines generates. With an empty weight of 32,081 pounds plus 7200 pounds of fuel and a missile load of 2762 pounds, I come up with a weight to thrust ratio of 1.5 based on dry thrust of WS-10 Chinese engines, and wing loading of only 84.06 pounds per square foot. Based upon those numbers, if the J-11s are a problem, they are somewhat less of a problem than the Su-27and Su-30 Flankers. Both the F/A-18C and the F-35B should not be afraid to go into a vertical fight with a J-11 even if it has the WS-10 engines. Further, the F/A-18 can go into a turning fight with a J-11. However, the F-35B should avoid a turning fight with a J-11 because the F-35 has a worse wing loading than the J-11.

The J-20 is not an air superiority fighter. It is designed for long range missions to take out our AWACS and tankers with missiles. As a result, it has stealth from the front but not as much from the rear. That may have changed for reasons I am about to explain. Chinese hackers are believed to have stolen about 24,000 design files pertaining to the F-35 in 2011 from our dumb ass defense contractors. The defense contractors actually had computers with this information on them coupled to the internet. There were three defense contractors involved in the JSF program, and two of them had their networks hacked. The data the Chinese hackers stole is supposedly mainly about the design, construction and self-testing systems of the F-35. The DOD says no highly sensitive information was stolen. I am not sure I believe that since the hackers inserted technology that encrypts the data being stolen as it is being stolen. Therefore, our people investigating the theft do not even know what was stolen.

Breaches of computer systems holding F-35 design data that have been discovered so far extend all the way back to 2007 with more breaches in 2008 having been discovered.

The F-35 has 7.5 million lines of code running its computers. Luckily, the most sensitive code pertaining to the flight controls system and the IRST sensor system was supposedly not on computers coupled to the internet, and the Chinese are not believed to have gotten those files. Air Power Australia published one hypothetical scenario however where a Chinese cyber hacker chieftain asserts that her hackers actually went into the F-35 code and made changes. I guess we won't know until that trap door springs. Hopefully, that is just a myth.

According to reports, the defense contractors did not make much of an effort at computer security which leads me to believe the design data that was stolen was bogus and planted there by the CIA. I have no independent verification of that since that is way above my pay grade. So basically I am just starting that rumor to screw with the Chinese so they won't know whether to copy the design or not.

In any event, the J-20 wing loading is 126 pounds per square foot at 80,000 pounds max takeoff weight, and 104 pounds per square foot at 66,000 pounds takeoff weight. Empty weight and internal fuel capacity are unknown, so these figures are just a guess. Either way it is a dog on wing loading based upon these takeoff weight numbers, and any F/A-18 or F-35 should be able to out-turn it. The J-20 will only have 40,100 pounds of thrust if it uses the WS-10 Chinese engine, but the Russians supposedly are going to supply 117S engines which would provide a total of 64,000 pounds of thrust. In that case, weight-to-thrust would be 1.25 at 80,000 pounds, so the Chinese J-20 stealth fighter would operating up there in the double inferior zone with the Thud. If these numbers are correct, the J-20 will not be used as an air superiority fighter in dogfighting and even an F-35 should be able to out-turn and out-climb it. At 66,000 pounds with the 117S engine, a J-20's weight-to-thrust ratio would be 1.03, so that would be a problem for both F/A-18Cs and F-35B in a vertical fight, but a turning fight could be fought with a J-20 by both the F/A-18 and the F-35.

The F-35A weight-to-thrust ratio is 1.44 with half fuel and a full missile load of 6 sidewinders and 2 AMRAAMs. With a wing loading of 87.69, the F-35B should be able to go into turns with a J-20 even in the best case scenario for the J-20. I just would not try to out-run one or out-climb it based upon this sketchy data. Admittedly, our data on the J-20 is sketchy and the Chinese have been pretty good at keeping it under wraps.

However, if my numbers are right, an F/A-18E Super Hornet should be able to smoke any J-20 in a turning fight, but with a weight-to-thrust ratio of 1.5, the Super Hornet should avoid a vertical fight. In fact, a Super Hornet should avoid a dogfight with a J-20 altogether if possible unless you have friends with you and you can gang up on it. That advice goes for the F/A-18C and F-35B pilots as well. Having numerical superiority is always a good thing.

The Chinese J-20 stealth fighter is believed to have 360 degree coverage on its IRST and plenty of payload capacity for missiles. However, it may sneak up on you with its stealth and smoke you before you even know it is there. Our AWACs won't be able to see an inbound J-20, so unless we have a VHF radar setup on the ground that can see it, the inbound J-20 stealth will be invisible to you F/A-18 pilots. The F-35B will be able to see it though on its IRST, so if you F/A-18 pilots have an F-35 with you, you won't be up there completely naked, and that is an advisable way to conduct your operations. I re-emphasize, the best plan would be to tag team the J-20 with one or more F/A-18Cs and one or more F-35Bs. You can take him out as a team. The truly ironic thing is that for the cost of one F/A-18 and one F-35, would could have built another King of the Sky F-22 Raptor which would be able to steal the J-20's milk money and push it down to the ground. But I digress yet again.

Now lets complicate the situation a little. Suppose the opposing force is two Flankers, a J-20 or two and several Unmanned Aerial Vehicles like our X-47B. The new X factor is the X-47B-like UAVs and their capabilities. I think it is a good assumption that no country has yet developed a UAV that is autonomous and more capable than our X-47B. That is good news because our X-47B cannot dogfight close in. It is too complicated and there are too many possibilities of maneuvers based upon the number of opponents and what they do for the programmers to have programmed the machine to dogfight in every possible scenario. If somebody has tackled that very complex problem and conquered it, you are toast if you run into one of those. Why? Because a UAV has no pilot and is much smaller and lighter than your plane so it will be able to out-turn you and out-climb you in every scenario. It can be stressed for 12 Gs or more and you simply cannot turn that hard but it can. It can be designed with a better thrust-loading ratio also so it can out-climb and out-accelerate you every time. So if somebody has programmed its little robotic brain to dogfight properly, you simply have no chance and it is best to disengage and save the plane and yourself from certain destruction. But we have not been able to program our X-47B autonomous UAV to dogfight in every possible close in scenario with every combination of numbers of Red Force opponents and numbers of Blue Force fighters and all the possible combinations of moves everybody makes. If we cannot do it, I dare to say, nobody else can either. Call me crazy.

Aside from the fact that the UAVs cannot be programmed to dogfight, the most advanced UAVs today are also slow. Their top speed, at least for the carrier-based X-47B is 0.47 mach, so you can outrun one anytime. That is because they are designed for long range and long loiter time. Our X-47B has only one Pratt and Whitney F-100 turbofan. They are also pretty heavy with a max takeoff weight of 44,457 lbs.

The autonomous UAVs can be programmed to fly pre-programmed routes, drop bombs or fire air-to-air missiles or air-to-ground missiles, rendezvous with a tanker and fly back to the carrier and land. But they cannot dogfight in close-in, visual range combat.

Therefore, the strategy does not change much in this scenario. I would recommend engaging the Flankers with an F/A-18 or, preferably two F/A-18s to keep them busy with an F-35 in trail. Use the F-35 IRST and radar to keep track of the UAVs. If they attack, fire missile at them to make them scatter. If they persist, use the F-35 to engage them and shoot them down with sidewinders or guns. They are slow and won't know what to do with a skilled human dogfighter. Hopefully the F/A-18s will be able to stay alive against the Flankers long enough for the F-35 to sneak up on them and take a close in shot with guns or a Sidewinder. Unfortunately, if the F-35 has to engage the UAVs, the chances of it being spotted by the Flanker's IRST increase since there is no telling at what altitude and range relative to the Flankers the F-35 will have to fly to take care of the drones. The J-20 will probably be used by the Flankers as a trailer like we will use the F-35. It will be up to the F-35 to take out the J-20, preferably by sneaking up on it if possible and taking a Sidewinder shot. This will not give the J-20 much time to see the missile on its 360 degree IRST and make a break turn. If the trailer can sneak within guns range, the J-20 will never know what hit him if he does not see the F-35 on his IRST. Incidentally, with its heavy wing loading at 80,000 pounds, I am not sure a J-20 can break hard enough to defeat an incoming missile anyway.

Note that if we were flying F-22 Raptors, with their superior wing loading, thrust loading and stealth, we could smoke everything else in the sky. But I am afraid that Secretary Rummy killed that dream for everyone. Some dreams must die. This was not one of them. Now some of our good pilots are probably going to die because of it.

You will be divided up into teams of four jets each for the hops this afternoon. Two F/A-18Cs and two F-35Bs. You will be engaging two Su-30MKK Flankers simulated by F-4Es. The F-4Es actually have a better weight-to-thrust ratio than the Flankers, so have fun. Get in your teams and devise your tactics now. You have 1.5 hours to wheels up. Good luck.

Thank you gentlemen. That is all. Dismissed."

POST ICE PICK LECTURE SHOCK

After a moment of stunned silence in the room, Ricky looked at Carmen and raised his eyebrows with that "What the Fuck Just Happened" look. Carmen looked at J.J. and Neil, Taco and Ricky and said, "Well that was about as much fun as having a rock in your shoe for a 10 mile hike. I need a drink." They all laughed and agreed.

POST ICE PICK LECTURE FURBALL

Ricky and J.J. were assigned to the same team with Carmen and her wingman Tim "Tequila" Randall. Swat and Tequila were the F-35B contingent on the team.

Ricky said, "O-club. 2000 hours after this fur ball is over." They all nodded in agreement, now with serious looks on their faces and headed to the locker room to suit up in the G-suits for their afternoon hop and make their plan. Today, it was all up to them to decide what to do. They decided on a sucker fight.

"This the end of book 1. For the exciting conclusion
of this story, including the dogfight at Top Gun and the
gripping battle between China and the U.S., go to book 2."

Ron in Dress Blues

Ron, son and Dad

Ron as lawyer